A Scourge Of Zombies in America

One Mission to Unite a Haunted Nation

A Novel by
T. S. Kasely, Ph.D.

Copyright © 2020 T. S. Kasely, Ph.D.

All rights reserved. No part of this publication may be reproduced, distributed, or transmitted in any form or by any means, without prior written permission of the author, except in the case of brief quotations embodied in critical reviews and certain other noncommercial uses permitted by copyright law. For permission requests, write to tskasely@gmail.com.

tskasely.com

This is a work of fiction. Any references to actual events, people, places, locales, businesses, companies, public agencies, or entities are used fictitiously. All characters and inventions are products of the author's imagination and any resemblance to actual persons (living or dead), is entirely coincidental.

First Edition 2021

ISBN: 9798711094821

Independently Published

Book Design: Gibbons Business Solutions, LLC.

Cover Illustrator: Dee Fish

Editor: Julia McCray

*This book is dedicated to my grandchildren,
with the hope that their lives will be guided by a dream of their
own creation.*

A special thanks with love to my wife, Karen.

Contents

Part I: The Scourge of Zombies

Chapter 1 - Perspectives of the Original Crisis
Chapter 2 - Tim's Personal Flight from Zombies
Chapter 3 - A Shared Experience of Zombies
Chapter 4 - The Vision for a Better World
Chapter 5 - Children Playing in the Shadows of Zombies
Chapter 6 - The Scourge of Zombies
Chapter 7 - The Source of Shared Experience
Chapter 8 - An Inconsistency in Shared Experience
Chapter 9 - A Psychoanalytic Account of Zombies

Part II: Diagnosis

Chapter 10 - A Material Discovery
Chapter 11 - Tim's Enlightenment
Chapter 12 - The Power of Empathy
Chapter 13 - Tim's Search for Understanding
Chapter 14 - Seeking Material Evidence
Chapter 15 - The Matter for Creating Zombies
Chapter 16 - Lyndsey's Search for Understanding
Chapter 17 - Seeking the Source of the Zombies
Chapter 18 - The Unconquerable Forces of Nature
Chapter 19 - The Zombies Unmasked

Part III: Therapy

Chapter 20 - Tim's Vision of Social Unity
Chapter 21 - A Healthy Perspective on Nature
Chapter 22 - Removing the Flagrant Deceptions
Chapter 23 - The Search for New Leadership
Chapter 24 - Founding a New Coercion
Chapter 25 - Leaders with Compassion and Insight
Chapter 26 - Respect: Society Without the Attitude of Domination
Chapter 27 - Crisis in Paradise: The Problem with Self-Comparison
Chapter 28 - Crisis, Catastrophe, and Our Unity with Nature
Chapter 29 - The Ruling Power

Endnotes

Bibliography

Part I : The Scourge of Zombies

Chapter 1

Perspectives of the Original Crisis[1]

"Ooohhh…!" Clare wailed as she pushed with all her strength.

"I can see the crown of his head," her doctor declared with a calm that seemed to betray the reality of the situation. The epidural, as far as Clare was concerned, had failed to ease the pain as promised. She had a fleeting thought that she might as well had continued with her endeavor for a natural childbirth. That thought passed quickly with the next breath. She throbbed with an ache. The tension that she felt in her back summoned a freakish image to fantasy, and she envisioned herself turning inside out. That image "popped" and disappeared, but the pain was still there. The numbness she had hoped for was cruelly replaced by a deadening of the joy she had felt during her pregnancy. That joy had been banished from her immediate conscious experience.

"Ohhh…my god it hurts so bad!" She secretly wished that she could quit this delivery, but that wish didn't survive the next throb of pain. It vanished before she could feel any guilt for turning her back on the love and happiness promised by the life that she had imagined with the new son she was expecting. Right now, the pain was all-consuming, and she could no longer envision the possibility of a life without it.

"You're doing just fine," Doctor Elisa Taporo tried to assure her. The doctor could no longer speak with her usual tone if she was to be heard over Clare's groans and cries. So, she raised her voice and deepened its tone. "I can see the whole top of his head. It shan't be long now." Her assistants gathered the necessary items and stood prepared for the emergence of the newborn. Doctor Taporo readied herself to perform the final tasks required to empower the newborn to take its first breath in a world where it would have to adjust quickly to being cold and dry. The warm and wet world of this fetus was about to end. He was to be ushered into a new stage of life, beginning with expulsion from his mother's womb, followed by being cut off from his continuous supply of nutrients. This would be the first major crisis in a new and independent life. An intimidating reality had begun to disclose itself to another human being. Certainly, this newborn would wriggle and writhe in the depths of his being like a fish out of water. But, like the vast majority of those before him, he would adjust and survive to face numerous crises within which he would be haunted by the same disruptive feeling of helplessness.

"You're doing fine, Clare, if you could just push a little harder." Then Doctor Taporo spoke even louder, "His entire head is nearly visible. Push harder! You're almost finished." As she said this, she took care to surgically enlarge the vaginal opening to avoid any tearing. Clare's sense of urgency had peaked. She held her breath until her face turned red and pushed with every ounce of strength that remained in her. The son that she had desired slowly but surely made a complete exit from the womb. As he did, Doctor Taporo clutched onto his shoulders and head, wiping the thickest of the blood and other fluids from the newborn's face. The nurse-assistants quickly and expediently provided the doctor with the necessary instruments to complete the job. Doctor Taporo carefully snipped the umbilical cord, and extracted the mucus from the newborn's nostrils, giving him a gentle tap on the backside.

A profound and meaningful reality permeated the pain and confusion of Clare's birthing experience. Another human being had entered the world. Clare had a variety of fleeting thoughts as she cried tears of joy and relief. "I did it," she mused with a pleasure that seemed quite out of place amidst the infant's cries, the blood, the amniotic fluids, and the reverberating echoes of the pain that had wracked her body only moments before. As Doctor Taporo finished her work, and her assistants finished cleaning the newborn, turning him all around and inspecting him to make sure that everything looked satisfactory, Clare had returned to her senses enough to try and grasp the full significance of this unique experience. She began to reflect on what had happened. As she was on the verge of passing into a more restful state, thoughts and feelings about the reality of her birthing experience crossed her mind. *"We were a biological unity. He and I were one living thing."* But her attentive gaze faded in and out, until she suddenly became apprehensive. "Oh, I have to feed him!" She was physically exhausted, and for a moment it seemed as if it was not possible to stay awake any longer, but she felt anxious to suckle her new child.

"Everything is fine Clare. The boy looks quite healthy, and he already has a full head of hair!" The doctor's words provided welcome reassurance, even though Clare had the strangest feeling that perhaps she was dreaming. Then the doctor placed her new son into her welcoming arms. At that moment, the newborn felt a sense of relief that was visible to the immediate spectators. It was as though he was able to return to his own body from some alien world and the internal quaking could cease. Certainly, his sense of his mother's caress, her touch on the surface of his body, provided a calming affect that he desperately needed to stabilize his anxious feelings, and ultimately affirm his identity.

"His name is Michael James Austin," Clare announced with a pride that exuded from her spirit through her entire body and transferred through her son's new and mysterious sense of touch to his most private self. His external senses, the tentacles of his new life, were already awakening and discovering paths into the new world. And, for now, a sense of relief had begun to settle into his bones.

Prior to sensing his mother's caress as he rested within her loving arms, he had lived through the most horrible nightmare. No one present in the room could sense what this experience of birth felt like for Michael. Immediately following his expulsion from the safe haven of the womb, though he felt totally exhausted and cold, he flailed, twisted, and writhed, not only with his arms and legs and hands, but with strange and undesirable feelings burning inside of him. He felt as if he were jolted awake from a pleasant slumber. But worse, something was happening to him that he was in no way prepared to deal with. There was an aching, an eerie new feeling unfamiliar to him. It was not only discomforting, but all-consuming! He had no way to cope with it. His stomach twisted with pain as he groped aimlessly for something he had lost. It was his food supply – it was gone! And what had happened to that warmth, and the comforting feeling? That had been replaced with a feeling of absolute emptiness, separateness, absence, lack and abandonment, all rolled into one. He had never felt anything like this before. All he could do was to scream for help from the depths of his being. His newly developing senses indicated that his world had changed dramatically. He was alone. Lucky for him, he could not anticipate that all his anxious feelings, especially the loneliness, would return to him again and again throughout his entire life. The only thing that was real for him in the immediacy of the birth trauma was an icy exhaustion, coupled with anxiety in the face of life-threatening danger. His exhaustion was vying with this anxiety for dominance. Somehow, he felt as if this unwelcome intrusion of tension was striving to transport him back to what had been prior to this frightening experience. He tried with all his strength to go back, but it wasn't happening.

Despite his efforts, he did not manage to return to his prior condition in the warmth and safety of his mother's womb. He was about to surrender to the exhaustion, but he had to make one last try to get back home before he lost all his strength. When this failed, he made his first *intentional* act as an individual, conscious being, just like every other newborn. Before succumbing to the overpowering weariness, he rejected the totality of his birth-experience with the whole of his being.

Here is the origin of self-alienation. Michael had cast out the horrifying impotence and anxiety with all his organic powers. *"This suffering is* other *than myself!"* was the active expression essential to his willful banishing of his helplessness and anxiety. These had to be expelled from his immediate awareness so that he might give in to his exhaustion and sleep. *"This is not happening to me!"* echoed throughout the biorhythmic quaking that pulsated in his most vital organs. These organic rhythms were the source for the willful rejection of the real self with its weakness and anxiety. The terrifying feelings had been magically and effectively cast out along with his real self as an alien entity.

Obviously, the newborn had no capacity to express his suffering in words, but the indications were apparent, nonetheless. These signs were exuding from Michael's sensible surface. Any sensitive person who witnessed the miracle of his birth could feel and penetrate the absolute depth of the trauma. Before the infant had entered his incipient restful state, anyone could have sensed the gesticulations that indicate the utter forlornness at the very foundation of human life. Therein, it was apparent that the real self, had been cast away and disowned. These had been banished to the outside world. But later he would be haunted by his real self once again because, in fact, it does return. It does *not* manifest from within. No! It has been rejected completely. But it *will be* returned to him by others. He will be forever dependent upon others to bring his real self to his immediate conscious life. While mother brings it home with love, others might have different designs. In the meantime, it will survive on the outside as though it were a ghost awaiting its chance to haunt the pain-free, ideal self that one learns to nourish. But, at least for now, having cast away all his pain, Clare's new baby boy could sleep in the temporary comfort of her arms. However, when he awakens, his newly activated external senses, combined with his internal sense, will introduce vague reminders of what had happened to him. He will need continuous reassurance and help with his nourishment. His cry will be the call for both.

Clare suckled her son to the point of totally relaxing his

anxiety, and he rested in his mother's affirmation of his being. One of the nurses took Michael from her, as he slept, and placed him in the temporary crib set up next to her hospital bed. "Get some rest, Clare. Michael will sleep now. He will be right here beside you."

At last, Clare allowed herself to relax and she passed into a dream state. Her images were eerily vivid. She had a pleasant feeling, but it was mixed with painful concern, as she had a vision that she was having dinner with her son at a table in a restaurant. She saw him as a young boy. They were so happy and expressing their mutual love. But suddenly, while they were eating, the boy was taken away by some people who assured her that they would bring him right back. Michael cried and reached for her as he was taken away, and Clare feared that something terrible had happened to him. She could not finish eating and continued to feel quite unnerved by his absence. Her dream moved her to toss and turn in her hospital bed, restful sleep eluding her. She seemed to realize that her dream had provided her with an insight into a hidden reality about her birthing experience. Her beloved fetus, whom she had known so intimately during the time of his growth in the womb, had been cut off from her. It was as though the dream made her vividly aware of *Michael's* experience of his traumatic birth in the expulsion from the womb. No wonder his first breath resulted in cries! She seemed to have visualized that he had been separated from the warm and wet womb, and his lifeline. This feeling made her uneasy in her sleep, and she jostled as she mumbled incoherently.

The dream continued, but the anxious feeling was quelled as she envisioned that her son was brought back to her by the very people who had taken him away. Suddenly, she had a warm regard for those people who returned him to her. She also had a loving feeling for the son who seemed to be different from the boy she had known before he had been taken from her. She began to feed him from her own plate, and it were as though they shared a feeling of love that was utterly new and enigmatic. She wondered why those people had taken him away in the first place. Then, abruptly, she was concerned over *what* had changed. Before they took him away, their mutual feelings for each other had been indistinguishable; as if they had but one emotion between them, and it was fully comprehended by both. The confusion she felt in the dream was motivated by a new feeling of *empathy* after he was returned to her. It was as though she realized for the first time that they were sharing feelings from a distance, and she felt as though she had experienced his own feelings in a way that was incomplete. She had an overpowering sense that something was missing. Then, her son offered her food from his plate. As she accepted it, and ate, she felt even more uncomfortable. The food didn't taste right. She was agitated enough to open her eyes, turn her head, and realize that she was just dreaming. That was all she needed to relax and let herself fall into an image-less sleep.

Chapter 2

Tim's Personal Flight from Zombies

Tim ran as fast as he could down the back streets behind 5th Avenue. He was afraid that those diseased monsters might remain on his tail all the way to the hospital. It was only a few more blocks away. He wanted so much to be with Clare when she delivered their son, but the obstacles he had encountered were insurmountable. The first distraction was that his friend Jake had called from a gas station with a story about having been run off the road. Tim rushed to the gas station to get him. Lyndsey, Jake's significant other, was at work, so her brother, Tim, was the next person whom Jake thought to call to help him become mobile again. As if that wasn't enough, on the way to the hospital he had encountered a demonstration forming in the streets of Shadyside. When it looked as if he might be detained by the sheer masses carrying their signs and chanting their collective support for saving our planet, he pretended to be an emergency manager. He slowly, but gradually, escaped in his car through an alley behind the hospital. Then he drove over a grassy area surrounded by low curbstones that he had to traverse to get to the next road.

Unfortunately, even after evading the protest, he was unable to get much farther before he encountered the monsters just outside Oakland. At that point, he decided to make a last ditch run for it. He was determined to run all the way to the hospital, some six or eight city blocks. His internal senses still feared the presence of the gruesome monsters that he had encountered, even though none were readily apparent to his external senses. Sightings of these things had been completely non-existent until a couple of weeks earlier, but they seemed to be on the increase, and now he had seen them for himself. He wondered how these creatures could suddenly show up out of nowhere to terrorize people when they least expected it. "What the hell are these things?" he wondered out loud. For only a moment he understood how someone could get the notion that they are the dead victims of the Ebola virus. "No way!" he again thought aloud. Ultimately, he began to run with increasing confidence that sanctuary awaited him at the hospital.

Suddenly, a car was exiting the parking lot at the psychiatric institute right in front of him. It came closer and closer until he side-stepped his way past it. The old Buick did a nose-dive as the driver slammed on the brakes. It was one of the older models, lacking the modern safety devices that made collisions of any sort much less likely. "Holy shit!" he cried as he leapt, feeling some relief at having barely escaped harm from a driver who was probably every bit as frightened as he was about the near miss. Again, he looked around, realizing that the monsters that had been chasing him were gone. "Just a couple more blocks to go." Then, he thought to himself, "*I haven't seen a zombie since I left my car!*" That had happened several blocks back in the residential area on the edge of Oakland. "*Now* I'm *calling them zombies!*" he admonished himself. He felt disgusted that he had succumbed to the most popular rendering of the monsters as zombies. But he had been dangerously close to one of them, and he saw the sickening open wounds all too clearly. There was no blood, only a brownish puss that looked like infection. And the stench! It smelled like a rotting corpse. And its empty eyes stared off toward nothing. But the monster was reaching and trying to grab him! His own encounter had seemed to confirm the similarities of these things to zombies. They did look as if they were "undead".

His terrifying ordeal had begun as he was waiting at a stop sign for an ambulance and fire truck to pass in front of him with sirens wailing. In a flash, several zombies seemed to appear out of nowhere. They were stumbling around the cars and falling against them. One approached the passenger side of his car and he quickly surveyed the area around him. The traffic had stopped, and it showed no signs that it might be moving any time soon, making it impossible to drive forward or backward. His fear was rising to the point of flight. It was then that Tim freaked, and decided to abandon the car. He made a dash on foot all the way to the hospital to outmaneuver the slow-moving monsters. Now he could envision the previously hoped-for success of that plan. As he approached the door beyond the valet parking, he saw two armed guards inside. He slowed his pace to try and catch his breath, then reached for the door, opened it, and entered the hospital screening area just outside the lobby.

The guards at the door were ready to protect with force against any unwelcome intruders. They could see this was a living being, sweaty and breathless from running, but they heightened their defenses, nonetheless. Like Tim, they did not expect to encounter zombies near the hospital, but they were still apprehensive. "Why are you here?" the larger man asked of Tim, whose heart rate was beginning to settle back toward a normal rhythm.

"My wife is giving birth to our son," Tim replied between breaths, wiping sweat from his forehead.

"What is her name?" the questioning continued.

"Clare Austin." Every word spoken during this encounter was automatically posted at the top of the giant video screen erected upon one huge wall in the hospital lobby. His entire conversation with the guards was visible to anyone who watched the panels on this wall in the lobby. Tim's full name, profile, and his conversation with the guards was displayed for everyone inside the hospital to see. That was only one safeguard of the hospital's monitoring system. Much more information about Tim was available to people who had immediate access to system software. The cyber monitors present in the building had relatively limited access, and mostly for security purposes. However, a licensed data monitor had to be in the building in case someone's virtual file had to be opened to acquire specific information from it. As Tim had entered the screening room electronic sensors had begun the probing. They recorded his fingerprints, photographed his eyes, face, and anything else that could indubitably identify him and connect him with his virtual file. His personal information was retrieved from the data base, VISPI, an acronym for Virtual Identification System and Personal Information. The new data gathered by the electronic surveillance devices upon his entrance was matched with Tim's pre-existing file. The latter was a compilation of the entire known history of Tim as recorded electronically. Every American citizen had his/her own virtual file, which contained all records of him/her, beginning with birth – or at least whatever information could be uploaded about each person since the data base had been established.

Every government building, whether local, state or federal, as well as hospitals and educational institutions, had a similar security system and access to VISPI. Cyber monitors reviewed these files whenever someone entered one of these buildings. The attending cyber monitor was alerted to the most pertinent information about the entrant, while the security guards at the entrance to the building conducted the necessary questioning. If there was any reason for caution, a warning would flash to the cyber monitor, and it would be necessary to immediately notify the guards at the door to apprehend or otherwise detain and depose the entrant. These screening devices were originally intended to provide basic security. They were instituted to rebuff terroristic acts and to prevent identity theft. While they had evolved quickly as part of a comprehensive building security package, they were never intended for preventing unwanted encounters with zombies. The latter was only a recent concern.

These security systems were, allegedly, designed to protect

the privacy of individuals. Everyone was permitted access to one's own file to verify the accuracy of the data, but the application process was tedious and could take weeks for each request. Ultimately, people were concerned that abuses of one's private information could pose immediate, personal danger. However, the government did its best to structure the system for the protection of the citizen. One was precariously dependent upon the state and federal governments as overseers of this personal data.

The cyber monitors were unable to access anyone's virtual file. They only received enough information to identify individuals entering the building, primarily to determine who might be dangerous. Neither could they alter the data in these files. Only certain agencies and licensed professionals could enter an individual's virtual file to introduce new information, or to peruse the file for some specific purpose. Even then, one first had to apply for a passcode, identifying the reason for opening the file, to receive permission from the Federal Communications Commission. The FCC was careful to issue a passcode only to those with a license to receive it.

As the calendar turned to the year 2036, legislation had been adopted to expand access to this data base, and to equip more and more institutions with the necessary hardware, including banks and other major corporations. It frightened Tim to think that in milliseconds his personal history was summoned upon the identification of his defining physical traits. On this occasion, the hospital security system had identified Timothy John Austin as the man who had entered the building. His relationship to Clare Austin was confirmed by the cyber monitor, and no warnings flashed to suggest danger. That fact was signaled to the guards at the door. As this transpired, Tim was catching his breath. He felt an alienated sense of security, for the moment. However, he had serious misgivings about his privacy, given the fact that his entire personal history could be accessed by complete strangers, and his personal conversations were instantly displayed as public knowledge.

Some of his friends, particularly Jake, had joked with him, calling him a paranoid type. *"Maybe so,"* he thought to himself. But he couldn't help recalling how the United States had been influenced by the Chinese during the isolationist policies of the administration several years earlier. It was during the endless trade negotiations with the Chinese that security measures in the United States had begun a significant change. Around that time the United States government had begun to employ security technology similar to that used in China, along with some of their techniques for its use. For this reason, Tim was wary of the rapid spread of these security systems across the nation over the past ten years.

"Alright, Mister Austin, you can find her in room 1345." The voice broke through Tim's musings about the privacy which he felt slipping away from him. He thought himself lucky that these *thoughts and emotions* weren't displayed for all to see, but he put those concerns aside. For the moment, all was right with his world. He was safely hidden away from the zombies and he was going to see Clare and his new son. He turned his tall, slender frame toward the lobby.

The guard opened the door leading out of the fortified screening room into the lobby and suggested a path toward the room. Tim smiled, thinking only someone lacking common sense could fail to find 1345. A child could follow the signs. As he walked, his thoughts went back to his experience with Jake. He knew he would have some explaining to do at some point, but he really didn't want to discuss this with Clare in any detail at the hospital.

He gently pushed open the door with the number 1345 on it. He saw Clare, sitting erect on the hospital bed, her long hair hanging neatly over one shoulder. She held her phone to her ear with a slight look of concern on her face. Little Michael laid quietly in his own private plastic box, tightly swaddled. He was sleeping soundly.

"Is Jake alright? Lyndsey can't get ahold of him," Clare asked without the traditional hello or kiss.

"He's fine. His truck went into a ditch because of a reckless driver." That was the most he wished to say at that moment.

Clare continued, on cue from Lyndsey who was asking the questions, "Did he get the truck out of the ditch?"

"He said a wrecker towed the truck to the garage. That's all I know." Tim saw Clare gaze over toward Michael. Her face beamed with joy. He was ready to share some of that with her now. He wanted to pick up Michael, and hug Clare.

But Lyndsey still had more questions. She was concerned about Jake. Tim could hear her ask this time, "Did he make it over to see Jim Wallace?"

Tim was waiting for that question. It made him feel on edge. "No, but he asked me to take his things, so I did, and I left him at the car rental. I'm sure he'll be contacting you as soon as he gets a new phone. His was broken. I'll talk to you later, sis, okay?"

"Sounds as if there is no problem, Lyndsey," Clare tried to reassure her.

"Okay," she said, "No reason to worry. Love you. See you later."

Clare put down the phone. Tim looked at her with concern, but he set it aside for a hug and a kiss. Then, he approached Michael. "I can't interrupt that peaceful rest!" he whispered with an ear-to-ear grin.

"What happened to Jake, Tim?" Clare queried.

"I'm not sure. We can talk about it later." Tim suggested.

Tim didn't want anything he had to say finding its way to surveillance devices. He was an active part of what had become a vital underground movement in America. It had been born several years earlier from the collective concerns about climate change. The warnings from scientists before the turn of the century had proven prophetic. In fact, in some ways global warming had exceeded the expectations of the scientists who were sounding the alarm thirty years prior. As a result, political leaders were facing increased international pressures with regards to a whole spectrum of actions that were harmful to the environment. There had been serious discussions, and legislation had been proposed in the international forum, to try and enforce the preservation of nature. Various proposals had been drafted and shared. Among these were severe restrictions on the production and use of all sorts of weapons, the total elimination of all forms of nuclear power, and a curtailment on the use of oil in production and manufacturing.

There was a growing effort by many leaders of foreign countries to expand this international agreement throughout the world. Attitudes had also begun to change in the U.S. The most recent generations of American youth were insisting that "the good life" was not dependent upon a growing economy and increasing corporate profits. New priorities were ascending in the hearts of the youth. Specifically, the *health* of each new generation had attained a higher priority than it had within the greedy capitalistic endeavor to increase wealth and rule the world. It was long overdue but, finally, the *preservation* of nature and mutual respect for people all over the world was becoming more important than the domination of nature. This underground movement had only just begun to surface in the political arena.

The strength behind this new attitude in the U.S. had to be reckoned with in Congress when several members called upon its underlying philosophy of cooperation and mutual respect to solve the most pressing problems of Americans. Many traditional capitalists were talking as if this movement was nothing more than another '60s fad. Some said it was merely "nature lovers on a high". However, several of the younger and more progressive appointed officials had begun to assemble amongst themselves. Many of them were young *women* who had been elected to Congress. Empowerment of women in the business world had been eclipsed only by their growth in numbers in the realm of elected officials. This was critical for changing the American political landscape. Further enabling the change, many of the old, crony representatives had retired or died, while the newcomers were increasingly younger and more focused on solving problems without the typical guilt-slinging from one party toward the other.

Gradually, the American people were becoming more appropriately represented by their peers in respect to age, gender, and color. It was this more youthful, feminine, and diverse coalition who assembled among themselves and worked to inspire an atmosphere of cooperation in the Congress as a whole. They were applauded worldwide for their instrumentality in achieving the great compromise on health care, and the Ebola vaccination. But in the end, they were condemned by traditional democrats and republicans for publicly expressing their growing eagerness to participate in the International Alliance for the Preservation of Nature (IAPN). This created quite the schism in Congress. Many of the elders were casting stones, and members of this youthful coalition were being depicted as socialists and communists, or simply as dangerous to the U.S. Constitution. The elders defended their claim by emphasizing that the new champions of cooperation were not defenders of the corporation. This placed the youthful coalition in direct opposition with many democrats and republicans who, for the first time in recent history, were able to agree upon something. Both parties continued to defend the stale, traditional form of capitalism that was being threatened by a new priority to respect the life and health of the planet.

Ultimately, the new coalition in Congress had secretly decided to establish their own party in opposition to the traditional democrats and republicans. Tim had been working with some of these representatives to structure a platform that was founded upon the tenets of the IAPN. It was by coincidence that he met two members of this new coalition at the university while he was studying the brief history of the IAPN. Jim Wallace and Kayla Bruster were Representatives from the state of Pennsylvania. They just happened to be researching the origin and formation of the organization. Wallace introduced himself when he found Tim perusing the very same literature as he and Kayla Bruster. They became friends immediately, and Tim was pleased to find practical value for his philosophy degree. Since then, he had worked to present a valid and convincing argument, aiming to entice the democrats and republicans to set aside their greed and power-mongering to listen to the changing preferences of the American public.

The number of countries favoring participation in the IAPN was growing globally, and a discussion of the impediments for implementation of a radically different way of life was underway. But the topic had been mostly ignored and averted in the United States Congress. Congressional leaders had refused even to discuss the issues surrounding much needed changes in the structure of American life. The changes discussed internationally were generally conceived as a threat to the status quo. But finally, this new coalition had become emboldened to represent the growing number of Americans who preferred to respect natural life rather than to dominate it. The group aimed to force discussions that would change American capitalism. Their ultimate intention was to fully participate in the International Alliance and begin the cooperative effort to save what was left of the natural world. They would strive to replace those institutions that harmed and exploited nature with institutions that preserved nature. Tim's most recent writings were oriented toward persuading Congress to face the existing problems in earnest. An excerpt of his most recent exhortation read as follows:

"We must recognize, and respond wisely to, the distressing crises in our natural environment. We cannot fail to notice that we are increasingly destroying the elements of our world that nourish us and sustain our health. The future of life on earth demands that we evaluate our circumstances carefully and work together as a supporting member of the global community to prevent the continued squandering and destruction of our most valuable natural resources.

The rapid melting of the glaciers in the Arctic and Antarctica has more than verified the warnings echoed by climatologists earlier in the century. The melting of the polar icecaps has redefined our coastal boundaries, not only in the United States, but all over the world. Our central plains have flooded, submerging large areas of our farmland. We have seen temperatures rise worldwide. Fires constantly scorch the dry lands of the Western U.S.

What is, perhaps, most distressing is that we continue to make careless decisions and commit irresponsible actions that result in local disasters that lower our quality of life. We have created catastrophes with our aging nuclear reactors and caused accidents by transporting plutonium. These sad occurrences have irreversibly contaminated large portions of valuable land with radioactivity, forever altering the lives of millions of people.

Worldwide, the endless battles and skirmishes of various armed forces have created vast wastelands. The Persian Gulf and its surrounding lands have been destroyed by the deployment of nuclear missiles in so many foolish battles over oil. We continuously add to the number of cities in the Middle East and Northern Africa that lie in ruins from the continuous tracking and warring against so-called terrorists. Innumerable towns and cities that had been thriving social centers have been reduced to giant desert graveyards. These calamities comprise a collection of catastrophic events that have caused irreversible harm to our life source. At the same time water is rising and flooding our lands from every direction, we have been recklessly contaminating what remains of the land where we can live and farm. We must act now to cease our destructive tendencies and replenish the losses of our arable land. We must take immediate action, and follow the lead of the IAPN, making public health the top priority for all our institutional endeavors.

Our intention to dominate nature, and the people who comprise a vital part of it, must be overcome. We are slowly closing the window on our future. For the future of our children and grandchildren, and their children, let us join the global community to work together with the intention to respect and preserve all that nourishes life and produces health."

"Isn't he beautiful?" Clare asked Tim, ogling Michael with a look of adoration.

"Of course! He is our son!" Tim felt warm inside, but he cooled quickly as he realized that the birth of Michael had created a new responsibility for him. "I saw those zombies," he mumbled out loud as he recollected in a daze. He was thinking about the added defenses he would have to prepare in the face of these changing realities.

"Are you alright?" Clare asked him while he was in his reflective fog, "You look disheveled."

Tim considered this to be an invitation to express some of his recent frustrations. So, he let go of any inhibitions. "Dunno what's gonna happen with the car. I abandoned it and ran here."

"What?" Clare chirped.

"I ran my ass off to the hospital…only a couple of miles. I almost shit my pants when I realized that a walking dead thing was leaning against my car and I had nowhere to go. I saw a few more of them around the other cars, stumbling into fenders, reaching for something." Tim was quite animated as he spoke. He knew Clare would understand he had to release some tension. "I thought 'Fuck this!' I saw a clear path, got out and ran." he added, with a feigned nonchalance betrayed by his wide-eyed expression as he nodded agitatedly.

"Oh, my word!" she shivered as she thought about it. "I didn't realize you had such a hard time getting here! Are you alright now?" she asked, reaching for his hand.

"I'm fine now," Tim said with a smile, "but I would like to get out of here and head back home."

"Michael and I have yet to be discharged." Clare collected the facts for Tim. "Our doctor won't be here until tomorrow. I expect that's when we can leave." Then she added with a concerned frown, "I hope we don't meet any of those things."

"I suppose I ought to try and arrange our transportation. I'm not sure when or where we might find our car." While Tim expressed this concern, he knew his sister, or Jake, could take them home.

The new parents took some time to show their mutual affections in the presence of their new joy. Neither of them was able to shelve his or her concerns, and thoroughly enjoy the moment. But they embraced, and that reminded each of them of the affection that had resulted in the birth of a new son. They lingered as long as possible within that feeling.

Chapter 3

A Shared Experience of Zombies

Kaboom! Lightening lit the sky, followed by a rumbling that was enough to move Jake to imagine an earthquake. Giant raindrops began to fall in short order, and it wasn't long before he could hear and see hail pelting against his windshield with such force that he expected it to break.

Suddenly, he saw two zombies before him on the country road that would eventually take him home. He braced for contact and steered recklessly to the left. Somehow, he had missed them completely. "Damn," he thought out loud, "don't wanna crash twice in the same day! Shit!" he cursed as golf-ball sized hailstones began to bounce off his newly rented truck. One of them had created a spider web on the windshield directly in his view on the driver's side. He wanted to speed up, but he tried to remain calm, realizing that he was nearly home. His "most significant other", as he liked to call her, Lyndsey, and her daughter, Rinna, were expecting him soon. Even though Jake's phone had been crushed when he crashed into the ditch, he made it his first goal after renting a truck to replace it, then he contacted Lyndsey. They were expecting some friends to come to their house. He wished it could be a pleasant social engagement, but he thought otherwise. Zombies had been increasingly encountered in his neighborhood over the past couple of weeks, and this get-together had a purpose.

Another loud *kaboom*! A lightning bolt shot down from the dark sky and exploded as if it had just hit something over the hill beyond his house. Then thunder pounded the road beneath him. As he turned onto his street, he thought he might have glimpsed more zombies slogging through a corn field to his left. His wipers on full speed, he stepped on the gas. "*Only a little farther!*" he thought. He reached the top of the hill and began to descend the other side. Now he was in the home stretch. As he approached his driveway, he hit the brakes hard and turned onto it. He could feel the antilock brakes functioning as they were designed to work. He looked carefully about his property as he steered around the bend toward the garage at the end of the driveway. Peering beyond the speeding wipers, and the crack spread across his windshield, he saw an accumulation of hailstones in the grass through the pouring rain, but nothing else terribly unusual, so he pressed the button to open the garage door and waited impatiently as it opened. It seemed to take an eternity, but it took less than ten seconds to fully open. He rushed in with the truck and pressed the button again, watching intently behind him. Slowly the door went down. With a feeling of relief, he got out of the truck and locked the garage door. Then he went to the door that allowed him to enter the den. He shut it behind him and bolted the locks tightly.

Lyndsey was there to greet him. She stood erect at the door, with her usual charm glowing in her face. While she was not beautiful at first glance, the longer one remained in her presence, the more attractive she appeared to be. She extended her petite frame upward, raising herself on her toes. Jake hugged and kissed Lyndsey as if they had just been reunited from a long separation. To Jake's surprise, Alan, Zack, and their families were already there.

"What are you'n's doin' here already?" Jake queried. His Pittsburghese showed in his choice of pronouns. Jake set himself apart in this respect. Many Pittsburghers would say "yinz" as trained by the followers of the Steelers football team.

However, Jake had always insisted on "you'n's" claiming that it means "you and everyone else there with you", or "you and yours." Thus, he formed his contraction with "you", adding the "n" from "and", then the "s" to stand for "all the others who are with you." He always teased that "yinzers" were Steelers fans, suggesting that they had no right to decide the proper spelling and meaning for the more civil Pittsburghers who used a phonetically similar pronoun.

"We just got here," Zack replied. "I got off work early today because I had to take Jeffrey to get his vaccination. There he is!" Jeffrey came running from the playroom down the hall and jumped into his Daddy's arms. "How's my little man?" Zack spoke with pride as he picked him up above his head and tossed him into the air, then caught him and spun himself around and hugged him tightly. He was not a baby anymore, having just turned seven the week before. Zack's wife, Karen, came into the den with Alan and his wife, Greta.

"Don't throw him around like that, Zack." Karen objected to his playful manner. "After all, he just had that damned vaccination, and you don't know how he might react." Karen was still bothered by the prospects, no matter how slim, that Jeffrey might have an adverse reaction to the Ebola vaccine. After all, bad reactions were rare – less than 1% of the public had one – but not impossible. However, most of the adverse reactions seemed to happen in people who were already ill, not children. The worst reactions tended to occur in the elderly, among whom stroke was most common. For that reason, it had been decided that those who were very old or unhealthy could opt out, provided that the doctors acquire the necessary permission for each patient and make a thorough report to the health department. This would be recorded on one's permanent health record, which was an integral part of one's virtual file to be found on VISPI.

Once the Ebola virus had found its way into Europe and the United States in 2032, it had become more prolific. The strain was mutating. People could acquire a weaker version of it, and suffer for weeks or even months, while others died quickly. An incredible number of people had suffered horrible deaths in Africa before it had spread to other nations. Researchers had begun working more feverishly to develop a vaccine as the disease crossed borders around the world. Later in 2033, when the disease and fear of it had reached frightening proportions in the United States, a vaccine had been produced and administered after minimal testing. Subsequently, Ebola seemed to have been completely eradicated within one short year, until several cases had turned up once again in the U.S.

Ultimately, a new and improved version of the vaccine had been concocted by the Eternity Corporation, an American pharmaceutical company near Columbia, South Carolina. It was first available to the public in February 2036, in coordination with the establishment of the new health care system that had been deemed necessary and hastened into existence by the Ebola epidemic. It had been legislated that every American citizen had to have the new vaccine, and the scope of its application was extremely broad. While the disease was widely feared, and many people were motivated to get protection, anyone who did *not* get the vaccine would be easily identified through one's virtual file. One of the threats made had suggested that one might have to be vaccinated just to be allowed to purchase food. After the first month of administering the vaccine, exceptions were made for the very old and those in bad health. It was determined that these exemptions posed no risk to anyone who had already received the new vaccine. And so that no one would complain about affordability, unlike any previous medication created in the history of corporate America, it was administered at no cost to the citizen.

"He's fine, Karen. Look how happy he is! Not a sign of any problem." Zack was probably right to assume there would be no adverse reaction because most negative reactions that occurred happened within minutes after the intramuscular injection. Zack had barely made the deadline for getting the shot for Jeffrey. He was still a little upset with Karen that she had wanted him to wait until the last minute to get him the shot. The government had instituted a stiff penalty which included a substantial fine, and the withholding of the personal health care subsidy for one year, for anyone who had not gotten the injection by this day, June 7, 2036.

The new health care plan and the proposed solution to the Ebola virus were decided as part of one and the same bill in Congress. The usual bickering between democrats and republicans was miraculously overcome to forge an agreement. The defenders of corporate America were willing to compromise. They would agree to accept a national health care bill with the stipulation that the exact costs to the public would be specified after Congressional debate, but if and only if the Ebola vaccine were to be immediately mandatory for everyone. There was public resistance against making the vaccine mandatory, particularly from those who didn't trust the American government. But the upstart coalition intent upon restructuring the American way of life had carried their argument to the people. They emphasized that, although the vaccine was mandatory for all citizens, it was necessary for life-long immunization and expected to be 100% effective this time. Not only would the Ebola concern be permanently eliminated, but everyone would gain from a national health care program that would substantially lower the cost of health care for all citizens.

Health care had been a major expense for everyone, and the source of contentious arguments and debates for decades. The new coalition had argued for the acceptance of the mandatory vaccine as an integral part of a universal health care package. If it were not for this coalition urging and facilitating cooperation within Congress, and convincing the general population, Americans might have been forever entrenched in the old, inefficient health care system with no hope for progress due to political gridlock. The final agreement was achieved with the help of health care professionals of all sorts, and youthful leaders dedicated to supporting a healthier way of life for Americans. Support from doctors and nurses was crucial because medical professionals would be among the first to feel the compromise in their wages.

While making their argument to the people, the new coalition had emphasized the necessity of cooperation, making a direct reference to the inspiration of the International Alliance. This is what enabled a new group-consciousness to gain influence and begin to establish political viability. The defenders of the International Alliance made their presence felt at a moment of profound importance for the American citizen. As a result, the Alliance had become more widely known to the American public.

The divisive speech and infantile behavior displayed among the two parties in Congress had peaked during the Ebola crisis. Deep divisions had to be overcome to find an equitable solution to a very serious problem. For decades, every disagreement in the House and Senate would end in the familiar blame game that had become the hallmark of the two-party system. Too many important decisions had either been delayed, or even aborted, because of selfish behavior. The traditional system had wasted its substance. One party would claim that their own shit didn't stink, and that it was the opposition who was emitting the foul odor. However, the proof was obvious in the utter lack of progress, and so many failures to solve America's most vital problems. The superiority and dominance of one party over the other was the overwhelming force behind the attacks and counter attacks. No one would focus on the problems at hand! During an interview with a popular news source, one member of the new coalition epitomized the problem with a joke. She said, "There are too many parties in Congress! We must demand sobriety!" Then she added, "No more parties! We simply have too many problems to solve!" That truly said it all.

The health care system had been in tatters for years, because only a minimum of concern was actually oriented toward public health. Many wondered why something had not been done to support the health of the American public. After all, good health should be *the* most highly prioritized thing in life. The opposition between republicans and democrats on health care would continuously thwart rational discussion that might allow for compromised agreements.

The tension hit its highest point when the divisiveness amidst the parties dominated the discussion of how to deal with the renewed Ebola problem. It had happened during a debate of the questions, "Does everyone have to get the vaccine? Or does someone have a choice?" Finally, an agreement was made in the face of the gravity of the situation, and the health of Americans was able to gain a higher degree of importance. The great compromise was made to adopt the Universal Health Care Plan, while also requiring every citizen to have the vaccine.

But it was not only political opposition that had fought against a health care bill. The drug-makers and the medical profession as a whole were not making health care affordable for people who needed medicine or surgery just to stay alive. In fact, it was only those who needed medicine and services who wanted to discuss the issue of affordability. All others wanted to dictate the costs. Insurance companies exacerbated the problem. They were reaping huge profits with ever-increasing deductions from salaries, while simultaneously lowering the amounts that they paid to doctors and hospitals, even for preventative measures like regular check-ups.

Besides the compromises that these institutions and health-care professionals would have to endure, technological advances in the field of health and science had also helped to overcome the differences. Because so many procedures had been conducted by robots, the costs had become more affordable, or at least more transparent. The cost of surgery and other treatments were mostly measured in terms of the performing equipment in addition to the medical staff behind the operations. While these costs had stabilized, and were shrinking, the drug companies still expected a whopping profit from sales to fund research. But, finally, it seemed that their profits would also be subject to reductions within the new health care agreement.

"Alright," said Jake, "let's get started with the task at hand." He went over to the covered windows in the living room, checking the makeshift barricade he had built in the past couple of days. It was Lyndsey, actually, who motivated him to install these home defenses. She kept insisting that these crazy encounters with the "diseased people", as she called them, should be taken seriously. She seemed to know more about these attacks than most people, so he took her words as a warning. He had made special safeguards to protect his loved ones, including boarding his windows. One by one, he and the other men went around to each room in the house checking these defenses to guarantee their safety. Each of them had become concerned for their families since the zombies had been seen in numerous suburban neighborhoods. None of them wanted to have a close encounter.

Informative reports about these frightful encounters were still few and far between, and the reports were strangely variable. Because most people who saw the monsters were comparing them to zombies, the popular decision was to glean what was known about zombies from the many works of fiction in which they were depicted, just to learn about them. Moreover, some of the reports they had heard on the local news, in the papers and on various online news services, including Fraternizer, had consistently identified these creatures as zombies. And most people had agreed that they were quite like what they had been imagined to be in the fictional writings.

It had been only a couple weeks prior that the zombies had first been encountered in the Pittsburgh area. It was about the same time that these encounters were being reported across the nation. Now everyone thirsted for a better knowledge of where they were coming from, how to defend oneself against them, and for that matter, anything else one could learn. In fact, that was the reason that Alan and Zack had come to the home of Jake and Lyndsey. They were going to collectively search every available source and gather any information that they could about the zombie attacks. They all agreed that Jake's attic would be a good place to coordinate their defenses. They could adjourn to his "control center", as he liked to call it, to research as a group.

The three children, Rinna, Jeffrey, and Phillip, ages seven, seven, and eight respectively, could play in the game room. It was one of the safest rooms in the house, centrally located on the main floor with no windows to the outside. Greta stayed with the children while Karen and Lyndsey went to the kitchen to set the table for a group dinner. Zack and Karen had picked up a family styled dinner from the Chinese restaurant near the pharmacy where they had taken Jeffrey to get the vaccine. It wasn't long before the table had been set for all nine. They gathered and dined, eating heartily, leaving practically nothing to be collected and repackaged as leftovers. Jake insisted that the used dishes and utensils be left at the table for the time being. "We can clean up these dishes later. Let's go to the control center and see what we can learn about these damned zombies!"

Lyndsey went upstairs with Jake, Zack, and Alan. Karen and Greta stayed close to the children on the main level. "What the hell happened this morning?" Alan queried of Jake.

"Some big cowboy in a raised four-wheel drive truck ran me off the road," Jake said, holding his hand to signal a level above his head. Jake, himself, was over six feet tall and ripped with upper-body muscles. So, for him to call someone else "big" was unusual. "I was on the way to Representative Wallace's office. I'm almost certain that I was being followed."

"Aren't you the guy who brands Timmy as the paranoid?" Zack took a jab at Jake, even as he was recounting an experience of his own vulnerability.

"But I *was* being followed!" Jake insisted. "I decided to take a circuitous route to the office, and this big-ass Chevy came flying out from this alley, and just slammed right up against me and knocked me straight into the ditch on the side of the road. It was a deep fucking ditch! My truck was laying on the passenger side, more or less, right near the stop sign on Beacon Avenue. I was lucky not to get hurt."

"Anyone you recognize?" Alan asked not expecting that it was.

"It was hard to see inside, but I did see a big guy with a cowboy hat. That's all."

"Well, thankfully you didn't get hurt," Lyndsey interrupted. "Everything will get to where it needs to go. Just a temporary setback."

"Yeah. Right now, we need to get going with the research on these zombie attacks," Jake reminded them. "We are under attack on multiple fronts. We have to focus on them one at a time."

Jake had equipped his attic with a highly sophisticated computer system. There were several video devices and separate control boards attached to the main computer. Each wall was a giant video screen that could be linked to the others to give the impression to anyone present that he/she was surrounded by, and even actually *within* the scene depicted. One could imagine himself/herself anywhere that could be accessed via the internet, or satellite. The video devices on each wall could also be divided into smaller monitors to visualize just about anything, e.g., a multiplicity of events, scenes, or broadcasts at the same time.

Jake picked up one control board, pointed to the west wall, and said, "I am going to take this panel and search the local and national news reports. Each of you can grab a control board and take a panel for yourself. Maybe you could research what our friends are reporting on Fraternizer," he said to Lyndsey.

"I could do that. There were some strange postings yesterday," she replied as she took the controller from Jake, facing her chair toward the adjacent wall.

"Would you wanna try to find out how these monsters are being successfully repelled?" he asked Alan. "I'd hate to be shooting at them if bullets won't stop them," he added, handing him a controller as he uncovered another seat. Jake's reference to "bullets" was intentional. He meant to remind his friends about the new collection of guns and ammunition hidden away in the attic closet.

"You bet!" Alan responded. "And anything else I can learn. I know so little, because I have been able to keep my distance so far…knock on wood."

Zack had already grabbed a controller and faced the wall with the panels opposite Jake. It was not the first time he had been there. He and Jake were close friends. "I'd like to know what the hell these things really are. It makes no sense to think that they are the victims of Ebola," Zack claimed. "How could they be resurrected victims of the Ebola virus?" Some people thought that made sense because the monsters resembled those diseased victims. "Anyone with a little intelligence has to realize that their remains could never magically reform from ashes back into something that looks like a human being." He began searching websites where the theme was zombies.

"What do you expect? If you can convince people to believe that the dead can rise again, it's just as believable to imagine that they rise as zombies as it is to send them off to heaven," Jake chuckled with a devilish tone.

"Hey, that's what I believe, man!" Alan stated with sarcasm, and all four laughed out loud. It was widely rumored that a Christian group had concocted the idea about the Ebola victims rising again as zombies. No one gathered at Jake's house was disposed to believe anything of the sort. All of them treated superstitious belief with disdain and kept their children distant from such teachings. "I don't want my kids to grow up to be gullible, believing that nonsense. And that is exactly what it is – 'non-sense'! Seriously, there has to be a more plausible explanation about where these monsters come from," Alan insisted.

"We need a reliable source" Zack demanded, "that tells us what they are and where they are coming from. Some of these reports are so strange that I'm not sure what can be considered reliable. Zombies don't just appear outta nowhere!" He was growing impatient. "There is so much here to scan, it's like information overload," he complained after he discovered the volume and diversity of reports about zombies.

Each of the four quietly conducted a search for a few minutes until Zack exclaimed, "Listen to this! Would you believe that I'm finding more than one person who claims that their bite is not as harmful as you might suppose? One guy claims he was knocked down and bitten. He says that the bite was painful, and the monster had a stench about it and a lot of disgusting open sores, but…and get this…the zombie disappeared after he was bitten."

"Does he say what kind of drugs he was taking?" Alan quipped as the others simultaneously expressed their amusement at the thought.

"I've actually heard that before," Lyndsey declared in a serious tone.

"No, really," Zack added, "and the bite also disappeared in a short time. The man said that the anxiety he had during the attack was bad enough, but later he was crazy with fear as he laid in his barn, expecting to die a horrible death. He says he was afraid that he might even become a zombie himself. He adds that this happened two weeks ago, and he has no scar or anything where he was bitten."

"That is unbelievable!" Jake retorted as he opened the cabinet with the fine spirits. He took out four glasses and welcomed his guests to help themselves. He poured a shot of salty caramel whiskey for himself, held it in the air, and said "Here's to the good life…without zombies." As he downed the whiskey, he was listening to daily news reports. The others poured shots for themselves. "Are you kidding me!" he objected. "All I'm hearing in these local news reports is D-Day anniversary commemorations!" As Jake uttered this complaint, the President was to be seen on three of the four different newscasts that he was surveying simultaneously on his wall. He thought he should listen, so he silenced the others, and increased the volume to hear the President exalting those who rushed the beaches at Normandy.

"These men are the great heroes of freedom whom we must never forget. With great courage they gave their lives for the rest of us who owe them the honor and respect that all heroes deserve. We are forever indebted to their memory for they have preserved the power and honor of our nation." As Jake moved to silence the broadcast and search the others for any news about zombies, he noticed that every channel had a report about national heroism.

"Holy shit!" Jake complained. "Is there nothing about today's battles or today's heroes who are fighting zombies?"

Alan wheeled around in his chair and pointed to the section of screen in the upper left corner of Zack's wall. "There's a report about zombies." But, before Zack could set the controls to focus on it with volume, it had finished. It was quickly replaced by an ad for a drug used to fight diabetes. The ad showed an older woman looking at herself in a mirror apprehensively. Magically, in the next frame she was transformed, happy and carefree, dancing at the town square with her friends. Everyone in the ad was so happy and joyful. Then, all the possible side-affects were enumerated while the advertiser showed a video of people dancing and smiling. This amounted to the greater part of the ad. Alan couldn't resist a wise crack. "How the hell can she be so God damned happy, and dance through all those side-affects? She'll probably shit herself before she can finish the two-step!" Again, the whole group busted out in laughter.

"What did people do years ago, when none of these drugs existed?" Lyndsey asked. She had learned from her grandmother all sorts of natural remedies. As a result, she developed a preference to avoid medicines, especially any sort of pill, whether a vitamin or whatever. "There were a lot less surgical procedures, too," she noted, as if to question the validity of too much reliance on either one.

"Well, people think they're gonna find a cure for every ailment," added Zack, "and live forever. Advertisers will help them go on believing."

Lyndsey didn't pay much attention to Zack's sarcasm. She was taking the responsibility for learning about zombies quite seriously. The stories about zombie attacks that she had heard firsthand made her wonder, "*Why zombies?*" She had been searching for clues from a time when zombies were nothing more than fictitious entities in video games and spooky novels. "Do you suppose we could learn anything from novels about zombies?" she asked the others.

"I doubt it," Jake replied. "What could they teach us?"

"Maybe we could learn where they come from, and what they really are." She was struggling to learn what was most important to her. Lyndsey was an extremely reflective and well-cultured woman at age 38. Ever since entering therapy, she had placed a new and meaningful value on self-knowledge. Therapy had shown her that, without a doubt, one could further penetrate the mysteries of one's own self. Her strong desire to build her own self-knowledge also strengthened her professional ability to help other people work out difficulties that might otherwise consume them. She constantly learned from her self-reflective practice. These zombies could never make her lose contact with her own good sense.

"We ought to focus on today's zombies...the real ones," Jake retorted. "I thought you were gonna see what our friends are saying about the zombies on Fraternizer?"

Lyndsey responded, "Most conversations rotate around the fact that the sightings and conflicts are taking place at people's homes and in residential areas. Here is one strange incident: A group of people went to the hospital for aid from an alleged zombie attack outside of their house. They said that zombies just came up to their porch and started hitting and grabbing them. Two of them were bitten. They somehow got away and made their way to the hospital. But they were turned away from the hospital and treated as if they were psychopaths by the guards. All of them were frantic and expressing their distress over the attack, but they had no visible wounds where they had claimed they were bitten."

"Zombies appearing and disappearing?" queried Jake. "Wounds disappearing? That seems to be consistent in many of these reports. Maybe we don't have to fend them off at all; we could just wait for them to disappear." He said that tongue in cheek, but no one laughed.

"Yeah, we'll just…" Alan didn't get a chance to finish expressing the sarcasm he had planned. A sudden loud crash and the sound of breaking glass could be heard on the main floor. Greta screamed, and a muffled groaning could be heard amidst pounding against the wooden barricade that covered the broken living room window. Jake took Zack to the weapons cache as the children ran fearfully into the back room of the attic with Karen and Greta. Jake pulled out three 12-gauge shotguns, giving one to Zack and handing the other to Alan. Then he looked out the upstairs window and saw a couple of shadows moving below in the early evening dusk.

Bamm! Something slammed against his barricade at the living room window. His heart was pounding in his chest. Fear was rising in him. He grabbed as many rounds of buckshot as he could, dropping one, and loaded his gun. His friends did the same. He felt an aggression building inside of him as he readied to bolt downstairs to kill some zombies.

Karen and Greta were trying to stay calm and hide their fear from the children. But it was too late for that. All the anxiety directed toward the danger of the moment had filled the house to the point where it had its own current that flowed through the children like electricity would through any copper conductor. It transferred directly into the children despite the fact the little ones had no real sense of what was happening. They could all feel the anxiety, but it was the fear of death that motivated an aggressive response against the zombies.

"Go to the back bedroom!" Jake had ordered Alan. "Yell if it's been infiltrated, and we'll yell for you if we need you. Come on, Zack." He motioned for Zack to follow him into the living room. He told Lyndsey to stand guard in the den. She had grabbed a loaded handgun from the weapons cache and descended the staircase. Jake had taught her to fire both a pistol and a rifle at a target. She handled both weapons admirably. Lyndsey had also carried a rifle when she had been hunting with Jake in the woods behind his house. But, despite having reached some level of familiarity with guns, she did not feel comfortable holding the pistol now.

While this was going on, the women upstairs were perusing the arms in the weapons supply. It was prepared just a couple of days earlier when Jake had noticed the existence of zombies in his own neighborhood. These recent sightings made him want to have weapons with plenty of ammunition. There were enough guns for every adult to have at least one. Greta and Karen were not comfortable with any kind of weapon. Nevertheless, Karen extracted two 9mm semi-automatic pistols from the case, handed one to Greta and showed her the safety catch.

"Just push this lever up like this and it will be ready to fire," she told Greta, hoping that there would be no reason to take off the safety. "Be sure and aim with both hands only at a target you intend to kill."

"I don't want..." Greta was interrupted by the echo of a shotgun blast. She screamed again, and the children cried louder.

"Be careful with that weapon around these children. I'm going to the bottom of the steps," Karen told Greta as she grasped the pistol with both hands and made her way down the stairs.

Greta returned the 9mm pistol to the case whence it came,

then she told the kids in her calmest voice to sit down for a few minutes and wait, and they would go back to playing shortly. But the children would have none of it. Jeffrey and Phillip asked for their Dad. Greta told them everything was going to be fine. "Sit down, please." Rinna began to run toward the stairs until Greta grabbed her by the arm and dragged her back with the boys. She was screaming anxiously for her Daddy. "Just sit here with Phillip and Jeffrey, Rinna. Daddy…."

Pow, pow, pow. One of the men had unloaded his shotgun through the barricade. It was Jake. Zack stood ready in his defense. The pounding against the barricade seemed to have stopped, so Jake walked up to peer through the peep holes that had been enlarged by the shotgun blasts. He could see two grotesquely disfigured zombies lying in the front yard after he turned on the spotlights. He put his face closer to the holes to try and get a closer look, but he could see nothing moving.

Suddenly, *bam*! The barricade was loosened by something slamming it from outside. It knocked Jake on the head, and he fell backward, bloodied and dazed. *Pow, pow*. Zack didn't wait to see what was on the other side. Now the barricade was severely compromised. Zack bent over to check on Jake. "I'm fine," Jake demanded as he wiped the blood from his left eye and got up to glance outside. He could see outside through the broken window where the barricade had been. No movement. He and Zack grabbed the hammer, nails, and spare boards that Jake had conveniently left just beneath the window. They had begun to secure the window which was now open to the outside when…*crash*! Again, breaking glass; this time at the back of the house.

"Back here!" screamed Alan from the back bedroom. The fright from the window breaking on the other side of the barricade directly in front of him made him errantly discharge his shotgun into the ceiling, narrowly missing the floor of the upstairs room where the children were huddled. Zack ran back to help him, while Jake continued trying to secure the living room window, blood flowing down the side of his face. Before he could nail up enough boards to close the opening, he could see another zombie approaching, slogging around the side of the house. Now the war was being waged on two fronts. Jake aimed at the approaching undead and squeezed the trigger. Click. His heart stopped. Again, he squeezed. Click. Click. He opened the breach. Nothing was there. He reached into his pocket nervously at the same time he heard pounding and shots in the back bedroom. Then there was silence for just long enough to hear the moan of the zombie approaching the partially barricaded window. Blood was blinding his left eye from the gash on his forehead.

"Fuck!" he yelled at the top of his lungs. He heard two more shots in the back room, then he saw Karen running toward him.

"Jake...oh, no!" she saw blood and started crying. The blood on his face caused her legs to weaken. She nearly collapsed but Jake grabbed her and shook her before she went to her knees. He was happy to see the 9mm in her hands.

"Gimme that and go upstairs for more ammo for these shotguns." He could see that she might not be able to carry out that command because she was paralyzed with fear. But his aggression and determination moved him to stick the pistol out the opening at the top of the barricade and fire two shots. They were accurate head shots, and the zombie went over backwards twisting and contorting for just a moment before lying motionless.

Jake bent over and helped Karen from her knees. "Please, get up, Karen! Get me some more buckshot." He partially dragged her back toward the steps until she realized that he must be alright. Then she seemed to get a hold of herself and ran back upstairs. During that time, he had heard shots echo in the back bedroom. He ran in with his empty shotgun in one hand and the 9mm in the other. Alan had withdrawn his weapon from the opening in the protective cover that was now badly damaged on one side.

"I don't s...see any more," Alan stuttered slightly. Jake

shined a flashlight out the window. Three hideous zombies were lying on the ground outside the back bedroom. They were covered with festering sores all around their necks and naked torsos. Nothing could be recognized of their faces because large parts of their heads had been blown off.

Karen had just returned with a supply of buckshot shells. "I think we got 'em all," Jake said triumphantly as he wiped blood from his face.

"I wouldn't be so sure. What the hell happened, Jake?" asked Alan, noticing his wound.

"It's nothing. Just got smacked by one of the boards from the window." He was still bleeding from the open gash on his forehead. "It didn't hit me very hard."

"Let's go clean that wound," Karen said taking him by the arm. Just then another moan was heard outside.

Jake pulled his arm from Karen's grasp. "I got this." He grabbed three rounds of buck shot to reload his shotgun. As he did, Karen just had to look and see what was outside of the window.

"Jake!" she cried.

"What?"

"Don't shoot, Jake. That looks like your crazy neighbor who lives down the street!"

"So, what! It's not human, Karen!"

Jake used the flashlight to get a better look. "Unnnngg," was the sick sort of growl that came from the oncoming thing. He was shocked to see what appeared to be the face of Paul Branch. Paul lived in the next house down the street, and he was not exactly friendly to Jake. He made a foolish scene one night when Zack and Karen were over for a party at Jake's fire pit. He was complaining about the smoke and acted as if he wanted trouble. Although he would not admit it, Jake felt a strange pleasure at the thought of having to shoot him.

"Looks like a zombie to me, Karen. It has a body full of lesions." Just then he saw it raise what looked like a pry bar that is used for demolition.

"That's Paul Branch!" she insisted.

Pow! The shot had to travel no more than twenty feet to its target. It left the head of the zombie in tatters as the rest of it lurched and fell backwards.

"Jake!" Karen gasped hysterically, her hands grasping her throat.

"Get a hold of yourself, Karen! If that was Paul, he was no longer human." Jake peered out the window but saw nothing else moving.

Zack had gone back into the living room to make sure nothing was trying to infiltrate there. On the way, he saw Lyndsey standing alert in the den as if frozen there but staring down the hall toward her friends. The barricade in the den was untouched. Then he looked out the living room window. Nothing moving. Just four motionless corpses that had been zombies. Zack put several more nails through the boards to reconstruct the damaged barricade. Jake did the same in the back bedroom. Karen had counted four motionless corpses outside of that window, one of whom she swore was Paul Branch, Jake's nearest neighbor.

Jake finally went into the bathroom for some medical attention. Lyndsey followed to provide it. Zack continued guarding the window in the back bedroom until Alan returned with the last piece needed to reconstruct the barricade. As he lifted the board to put it in place, Zack stopped him.

"Hey, hold it!"

"What?" asked Alan.

"What the…? Look on the ground out there! Where are those zombies?"

"What?"

"They're fucking gone! Hurry and nail up that board. They might be coming back. I'll go check the living room," Zack shivered as the fear of death had crept into the depths of his being.

Chapter 4

The Vision for a Better World

Jake was happy to have traveled into the city and away from the rural neighborhoods like his own. He had begun to feel a comfort, since no one had seen any zombies along the way. He and his friends had a harrowing night, even after the shooting finally stopped. He was worried how he might explain the shooting and broken glass to the authorities. *"What would I have said we were shooting at?"* he wondered. There was no evidence to be found that could defend what he would have claimed had happened. Ironically, no one from the police department or the fire department, or any of the locals for that matter, seemed to have found it necessary to investigate what might have happened there last night. *"Did no one hear the shooting? Or have other people become too shocked and afraid to do anything but mind their own business?"* he asked himself. At any rate, once the sun had risen for a new morning, he was relieved that no explanations were required. He wasn't even certain what to believe himself.

Jake entered the hospital drive and proceeded toward the front door. "Let me out over there," Lyndsey said, pointing to the right. "You might as well park in the lot for a few minutes. We should be out soon. I'll be right back, Rinna." Jake drove his new Marauder beyond the security gate while Lyndsey went into the hospital to find Clare and Tim.

As she walked in the door, the probing of electronic sensors went to work to identify her. VISPI had retrieved the file of Lyndsey Austin within milliseconds after she entered the door. Lyndsey was a regular here; she worked for the State Psychiatric Institute a couple of blocks from the hospital and had extensive experience with this hospital in her work. The cyber monitor knew her well, and the guard at the door was quite attracted to her.

"Hello, Lyndsey! Alone today?" asked Raul as she entered. He loved flirting with her but had decided to behave himself today for some reason.

"Right now, I am, but my girlfriend and her men will be leaving with me," Lyndsey smiled, preening herself for Raul.

"Her men?" Raul questioned. "How many men does she have?" He wasn't sure what her tease might entail on this day.

Lyndsey, with her comforting smile, said to Raul, "One adult, one infantile."

He knew she had a wild sense of humor, and he decided not to mess with her this time, so he just smiled and said, "Bring your friends, and I shall make sure you get safely to your ride."

"Thank you, Raul." His inhibited behavior inspired her to pick up her pace; Tim, Clare, and Michael were waiting for a ride. Tim had tried to call the local pound, where he thought that his car might have been taken. No one seemed to know whether it was there, but he was warned that if it had been towed there, it would cost him at least $700. Finally, his wait to leave the hospital was about to end since Michael's discharge was confirmed. The infant had gotten a social security number and his vaccinations, which were necessary for him to leave the hospital. He had gotten all that he needed to begin his new life. That would have been quite enough, but he suffered at least one thing that he didn't need – a cruel and inhumane carving of the head of his penis. Michael was declared to have survived that folly, then he and his mother were discharged into the world. Tim made the needed adjustments to the new baby carrier and strapped Michael in tightly, so they were ready to go.

"Hey, Sweetie!" Lyndsey beamed as she opened the door. She bent over to hug Clare. "Ready to go home?" Lyndsey turned her attention to Michael. "He's so adorable," she swooned as she reached to free him from his secure carrier.

"It's been a long time since you held Rinna at that age," Clare mused out loud.

"True, but I have gained a more youthful outlook on life through the eyes of a child! More than anything, I realize the significance of helping Michael to establish his identity right from the start. Too many people would like to tell him who he is! Haha!" She had to laugh at her own wise crack because she would be the only one who did. Lyndsey had her own theory of self-identity, partially derived from Freudian psychoanalysis. Her theory was the result of years of research, which had begun with her doctoral dissertation. She had focused on anxiety and its relation to how one thinks about death. Freud's ideas of repression and the unconscious were forefront in her research. And whether she agreed with Freud or not, his insights were critical for the development of her theory of selfhood, and her therapeutic method.

"Well, let's get out of here," Tim said, taking Michael from Lyndsey to put him back in his carrier. The baby's baggage had already become attached to his arm. "Is Jake out front?"

"Yes. He and Rinna are waiting for us. Let's go."

On the way out, Raul, the security guard at the door, recognized Tim from the prior day. He spied the rest of the group coming to the exit, so he cleared a path for Clare to be wheeled out with the baby. Then he smiled and said, "Congratulations on your beautiful little infantile." Then he winked at Lyndsey as the two of them shared a private joke. Clare looked at them both and smiled, then Tim caught on.

Tim laughed and said, "You must have been talking to Lyndsey."

They were heading out to the Marauder. It was the most common version of the giant electric SUVs and would easily seat the six of them with an unused row of seats to spare. Clare decided that she and Tim would sit on each end of the third row of seats and snap the baby carrier into the kiddie cargo between them. Rinna sat right in the center of the second row. Her seat was able to face either forward or backward. Needless to say, which way she adjusted her seat; Michael had her full attention.

"So where *are* we going?" Clare asked as they settled into their positions. Lyndsey made it clear that they still had to deliver Tim's documents to Representative Wallace, as Jake had been trying to do the previous day when he encountered some resistance. "We never got the documents to Jim Wallace." She turned toward Tim.

"Let's go then," said Tim. "He intends to discuss them with the coalition, and clarify the platform for our new party, making certain it is coordinated with the fundamental tenets of the IAPN."

"Has anyone from the Alliance commented on your work?" Lyndsey asked.

"Some, but I should get more feedback soon. The International Alliance has been in discussions, aiming to draft 'Rules for the Preservation of Natural Life'. They have been busy delineating guidelines to honor and respect nature. As you know, their exclusive aim is to preserve and protect the resources that nourish and shelter us."

"It makes too much sense!" exclaimed Lyndsey. She was bothered that this philosophy was so quickly and easily dismissed by the administration of the United States. In her judgement, mankind's most powerful ears needed to listen to these people with the utmost urgency. Rather than simply watch mankind teeter on the edge of self-induced destruction, the United States should defend the countries that had convened to take action to preserve nature and public health. She believed it was time to heed the warning that the modern history of domination was bound to end in self-destruction.

"It might sound as if they want to revive some archaic form of civilization," Tim added, "but the group, and its philosophy, is slowly building its reputation around the world. European scholars are also discussing the major impediments to adopting a new and radically different lifestyle. Hence, some very important, life-impacting questions are being addressed quite seriously."

"Like, for example?" asked Clare.

Lyndsey was pleased for the inquiry. "Well," she began, "can we as a species re-orient our attitude toward natural life? Can we re-configure conscience to command respect and cooperation? And ultimately, could we re-structure our institutions in accordance with an architectonic of public health?"

"Sounds like a complicated chess match that cannot be won with a minimum of sacrificial moves," Clare waxed metaphorically.

"Probably not; chess is logical," Lyndsey quipped with a wry smile.

The U.S. had been invited and urged to join various organizations aiming to protect the planet in past decades. There were many opportunities for it to take the lead in these endeavors, but the administration always projected its misgivings publicly. The answer was absolute, and it could be summarized as such: The necessary changes that would have to be made to conform with the Alliance would be draconian and impractical under current economic standards. It was obvious that the economy always had top priority over what is most important in life, especially the health of the American people.

No doubt, difficult structural changes to American institutions would be necessary. The International Alliance had suggested specific guidelines. For example, the manufacture of weaponry is to be subjected to severe scrutiny, and the sale of weapons between nations is forbidden. Moreover, the dismantling of many existing weapons would begin immediately, to prevent the temptation to initiate any new destruction. Power grids would be absolutely restricted to green sources, among which solar power had been a clear winner. All nuclear power plants would have to be dismantled and replaced. Just what we would do with all the parts from weapons and power plants was a gigantic recycling problem. Finally, and most importantly, our remaining natural resources would be used only with a plan for renewability.

Rebuilding the infrastructure would prove very costly and forever change the existing economy. Several lines of business, and their corresponding jobs, would be sacrificed without regard for economic growth and corporate profits. Ultimately, the competition essential to capitalism would have to come under a new framework of governance. All business proposals would be evaluated for their uses and abuses of our natural resources with a long-term view for supporting life and health. Indiscrete aggression, and the domination of nature, would have to give way to respect for nature and protection of our resources. Such changes to our national institutions would impact our daily lives and jam the cogs of the traditional capitalistic machine. But life on earth is in grave danger, so these changes should be understood to be wise and necessary.

"There's no doubt we need all the help we can get to represent the growing voice of the American people who are concerned with protecting our planet," said Jake. "We can't simply continue to repeat the same self-destructive habits generation after generation."

"I'm with you 100% on that!" Tim concurred. "But, right now, we have more immediate problems," he added as the reality of the zombies came back to mind. He was hesitant to speak with Rinna present, but her attention was absorbed with Michael.

"Well, I certainly do not wish to see the monsters that I've been hearing about," Clare said with a certain finality, looking toward Lyndsey.

"What are these things?" Tim asked rhetorically, and with an air of confusion that could be sensed in the sound of his voice.

Jake was exiting the parking lot. Everything seemed to be normal. Traffic was moving, and people on the sidewalks were walking rather quickly, but no zombies could be seen. "I don't know what they are," Jake said noticing their absence. "I do know that they look diseased and dazed, and act like they aren't even conscious in their bodies. And the strangest thing was that Karen and I saw one zombie that resembled a much-disliked neighbor of mine."

"What?" Clare and Tim said simultaneously.

"Yeah, Karen was frantic when I shot him," Jake said, studying Rinna through the rearview mirror. She seemed to be oblivious to the world.

Suddenly Rinna surprised them all. "There were a lot of shots!" she interrupted with a slight whine in her voice that indicated fear.

Lyndsey turned and grabbed her hand. "Honey, we need to talk about this. If it bothers you, let us know." She wanted her to know they *all* needed support. Then Lyndsey's eyes met Jake's as he glanced in her direction. He knew to speak more carefully.

"I don't like guns! But I'll let the adults talk while Michael

is awake," Rinna thought to herself. She knew that, sometimes, adults have to talk without the children speaking. She reached toward Michael and gently brushed her hand over his.

"So, the zombies are not Ebola victims," Lyndsey added, "unless that neighbor had died of Ebola."

"How *did* that neighbor die?" Tim asked.

"He didn't, as far as I know," said Jake, looking to Lyndsey for conformation.

She nodded, "That's what I heard."

"I still can't get over seeing them gone!" Jake shook his head and looked in the mirror at Tim. If the police *had* come there afterwards, there was nothing, only bullet holes from shooting through barricades and windows. Someone would have thought we were crazy, had we told our story." He said this realizing that similar stories were accumulating.

"Did you have to shoot a gun, Lyndsey?" Clare wondered.

"No. The room I was guarding was never compromised and I stayed put. I saw no zombies!" She hesitated. "We really need to find out where these things are coming from and how to avoid them," Lyndsey said calmly. "Have either of you heard any such thing?"

"No," Tim and Clare answered simultaneously.

"No one seems to know where they come from." Lyndsey said shaking her head. "We did not see a zombie today on our trip here. But, frankly, we are worried about Karen and Zack. They are taking the boys to a Little League game tonight. Zack thinks that he'll be able to confer with other parents to find out more about these things."

Jake had driven from Oakland to Duquesne Boulevard to cross the river to the North Side. As he made his way across the Allegheny River toward the North Hills, he was looking at the river levels. Not too long ago the rivers had risen so much in town that The Point, and the rest of the city, had to be protected by building retaining walls along the riverbanks. Without them, the city streets would be flooded. But the water was not terribly high today. Jake was approaching the exit that would take them to the office of Representative Jim Wallace. As he got closer, it was apparent something was amiss. The smoke that he had not paid much attention to had become thicker as they crossed the river, and now they could see emergency vehicles converged around the general vicinity of Representative Wallace's office.

"Oh, man!" Tim exclaimed, gaping toward the office which had been reduced to charred remains, black and smoldering on top of an otherwise level concrete parking lot.

"It's burned to the ground," Lyndsey lamented.

"Wow! Did we have a 'Plan B'?" Jake asked as he maneuvered around the pylons protecting the emergency vehicles.

Chapter 5

Children Playing in the Shadows of Zombies

"Strike three!" the umpire threw his right hand in the air, adding to the frustration of the batter, who was Zack's son, Jeffrey. He turned away from the plate, put his head down and began to walk back to the dugout.

"That's alright Jeff," Zack yelled from the bleachers. He was surprised to see such a large turnout for the game, despite the fact they usually had large audiences for playoff games. Nearly all the kids who came to play had been brought by his or her own parents. It was quite clear that families were keeping closer together than usual. Zack could feel a high level of apprehension flowing through the bleachers and the field. It had a smothering sort of presence. One need only watch the kids on the field to sense it. Several of the boys and girls were looking around, as if they were expecting someone to come and make them leave the field. In the stands, the parents were having conversations about their fears and specific encounters with zombies. Zack and Karen had discovered no less than five other people involved in two separate incidents in recent days. They were exchanging stories and talking about these monsters as though they were certainly zombies, just like the ones of fictional repute. As some parents tutored each other on the nature of zombies, they watched carefully whenever anyone entered the long drive into the parking area.

The field was located in a small town about thirty miles northeast of downtown Pittsburgh. It was on the corner of a community park that contained three separate baseball fields. There was a gravel alley between each of the fields for those people in charge of setting up and preparing the field. Anyone could walk through these alleys, if they were not blocked by the field crew, but someone intending to park a car would have to travel to the end of the road and turn right to enter an alley to get to the parking area behind the fields. The gravel road through the parking area was nearly as long as the paved road in front of the fields, except that it doubled back toward the direction whence it came before reaching the end of the last field. On the other side of the horseshoe road was a wooded area that ran the whole length of the road. Usually, when a vehicle entered the parking area, you could see dust flying, but today it was still damp with puddles from the previous day's rain.

Zack was closely attending to what was being said in the bleachers. One of the parents was speaking authoritatively about a zombie attack. "It's all about surviving a zombie apocalypse. These things come from the land of the dead, but they aren't dead. They are un-dead. We have to destroy them just to save ourselves and send them back to the crypt!" the woman was ranting.

Zack, and others, could feel the sentiment underlying this woman's warning. "Have you encountered them?" he asked her.

"Yes, I have!" she scowled and squinted as her eyes bulged with horror. It was apparent that some of the other parents either thought she was crazy, or they just didn't want their kids to hear what she was saying. They were moving away, heading elsewhere, but there wasn't far to go. This problem could no longer be avoided entirely.

"Did you have to kill them?" Zack had to ask.

"I did!" the not-so-crazy lady spoke quickly, eventually identifying herself as Matthew Lombardi's Mom, Sylvia.

"Were you, or anyone else that you know, bitten?" Zack had to ask that too.

"No! Well...I thought Matthew and maybe his Dad were, but I guess not."

"How did you get away?" Zack pressed on.

"I heard them screaming in our front yard." She pointed toward the field at no one in particular. "James was yelling for me to get the gun, so I went for the shotgun. When I got back, Matthew was running right at me, crying and holding his shoulder. James was getting himself off the ground, and once I saw it was safe to fire the weapon, I shot 'em both...the zombies." She clarified. "I needed three shots because I aimed for the chest at first. That didn't stop it. I had to shoot them in the head."

"And none of you have any injuries?" Zack was trying to be as thorough in his questioning as possible.

"No...but we had to build a blockade to sleep in. We're afraid to leave the house," she added, beginning to sob. "James insisted he would coach this game for the kids. But we are driving around armed, and afraid for our lives."

"What did you do with the zombies that you killed?" Zack wondered whether they had disappeared.

"I let James take care of that. I took the boy to tend to his shoulder."

"Was he okay?"

"Yes, he must not have been bitten. He's just scared now,"

was her response as her sobs abated.

Zack made a mental note to ask James after the game what he did with the bodies of the zombies that his wife had shot. Karen wanted to say something to this woman the whole time, but she had kept quiet. Finally, she blurted out "Did you recognize any of the faces attached to the monsters you shot?"

Matthew's mother looked at her abruptly with scrutiny. "No, I didn't." She lied out of shame, because she remembered a feeling of *Schadenfreude* during the shooting and after seeing the zombies lying dead. She actually did see faces of the Masons on the zombies. She thought they were Wally and Bridgett Mason, Dennis' parents, but she couldn't bring herself admit this in public. She had already made her dislike for that family known to other parents. Karen was evaluating her response.

Ping! Dennis Mason barreled-up the ball and launched it between the center fielder and the right fielder. The ball was retrieved quickly and flawlessly, then thrown toward second base. The throw was off target just a little, but enough to allow the imposing Dennis to get back to second base before he could be tagged. He was a whole head taller than any of the other boys, and thirty pounds heavier, but he was just nine years old and thus eligible to play Little League, which ranged from ages seven to nine. He had quite the heroic image of himself as a giant among boys. He didn't think himself vulnerable, at least in the company of his peers, and he had a tendency to talk too much about his achievements and act out his superiority.

In defense of Dennis, this kind of behavior had been building in American sports for years. Players were becoming more and more self-absorbed. In the not-so-distant past celebrations happened only as a *team activity*. This was simply taken for granted. In the early years of sports, anyone celebrating his individual accomplishments during a game had to face admonition in one way or another. But times had changed. Maybe it started way back in the 1960s with the spiking of the football by someone who ran untouched into the end zone. Or perhaps it began with a celebration from a player who just dunked a basketball over his opponent. Nevertheless, individual celebrations had become more commonplace and acceptable in recent times. Baseball players acted out their frustrations for their many failures when they simply got a hit. The sheer quantity of individual celebrations had increased exponentially, particularly since the age of the selfie. This behavior epitomized the state of competition in American society. It had become more intense and "in your face", or, simply put, disrespectful. "Express yourself!" had become the new motto for athletes. It showed how competition had fractured the team into individuals, each of whom was in danger of becoming poisoned by an addiction for expressing one's own self-worth in the face of one's opponent. Even the children were determined to demonstrate how they felt about their own personal accomplishments. Boys like Dennis had little alternative but to imitate the leadership of their heroes. After all, that was how youth step forward to become the next generation of "winners".

"Get outta here with that ball! Throw it to the pitcher." Dennis made the command to the second baseman, Phillip, whose brother, Jeffrey, was on Dennis' team.

"I gotta try to tag you out Dennis," Phillip retorted, although he was a year younger, and almost thirty pounds lighter than Dennis.

"Yeah, you couldn't do it little fella." Dennis came back.

Zack could see from his seat in the bleachers that Dennis was antagonizing Phillip at second base, but he was only half attending to what was happening on the field. He was more interested in the story about a zombie attack coming from a different couple. He wanted to ask them questions like those he had asked Sylvia Lombardi, so he moved closer, leaving Karen in her seat just a few feet away.

Ping! A hard-hit ball one-hopped to Phillip. It knocked him down and rolled several feet away from him. As he got up to get it, Dennis was barreling toward third base. Pete Thompson was standing next to third awaiting a throw. No throw was coming, and, to his own demise, he was too late to see Dennis bearing down on him. Dennis went to the base but slammed into Pete on the way. Being nearly forty pounds lighter than Dennis, Pete went for a quick fly into foul ground beyond third base. Dennis, hands on hips, stood on the base, laughing.

"You're a real lightweight, Petey," Dennis snickered, hovering over him like a boxer who had thrown a knockout punch.

Along came Phillip from second base, and Jason from shortstop, then Leah from left field. Jason got there first and reached down to help Pete get up. The other players surrounded Dennis. While none had any plan to touch him, Jason asked "What's wrong with you, man?"

"What's wrong with *you*?" asked Dennis of the players collectively. "You're a bunch of wimps, and you stink!" He reached out and pushed Jason, who went down on the seat of his pants.

"Well, you got shit for brains, Dennis!" Jason couldn't help but retort from his backside. He wondered whether Dennis might try and hurt him.

It looked as if a mini brouhaha might develop among the players. Then, Jason's dad yelled something at Dennis. The kids really weren't listening to the parents who were yelling advice to their own children. The team that was playing defense was now twelve players strong on the field, all of them gathering in the vicinity of third base. Ironically, Dennis' team, led by Matthew's dad, James Lombardi, had not come out from the dugout onto the field. But then, Dennis' dad, Wally Mason, began to express his anger that the other team had ganged up on Dennis. Hearing his complaints, Jason's dad told Wally that Dennis needed to learn some respect. It looked as if some of the parents were about to pour gasoline on the flames of the situation.

Dennis didn't realize that he alone could douse the flames of competitive aggression and end this calamity. He continued in ignorance, "I'm way better than any of you buttercups will ever be." Moments after he said this, Dennis buckled to his knees and lurched forward with a grunt that was a result of the air being forced out of his lungs from a blow to the area of his groin. His dad had seen the foot that dropped Dennis. A couple of other dads jumped up to make sure Wally didn't do anything stupid, but before they could stop him Wally hopped over the four-foot cyclone fence and was running toward the kids gathered near third base. The umpires and coaches also ambled in the same direction. Assuredly, they were giving a new meaning to the term, "hot corner".

James Lombardi was the first to provide resistance against Wally Mason. "C'mon, Wally! Let's just separate the kids," Lombardi demanded as he put him into the gentlest hold he could. Little was happening amongst the children with Dennis rolling on the ground and moaning, hands between his legs, because none of his teammates went to his defense. All the players were just standing together on the field watching what was transpiring in front of them. Most of the kids noticed the group of dads who came onto the field pushing and shoving with Wally Mason. A couple of the dads authoritatively suggested how Wally should correct the errors of his son. Some of the children who witnessed this were indelibly marked by what they saw and heard.

Pow! Pow! Pow! Zack's problem was solved! His attention had been divided between the behavior on the field, and what this couple had been saying about *their* physical struggle with zombies, until he heard the shotgun blasts in the woods behind him. The kids and their parents stood frozen on the field with looks of fear and confusion. Zack hopped the fence and grabbed his boys one at a time, then left the field. The shots came from behind the parking lot, beyond the wooded area.

Pow! Pow! It was heard again. Zack took the boys to the truck and Karen followed right behind. He opened his tool kit on the side of the truck, pulled out a drone equipped with camera, and launched it to survey the nearby area.

James Lombardi ran over to Zack. "Watch after Matt and my wife, please. I'll be right back. I have to see what's going on. I have my shotgun."

"What did you see yesterday?" Zack had to yell at him as he sent off his drone.

"She shot 'em! I saw it!" James yelled back. He ran past the parked cars, some of which had begun to move as people frantically started to leave. Nevertheless, as he hopped around the cars in the lot, James Lombardi was careful to keep the barrel of his 12-gauge shotgun aimed straight toward the sky.

In the chaos following the shots, the rest of the parents gathered their children and retreated toward their cars. "A vehicle might be the safest place out here right now," Zack said to Karen and the boys. He made sure Matthew and Sylvia got in too. From his truck they had a clear view toward the wooded area. The edge of the woods was still for a while. Besides closely monitoring that space, Zack watched his phone, which showed him the video coming from the camera on his drone. The wooded area pictured from the drone was fairly thick with trees and brush. An occasional opening revealed no unusual activity below.

Then he saw branches rustling on the edge of the woods. Zack started the truck in case he needed to get away fast, but it was James Lombardi, who was moving at a moderate pace in Zack's direction. "I don't see anyone else," Zack said to anyone in the truck who might be listening. He summoned his drone to return, then lowered the window in the truck. "What happened, James?"

"There's a house a few hundred feet in, and more on the other side of the woods. Some guy said the kids were playing in the back yard when he saw monsters slogging around just beyond his yard." James was slightly out of breath, but he continued, "He said they looked sick and dangerous, so he got his rifle and went out to shoot them. He fired several rounds into them, until one got close to him. He said it was his captain. I dunno what he was talking about. Said he shot it in the head, and it went down motionless."

"How many are there? How many did he see?" asked Zack.

"He said there were three, then he tracked down the two he missed and shot them. But when we went back to his home, the first one he had killed was gone. Then he went back to look for the other two where he shot them, but I left. He won't find 'em!" James lamented.

"Why not?" Zack expected the reply.

"They won't be there." James figured, "Sylvia shot two. It wasn't long after they weren't there anymore. Just gone! What do they do…just get up and leave, or what the hell?"

"I don't know," pondered Zack. "I'd rather not have to find out!"

"Well, I have found out! And I'm scared shitless for my boy and my wife, and I feel so damned helpless." His voice trailed off as if he had cowered behind a wall, even as he stood next to Zack. "C'mon honey, let's go face these demons." Sylvia got up, forced a smile toward Karen and thanked Zack as she hugged Matthew.

"You have our address and phone number, if you ever need anything." Zack reached out because he wanted another human connection. "Just come over, announced if possible," he joked. James couldn't muster a smile. He left for his truck with Sylvia and Matthew.

Zack brought down his drone, put it in the truck, and took his family home.

Chapter 6

The Scourge of Zombies

"Hello, Elizabeth," Lyndsey said to the secretary.

"I guess you've heard about the special appointment...?" Elizabeth queried back.

"That's why I'm here. I had just taken home my Sister-In-Law, her beautiful baby boy, and my brother, Tim." Lyndsey walked around the office. She tried to get a sense of who else might be there, but there was no one.

"The group should be here within the hour." Elizabeth considered searching Lyndsey's mind to find out how much she knew. "There are three adults, all between 34 and 37 years old."

"Yes, and they've all been attacked and bitten by zombies. They are scared to death and they wonder what happened to their wounds. They have decided that God has saved them by some miracle." Lyndsey made sure Elizabeth understood that she had been sufficiently briefed. After all, Lyndsey had already seen three other cases where people claimed to have been attacked by zombies. The reasons for being saved always seemed to differ among them, but consistently she heard of harrowing experiences of being attacked by living corpses that somehow resemble human beings. Either they escape harm, or they are bitten, but, in every case, there are no bite wounds and no evidence of zombies having been there. The evidence that zombies were encountered by these people showed only in their crippling fear for their own lives, coupled with a pathological need to kill zombies. She was trying to make psychoanalytic sense of it all.

"They will be here soon. You have your props and some staging. If you need me, just ring." Elizabeth was referring to the secret button under the top of the desk which Lyndsey could use for her own personal safety, or for liability sake.

Something about these people was particularly bothersome to Lyndsey. She was struggling to learn what had made them so fearful. She reflected upon the problem in her own unique way. *"The zombie attack is a recent crisis in their lives. Each person who has been attacked has definitely experienced a return of the real self. It marks the reliving of primordial anxiety[1] in a new crisis."* Lyndsey believed that one's anxiety and feelings of vulnerability return despite having been cast away with the newborn's first quasi-willful act. However, these feelings return to one's conscious awareness as *other than one's own*. They return to awareness from the outside world by means of the external senses. Suddenly, she had an insight into the connection of zombies with this psychological haunting. *"There is no irony in the fact that it feels* as if the real self came back from the dead. *In that sense, maybe this real self is like the undead? Its appearance marks the return of a profound alienation. Certainly, one must be at least marginally aware that this feeling had been rejected before. These zombie victims, in particular, suffer horribly from guilt and self-rejection, and they harbor contempt for others. They seem to think they have to destroy zombies to justify their own being as an* ideal self *– a hero who defies its own human reality. It's a classic form of self-deception. Most people prefer this, rather than face the reality."*

What bothered her the most was the intense and lasting fear

of death these victims had suffered. She began to recall her research on the topic of the fear of death. She had disagreed with the theory asserted by some psychoanalysts; particularly that fear of death is *natural and universal*[2], and ultimately necessary. Her research on "death-consciousness" had begun with a phenomenological investigation but was unavoidably derailed into psychoanalysis once she had learned of this bold and unproven claim. She questioned whether one could be born with a fear for something that had never been sensed in any way.[3]

Lyndsey struggled to determine how fear of death could come to be at all and sought proof for the claim that it might be natural and universal and distributed to every member of the species. But she could find no proof, and she seriously doubted that one could be born with this fear. She even wondered whether a newborn could have a "sense" of death with no experience of it. Ultimately, she concluded that if it is impossible to have a perception of *one's own death* prior to its actual occurrence, then conscious awareness of one's own death would have to be some form of imaginative anticipation.[4] Her conclusion was that one's own death can be represented consciously only in fantasy and, moreover, only in the mode of *alienation*. In other words, every conscious representation of death requires *the other* to give it meaning. She had become staunchly opposed to the claim that there is a *natural fear of death*, and she was certain that if someone has a fear of death, it must be a result of social experience.

She also wondered how a fear of death could be repressed. Could it be in the same sense as the newborn's anxiety and helplessness? No, the repression of a fear of death could not be a "primordial" repression in the same sense. Lyndsey had conducted extensive research into these difficult philosophical questions. She was certain that Freud's concept of "repression" was used in different senses. Similarly, his notion of "unconscious" was used ambiguously. To avoid confusion, she preferred to begin with birth trauma as the original crisis in a human life. The trauma is lived at the awakening of human life, and always ends with self-denial. Self-denial is *the primordial repression.*[5] To Lyndsey, this meant that the real self is cut off and rejected. The anxious feeling of helplessness is cast away with the incomprehensible event that brought it on in the first place. Anxious vulnerability is "unconscious" *because* it is "outcast". It has been expelled from self-consciousness; it is exclusively *other*. But the incomprehensible event with which this anxiety was originally united will always be "unconscious". The newborn was not able to organize it in perception or store it in memory in a meaningful fashion. Consciousness is an organizing principle; it organizes perceptions on the grounds of past experiences. But the newborn's senses and capacity for conscious organization of the world are newly activated within the trauma of birth. That is why birth is a thoroughly alienating experience. Self-alienation is a negation: *"This pain and suffering is not mine."* Later in conscious life, the real self – this anxious and helpless being in crisis – returns to its conscious source, but only through the medium of the other. Lyndsey had ultimately concluded that whatever is meant by "fear of death" must be *related* to this rejection of the real self. However, in the reality of birth, there is no experience of death to be feared.

Furthermore, she had concluded that fear of death could not be repressed in the same sense as the incomprehensible experience of birth. If there is a repressed fear of death, then it must come later in life. Moreover, it must come from the other over time via social experience. Personal experience provides little or no information about one's own death very far in advance. But personal experience *has* provided an immediate experience of one's own weakness and vulnerability, and the death of *others*. Anxiety over one's own weakness *is arguably* natural - universal and necessary in the situation of crisis. Lyndsey preferred to think that "repression", in the original sense of the term, happened only as a result of birth trauma. But this traumatic experience is *birth*, not death. There is no fear at birth of anything that is to come later. Birth trauma is the primordial anxiety over a *present* danger.

The return of the real self to the consciousness which had rejected it is essential to every subsequent crisis experience.

Multiple experiences of this sort must be endured over a lifetime. When one comes to face one's real self in these situations, a conscious decision is made that will determine whether one continues to nourish the ideal self and a false identity, or whether the real self can be accepted in conscious life. Acceptance of the real self initiates the reconstitution of one's natural identity. Lyndsey believed that accepting one's natural identity was the only way to overcome "primordial guilt."[6] The latter is a feeling of malaise resulting from the awareness that one *is* this anxious and vulnerable organism, in combination with an awareness that precisely this fact has been rejected, and/or that one continues to reject it. In other words, one realizes that one is not the ideal self, as one had wished oneself to be. Lyndsey felt strongly that anyone who faces the real self in conscious life, and accepts it, can avoid a lot of self-deception.

Lyndsey went into the encounter room as though it were her theater, checking to see that each of the props were in their place. She had things that could quickly introduce a stressful situation, some that were comforting, and others, strategically located within the room.

Suddenly, she was interrupted by the members of the group for whom she was preparing. Three perfect strangers came directly into her theater as if they were the main characters in a play. Elizabeth had followed them in, introduced them, then smiled, secretly rolled her eyes, and eased the door closed at the gesture of Doctor Austin. Lyndsey welcomed the group and offered each of them a seat in the encounter room. It was a large room that was often partitioned. Each participant perused the comfortable furniture intended to get the session started on friendly terms. There were two large sofas, which had seats on either end that would recline. There were five petite recliners that could swivel, or rock, arranged near the center of the room, and there was a beautifully carved oak table with six comfortable chairs, suitable for discussion groups.

Lyndsey was looking at identification cards with their names printed upon them, but their virtual file was what she was remembering. She had prepared by perusing the electronic history of these three people who were from an area not far from her childhood home. She had to obtain the necessary passcode to enter their virtual files on VISPI. It was her job to question these people about the zombie attack and to record her findings in their files. There was nothing terribly unusual about them in their histories: No criminal or civil disobedience, fairly normal health, nothing in the state history of past therapy, only the typical information important to the welfare department, among other things.

Now she was meeting them in person. There were two men, and one woman, all siblings. Lyndsey noticed immediately that the large man who carefully controlled his demeanor was a sort of leader of the three. She immediately recognized him as the oldest. The other two seemed to follow him, but they appeared to Lyndsey to be quite shy and inhibited. So, she did her best to invite them to speak of their ordeal.

The encounter seemed to go on forever, until Lyndsey had begun to feel that she just wanted to go home. These people fit squarely into the parameters of what had been discovered in her previous sessions with other victims who suffered zombie attacks. Her mind began to wander. She wanted to be with Rinna and Jake or spend time with Tim and Clare and the baby, so she began to indicate with a group of subtle gestures that the session had come to an end.

But suddenly she was surprised by something she had heard. The smaller of the two men claimed to recognize a face on one of the zombies that attacked them. The woman nodded as if in agreement. This man said that he thought one of the monsters looked like a neighbor whom he had fought with in the past. She needed to hear that again.

"You thought you recognized one of the attackers?" Lyndsey asked him.

"Yes," the man behaved as if he were ashamed. "I wanted to kill him when I saw his hideous face and realized that he and the others were trying to kill us."

Lyndsey remembered that Karen thought she had recognized one of the zombies during the attack at Jake's. She was learning that it might be common for victims to recognize a zombie as someone he or she did not like. This man had said that he knew for a fact that this face he saw on one zombie really belonged to a man who was every bit alive. *"What on earth could this mean?"* she wondered as she tried to make sense of the familiarity.

Finally, the group session had reached a point where she could move to end it more openly. Lyndsey turned toward the door and lifted her palm gently upward. At first, not one of her clients gave the smallest sign of confidence in a newfound freedom. She knew that if they were to overcome what had happened – if it were possible at all – they would need several therapeutic sessions. It was not her responsibility to help these people overcome personal issues, although Lyndsey always worked toward that as a high priority. Still, the sooner she could get them out, the sooner she could document her findings and go home to her family.

"Alright," the larger of the two men took the cue and rose from the sofa. Lyndsey had learned that he was the one of the three that held them all together in a sane place. Lyndsey reached for his hand and let him know with erect posture and a nod of her head that she recognized his leadership.

"Thank you," Lyndsey held her hand toward the others. She knew that none of them would be back unless the state were to decide upon a second interview for some reason. The state and federal government cared only to gather information on these victims. And they seemed to be reticent to make any kind of statements about the attacks.

In her report, Lyndsey would say something similar to what she had written in the previous reports about zombie attacks. Then she drifted, thinking that these events should be the primary concern for the entire nation. The attacks certainly appeared to be increasing in number and occurring in more and more locales. The whole thought of zombies attacking people, wrestling them to the ground and biting them, and then the zombies and all evidence of bites absent...that absolutely befuddled her. *"What about people shooting them dead, but then dead zombies disappear? They must not be dead!"* she thought. It was straight out of a Hollywood horror movie. But *this* was too real! Thankfully, she didn't need to determine exactly what had happened to these people. She *would* be sure and report the fear of death, the built-up aggression, and the desire to kill the zombies. "Strange," she thought out loud, "but these seem to be the *only* lasting wounds for the victims of zombie attacks."

"No calls please, Elizabeth," Lyndsey requested as she adjourned to her own office and awakened her computer. She logged onto the FCC licensee website to apply for a passcode to open three files to enter information on a zombie attack.

Chapter 7

The Source of Shared Experience

Tim was looking out his living room window onto the front porch. It was eight steps higher than the sidewalk in front of his house. He knew the neighborhood like the back of his hand, having been born and raised in this home. The houses on his street stood side by side with small yards in the front and back. Narrow walkways defined the distance between the houses. Beyond the sidewalk, cars were parked curbside all along the street. Only a few neighbors had a garage and a driveway.

For the time being, there were no zombies to be seen. Still, it had been apparent to Tim that more and more people in their neighborhood had begun to fear for their own safety. He had noticed changes that he was certain were attributable to the recent zombie attacks. Some people had covered their downstairs windows with boards or plywood. Others, who never used their garage for parking their cars, were now doing so. No one had their front door open, very few windows could be seen to be open, and no one was outside on the porch. Usually, children could be seen and heard running and playing in the streets, especially on the weekends, but even that was non-existent on this day. He watched his neighbor across the street drive to the front of his house, park the car, carefully survey the surrounding area, then hop up his stairs two at a time, unlock his door, enter the house, and close the door immediately.

At that moment, Tim became concerned that he had not made sufficient preparations to defend himself, Clare, and Michael from attacks on their home. So much was going through his mind that he was frazzled and didn't know exactly what to do first. He went to the gun case that had been left to him by his father. It had been locked ever since he had inherited the weapons following the death of his parents from the Ebola virus. He pulled his keys from his pocket, unlocked the case, looked over the guns, and acquainted himself with the ammunition in the drawer below. As he loaded each weapon, he called to mind what had happened to Representative Jim Wallace. He wondered whether zombies had killed him. *"Certainly, our endeavor to create a new party founded upon the same philosophy as the IAPN was not the motivating factor for his death. Could it be?"* he wondered. It was not entirely clear how the explosive device had avoided the detection of building security and started the fire at his office, and why he and his secretary were unable to escape. It was sad and frightening, but his death would not sidetrack the plans to establish the new party. Then there was the incident where Jake was run off the road. Was someone wanting to kill him, too? After all, he was taking the documents which defined the party platform to Jim Wallace. Who could have known that?

These questions nagged at him. Preventing the delivery of these documents would have no effect on the establishment of this new party, other than to delay it. There were several other representatives working on the very same project in other locations. At worst, there would be an inconvenience of having to meet with these people outside of the local area. He had already received numerous texts from others who were prepared to pick up the work that Representative Wallace had been doing. In particular, Candice Frandell of the District of Columbia and Jean Bartok from Arizona had already suggested a meeting to discuss the philosophy and the plans for instituting it as the fundamental party platform. The group was reluctant to use email or online group meetings to discuss the details for implementation, preferring private meetings and the use of private computers, at least until the final documentation was prepared. Now it appeared as if a meeting was about to be arranged with several representatives, including international correspondents who were major proponents of the International Alliance. Tim would soon know the details of that meeting – once they were worked out.

Suddenly, a faint cry from Michael broke through his thoughts. "*Yes, another concern and a new distraction,*" he thught to himself. Clare had also been upstairs sleeping, making up for the rest she had been denied over the past few days. She and Michael had a nice long sleep this morning, so hopefully she would feel more like herself again. He started to ascend the steps when his phone signaled the arrival of a new text. It was from Representative Bartok in Arizona. "I have disturbing news." the text began. "Get back to you with details of meeting."

Tim sat down on the top step wondering what was happening. He simply responded, "Okay." Michael's cries were getting louder. He could hear Clare moving in the room behind him.

"Honey?" she called.

"Yes Clare, let me get him. I'll change his diaper, then bring him to you. Are you feeling alright?" He wanted to make sure she was ready for a feeding. Her episiotomy had been the cause of pain and discomfort for a couple of days, so he didn't want her to do anything to aggravate the healing process.

"I do feel good," she said, reassuring Tim that she was at least ready to feed Michael.

Tim attended to Michael with special concern for the wound he had on the head of his penis. "I can't believe that we still do this butcher-job to a helpless infant. Does it serve any practical purpose or is it just another stupid tradition?" he wondered out loud.

"What, Tim?" Clare thought he might be talking to her.

"Nothing. I'm bringing him now."

Michael was squirming and crying until Tim carried him over to Clare. As he passed Michael to Clare, a visible change took place when the infant sensed his mother's touch. He knew what was coming. His cries became short, and his squirms became centrally located around his head and mouth as he searched for the source of his nourishment, ready to grip Clare's nipple with his lips and begin sucking. Clare had already sat up in bed and lifted her gown, exposing her breast to start the feeding. Michael had anticipated the coming of an early lunch. His newly developing olfactory sense provided the clue. He latched on and began sucking hard. "Whew! The poor boy must be starved!" Clare said with a bright smile as she looked over toward Tim, her eyes beginning to see more clearly.

"I guess he found what he wanted," Tim tried to return the smile genuinely, but he couldn't help wondering what was bothering Representative Bartok. He decided not to share the concern with Clare right away.

"Everything okay?" Clare asked as if he were hiding something.

"Well...some of us are going to get together to discuss the platform and our future plans. I don't know when or where, but I should find out soon." He walked over to the upstairs window. His heart dropped in his chest. He could see three zombies dragging themselves along the street a little more than a block away. Fear began to rise from his stomach into his chest. He calmly turned to Clare and said, "I'll be back shortly." Tim kissed her forehead, then Michael's, and ran downstairs, grabbed a .38 caliber semi-automatic Smith and Wesson and stuffed it into his jeans. Then he made sure the front door was locked and drew all the curtains. He didn't see any zombies out front. He ran to the back door to make sure it was locked. No zombies there either. He decided to wait quietly in the hall at the center point between the front and back doors, after silently lifting a Remington shotgun from the gun rack. He could hear Clare talking to Michael, so he did his best not to alarm her, at least for the time being.

Clare was keenly aware of her senses – both her external and internal ones. She could feel Michael drawing mother's milk from her breast. At the same time, she felt a calm exuding from the surface of his body through her sense of touch. His calm ultimately touched her internal sense. She suddenly flashed back to the dream she had in the hospital just after she had given birth. She remembered an uncomfortable feeling of alienation, but now she was attaining further insight into what it meant. "*I can feel his calm right now,*" she thought, "*but I feel it more with my fingers and hands, and the tactile sense of his body touching mine. Yes, I can intimately feel his calm. But when he was inside of me, I felt him in a different way. Our blood, our biorhythms were a biological unity, and our feelings were truly one. It was by means of a peculiar internal sensation that we shared our feelings in totality. It was as if we experienced some ideal and perfect form of empathy between us. But now a distance has been established. At birth Michael was literally and figuratively cut off from me. We are two entities now. While I am sure that I can feel his calm right now, the transfer of his feeling to me seems to occur by means of my external senses, especially the sense of touch. Was our* perfect sharing *of feelings within one integrated internal sense forever changed upon his birth? Must we now* indicate *our private feelings through our external senses? If so, then my innermost feelings are transferred to him via his external sense of touch, and his internal sense must be derived therefrom. As my baby, does he nevertheless have minimal difficulty accessing my feelings in this way? Or do we somehow still share one internal sense?*"

She continued to reflect. "*What about Tim? He was never my baby like you, Michael. It seems that he must comprehend my love for him from his external senses. Could it ever be the same feeling for him as it is for me? He could never sense the feelings of love that I have for him as you had sensed the feeling of love that I have for you. His blood and biorhythms are distinct from mine, and always have been. Our feelings can be shared only by empathetic experience through our external senses. Are you and I limited in that way now, Michael? I wonder. Do we not have the same blood? Are our biorhythms essentially the same, or at least closer for us having once been a physical unity? I do believe that prior to your birth we had lived through a perfect sharing of feelings. But empathy is something different. Is it an experience between separate people that attempts to emulate a perfect sharing of internal feelings, similar to the experience in the womb?"*

Michael had let go of Clare's breast as he faded into a much satisfied, peaceful rest. Clare lifted him to her shoulder and began rubbing his back gently, hoping to push out any air that had accumulated during the feeding. Right on cue Michael belched out loud, then his body slumped against Clare as he drifted into a sound sleep. Clare continued rubbing his back for a few more minutes, until Michael forced out the remainder of the air in his stomach with a couple of soft, almost silent burps. Just then Tim could be heard ascending the staircase. He entered the room to see his beloved wife sitting up in bed with Michael asleep on her shoulder. He went over to the window again.

"How are you feeling?" he asked Clare as he spied two zombies on the street at about the same location where he had seen them earlier.

"I'm feeling much better than yesterday," Clare asserted. "Can you take him and put him into his crib until he awakens?"

"Sure, babe." Tim carefully lifted Michael from her shoulder and carried him over to the crib. "You might wanna get dressed and have everything ready to go in case we have to leave quickly," he warned. "There are a couple of monsters outside on our street."

"Where?" Clare said with surprise as she climbed from the bed to prepare the diaper bag and get dressed.

Just then Tim's phone buzzed with a text. He was heading back down the steps to get to his shotgun as he looked at his phone. It was Representative Bartok.

Clare peered out the upstairs window expecting to see zombies for the first time, but she saw nothing other than a couple of neighbors getting into their car. She watched as the car pulled away from the curbside and accelerated down the street at a pace that was much too fast for this residential road. She finished loading the bag with the necessities for a new mother. As she did, she sensed that her range of motion was increasing, and she had become relatively pain free. That was a most welcome feeling. As she gently pulled the bedroom door shut behind her, she went down the steps to find Tim with a pistol on his hip looking at his phone.

"What's goin' on?" She asked.

"A meeting is being arranged…" Tim began. "Representative Bartok says something is disturbing. She wants me to be ready to travel, but she doesn't yet know where. I am to bring the documents, preferably on a disk, but also a paper copy." He put the phone back into his pocket.

"When will you know where to go?" Clare wondered.

"She is still working on that. There are important others with whom to coordinate a time and place. I should know relatively soon."

Clare interjected, "I didn't see anything outside that looked unusual."

"That's good. Just be ready to go, Clare." Tim was happy that he had decided to ask Jake to take him to the city pound where he found that his car had been towed. It was no worse for wear, but besides the towing fee, the city levied a hefty fine upon him for having abandoned the car in the middle of the street. At least he got it back. "Right now, I want you to pack enough clothes for yourself and Michael to last a few days.

Lyndsey and Jake are expecting you to stay with them while I attend this meeting." Tim walked to the front door and peeked around the curtain, then he went to the back window and did the same.

"Any problems?" Clare inquired as he returned from the back of the house.

Calmly, and forcing just the hint of a smile for Clare, he said "No," and placed his arms around her, hugging her. He found the physical contact with her very comforting, so he allowed that feeling, and the hug, to linger for several seconds. "I love you, babe," he spoke from the heart, kissing her gently on the lips, then rubbing his head against hers. Another text interrupted before either one of them could thoroughly enjoy a passionate embrace. It was Lyndsey. "Jake wants to come and get you now. He wants to know what the situation is like in our neighborhood."

Another text. This time it was Representative Bartok. "Jean Bartok wants to know how soon I can travel to Phoenix." Tim went to his desktop computer and logged on to his favorite travel website. There were enough flights to Phoenix from Pittsburgh that he would be able to leave as soon as he was certain of the safety of his wife and son. "Do you mind that you and Michael might have to stay with Lyndsey for a few days? I'll take the car to the airport after Jake comes to get you. Alright?" He asked Clare with his arms outstretched and hands on her shoulders.

"I suppose," Clare didn't really want to agree, "but, how long will you be gone?"

"I dunno yet, babe, but I suppose only a few days." Tim lamented, wondering whether he would ever get to spend quality time with his new son. He removed his hands from Clare's shoulders to send a text to the representative in Arizona, "I can be there sometime tomorrow. Okay?" Then he looked out the windows once more before sending a text to Lyndsey. "No immediate threats. Saw monsters earlier. Gone now. I have to travel. Clare and Michael are ready to go with you."

Little Michael began to awaken once again. He immediately sensed the absence of his mother. He had been certain that he was in direct contact with her, so the recognition of her absence motivated a sharp, short cry. Then several whimpers followed, until he let go and began to cry out loud. Clare immediately turned away from Tim and moved to ascend the staircase slowly and carefully, knowing full well that even though she was feeling no pain between her legs, she was still not fully healed. When she arrived at the crib where Michael lay, objecting to his temporary loneliness, she smelled something foul and pungent. She went into the diaper bag for the necessary items. As she removed the diaper and wiped away the watery discharge from his little butt, she saw something that alarmed her. "Tim!" she cried with a somewhat urgent tone.

"What's wrong?" Tim queried as he ran up the stairs two at a time.

"There's something on the cheek of his ass," Clare asserted with concern. Tim peered carefully as Clare lifted Michael by his legs. A small nodule that looked almost like a tumor was protruding ever so slightly from the surface of his left cheek.

"What the hell is that?" Tim expected an answer from Clare because he figured that eleven years of nursing provided her with more knowledge on the subject of health than did his education in philosophy.

She moved the nodule from side to side with her index finger, and Michael did not seem to be disturbed by the touch. Then she said, "I don't know. I'll see if Jake can take us to the hospital to have it examined."

"Would you rather that I stay and take you myself?" Tim asked.

Clare didn't answer immediately. She pulled off Michael's clothes, and closely inspected the entire surface of his body. Just then he surprised her with a spray that was a lot more powerful than she could have expected. She naturally pulled her head back as the spray landed on her chest and neck, and she quickly covered his penis. Tim laughed from deep within his chest. Even Clare couldn't help but chuckle. She playfully admonished Michael, telling him there was no fire to douse. The two enjoyed a moment of pleasure that momentarily interrupted and overpowered any anxiety that had arisen after finding the nodule.

"It doesn't seem to be serious," Clare said more with hope than certainty of her diagnosis. "I'm sure Jake can take us to the hospital. You go ahead to the meeting, and I'll let you know the moment I learn something."

"Are you absolutely sure?" Tim sought some conviction from Clare because he was again beginning to feel frazzled.

"Yes. I will be sure to contact you. Take care of this business. We shall be fine until you get home." She leaned into him and kissed him on the cheek.

"Okay, I'm going back downstairs to book a flight. I'll call Jake and give him the update. He should be here soon. I love you, Clare."

Clare smiled and showed her affection with a warm embrace. Finally, they separated with reluctance, and prepared for the tasks at hand.

Chapter 8

An Inconsistency in Shared Experience

Jean Bartok popped pills into her mouth that her doctor said she needed to survive the disease that she had recently been diagnosed with. Then she reached for the bottle of water nestled in the rear console of the Galactic Chief in which she was a passenger. She was in the third row of seats with Jan Greisfeld, a German national and President of the IAPN who had made the trip to Phoenix. In the second row of seats were Senator Leann Gomes from Minnesota, Candice Frandell, a Representative from the District of Columbia, and Zhi Mingzhou who had travelled to Phoenix from a previous engagement with colleagues in Los Angeles. He had hoped to acquire information to persuade his comrades in China to join the people of Hong Kong and give due consideration to the International Alliance. The driver of the SUV was Representative James Clark from California. To his right, in the passenger seat, was Representative LeShaun Brinson from Alabama.

The Alliance had dispatched Jan Greisfeld to determine whether the party platform proposed by the upstart coalition was consistent with the fundamental principles of the IAPN. The Germans were blazing the trail in the endeavor for the institution of these principles across the globe. His feedback on the progress of the developing platform was important to the other members of the Alliance.

But it was, perhaps, the Jewish people who had made the most significant contribution to support the Alliance, much to the chagrin of leadership in the United States. For several decades, the nation of Israel had been a reliable ally of the United States, but they shook the world with the public renunciation of the claim that "The Jewish people are the Chosen Ones of God". This decision was made by the new leaders of Israel. They had acted on the advice of scholars, and on behalf of a growing number of the Jewish people who wanted the daily wars with the Palestinians to end once and for all. The renunciation was quite controversial. Many riots and protests followed in Israel's major cities. But the authorities had argued that this religious belief was an expression of superiority which sustained the attitude of domination, and this was precisely what had to be overcome and replaced with a new attitude of respect and cooperation.

Israel was welcomed into the International Alliance with great fanfare and celebration. Their membership would prove to be a powerful influence upon other nations that were not yet willing to join. This, in particular, was a powerful kick in the ass for the leadership of the United States, which had always insisted upon its superiority over the other nations of the world. This claim to superiority was one of the binding threads that connected the United States with Israel. Hence it appeared that, because of this renunciation, the U.S. would make a clean political separation from Israel.

The United States was among the largest of nations which still openly refused participation in the IAPN. Along with the Chinese and the Russians, the ruling authority of the American government continued to express its economic and military superiority based upon the strength of its technology. The leadership of The United States had no plans to proclaim equality with the other nations of the world, even though its people were suffering the same fate as the people of every other nation. Every earthly inhabitant would need to unite to address the growing scarcity of the resources that nourish and sustain the lives of humans. But these giant nations were not yet guided by this goal.

However, as was the case in the U.S., so it was in China that a growing insurgence from the citizens was gradually moving the authorities to consider the spirit of the International Alliance. Had the decade-long struggle in Hong Kong for the institution of democratic policies not succeeded as well as it had, the leadership in mainland China might never have heard the rising concerns of their people. Nevertheless, they remained as unlikely as the U.S. to renounce the attitude of domination, despite the growing problems with loss of farmland from flooding and pollution that had resulted in devastating food shortages for many of the Chinese people.

Those Congressional members in the U.S. who were coalescing for the development of a new party platform were charged by their opposition, the defenders of traditional capitalist politics, with colluding with foreigners to destroy the U.S. Constitution. There were, in fact, arguments that defended this claim. However, because environmental changes were evolving to the detriment of the entire human race, the time was ripe to revise the Constitution to fit into the natural order. But the hard-core capitalists were dead set against any sort of compromise that would weaken American corporations. Their words and behavior forcibly reflected this fact. That placed not only the visiting foreign delegations at risk, but anyone who was perceived as complicit with the upstart coalition.

Meanwhile, the team who was traveling together in the Galactic Chief faced more immediate problems that would command priority. As they were on their way to the meeting at South Mountain to correlate the new party platform with the guidelines of the IAPN, the charges of foreign intervention into the politics of the United States were not a pressing concern. For some reason, the Roosevelt Dam had been opened to release a surplus of water from the lake, and the Salt River had risen beyond its banks. It was flooding the surrounding areas.

About ten years prior, the Salt River had to be managed to a constant flow. Decades ago, one could drive through the dry gulley where the river would occasionally flow. But rising water levels in the western states had changed that.

Representative Clark had been planning to drive the large SUV into Tempe across the Mill Street Bridge, until the encounter with the rising river forced a detour. The Mill Street Bridge was closed. It even looked as if Arizona State University might have experienced some flooding. There was no time to survey the damage. Clark would have to find an alternative route to their destination through some residential neighborhoods where bridges had been constructed to pass over the river at points where it tended to flow with less urgency. Unfortunately, many roads heading back toward Phoenix were congested. An excess of flowing water had stopped traffic and left the rush hour drivers in search of a clear path around the impediment. Now they were stuck in bumper-to-bumper traffic, waiting in line to cross over the river.

Suddenly, there was one more problem they didn't need: zombies! Several of them just seemed to come from around the sides of houses and were approaching the cars. James Clark began surveying the area for a possible means to escape. He wondered why the traffic had stopped at the bridge, and whether it would move soon. He couldn't get an adequate view of the bridge because he was about fifty cars back in the line. All he knew was that traffic was not moving, and three zombies were approaching.

"Oh my God!" cried Jean Bartok. The others had begun to offer advice for escape, except for Zhi Mingzhou and Jan Greisfeld. Mingzhou gazed at everyone in the SUV with a befuddled look as he said something into his phone in his native Mandarin. Suddenly, the translation blurted out: "What is happening?" The question was directed toward anyone who would answer.

At the same time Jan Greisfeld was trying to position himself in his seat so that he might get a better view through the windshield. "What is wrong?" he asked. He, too, could sense the fear and panic that filled the SUV. But he settled back into his seat, believing that he understood what was happening. He sat quietly, hoping that James Clark could manage the situation without anyone getting hurt.

"Get the fuck outta here!" LeShaun Brinson screamed with urgency. His apprehension peaked, and time lapsed into a past when football was his passion. He was sitting high in his seat, ready to initiate violent force if necessary. Zhi Mingzhou held his phone closer to his ear, hoping that his foreign language software might provide a translation of Brinson's remark. Zhi had no trouble feeling the panic, however he relied upon his phone for an accurate translation because he believed his English to be insufficient. But no meaningful translation was forthcoming for Brinson's comment.

"Swing around and cut through that yard!" Brinson demanded, pointing out a means to escape to his right. As he said this, one zombie was leaning against the hood of the SUV. Another had approached the passenger side. Even though its face and torso were pocked with festering sores, Brinson claimed to recognize it. "That's Jeff Thomas!" he yelled. "Run the mother fucker over!" He insisted as the zombie began pounding on the window of the passenger side door. Both Jean Bartok and James Clark looked toward the hideous face to see whether Brinson was right. Jeff Thomas was a Senator from the state of South Carolina. He was a wealthy businessman, a staunch defender of traditional capitalism, and adamantly opposed to the new coalition that had been forming in the United States Congress. He was an enemy to the new party and its platform.

"I can't run him over!" James Clark exclaimed with moral fervor.

"Just get us out of here!" LeShaun Brinson was ready to jump onto Clark's lap and take control of the SUV. The hideous zombie pushed his face onto the window as two others walked around the driver's side of the SUV.

While this was happening Zhi Mingzhou was studying each person in the SUV one at a time as his phone provided translations that he was no longer trying to hear.

Finally, fear of the zombies approaching the driver's side window drove James Clark to a momentary madness. He lurched the Galactic Chief forward knocking over the zombie that looked like Jeff Thomas, then slammed the rear corner of the vehicle in front of him and made a u-turn and drove through the yards of two homes. He sideswiped a fire hydrant just enough to cause a narrow waterspout to shoot about thirty feet in the air. Once he made it back onto the road, two more zombies were in his lane about fifty feet ahead. He smacked into the first with a loud thud against the SUV. That zombie went flying into the one behind it like one bowling pin taking out another. With no more zombies in front of him, he only had to beware of other cars that were making similar maneuvers to escape the zombies. He glanced in his mirror for a moment to see the chaos behind him, then he drove onto the open road.

"Jesus Christ, I thought we were goners, James. Why treat those monsters with kid gloves? Just run 'em over!" LeShaun Brinson was entirely unsympathetic.

As they escaped the apparent trouble, no zombies now to be seen, Zhi Mingzhou was still as befuddled as could be. He had temporarily silenced the electronic voice on his phone, while he made gestures to indicate his confusion to Candice Frandell and Leanne Gomes.

Jean Bartok saw his request and spoke his name to gain his attention. He turned toward her and unmuted his translator. She spoke toward his device. "Those zombies were pounding on the windows and threatening us. We had to take action to escape them." She waited for the translation so the Chinaman could respond.

"Zombies…? What is 'zombies'?" Zhi Mingzhou asked in English with the innocence of a child.

"Didn't you see those hideous creatures pounding on the glass of the SUV?" Leann Gomes asked.

After the translation was expressed for Zhi Mingzhou, he peered at Ms. Gomes then Jean Bartok with an expression of utter confusion. He spoke in Mandarin toward his phone, then the translation repeated in English, "I felt great panic of colleagues. I saw no reason to panic just because traffic was stopped. We wait or turn around. No threat, right?" He looked at them, shook his head, and held his empty palm in the air as if to imply that either he or they were crazy.

"Didn't you see the monsters leaning against the windows of the SUV, trying to get in?" Jean Bartok asked, hoping that he would understand the question.

After a pause, he heard the translation. He simply shook his head. "I saw no monsters, only felt great fear among you."

"*Holy shit*," Brinson muttered to himself. "He couldn't have been looking out the windows."

"Just apologize to him, and try to explain what happened," James Clark suggested. "Can you do that Jean? I gotta find a bridge across the river so that we can get to South Mountain. I might as well go back to I-10."

"*Yeah,*" Brinson muttered under his breath sarcastically. "*He must have some kind of problem with his vision.*"

Chapter 9

A Psychoanalytic Account of Zombies

After Tim had made his way around the east side of South Mountain in his rental car, he had come to a place where only various cactuses were scattered about the desert landscape. He had been driving through an idyllic scene along the base of the south side of the mountain. There were no homes to be seen, only an endless flat desert to his left, and a variety of cactuses and bushes adorning the rising hillside to his right. In most areas of the United States anything called a "mountain" was recognizable as such by steep, rugged terrain with peaks that were measurable in thousands of feet. That was certainly not the case with South Mountain. It was more like an expanse of moderately high rolling hills grouped together in the middle of a desert plain.

As he drove along the foothills, Tim ogled the saguaro cactuses that gave character to the ascending hillside, which someone had called a mountain. The scenery made him feel high. Then he caught a glimpse of the cabin. It was nestled into the side of South Mountain, elevated somewhat above the desert floor. It was a recent construction, partially hidden by a forest-like landscape that served to provide a sense of seclusion.

The cabin resort was just far enough up the side of the hill so that on most days one could see for miles across the southern desert toward the city of Tucson. The general area was still relatively pristine, noticeably lacking the usual conveniences, and for that reason the cabin looked out of place. Tim had passed some stores several miles back on the east side of the mountain. They included charging stations with gasoline, a couple of restaurants, a smaller version of Walmart, and a few other stores. So, he knew that were he to travel back around the east side of the mountain north toward Phoenix he would return to civilization. Besides the commercial amenities, the north side of the mountain also had a stable with horses that were available for public riding. One could purchase guided tours on horseback. But, in his immediate location on the south side of the mountain, he could imagine that he was completely cut off from civilized life and living in some kind of dreamworld.

As he approached the cabin, the road curled around a bend through a narrow valley leading to a parking area. There was a giant SUV parked in the lot, flanked by a couple of smaller ones. Tim parked his car alongside the others, got out, stretched his legs, and briefly walked around, taking in the scenery.

The desert heat was quite dry, though oppressive. But his attention was directed mostly toward the cabin. It was a huge two-story building made of logs that must have been imported from some far away forest. He tried to imagine what might be inside. What he could not see was that the second floor had twelve guest rooms with lavish accommodations and the first floor had a kitchen, an elaborate formal dining area, a conference room, and a gym and pool for exercise. In the back, there were indoor tennis and handball courts surrounded by glass walls and a paved path that led the way toward a hiking trail that went over the top of South mountain to the other side. Presently, though, the desert heat would forbid a long hike on the trail.

Before he could wander too far from his car, and get lost in the idyllic surroundings, he spied an armed guard walking in his direction. He was a large man wearing a brown uniform, and a matching cap with a green saguaro cactus on it. He walked briskly toward Tim. As the man approached, Tim could see that he was Native American. The guard produced a faint smile and asked, "Can I help you, sir?"

"Yes," Tim replied, "I am Timothy Austin. I am here to meet Jean Bartok, among others." Tim opened his jacket wide with both hands for the man to see, saying "I have identification in my pocket," gesturing with his head toward his left side. Then he reached into his inside pocket. He produced a passport and his Pennsylvania driver's license. Extending his arm with these in hand, the guard came closer to accept them. He looked them over, glanced back toward Tim, then a grand, welcoming smile came over him.

"We are expecting you, Mr. Austin. Representative Bartok and her entourage have yet to arrive. However, Representative George and Senator Paulson are already here also awaiting their arrival, along with a dignitary from Israel." The guard reached out to hand something to Tim. "Please attach this tag to the front of your jacket in a conspicuous location." Then, he added, "My name is John Redfeather. I am one of three guards who is presiding over the property. Be sure that we are able to see your tag at all times. Please, gather your things and come in. Enter the glass doors and place all your belongings on the conveyer inside, then just follow the instructions. We hope you will enjoy your time here."

"I will. Thank you." Tim went back to the car and collected his briefcase and a small backpack, then made his way to the door. He was surprised to see that this cabin had security measures that would rival government buildings, hospitals, and the like. As he entered, the electronic sensory devices began the process of checking his identity. It was mere seconds until a green light lit and an artificial voice instructed him to place his belongings, which were not part of what he was wearing, upon the conveyer belt. He did so. The conveyer relayed them through a large metal box that inspected the contents. Then the voice returned, asking him to walk through the tunnel adjacent to the large metal x-ray device. On the other side he was met once again by John Redfeather.

He spoke with a gentle, relaxing voice. "Welcome to our desert resort. Feel free to go anywhere inside. If you want to go outside, please use the rear exit to the mountainside. Please do not try to go out the front entrance without the assistance of a guard. You can acquire a key for your room at the concierge's desk right over there. Enjoy your stay."

"Thank you," Tim said, feeling quite safe for the first time in a long time. All he really wanted to do was to talk to Clare and make sure all was well with his family. He had tried to call her prior to driving to South Mountain, but for some reason the call would not go through. So, his first point of business would be to call her from the privacy of his room, assuming it offered privacy. As he took his key in hand, getting directions to his room from the concierge, he spied an SUV that had just entered the lot. It parked near the others. *"That's probably Jean,"* he thought to himself. He picked up his pace to get to his room.

Upon entering the room, he was in awe. It was a lavish suite with a 15-foot ceiling and every convenience that one might expect in a luxury hotel. The room was quite large, approximately forty feet square, with two picture windows about ten feet square. One window offered a view over the parking lot, which was out of sight. Tim could see for miles across the desert. Out the other window he could see saguaro cactuses on the hillside. One of the walls that had no window was lined with small kitchen appliances, a vanity, and a door leading into a bathroom that included not only a large shower and a bathtub, but also a hot tub. The other wall had video equipment and control panels.

Tim was overwhelmed with the accommodations. But he didn't want to linger within the awe that moved him to examine all of the amenities one at a time. He wanted to talk to Clare. He grabbed his phone and said, "Call Clare."

"Hi, honey," Clare answered immediately as if she were sitting with the phone in her hand waiting for his call.

"Hey, babe! How is everything?" Tim expected her to begin by addressing Michael's butt.

"We are fine." The confidence in her voice made Tim feel somewhat more at ease for having left her behind. "How are you?"

"I'm fine. I'm at an incredible log cabin at South Mountain near Phoenix," Tim wanted to tell her about the accommodations, but he felt guilty that she wasn't there to enjoy it with him. "I just got here."

"We are still at the hospital, but we shall be leaving soon, I hope. Jake brought us here yesterday directly from our house. Doctor Otani, whom I know well from having worked with her many times, looked at Michael soon after we arrived. She was so concerned about the nodule that she decided to remove it right away."

"What did she say it was?" Tim asked.

"She didn't know for sure. She sent it to the lab. We should know more in a couple of days. Michael has only a little mark on his butt. It has to stay covered for a while to keep the poop off it," Clare concluded without an air of worry.

"I hope it is nothing!" Tim still had his own concern.

"Lyndsey and I were talking to Alan Gustavsson. He is a lab technician at the hospital. He works at the lab tonight, and he said that he would try to examine it personally. So, I feel lucky that we have such good friends who would make special consideration for us."

"That's great! We *are* lucky. How are you feeling?"

"I'm nearly 100% now. No more pain," she added with joy.

"I'm really happy to hear that, Clare! I sure miss you!"

"I miss you, too, Tim. We can't wait for you to get home," Clare added speaking for both herself and Michael.

"We should be getting together here soon. Jean has just arrived. I'll let you know our plans and when I'll be returning home. It should only be a couple of days, I hope." Tim emphasized his desire to return home.

A knock at the door interrupted his thought. "Be right there," he yelled. "I gotta go, babe. I'll call again later." He mimicked kissing sounds, and added, "Love you, babe."

"I love you," Clare responded in kind.

"Talk to you later. Bye." Tim went to the door to find John Redfeather. "Your colleagues have requested your presence in the dining area at 5:00 pm. Just go down the staircase and turn left. You will see a sign there. You have about an hour and a half until then."

"Thank you, sir!" Tim showed as much respect as possible.

"Please, call me John during your stay with us. We try to be informal so that our guests can relax." He smiled a wide smile.

"Will do, my friend, thank you so much." Tim returned the smile as he closed the door. He was happy that he had time to shower and relax for a spell before dinner.

After a brief nap that rejuvenated his spirit, Tim adjourned to the dining area where there was a feast fit for royalty. He felt slightly out of place with all these members of Congress and international correspondents. However, he had only to remind himself of his place among them. He had been instrumental in communications with the German nationals who, themselves, played a key role in drafting the official guidelines and philosophy for the IAPN. The Germans were leaders among the Europeans and their neighbors in Scandinavia for creating and recording the documentation, organizing debates, and promoting the Alliance worldwide. And now Tim was in the honored position of being able to meet directly with Jan Greisfeld, President of the Alliance, for the first time. Tim was pleased that the man spoke fluent English, because he feared that his German would prove inadequate where important details were concerned.

When the dinner was complete, they adjourned to the conference room. After-dinner drinks were prepared before the panelists had taken their seats. First were the introductions and an informal period of getting acquainted. Tim hit it off right away with Jan Greisfeld. After all, they had been corresponding for a short time. In fact, there were occasions when it had been deemed wise that Tim should contact members of the Alliance, rather than having Jim Wallace or any other representative correspond directly with them. The last thing that this coalition wanted was democrats and republicans publicly crying foul, claiming a foreign influence on the American elections. These interactions would become public knowledge soon enough. It was preferable to establish a foothold for the new party before any public condemnation of the coalition could begin. As it was, the truth had already begun to surface. The saving grace, so far, was the fact that more and more Americans were vocal about their support for the International Alliance. It was now a matter of making their voices relevant within a Congress which, to this point, had failed to adequately acknowledge common voters over the corporate leaders whose lobbies were infinitely more powerful.

The eleven people present at this meeting sat down at a round table that was assembled specifically to accommodate this group. It was placed in the middle of the conference room, which was centrally located on the ground floor of the cabin. It was without windows, but brightly lit by a giant crystal chandelier that hung directly above the round table from the high ceiling. Each member was able to face the other in a way that would enable every gesture and facial expression to be clearly seen. At this meeting, there would be nothing to conceal, and the spirit of cooperation would guide every communication. This was precisely the spirit that the new party intended to carry into all future Congressional assemblies. Before the most pressing issues that had convened this meeting could be addressed, Zhi Mingzhou had raised his hand. When he was recognized as wanting to speak, everyone fell silent. He spoke his native Mandarin into his phone, then raised the volume for all to hear.

"Please, forgive me for not speaking to all of you directly in English. I would rather trust my software for an accurate translation," he said, forcing a smile with difficulty. "Before we share the spirit of the International Alliance, and address important matters, I wish first to thank you for your invitation and your consideration of the Chinese people, despite the fact mainland China is not yet committed to the Alliance. While I represent a growing number of Chinese people, I wholeheartedly represent the people of Hong Kong. I, and my colleagues, have the ear of the Chinese administration, which has to this point failed miserably to address the growing problem of hunger resulting from devastating pollution and flooding that has destroyed our most fertile farmland."

Zhi forced another smile, then continued in Mandarin. When he was finished speaking, the voice from his phone expressed what everyone expected to be his concluding words. "Your invitation provides hope that we might work together to seek solutions not only for Chinese problems, but for these global problems. I am very honored to be present." But to the surprise of everyone present, the subject was abruptly changed by Zhi, and he continued. "I am very concerned over something that happened today as we sought a path to our destination here. We were waiting in traffic when my respected colleagues present in the automobile frightened me. I sensed a fear that was driving a behavior that I could not understand."

Jean Bartok, LeShaun Brinson, and all the others who were the subject of this speech paid careful attention to Zhi Mingzhou, acknowledging his great concern. Their efforts to explain that zombies were pounding on the windows and leaning against the fenders and hood of the SUV had been unsuccessful. Zhi insisted that he had neither seen nor heard anything of the sort. He said that James Clark had really alarmed him when he slammed into the car in front of him, drove through private property, then hit a fire hydrant. Zhi wanted some confirmation of the story that Jean Bartok and the others were trying to get him to accept, because he found it difficult to believe. Unfortunately, Zhi was further befuddled as the passengers who had been in the car with him tried to explain to Tim and the other Congress persons what had happened. Zhi was now offering his phone to anyone who wished to respond, so that he might receive a translation of an explanation that made sense to him.

"I'm at a loss to explain to Zhi what happened. He simply did not have any sense of the zombies," Jean Bartok said with her hands in the air as if she were surrendering.

Senator Paulson asked, "Did everyone else experience zombies attacking the van?"

"Yes, all of us!" insisted Leann Gomes as the rest of them nodded, except for Jan Greisfeld who pretended to be busy sorting a pile of papers in front of him, as if he had not heard her.

"What is going on?" asked LeShaun Brinson, as if someone were playing a trick on him, "I believe him! He had absolutely no clue what we were doing! I'm not sure what to make of it. He thinks we are freaking crazy! I would too."

Tim decided to speak up. He reached out for Zhi's phone, took it, and placed it directly in front of himself, then looked directly toward Zhi. "Please forgive what must have seemed to be insane behavior on the part of my colleagues. We do not understand why you did not see the monsters that appear to be dead people walking." He waited for a translation. Zhi stared at him with his head tilted askew and furrowed his brow in bewilderment. Tim continued. "My friends at home in Pennsylvania have also been attacked by these creatures. They, too, had a most terrifying experience. They were attacked by monsters that broke windows at their home and threatened their lives. In the past month or so there have been many similar reports of these attacks in our country. Have you not witnessed any such attacks in your country?" He waited again for the translation to finish. Zhi gazed back at Tim and simply shook his head.

"That really bothers me," Tim continued, "because – and here is what is so strange to us – the evidence of the zombie attack disappears in a short time." Zhi listened to the translation, then put his right palm on his forehead and looked around at the other members of the meeting. Then Tim really stuck his neck out to tell the whole truth. "Some people have gone to extremes of collecting weapons to combat the monsters. On several occasions, zombies have been shot with guns. It is hard to blame the victims. These creatures cause great fear. They are hideous monsters with open sores all about their bodies, and they smell foul. It seems that the only way to repel them is to shoot them in the head. That's what many reports say, and that is how many people try to survive an attack. After being shot in the head, they move no more. But – and there are many reports verifying this truth, so, please believe me – after a short time the dead zombies disappear. Furthermore, no one who has been bitten has a wound to prove the bite. It is as confusing for us as it must be for you." Tim now feared that Zhi was going to think that they were all nuts.

After listening, Zhi laughed out loud, but his gestures still showed discomfort, including a shaking of his head as he hit it with his right palm. He took his phone back from Tim. "That sounds as if it were right out from a video game like my grandchildren play." He tried to smile, nodded, and forced a laugh.

Tim looked over at James Clark who said, "He's right about that!"

Then Jean Bartok asked, "Does anyone else know of someone having this same sort of experience? You know…someone who sees nothing during an attack?"

Finally, Representative George from the state of Ohio broke the silence. "I am ashamed to admit this, but I do."

"What's the shame?" asked Larry Paulson from Oklahoma.

"Well, until now I just assumed my Dad was feeble or blind or something," he lamented, momentarily acting as if he might sob. "I treated him so badly. My family was attacked one evening two weeks ago." Zhi Mingzhou pushed his phone over toward Dale George. He still needed some sort of confirmation to feel more comfortable with these people. He sensed that he might be about to hear it.

"We had just finished dinner and were relaxing on the back porch when several zombies just seemed to rise up from the ground in the back yard. At first, we were stunned and didn't react quickly. Then we heard the moaning and, as they approached, we smelled a stench of death. My wife ran into the house, and I wanted to follow, but my Dad just sat there like nothing was happening. When I urged him to get up and go into the house, he resisted me, saying that he wanted to sit on the porch. I told him 'we have to get away from these monsters', but he said, 'Leave me alone.' Then I said some things to him that I regret as one of the monsters swung at my head with his fist. I was so scared I couldn't think straight. I hit it in the head with my fist." Paulson was visibly shaking at the vivid memory he was reliving.

"It was so sickening! Its head was soft as if it had no bone. Just the touch of it was so disgusting, and it left part of its face on my hand. My Dad must have thought I was nuts, but I was scared out of my wits. Then the monster grabbed me by the arm and bit me on the shoulder. The other ones drew closer until my wife came outside with my 9mm. She fired two shots into the torso of the one that bit me, but it just kept coming. Finally, I pushed it away, took the gun from Jen, and shot it in the head. It went down, shaking all over until it quit moving. Others were getting near, and my shoulder was throbbing with pain." He paused to catch his breath and swallow, but his mouth was dry. He reached shakily for the glass in front of him and took a sip of water.

"My father was alarmed from the firing of the gun. He got up quickly and hobbled toward the door. My wife helped him get in. I yelled for her to lock the door, but she insisted that I come in first. I began shooting wildly toward the head of each zombie. I definitely hit two others, and they went down. At that point I feared for my life so much that I ran into the house and locked the door. I felt like I was having a heart attack. Jen helped me into the living room, then went to get first aid for the bite. My Dad was so confused. He sat with his head in his hands. When Jen came out to clean and bandage the bite…she could find no wound."

Zhi was waving his hand. His phone had begun to translate due to overload, and he wasn't ready to listen because he was watching intently as the representative from Ohio expressed his ordeal with genuine emotions, some of which Zhi recognized as similar to those he had witnessed earlier in the day. His eyes had even begun to tear, although he was not sure as yet what the distraught man was saying. He took his phone and stepped aside to listen to the long discourse as the others consoled Dale George.

"Your Dad didn't see any zombies?" asked Jean Bartok.

"No, but he was so upset about the shooting. He asked if we were losing our minds," lamented Dale George.

"What happened to the bite wound?" asked Leann Gomes.

"There wasn't one."

"What about the pain?" asked Tim.

"Gone, but it sure as hell hurt when it bit me!" repeated Dale George. "Then the zombies were gone. When I looked back outside, there was no one there. My Dad was so worried about us that we lied to him and said that bats were attacking us. Then my neighbors came to the door, and we explained to them what had happened. They were more sympathetic than my father."

Silence reigned for more than a minute, except for the Mandarin translation for Zhi Mingzhou. He came back to the table with watery eyes, speaking into his phone. Finally, the translation came: "I am so sorry for your ordeal. I also apologize for doubting the behavior of my colleagues on the trip here today. But this is preposterous!"

"I don't understand," said James Clark, "some people cannot see these monsters? After the attack is finished, the monsters just *vanish*? There are no bite wounds? All evidence of an attack is *gone*? Are we somehow being duped?"

"If we are, then we are not alone. These encounters seem to be more widespread in recent days and weeks," Tim added, "and most of the accounts are the same."

At this point, Jean Bartok was wondering how Jim Wallace's death figured into this insanity. "You know, Jim Wallace had told me that he had proof of a conspiracy just before he died. Could it have something to do with this?" She considered the possibility. "He had something that he wanted to show us at this meeting today, but he was apparently murdered for what he knew, and the evidence was likely destroyed in the fire."

"A conspiracy?" queried LeShaun Brinson. "You mean involving these zombies?"

"I don't know." replied Jean Bartok, "All I know is that it was his idea to have a private meeting so that we could determine the best course of action. He said something about conducting an investigation."

"I guess we will never know what he was talking about," Tim said regretfully.

"What are these monsters, and where do they come from?"

was the most pressing question echoed again and again, this time from the voice of Candice Frandell.

"They sure seem as if they might be victims of the Ebola virus," Dale George exclaimed.

"That just can't be the case!" demanded James Clark, "The victims of the Ebola virus are dead and cremated. They can't just resurrect from ashes! There has to be a rational explanation!"

Abraham Jahir sat erect in his chair and laid down the pen that he had been holding. Jahir was a 70-year-old citizen of Israel. His hair rose in grayish curls from a horseshoe shape around the top of his head, and a long, white goatee accented the deeply carved dimples on his cheeks. He folded his hands on the table in front of him and produced a weak smile for the others. None of the delegation knew him except for Jan Greisfeld, who had invited him to make a presentation about zombies. Little did he know that the incident on the way to the cabin would provide a segue to his presentation. Greisfeld explained his credentials to the group. Jahir had an advanced degree in psychology, and he was well published. He had become a distinguished therapist in his homeland, and he was currently employed by the Haifa Software Corporation.

He had been silent throughout the entire round-table discussion. Now he cleared his throat and prepared to speak. "First, we really must consider what we already know about zombies, since everyone seems to be convinced that these strange creatures are, in fact, zombies. Recently, I have done some research on the fictitious beings. Given my area of expertise, I am well prepared to explain their nature and significance in the world of art and literature."

"My friends had talked about the nature of zombies as they had gleaned from books and video games, but they didn't attain significant insight that was practically useful," Tim said, wondering whether it would be worthwhile.

"Well, let us see whether I have learned anything that you might find useful." Jahir began, "Zombies are always referred to as being 'undead' or 'living dead'. Right? Obviously, this is an oxymoron, and it must be taken metaphorically as there can be no 'living dead'. What is it that is 'dead', but keeps returning as though it were very much alive, again assuming that 'dead' must be understood metaphorically?"

Several members of the gathering searched the faces of their colleagues, but no one seemed to have anything significant to contribute. Finally, Leann Gomes said, "I think you must have an answer. Perhaps you can enlighten us?"

"Zombies have been a fixture in the imaginations of Western men and women for more than a century. They are found often in American film and literature, and they are famous in video games. But, arguably, the symbolic significance of zombies remains largely misunderstood. Truthfully, they represent a dark corner of consciousness that most people refuse to penetrate. We might even say that they represent something 'buried' in our conscious life. Instead of making a careful descriptive, or perhaps a psychoanalytic treatment, of that dark corner, what is 'buried' is brought into the light of day, so to speak, as 'zombies'. But does anyone clarify what they symbolize?"

"It sounds like you intend to offer a psychological interpretation of zombies," replied Tim, anticipating an education on the subject.

"Yes, that is my intention," responded Jahir with complete confidence. "Perhaps I can convince you that zombies represent the very foundation of conscience. Artists toy with this idea, perhaps without really understanding the basic referent of zombie symbolism. Consider this: What is it that is 'undead' in conscious life? How is it that zombies are already dead, yet when encountered in stories, video games, and now in our real lives, they must be 'killed' once again? If you consider this question as a starting point, I believe that we can attain meaningful insight to help us understand their presence today."

Jean Bartok looked around to find that everyone was listening intently to what Abraham Jahir had to say. "Well, Doctor Jahir, I think you have captured our attention. I hear no one interjecting an opinion of his or her own. Please help us to understand what you know about zombies."

"Perhaps we should begin our explanation with reference to the great insight of Sigmund Freud. I am referring to his idea of 'repression' and the related notion of the 'unconscious'. Is it not true that something that one represses is denied or rejected completely? Let us look specifically at what is repressed. I would argue that what is buried in every repression is our personal frailty. That is being rejected. I would call this the primordial repression.[1] It is this weakness, this helplessness, that we would like to make disappear. Is it not? May I suggest that 'repression,' understood in this way, is an attempt to 'kill-off' or 'bury' something essential to our being? Our frail nature is cast away from conscious life as something that is wished dead and gone, something utterly other than oneself."

"So, you are suggesting that zombies represent human weakness? I'm not sure that I follow," complained Jean Bartok.

"That is only part of the picture. If you will grant my interpretation thus far, then, you see, it is not unusual that our personal weakness returns to haunt our conscious life, despite our wishing it dead and gone. The common response when it returns to haunt us is to repress or reject it anew. What is repressed, therefore, might be interpreted as something that is 'undead.' It has been cast out as nothingness, but it returns again and again. It must be 'killed' over and over. Is this not what happens in the literature? Is it not the case that in video games zombies have to be killed to achieve some goal, or win the game?"

James Clarke responded with a bit of awe. "Yeah, that does seem to fit, metaphorically at least. Certainly, in our earlier predicament, we were moved to kill the zombies."

"Alright, good." Jahir was pleased to get some confirmation that his explanation actually made sense.

"But I'm not sure how that is essential to our conscience as you suggested at the start," added Tim.

"Very good. That is precisely the question to ask. You follow very well." Jahir continued. "The zombies are symbolic of one's personal weakness that has been expelled from conscious life. In life's vicissitudes, it returns, particularly in times of crisis. Zombies summon one's own weakness back into conscious life. However, as one faces this weakness in the form of the zombie, it brings about a change of feeling. Originally, facing one's own helplessness is a *private* situation that produces *anxiety*. This is difficult to live with for long, especially if it is a violent anxiety, and of course, different people suffer anxiety in different degrees of intensity.

"However, the zombie produces a meaningful change in the conscious life of anyone who refuses to accept this weakness with anxiety. And, in fact, most people cannot accept it, but rather struggle to repel it again and again." Jahir paused to look about the table for any signs of confusion before he continued. "The zombie motivates a more aggressive reaction because it brings a *fearful expectation*. In the endeavor to repel this monster, one's anxiety is transformed into a fear of death. A more forceful repression is needed to reject the fear of death. This new repression requires more sophisticated efforts of self-deception. Ultimately, one can see that perception of the zombies transforms one's private experience of helplessness into something quite public. It does so by producing a fearful expectation. The zombies must be killed to preserve a life of strength without weakness. Hence, the zombie is returned to the realm of the dead – the unconscious – whence it came, but not without a vigilant, aggressive employment of self-deception to ban this fearful expectation from conscious life. Once again, the zombies symbolize the anxious orientation toward weakness that one does not wish to acknowledge in the first place. Aggressive action against them transforms the anxiety into fear of death, and one is moved to repress this fear with even more strenuous efforts of self-deception."

"Wow, that's sick!" LeShaun Brinson blurted out.

"I'm sorry? You do not think it makes sense, symbolically?" asked Jahir, believing that Brinson meant that he was off-base.

"Are you kidding? The way you explained it, it makes *too* much sense," Brinson nodded in agreement.

"The theory is not quite complete. Fear of death, aggression and self-deception are not only the basic building blocks of American conscience, but also the essential elements intrinsic to an attitude of domination. This is precisely the attitude that we aim to combat as members of the IAPN. It is this specific conscientious orientation that aims for the domination of all natural life. This is our mortal enemy. We endeavor to unite all nations to respect and preserve our natural surroundings."

Most of the group sat quietly mulling over the account of zombies presented by Abraham Jahir. Finally, Tim wondered out loud, not really expecting an answer. "How can we ever change conscience, and overcome the attitude of domination?"

"That is the great problem we face," said Jahir. "At the university, we are working toward a solution…but it is difficult. That is why our nation has taken a first step, on the advice of scholars, to renounce the long-acclaimed superiority of the Jewish people over all others as expressed in the belief that we are 'God's Chosen People'. It is most difficult to embrace the humility necessary in making this choice. Needless to say, it has not been met with universal acceptance. Many of the religious in our country believe that this decision aims to destroy the nation of Israel. They cannot see that the attitude of superiority degrades not only other people, but all of nature. It is a classic piece of self-deception that blinds one to his or her own prejudice. In fact, religion in general is a primary culprit that deceives people throughout the world. Foolish beliefs distract us and prevent us from uniting to solve the real problems that we face. Religion preserves the attitude of superiority among peoples of the world."

"How might we ever overcome the natural tendency to consider oneself as superior to others?" asked Jean Bartok.

"Is it obviously a natural tendency? It seems more like a habit that one develops, despite the fact it is based on a natural tendency," replied Jahir. "We are working on a plan to 'neutralize', so to speak, this common tendency to constitute oneself as superior over others. It seems that this attitude is a habit based on a need for self-esteem. In our studies, we have been referring to the attitude of domination as the 'heroic attitude'. It involves a...."

Suddenly, John Redfeather rushed through the door of the conference room with a purpose. "What's going on?" asked Tim while the others sat erect as if to ask the same question with a change in posture.

"We have unwelcome guests in the parking lot. Three men dressed like ninjas and armed with assault rifles. Let's...."

Boom! A tremendous blast shook the whole cabin. The front wall of the conference room had been opened to the lobby with a gaping hole. Dust and debris filled the air, and chaos ensued. The giant chandelier fell from the ceiling and crushed the table with a crash that sounded like another blast. The crystal shattered and exploded outward with devastating effects. One shard impaled Leann Gomes. It went straight through her eye socket and out the back of her head. The force of the chandelier sent her flying backwards, along with other members of the discussion panel. Blood pooled around her head and flowed along the left side of her motionless body.

The legs of James Clark were pinned beneath the table which was crushed under the weight of the chandelier. He seemed to be sitting up and alert, but blood flowed from his mouth and down his chest as his torso slowly fell backwards onto the remains of his chair on the floor behind him.

The blast sent John Redfeather flying some ten feet onto Abraham Jahir, forcing him away from the shattered remains of the table and chandelier. They both struggled to regain their wits and emerge from the debris.

Everyone at the rear of the table, facing the wall that had been blown apart, was thrust backwards toward the rear wall by the force of the explosion. Jan Greisfeld and LeShaun Brinson were not too badly hurt, despite having hit the rear wall. Greisfeld was holding his head in a daze, but Brinson stood up and was trying to help Greisfeld to his feet.

Zhi Mingzhou and Dale George had their backs to the explosion and had been forced into the table by the blast. They laid motionless under the weight of the chandelier. Jean Bartok was lying on the floor moaning and crying not far from Redfeather and Jahir.

Larry Paulson and Candice Frandell were remarkably still sitting in their chairs with looks of horror on their faces, but now they were near the rear wall. They stared toward the front of the conference room as if in shock. Tim Austin tried to rise from beneath debris strewn off to the side of the table. His chair had been struck by a flying beam from the front of the room. He was knocked aside some fifteen feet from where the remains of the table and chandelier were piled. His head and back were lacerated, but he was conscious and alert enough to feel a terrible pain in his right shoulder. He was sure it was broken or dislocated, but he was able to arise, having no difficulties with his lower extremities.

Dust was floating all about the room, making it difficult to see exactly where everyone had landed. Only moans and cries made it possible to find the survivors. The rear wall of the conference room was basically untouched by the explosion. It was inviting those who were able to escape by exiting the very same way that they had entered. The back door provided means to the tennis courts, the upstairs via the rear staircase, and the dining area. Suddenly, it flew open, and one of the guards yelled, "Come out the back door! Gunmen in the front."

"Some of us need help," Tim cried as he went around to survey the injuries. His shoulder hurt like hell, but he climbed over debris to check on those who were lying around and beneath the table. He had found those who did not survive one by one. As he did, John Redfeather rose and helped Abraham Jahir get to his feet. His nose was bloody, and something had gotten into his eyes making it hard to open them and see, but otherwise he was not too badly hurt. "Stay right here," Redfeather told Jahir. "Let me help the lady." He bent over to attend to Jean Bartok.

She let out a long moan and asked, "What's going on?" It was apparent that she was not going to get up and walk away without some help. Tim went over to help Redfeather with Bartok. Paulson, Brinson, and Frandell all hobbled toward the rear exit where Greisfeld was still sitting against the wall with a severe concussion.

Suddenly, the rapid fire of an assault weapon could be heard toward the front of the building. It didn't last long, but it was enough to send everyone scrambling for safety. Redfeather grabbed Jean Bartok under the shoulders and started dragging her toward the east wall away from the rear exit. "Come on!" he urged her with force.

"What are you doing?" asked Tim, "Let's get outta here!" he demanded looking toward the rear exit.

"Help the old man," yelled Redfeather, gesturing toward Jahir, "and follow me."

Another brief splattering of shots from the assault rifle was heard in the front of the cabin in the direction of the blast. Now the urgency of the survivors had peaked.

"Let's go! This way!" yelled the guard at the rear door one more time. Brinson grabbed Greisfeld and threw him up over his shoulder. "Get going," he instructed Paulson and Frandell. Each of them hobbled toward the guard at the rear exit with all the speed they could muster; Brinson with Greisfeld on his back.

"Wait!" yelled Redfeather, calling toward the group exiting the rear door, but they weren't listening. "We have a safe haven through a door in this wall." He let Bartok gently drop to the floor to reach out and grab Tim to assure him of the best means to escape.

"Where? There is no door there!" Tim insisted.

"Come on, this way!" Redfeather demanded as he felt along the wall for the slot. Thankfully, it was undisturbed. He pushed his key into the slot and the door slid open.

Tim's eyes opened wide. He looked for the others, but they had already escaped out the back door. "Come on," he said to Jahir, who had to follow the voices of Tim and Redfeather with his arms and hands extended outward to find his way to the door.

"Hurry!" urged Redfeather. Tim bent over to help him with Jean Bartok, who was still unable to collect her wits. They followed, entering the open doorway behind Abraham Jahir. "Just a little farther," Redfeather demanded. Finally, they were in far enough to shut the door. Redfeather pressed the switch on the inside wall and the door closed. "Quickly, this way." John Redfeather led Jahir down a narrow hallway about twenty feet long, then through the rear of the kitchen pantry, where he stopped. The hallway was practically dust free, and there were no other impediments to slow him, so Tim continued supporting Jean Bartok on his good arm. She was finally coming around to realize that something terrible had happened. Redfeather was feeling along the wall underneath a piece of trim that was not merely decorative but hiding a slot for a key that was in his left hand. He found the slot and slid the key into it.

Another round of rifle fire could be heard; a longer burst than the earlier ones. The sound was slightly muffled, but this time it seemed as if it were coming from the back of the cabin.

"Step back," Redfeather pushed Jahir slightly aside and a steel door lifted from under the floor tiles to expose an underground ladder that had several steps. It went down about ten feet into a tunnel. "Come on." Redfeather went down first. "Now you." He pointed to Jahir, who started his descent slowly and carefully, still barely able to see. "Help the lady onto the ladder," he told Tim who helped Jean Bartok turn around. His shoulder was pounding with pain, but Tim held her hand until she found her footing and grabbed the top rung with both hands. Redfeather stood on the bottom rung of the ladder, reached up and grabbed her by the hips, while Jahir helped him to keep his balance. They slowly lowered her into the tunnel and backed away from the ladder so Tim could come down.

Tim sat down and dragged himself to the opening, saying, "Help me down. I only have one good arm." He managed with difficulty to descend the ladder with just one hand but got the help he needed as he approached the bottom.

Without further delay, Redfeather pushed a button on the wall to the right of the ladder and they watched the floor lower, hearing a bolting action that sounded like a vault locking. Spotlights came on to reveal the entire length of the tunnel. "Follow me. We will be safe here," Redfeather assured them as he led them through the tunnel. It had a low ceiling, only five and a half feet high, so they had to walk hunched over. They had to help Jean Bartok who was still unable to fully comprehend what was happening. Finally, they arrived at a room that measured about fifteen feet by twenty. It was cool and comfortable with thin padding on the floor – almost like a giant mattress – along one wall.

"Let's put her over here," Redfeather instructed Tim, gesturing toward a place on the mat. He opened a cabinet on one wall. It was replete with enough packaged and canned food, and bottled water, to last them no less than a week.

"What is this place? asked Tim.

"It's our salvation right now," Redfeather replied.

"I guess so!" agreed Jahir as he laid down on the mat and placed his arm over his head.

"We will be fine here until it is safe to emerge. This room is vented to various locations on the mountainside." Then, Redfeather went to a small door inside the food storage closet. He opened it, reached for the emergency contact button, and pressed it. "Now the local authorities know we are here. It's only a matter of time before they come to rescue us."

"Holy smoke!" Tim exclaimed.

John Redfeather opened one last door opposite the food storage closet. It was filled with first aid supplies. "We didn't forget anything," he said with a forced smile.

The men perused the medical supplies stored within the underground cabinet and began tending to their needs as best they could.

"One more thing...while we are taking care of our wounds," Redfeather said, reaching for what looked like an old-style canteen. "Have a swig of this." He gulped three times, then handed it to Tim.

Tim took a long swallow of the liquor and savored the burn in his throat as it warmed and calmed his quaking insides. After one more mouthful, he offered the canteen back to Redfeather, feeling somewhat relieved. Tim produced a feeble grin, then sat down on the mat next to Abraham Jahir, sighed, propped his left elbow on his bent knee and placed his head in his one good hand. Grimacing at the pain in his other shoulder, he wondered, *"How the hell do we get out of this mess?"*

Part II : Diagnosis

Chapter 10

A Material Discovery

Clare was utterly inconsolable. She hadn't heard from Tim for almost two whole days and had been sobbing uncontrollably for hours. Lyndsey had her arm around her. She, too, had tears in her eyes, distraught over the fate of her brother. The reports on the national news the day before had left them with no hope that they would ever see him again. Clare was certain that the cabin which had burned to the ground on South Mountain was the place from which he had last called her. Now she didn't even have the energy to eat or feed Michael.

The national news had indicated that it was a gruesome murder scene. Nine people had been shot to death with an AK-47 assault rifle. Their bullet-riddled bodies were found in various locations outside of the building. Apparently, they had been trying to escape the burning cabin when, unbeknownst to them, armed gunmen were waiting for them outside. Among those who were shot to death were three members of the United States Congress, two security guards, the concierge of the cabin resort, two additional personnel, and a German national who was identified as a governing member of the International Alliance for the Preservation of Nature. At least five others had been found inside the cabin. Their bodies were badly burned, so forensic labs were working to identify their remains. Only one of them had been positively identified thus far: Senator Leann Gomes of Minnesota; the other bodies were unrecognizable. And there were no leads regarding suspects.

The main theme of every news report they had seen concerned the question of whether there was some conspiracy transpiring at the cabin. At least one report had speculated that several Congress persons were meeting with the German national, and perhaps other foreign nationals, for the sake of undermining the government of the United States of America. However, there was no proof for any such claim. Some members of Congress were saying that there might have been an engagement with foreign nationals for the sake of tampering in the 2036 election. But this type of accusation was common since the 2016 election, so it didn't carry much weight with the majority of American people. However, making such an accusation in the first place moved one to think cynically regarding the murderers in this case.

Jake tapped lightly on the door of the back bedroom on the main floor of his house. That was where Lyndsey and Clare were trying to console each other.

"Come in," Lyndsey struggled to make her voice heard.

Jake opened the door and brought in a plate with two breakfast sandwiches. "Hey. You two have to eat some breakfast," Jake insisted. He set the plate on the nightstand next to the bed. "Come on, girls, please eat something. I fed Michael a bottle of the milk you left in the fridge. There's only one bottle left, Clare. You have to nourish yourself to feed the boy."

"Where is he?" asked Clare, her face smeared with tears, and red from the ceaseless crying that had been going on for several hours now.

"He is asleep in the attic. That's where I'll be if you want me. Michael misses you, Clare. He cried a lot before he finally fell back to sleep." Jake stepped outside the door and gently pulled it shut.

"Come on, Clare," urged Lyndsey, "let's eat some breakfast. Oh dear! It's actually lunchtime," she noticed picking up her phone.

The previous evening had passed without another encounter with zombies, despite the fact Jake had seen a number of them from the window in the attic. He and Alan had armed themselves and then gathered the women, Rinna, and Michael, and escorted them upstairs where he felt that they would be safe, at least as long as he and Alan could fight off any infiltrators.

They waited anxiously in the living room and den with their weapons. With all the barricades doubly reinforced over the downstairs windows and doors, they no longer had any view whatsoever to the outside from this level, so they sat quietly ready to unload their weapons into any demonic creatures that attempted to enter. The fearful anticipation lasted for hours, but nothing ever happened. Finally, they went back upstairs. Zack launched his drone from the attic, turning on the night vision. There were no zombies to be seen outside, so Alan and Jake went into the two-car garage and opened the man door to inspect the area outside of the garage. Seeing nothing, they locked the door and went back into the house.

Alan had taken his wife, Greta, to stay with Jake and Lyndsey the previous afternoon, so she would not have to be home alone while he went to work. When he returned early this morning from his shift at the hospital lab, he came with news about the mass removed from Michael's butt. He wanted to relay that information to Clare right away. However, when he heard the news about Tim, he had decided to delay telling her, since it was no threat to Michael's health. Nevertheless, he had found it so disturbing that he had told Greta and Jake while they sat in the control room keeping one eye on national and local news. Now they were all starting to discuss it again.

Suddenly, there was a noisy clamor in the downstairs bedroom where Clare and Lyndsey were. It sounded as if Clare was screaming, so the men bolted from their positions in front of the video screens and raced down the steps with their weapons. Jake was first to arrive. When he turned the corner toward the bedroom the door was opening, and Lyndsey was exiting the room, crying openly. Before Jake could ask what was happening, she exclaimed with great joy, "Tim's okay!"

"What?" asked Jake with joyful disbelief.

"He's on the phone right now. He called Clare." Lyndsey let go of her emotions, hugged Jake, buried her face in his chest, and cried tears of joy.

"Where is he?" asked Jake.

"I don't know. Clare's phone rang, she didn't recognize the number or the area code, but it registered as a call from Phoenix, Arizona. She got this blank stare on her face. My heart dropped. I guess we both expected the worst. Then, she answered, and he said, 'Clare? I'm fine, Clare.' Then she began screaming hysterically."

"Wow! What a relief!" sighed Jake, as Alan put his arms over their shoulders.

Lyndsey and Jake went into the bedroom, while Alan took the guns and went back upstairs. Clare was crying so hard that Lyndsey grabbed the phone and asked, "Where are you, Tim?"

"Is that you Lyndsey? Is Clare alright?"

"Yes, yes, yes!" Lyndsey replied with a wide smile. "She just needs to catch her breath."

"I'm at a hospital in Phoenix. My shoulder was dislocated, but it's much better now. I'm going to get some medical attention for it. I'll be getting a flight home as soon as the authorities release me. Clare…?"

Lyndsey returned the phone to Clare. She had not yet calmed herself enough to speak complete sentences between breathless sobs. "Oh, Tim!" Clare started crying again.

"I'm fine, Clare. Get yourself together. I'll call back in a little while. The doctor needs both my arms relaxed now. I love you so much, Clare! I love all of you. Talk to you soon. Bye, sweetie."

"I love you!" was all that Clare could say amidst the sobs that kept taking away her breath.

Just then, Alan came back down the steps. "Come check this out, Jake," he said with urgency. "A report on the fire in Phoenix is coming up shortly on the noon news." Jake went upstairs while Lyndsey stayed to help Clare calm down and catch her breath. As he arrived upstairs, he was so happy and relieved that he went to his liquor closet, pulled out the caramel flavored whiskey and poured two glasses.

"Here's to Timmy!" He said holding his glass in the air and handing the other to Alan. They gulped the whiskey, and Jake poured another.

"Enough for me, Jake," Alan said with his hand stretched outward to refuse a refill.

Jake poured two more glasses anyway. "Come on, Greta!" he said as he handed her the glass.

"Well, alright," Greta hesitated.

"Oh, man! Tim's alive! Woohoo!" Jake yelled, releasing some tension.

"Look, look!" alerted Alan. "Here's the report." They all turned their attention to the video monitor as Jake increased the volume.

As the same scenes from the day before showed the burned-out cabin once again, the reporter began, "The death toll at the South Mountain Cabin Resort near Phoenix, Arizona has increased to fifteen, as another body was found at the gruesome murder scene. But, in a curious twist, there is a piece of good news to report. This morning, four people were saved from beneath the rubble. Apparently, the cabin had been designed with an emergency tunnel, replete with the necessities that would enable their survival for several days. A member of the Phoenix Police Department had arrived on the scene with the local police, the FBI, and local fire departments, while the blaze was still ongoing. The officer informed the fire fighters that, subsequent to the blaze being extinguished, they would need to clear debris from the area to the rear of the kitchen near the pantry. He expected that there must be at least one survivor tucked away in the safety of an underground shelter located there. Several hours later, once the entrance was located, the door was opened by remote control and four people were lifted to safety. The identity of only one of them has been disclosed. That was Arizona State Representative Jean Bartok. All four of the survivors were taken to a local hospital for treatment, but none are believed to have any serious injuries. Representative Bartok is the fourth member of the United States Congress to have been found at the scene. Her name is now included among others thought to be complicit in a scheme to influence the 2036 elections coming in less than five months. In an unprecedented show of unity among parties, several congressional republicans and democrats have called for an investigation into the proceedings at the cabin resort."

That was the extent of the report. It was quickly followed with an ad that warned people of the dangers of not treating high blood pressure. Jake muted the volume. "Shit!" he exclaimed with disgust, "Those bastards will be looking to hang the opposition. I hope Tim isn't in too much trouble."

Lyndsey and Clare were making their way to the attic, but not soon enough to hear the report. Right on cue, Michael began to whimper, as if he smelled his mother's approach.

"You'n's missed it," Jake asserted.
"What did we miss?" asked Lyndsey with mild alarm.

"Just a report on the rescue of Tim and three others from an underground tunnel beneath the cabin."

"An underground tunnel? Oh my God!" Clare exclaimed not knowing what to make of the fact. "Did they show the rescue?"

"No," said Alan, "there was no new footage, only the same pictures from yesterday." He put his arm around Greta, hugged her, then leaned over to rub noses with her. "The report did mention once again that some congressmen think there is a conspiracy to fix the elections," he added with disdain.

Michael's cries echoed with more urgency. Clare went into the room adjacent to Jake's control center to find him lying there, eyes opening in search of something. "Hello, Michael!" she said with a voice designed to excite him to react to her presence. "How's my baby boy? I missed you! Mommy feels all better now." She tried to assure him as she lifted him from the make-shift crib. It was a twin-sized mattress in the corner against the wall with two old toy boxes pushed up to the side to prevent Michael from rolling off, despite the fact he was not yet able to roll. Michael remained silent as Clare drew him close to her face so that he could see her. His eyes opened and closed twice as if he were sending her a signal. Clare was so happy that she kissed his little cheek and rubbed it against her own.

After she had changed his diaper and checked the wound under the patch on his butt, she remembered that Alan had promised to examine what was removed from him at the lab. She quickly dressed the boy and exited the room, planning to ask Alan about the results. Before she could ask, Jake said, "Hey, Clare, get ready for another surprise. Alan…" he gestured to Alan to tell Clare what they had been discussing earlier.

"First of all," Alan began, "there is nothing of concern to report about Michael's health. What I found about the apparent tumor is that it was nothing more than fatty tissue."

"Oh, thank God," Clare declared with relief.

"Yes," added Alan, "his health is just fine. You need only care for the open wound to prevent stool from contacting it. However," he continued, "that's not the whole story."

"What?" asked Clare apprehensively.

"Don't worry," insisted Jake. "Go ahead, Alan."

"Well, there was something small in the tissue that looked almost like a speck of dirt or something."

"What was it?" Clare interrupted.

"Well…" Alan began, with hesitation, because he still couldn't believe what he had found. "I put the mass under the microscope, and I was a bit confused. It was some kind of foreign matter. After further amplification, and verification from my colleague…well, we determined that it was a microscopic circuit board."

"What?" Clare exclaimed in disbelief.

"Yep. In fact, there were two separate ones. I'm sure they are silicon chips."

"What the fuck were they doing on my baby's ass?" Clare begged with defiance.

"That I can't say," Alan replied. "All I know is that we found two silicon chips in the mass of fatty tissue. I asked Lance not to say anything because it was my responsibility to analyze the mass. I simply asked him to look through the microscope for the sake of confirming what I thought I had seen."

"What did you do with them," asked Lyndsey, since she had not yet heard the whole story.

"I returned the tissue to its vial and placed it in the bin to be destroyed. Then, I put the chips in a separate vial, and brought them here," Alan said with a mischievous grin.

"Do you have it now?" Lyndsey asked.

"Actually, you and Jake have it. I put it in your medicine cabinet downstairs," Alan said.

"Won't somebody know that they are missing?" asked Lyndsey with concern for Alan.

"I doubt it very much. I have submitted the lab report to my superiors, saying that the mass was nothing more than fatty tissue. The vial and its contents will be destroyed…if it has not been already."

"We have a real mystery on our hands, Clare," Jake stated. "We have to figure out what the hell silicon chips were doing inside little Michael. Let's act with extreme caution about this. It might be best to pretend like we know nothing of any such discovery, at least until we can find someone trustworthy enough to help us."

Clare was confused. She held Michael close to her, then went back into the attic bedroom, removed his diaper, and took a closer look at his wound. Lyndsey followed to see what she was doing. "It seems fine now, doesn't it, Lyn?" she asked.

Lyndsey bent over and lifted the bandage to glance once more at Michael's wound. She thought to herself that she wouldn't recognize anything anyway. After all, her expertise was *mental* health. "I'm sure he will be just fine," she tried to assure Clare.

Jake was using his control panel to flip through the local

broadcasts, searching for reports on recent zombie attacks. The past couple of days had marked an increase in the number of reports on both national and local news. Each was as baffling as all the others.

Interviews of persons who were attacked consistently revealed that people who suffered the horrific encounters were fearful for their lives and maddened to a furious rage that moved them to all sorts of violent actions to repel the evil creatures. Apparently, there were numerous methods that could render the zombies harmless, but all of them required a forceful attack against the heads of the monsters. Crushing their skulls and blowing their heads off were the preferred methods for stopping the zombies in their tracks. A couple of the people interviewed even bragged that sharp objects could be forced through their heads with the same stifling effect.

But, regardless of the method used to repel the zombies, the same strange results followed. No matter how much of the stinking, festering puss was transferred from the zombie to the victim under attack, not one of them had become a zombie. Every person who reported having been bitten had no physical wounds to prove the attack. And there were no dead zombies to prove the claims that any of them had been destroyed. Moreover, there was not one zombie shown on any of the reports! It was insane!

In fact, when these attacks first started, many people had begun to question the mental capacity of the victims. It was no wonder that some doubters had thought the victims to be mentally impaired. But the reports had become more numerous, and even the most skeptical of onlookers were becoming more sympathetic with these victims, ultimately concerned for his/her own wellbeing. Slowly but surely, the lasting effects of fear, coupled with murderous intent, were spreading to many people who had never even seen a zombie.

Chapter 11

Tim's Enlightenment

Tim wiped the sweat from his brow with his sleeve. Even though the temperature in the airplane was comfortable, he felt warm as he fully awakened from a short period of dozing on-and-off. He would have gladly welcomed a restful sleep, but none was forthcoming. He was absolutely overwhelmed by the circumstances of the past forty-eight hours. The dreams that he was having about Clare and Michael and zombies were making it impossible for him to rest comfortably, and he was feeling quite frazzled. He wondered how he would explain to Clare and the others what he had learned from Abraham Jahir. His interaction with the Jewish psychoanalyst had certainly put everything in his life, especially these crazy zombies, into an entirely new perspective. Presently, a lot of different questions were jumbled in his mind, and he couldn't stop trying to separate a plethora of confusing problems into their own respective mental compartments, so that he might deal with each one separately in its own due time.

His recent proximity to death and destruction had taken a toll on him. He couldn't wrap his head around the grand significance of the deaths of these people with whom he was just beginning to become better acquainted. Thinking about it too much caused his internal organs to quake, and simultaneously made him sweat. He was sick with anxiety whenever he focused on these deaths too closely. But so many questions were arising from these catastrophic incidents. He couldn't even keep count of how many members of Congress had been killed in the attack at the cabin, and also the burning of the office of Jim Wallace on the North Side. Was it five, or six? The numbers really didn't matter. These were human lives cut short by murderous intent.

More questions arose from the fact that the number of defenders of the International Alliance in the United States Congress was reduced by these deaths. Would they still have sufficient numbers to go forward with the plans to create a new party? Hopefully, the replacements for those who had been killed would have the same interests for the future of the U.S. government. Tim would have to rely on Jean Bartok, and perhaps also Kayla Bruster, to recruit new representatives in place of those who had died.

Then there were the deaths of Jan Greisfeld and Zhi Mingzhou. Would there be retribution coming from Germany and Hong Kong? How would their home countries respond to the murder of these prominent leaders? Would the relations between Germany and the United States become more strained, making it difficult to unite the intentions of the new coalition with the International Alliance? After all, Jan Greisfeld was the President of the IAPN. Tim wondered whom he would be working with to coordinate the party platform with the tenets of the Alliance. All these questions would be answered in time, but right now they were alerting him to some of the many problems he would encounter in the near future.

The thirty-six hours he had spent with Abraham Jahir had changed his life forever. Tim was struggling to assemble the facts and visualize the big picture. Jahir had suggested that the zombies were nothing more than an elaborate hoax. But who could be the source of such a grand deception? That was not clear. And how could he possibly suggest that events surrounding the zombie attacks, which seemed to be so real, were actually not real at all? Tim recalled the frightening perceptions that sent him running for the hospital. He was having difficulty weighing this memory against what Jahir had told him. Then there was Jahir's claim that, late last year, the Haifa Software Corporation had developed a new program capable of enabling computers to have feelings and mimic human emotions. Tim was astounded that someone had finally accomplished the grand design of making robots more like humans. He tried to ascertain the value of such a discovery. Robots performing surgery wouldn't need feelings, would they? Was it for some frivolous end, like making electronic household aids express emotion to those who employed them?

What he was sure of was that people would continue to invent more and more electronic devices, put them to work, and only later consider the moral ramifications. No one ever asked what possible problems might arise from their creation until after they witnessed some of the problems firsthand. As was often the case, when problems did surface, there would be some sort of mess to clean up and new dangers to beware. This time, a new technological discovery had grown an ugly Medusa head when the software was either stolen, or some reprehensible bastard sold it for personal gain.

Then he recalled his relief at having finally escaped what had seemed as if it might be endless questioning – not so much from the local authorities, but from the FBI. They wanted to know what he was doing at the cabin resort with so many members of Congress and foreign nationals. It was now public knowledge that there was ongoing correspondence between the governing members of the IAPN and members of the United States Congress. Tim did his best not to reveal that a new party was arising that was founded upon the tenets of the Alliance. But he wasn't sure what the FBI might have learned from Jean Bartok or Abraham Jahir. They were questioned as a group only briefly, and that interview was conducted by the local police who were seeking leads concerning those who orchestrated the mass murder.

When it was clear to the police that none of the four who survived had any knowledge whatsoever regarding their assailants, it was then that the FBI had questioned each one individually, trying to determine the group's agenda. Those interviews lasted for hours; more than four hours in Tim's case. It was all he could do to assure them that he was a philosopher who was invited to help with the discussion of complicated moral conflicts that exist between the United States and the International Alliance. Naturally, they pressed him to answer why *he* was invited and not some other academic who had more noteworthy credentials. He responded that he was a friend of Representative Wallace, who had recently died in a catastrophic fire in Pennsylvania, and that he was recommended to Jean Bartok as trustworthy and full of insight into key matters concerning the Alliance.

After a grueling test, the FBI was satisfied with the results of the questioning, although they seemed reluctant to stop, and finally allowed Tim to leave. Then, he was asked where he would be going from Phoenix and told to remain in the country, should they need to question him further. Tim felt an anxious anticipation when he considered that he might have to tell Clare about this.

What nagged at Tim the most was the disconcerting feeling that accompanied his belief that every ounce of privacy in his life had begun to flitter away like a sheet of paper in a gust of wind. He expected Jake would tease that he was some kind of paranoid neurotic. But Tim felt that his concern was totally justified. So much of his private discussion with Abraham Jahir during their time beneath the cabin, regarding the psychological aspects of conscious life, was beginning to assemble a new understanding in his mind. Jahir's account of human feelings, or what he kept referring to as "internal sense", was now commingling in his understanding with what he thought about personal privacy.

"What is solely our own, if not our feelings and thoughts?" wondered Tim. Then, he considered that question at length in philosophical contemplation[1]: *"My personal privacy is this immediate, conscious self who I am. I am always present as this internal sense, actively attending to the world around me.*

My privacy is my very self-identity, producing my thoughts, my feelings, all my sensations, and every kind of memory. My most private being makes its way into the world, showing itself in my behaviors for others to perceive. I reveal myself to others in innumerable ways, even if only partially and obscurely. Signs of my most private being are indicated by me continuously in the things that I say and do. Anyone can witness these signs as emanations of my privacy – my own self-identity. Others can not only sense various aspects of my privacy, but also feel my private self by means of their own internal sense. And my privacy can be appropriated by others. I know that, all too often, others influence me to believe things and behave in ways that I would rather not."

Tim proceeded to clarify for himself the manner by which his privacy might be influenced to become other than his own, i.e., as determined by something other than his own will. Certainly, this was common in all sorts of experiences. He wondered about love relationships, believing that he willingly shared himself with Clare. But there were other times when his privacy might be penetrated and influenced *against* his will. He was integrating these thoughts with what he had learned from Abraham Jahir about the zombies.

"While I willingly express my private self from my internal sense out through my external ones, by means of the surface of my body in general, my private self can be penetrated and determined by others from the outside in, so to speak. My external senses can be activated to influence my internal sense. The outside world in general can act upon my external senses to determine how I feel and think about things, and what I believe. Clare's beauty can move me to a feeling of love and adoration in the same way that a beautiful sunset can deliver a feeling of awe and move me to wax poetically. Alternatively, those disgusting zombies can move me to fear. They can steal my privacy by dominating my internal sense, thereby determining how I feel. Someone is intentionally trying to manipulate my external senses to dominate my internal sense and create a feeling of fear. And, if Jahir is right, specifically fear of death. But why? How might someone benefit by

motivating this fear in people?"

    Tim let go of his contemplative endeavor as he was interrupted by the flight attendant reminding him to secure his seat belt, as the pilot had begun the descent to the airport in Pittsburgh. He started to wonder, what was most important for Clare and his friends to know right away, and what information might be best withheld until the time was right. At that point, he realized his reflection had come full circle; he was back where he had started. Again, he tried to close his eyes and relax, but there was just too much to think about.

Chapter 12

The Power of Empathy

As he walked from the jetway to the ramp, then downward toward the baggage claim, Tim pulled his phone from his jacket and turned it on. He was glad that he wouldn't have to dally around the conveyers to retrieve any belongings. Everything he had taken with him was destroyed in the burned-out cabin, except for his phone. He had only a few basic necessities that he had gathered from Walmart to get him home, and these were stowed away in his new backpack.

As he enumerated to himself the items he had lost in the fire, Tim remembered something he had done as he hurriedly gathered his belongings before leaving the house to catch the flight to Arizona. This recollection brought a new sense of order to his state of confusion. Looking back, he thought himself wise, indeed, to have sent off both a printout and a digital copy of the documents he had created for the meeting. He was pleased with himself as he recalled that Kayla Bruster now had these materials, and he was sure that they were in good hands with her. He was also counting on his private laptop containing all his important documents, safely stowed away in its hidden location at his home. This laptop contained the totality of his writings, all the work he had done concerning the party and all his research on the International Alliance.

As soon as his phone had reset, it began lighting up with text messages. One was from Clare, one from Representative Bartok, and one from Kayla Bruster. He opened Kayla's first. She requested a phone call at his earliest convenience. Jean Bartok reported that she was feeling better. Although she had no serious injuries from the explosion, she had to remain in the hospital for a while longer so that doctors could make sure her illness was under control. She had not taken her medication as prescribed for two days, and she had to be monitored for several hours until her vital signs normalized. She, too, was requesting a phone call.

But Clare would get first priority. As he walked toward his car, he issued the command to call her. "Hi, babe!" he responded to her cheerful greeting. He so needed to hear her voice and get some good vibes from her to aid in purging the turmoil from his inmost being. "How are you? You sound really good!"

"We are all fine, honey. Michael has been so alert today. He must know you are coming home to us. We can't wait to see you!" Clare added with the joyful voice that Tim wanted to hear.

With tears clouding his vision, he said, "I can't wait to see you! Just hearing your voice has lifted my spirit out from the dark place it has been."

"Are you okay to drive, Tim? Jake said he would come and get you." Clare insisted, knowing that he had to drive some thirty miles to Lyndsey's house with a sore shoulder.

"No, no, no. My shoulder is fine, Clare. It practically reset itself. The pain is gone; I haven't taken any pain medication, other than aspirin. And now my spirit is coming back to life just from talking to you. I can drive," he added, trying to reassure her. He didn't want to leave the car at the airport, so he changed the subject, "How is Michael?"

"He's fine, and growing more alert by the day," she

responded.

"Oh, that's great, Clare." Tim was approaching his car in the short-term parking lot. Once he entered the car, he could put down his phone, and talk through the car phone. "I'm just getting to the car now."

"Well, honey, I'm gonna let you go so that you can focus exclusively on driving. Please be careful," she exhorted him. "I'm gonna feed Michael. It seems that he is always hungry! Or maybe he just likes sucking on my breast. He's just like his daddy," she joked. Tim laughed so hard that he nearly choked, then he cried tears of joy. She needed to hear his laugh as much as Tim needed to do it. It was curative for the both of them to unite in spirit. "I miss you, honey!"

"I miss you too, Clare. I'll be there in an hour or so. The morning rush should be over by now. Hopefully, traffic is light through the city. See you soon," he concluded, ending the conversation. For the first time in three full days, he felt a peace and warmth, calmed by the expectation of seeing Clare and Michael, and the rest of the gang. He had hoped that he could preserve that state of mind until he got to Jake's house. Then, he remembered that Jean Bartok and Kayla Bruster were both expecting a call from him. He decided that, since neither of them had expressed any urgency, they could wait until he felt more like the private person he was before the events of the past several days. He desperately needed to relax, and sort things in his own mind. And he wanted to spend time with his new son. Mostly he wanted to feel normal again. But then he became concerned that perhaps normalcy would elude him.

He rang Clare once more as he got close to Jake's. He wanted them to be ready to let him in as soon as he arrived…in case they might be fearing zombies. How would he ever begin to explain to them what he learned from Abraham Jahir? First things first: he needed to spend some time with Clare and Michael. As he came around the bend in the driveway toward the garage door, he stopped, and the door began to rise immediately. There was nothing unusual; no zombies that he could see. But the driveway had two other vehicles...one that belonged to Alan Gustavsson and the other to Zack LeVeille. Tim parked in the yard on the opposite side of the driveway, locked his car and ran into the garage, pressing the switch to lower the main door. Then he entered the house through the door that opened into the den. Clare was there to greet him with a warm embrace as soon as he walked in. They clung to each other passionately and Clare started crying. "I thought you were gone, Tim," she whispered.

"Well, I'm not, babe!" Tim grinned ear to ear, kissed her, hugged her, and messaged her backside over and over. The others waited in the living room to greet Tim, allowing him and Clare to embrace for what seemed like a brand-new beginning for their life together. It was a passionate reunion for them both. Finally, he wiped the tears from her eyes, kissed her once more and said, "Come on, babe, let's go in with the others." She wiped her face and took his hand to follow.

Lyndsey was next to wrap her arms around Tim and plant a big kiss on his face. Then Jake hugged him, and said, "I'm not kissing you like that." A joyous reunion continued for several minutes until Tim sat down and asked, "What do we have to eat?"

"Way ahead of you, Tim," said Lyndsey. They had already gathered enough food for a substantial party. She and Karen had prepared some of it for an early lunch. There was ham, potato casserole, cheesy pasta, green beans, assorted olives, wine, Italian bread, and lots of snacks like cashews, crackers, and assorted candies. The gang let Tim fill his plate first, then the others followed, and they ate heartily, enjoying a reunion meal.

No one said a word about any of the pressing issues that were plaguing the group, at least while they were eating. It was agreed unanimously among them before Tim's arrival that no one would raise the issue of the silicon chips, and definitely no one should bring up what had happened to Tim. He would have to initiate conversation about the events in Arizona himself.

Lyndsey had suggested to them that he might need some time to regather his wits. He might rather not remind himself of the harrowing experience he had endured, at least not right away.

As the meal was ending, everyone considered his/her plans for the immediate future. Tim indicated that he wanted to spend some quiet time with Clare and Michael, complaining that he had yet to enjoy any meaningful time with his new son. The three children rushed toward the game room the moment they were allowed to leave the dinner table, so Greta got up and followed, offering to stay with them while they played at the kiddie version of the control center. The rest of the adults would go upstairs to Jake's control center.

After the children raced for the game room, Tim had intimated to the adults that he had quite a lot to tell them about the zombies, but he'd rather hold off until he could relax for a while with Clare. He did warn his friends to cool their fear, because the zombies were not a concern, insisting that they could do no harm by themselves. They looked at him with a variety of puzzled faces, but he assured them that, if what he learned is true, then the zombies were absolutely harmless, and their potential victims were more likely to harm themselves going to extremes to combat the creatures. The group struggled to make sense of his assertion, but he ended by saying that he would explain later that evening.

As they climbed the steps into the attic, the group clamored over what he might be talking about. Each of them had his/her own opinions forming as they attempted to gather all the facts. As soon as he entered the attic, Alan declared, "I need some sleep." He had not slept since returning from the night shift at the hospital. He felt safer at Jake's, so instead of taking Greta home and leaving her alone while he slept, he accepted Jake's invitation to stay with them another day. He adjourned to the room where Michael had been sleeping while Clare was sick with the belief that Tim had been killed. "A couple of hours should be enough to rejuvenate me, since I am off for the next two nights." He closed the door, moved the items placed around the bed to keep Michael from rolling off, threw himself down on his back, and closed his eyes.

Jake grabbed a controller and tuned into several local and national news stations. Lyndsey dropped herself into the chair beside him like a rag doll. She was set to go to the institute for an afternoon session with a new client. Zack took a controller and faced the wall adjacent to the one that Jake was using. Karen decided that she would go back downstairs to be with Greta and the children. "We might go to the basement, Jake," Karen said. "The boys wanna ride their bikes down there." The house had a large basement with a relatively level concrete floor. Besides the bicycles, there were electric kiddie cars that they could drive and play bumper cars.

"Okay," said Jake, "just let me know when you go there." He was concerned about the safety of the basement windows, whether they could withstand an attack. He believed that they would be difficult to break because they were glass block. But he was afraid that a zombie swinging a steel bar, such as they had seen the night of the attack at their house, might be able to break the glass. Then he paused to compare these thoughts with what Tim had just told him about the zombies.

Jake didn't reflect on these conflicting thoughts for long before something caught his eye on the monitor. It was a report on recent zombie attacks. He raised the volume and attended closely to it. A collection of separate incidents was being reported. It began by showing damage at a property where several people had been besieged. In one segment, a reporter interviewed three people who were attacked, and it was clear that their fear had driven them to extreme measures to protect themselves. Two were still holding tightly to their weapons of choice: an axe, and a maul. The one man was absolutely mad! He claimed to have bashed in the brains of more than one zombie with the maul, while the other man nodded and raised his arm, waving the axe above his head. In a different incident, a woman was shot by her husband as he aimed to kill an approaching zombie. Another report showed the broken glass on the second floor of a house where a man had fallen to his death, apparently knocked through the window during an attack. Finally, Jake had come to the realization that there were no zombies actually shown in any part of the report.

Lyndsey was also watching intently. She sensed that the number of these attacks was on the increase nationwide. She remembered that her first evaluation of the victims of a zombie attack was that these people were psychotic. After all, none of the victims were able to *confirm* that zombies had attacked, because no fallen zombies had ever been found to reveal that there was an assault in the first place! Similarly, no one had any bite marks to show. The only wounds, or proof of physical harm, were incidental injuries that happened during the attack.

But, consistently, all the reports she had seen or read revealed two disturbing after-effects. The first, she had documented on more than one occasion. Specifically, there was an enduring fear of death and an aggressive desire to kill zombies that continued to haunt the victims long after an attack. The other effect was newly observed, but even more problematic. It was demonstrated in interviews with people who had *not* been attacked by zombies. These people either knew someone who had a frightful encounter, or simply had been hearing about these attacks. The enduring symptoms of zombie attacks were now spreading throughout the populace by means of *sympathetic experience*. People who had never been attacked by a zombie were frightened for their own lives and had also taken measures to combat a possible attack.

Fear seemed to be driving the majority of the population to build their defenses. Jake, himself, had boarded his windows and doors and accumulated guns and ammunition. In fact, gun sales, along with ammunition, had skyrocketed. This was a boon for the manufacturers of weapons. People were gathering axes, sickles, knives, iron bars, and anything else that one might keep ready-to-hand. These could be found in the living spaces of homes, where normally they would never be seen. People were actually bringing tools and other equipment from their outdoor sheds into their homes.

Jake, Zack, and Lyndsey listened as the reporter drew her

conclusions from the interviews. "The fear of these grotesque monsters seems to have spread throughout the country. Increasingly, people are preparing to defend themselves against vicious attacks. As you can see, even those who have not directly experienced the zombies have a sympathetic eye for those who have suffered attacks. They, too, know the fear that these creatures inspire, and they, too, are prepared for battle should the necessity arise."

"Man! This fear is spreading like a freakin' disease!" exclaimed Jake, shaking his head.

"Yep," agreed Zack, "it's no wonder. Right? It scourged this house, and all of us!" He asserted, as if to provide proof.

"It's no surprise." Lyndsey agreed. "Actually, sympathy is a means by which we can, so to speak, catch the ills of others. Phenomenologically, it…."

"Oh, shit, Lyn!" objected Jake, "Keep it simple for us, huh?"

"I only mean to speak from the perspective of anyone who experiences sympathy. I don't mean to intimidate you with the language," corrected Lyndsey.

"Are you being pedantic again, Lyndsey?" Zack teased her to feign being sympathetic with Jake.

"I'm sorry," apologized Jake, "please, go easy with the psychoanalytic jargon."

"I shall try and simplify the technical language," she said. "Sympathy is actually a special type of empathy. Humans share all sorts of feelings empathetically; some are more intimately shared than others. Sympathy is a sharing of the suffering of someone else, or others in general."

"I remember from my college days a professor who told us that the word comes from the Latin, *simpatico,* which means to 'suffer with'," added Zack, hoping to show that he understood what Lyndsey was talking about.

"That's right!" Lyndsey appreciated the response just to show Jake that Zack was willing to follow her reasoning. "Sympathy is a complex experience, but one thing it has in common with empathy is that it presupposes a *comparison* of oneself with someone else.[1] The sympathetic person is usually unaware that he/she is making this sort of comparison. One perceives the other suffering, then memory flashes to a past experience of one's own suffering, and the self is compared by this means to the suffering other. It is by means of this comparison – whether it occurs spontaneously, or one does it deliberately – that one shares the pain or suffering of the other. This association of personal vulnerability via self-comparison is essential to sympathy. The sharing of someone else's pain always presupposes it."

Jake wanted Lyndsey to notice that he was willing to follow her train of thought. "So, the spread of this fear occurs by means of this self-comparison, whether or not someone is attacked by zombies?" asked Jake.

"You can see that! That is the nature of sympathy." Lyndsey continued. "Human empathy, which includes sympathy, is a natural response, I believe, that developing humans rely upon to bridge a gap exposed at birth. In the womb, the developing fetus shares its mother's feelings in as complete a manner as such sharing is possible. You could say that feeling is shared within one complex internal sense. The same blood courses through both mother and fetus as a biological unity. They feel with one connected nervous system. They share biorhythms, and all the vitals that constitute one complex internal sense.

"At birth, the newborn is separated from the mother's internal sense. The crisis exposes a lack, and the newborn struggles with the dawn of its own private internal sense. Birth creates the need for empathy, not merely to share feelings, but the newborn *becomes* empathetic in the search for its lost nourishment. To compensate for its loss, the newborn struggles with its newly activated external senses in search for a means to reestablish the connection to the internal sense of its mother. It feels around empathetically in the search for what it has lost.

"Although empathy arises naturally to make up for the disconnect, it falls short of being able to achieve the same kind of sharing lived in the womb. In its developed capacity, human sympathy is a natural means for tuning the internal sense to feel the pain or suffering of another. It aims to share the internal sense of the other, reaching for it by means of its external senses. Throughout the course of our social lives, we are trained to share specific feelings under specific circumstances.

Lyndsey continued, "As a natural response to a lack, empathy aims to produce a unity of feelings among people. Obviously, the same is true for sympathy. In its developed capacity, empathy employs a self-comparison to share the internal sensibility of others. But, as I have said, this natural tendency can be developed by various techniques so that we share *specific* feelings. In other words, we can be trained to be sympathetic in specific ways. Consider how we use euphemisms about death, particularly at a funeral. Everyone is urged to make the self-comparison so that we 'feel the other's loss'. We have been trained to feel *with* others to the extent that all of us are expected to use the same innocuous language about death."

"I get the point, Lyn," said Jake. "So-and-so has 'passed on', and the like."

"Well," said Zack, "you wouldn't have approached Clare yesterday and said to her, 'Tim's dead.' Right? We are expected to be sensitive and anticipate what others might feel."

"It is by means of this self-comparison, essential to sympathy, that we make a tacit sort of agreement to think and speak publicly about death in this way, as if we must hide some grim reality about death from ourselves and each other. This serves mostly to veil the facts from our immediate awareness. Our society teaches us to repress thoughts about death by means of a careful use of language. I don't wanna get *too* cynical about this, but...why would we want to disguise the realities of death?" Lyndsey wondered.

"Yes, we are certainly trained to share similar feelings about death," Jake laughed. "I don't know if there is a reason why?"

"One rarely asks such questions. People just tend to do what others do. We are trained to use this self-comparison so that we feel for those others who suffer a loss, and we act as we are taught, to carefully disguise the facts with innocuous speech," Lyndsey concluded.

"Yeah, and it used to be you had to wear a sad face, too," said Jake. "But nowadays some people have a celebration of life as an alternative to the solemn funeral proceedings."

"I think we need to make changes in our orientation toward death in general," Lyndsey asserted. "We should probably avoid imitating what others do and learn to speak of it as it is. Perhaps each person could learn to express his or her own feelings, instead of bowing to the traditional public service, if you will." Jake nodded, then Zack.

"That's one way that we are trained to be *sympathetic*. Are we not also trained to be empathetic, and share good feelings?" Lyndsey asked. "Consider the so-called 'holiday season'. Everyone is urged to share the joys of Christmas with gift giving, the good feelings of an imagined savior of mankind, and so on. We all are urged to do the same things on certain days at specific times and have the same kinds of celebrations. Does that not facilitate the sharing of specific good feelings? These feelings are also shared by means of empathetic self-comparison. The latter dominates our daily lives, and it is taken for granted. As a result, it leads one to make a lot of 'traditional decisions', mostly without questioning our own thoughts and actions."

Jake cut her off to add his own opinion on this issue. "I am a cynic about holidays, especially Christmas. I am certain that American corporations and the political culture they gravitate toward are supported, and enriched, by means of everyone in society sharing the pleasures of gift giving for six full weeks or more. The urgency underlying the promotion of the 'holiday season' even appears as a form of desperation. If no one were encouraged to make a self-comparison to the people who promote and engage in these celebrations, perhaps no one would bother with such a holiday."

"Ha! Are you gonna legislate against Christmas? This is where you will find the limits of theory in the real world!" Zack poked fun at Jake.

"Gift giving would be more spontaneous and creative without it!" Lyndsey begged. "Imagine if we were trained to give gifts spontaneously, according to one's personal need at the time it is needed. We should dispense with the forced celebration! This is a case where the sharing of feelings is coerced through training and habituation to result in a desired outcome: corporate profits. When this practice has been repeated for generations, then it becomes difficult to change. Moreover, it is hard to distinguish what might have been a natural progression of empathetic experience in contrast with what results from coercion."[2]

Before Jake could interrupt, Lyndsey emphasized the conclusion to her line of reasoning. "Go back to the effects of the zombies. The natural tendency in sympathy to use self-comparison opens the door to more than just shared suffering. Because the comparison to others is encouraged, and common to life in the social world, a shared fear of death is inevitable. It is much more difficult, and personally challenging, *not* to share the feelings of others, because the majority can be so overwhelmingly persuasive. You can see that empathy as a whole – and particularly sympathy – has a power of its own over social behavior. Because of sympathy, fear and aggression are spreading among the people as if the zombies were everywhere. Now it would not matter if they were nowhere!"

Lyndsey insisted.

Zack concurred with Lyndsey. "I remember how the children felt our fear during the zombie attack here at the house. They were huddled in the attic, and never saw any of the things that we saw. They had no insight into what was happening, but they felt our fear as if the zombies had attacked *them*."

"That's right," agreed Jake. "They felt our fear as if it were their own. Our feelings transferred to them as if it had been conducted within electronic circuitry. They saw no zombies, but only shared the powerful emotions that we could not keep to ourselves. Our feelings overpowered their own private feelings about their environment."

"That's right, Jake," Lyndsey was happy that he was intellectually involved in this conversation. "But I'm still trying to figure this out. A person experiencing sympathy associates one's own anxiety and weakness with the suffering of the other. However, as sympathy is a social experience, that anxiety somehow transforms into fear. It seems that this happens as a consequence of the self-comparison in sympathy, and that sympathetic experience plays an essential role in one's orientation toward death. However, what we think and feel about death is learned directly from others, primarily through the feelings associated with it."[3]

"Yeah," said Jake, "and since we are taught to hide our feelings about death, we have our little deceptions and rituals to keep it concealed."

"But as one grows in the social world, it requires an increasingly sophisticated effort of self-deception to conceal the fear of death shared in society. More so than it does to repress one's private anxiety over one's own weakness," judged Lyndsey. "One's own weakness is initially concealed only from oneself. However, one's response to what is learned about death via social experience must also be hidden from others in speech and ceremony and the like. That's what really happens, no?"

"Because of the zombies we have an epidemic of fear and deception," Jake complained.

"That is what we have today, no doubt," Lyndsey confirmed Jakes concern. "The natural tendency to empathy can be a problem insofar as it fosters the spreading of feelings that one fails to adequately scrutinize. For that reason, unless one has the wherewithal to preserve one's own privacy, and maintain self-control over one's own internal sense, one is at the mercy of empathy determining how one feels."

"You will be moved about like a puppet," joked Jake. "No doubt our society is using more and more of our private information to create individualized persuasive techniques on the basis of empathy."

"It's all about getting your business!" Lyndsey replied. "Businesses entice people to begin celebrating Christmas earlier every year. They motivate that 'good feeling', and get it circulating as soon as possible so that the spending parties can begin!"

"And advertising goes extreme!" added Jake with disdain. "That is among the most despicable of professions! Creators of ads manipulate us to expose a lack, then try and persuade us to fill the gap with some specific product. Advertisements for prescription drugs and medical services, directed to the general public, are especially reprehensible. Anything goes in these damned ads! Advertisers, and the drug companies they represent, prey on reminding people of their own weakness, then suggest a possible cure and urge them to ask their doctor to help them. Drug companies that utilize advertising direct to the public are seeking profit by exploiting human weakness. These institutions benefit the most from a fear of death to increase profits and revenue. Generally, it is assumed people will cater to an ideal self and employ the common deceptions. Neither the advertisers nor the makers of drugs have a genuine concern for the health of individuals. They can't even know how a particular person will react to a specific drug! In my opinion," Jake exclaimed, "advertisers are comparable to the scam artists that try to trick you into forking over your cash. They abuse the freedoms of our country to manipulate the public!"

Zack laughed out loud. "You ought to run for president on the platform that you will clean up corporate America."

"Somebody needs to!" insisted Jake. "Our institutions have lost track of what is truly important in life. The health of citizens should be top priority, not manipulation and exploitation!"

Then, Jake noticed a picture of Jim Wallace on one of the video screens he was monitoring. "Hey, look at this," he said, asking the others to listen.

The report was broadcast from the station that Jake comically referred to as the "chronic neurotic buffoonery channel". A picture of Jean Bartok followed one of Jim Wallace. Jake raised the volume above the other sounds in the room. The report announced an investigation into the fallen representatives of the House and Senate, regarding a conspiracy against the United States. It included speculation that people, currently under investigation by the FBI, might have been attempting to undermine the political system, trying to rig the upcoming election. As it showed the picture of Representative Bartok, the claim was made that a new party, referred to as "The People's Party", had been covertly organized by members of the U.S. Congress. It suggested that one of the current candidates for the 2036 election had secretly adopted a new party platform that was aligned with the International Alliance for the Preservation of Nature. Defense for that claim was made with direct reference to Jan Greisfeld, the President of the Alliance, who was killed at the cabin resort on South Mountain in Arizona. It was believed that he conspired with these representatives to influence the upcoming U.S. election. The report concluded by saying that the FBI was trying to identify all the members of Congress who were complicit not only with Greisfeld, but also with a Chinese national currently unknown and a Jewish national, named Abraham Jahir, who was said to have escaped detention in Arizona.

"Holy shit!" exclaimed Jake as he rose from his chair, ready to race down the steps to inform Tim.

"Hold on just a minute, Jake!" demanded Lyndsey. "Let's think for a minute before you rush to spread any concern. What is…" Before she could finish expressing her thought, Tim was coming up the stairs. He opened the door and entered.

"You showed up right on cue!" insisted Zack.

"Why do you say that?" asked Tim.

"We just saw a report," Jake began. But before he could continue, Tim finished for him.

"Our plans have been exposed," Tim said with a feigned calm in his voice.

"How did you know?" asked Lyndsey.

"Kayla Bruster called me. She said that the FBI forced Jean Bartok to disclose the purpose of the meeting in Arizona. Apparently, Jean had contacted Kayla after the questioning. Kayla suggested that I steer clear of Jean, meaning don't return her calls," Tim said, running his hand through his hair.

"They forced her? How?" asked Jake.

"I'm not sure, but she is not well. She's back in the hospital. Her heart is causing her trouble." Tim was quiet for a moment.

"Now what's the plan, Tim?" Lyndsey asked, hoping that he knew what to do next.

"Well, obviously someone plans to depict us as enemies of the state, trying to crash the political party. They will go so far as murder to stop us." Tim was adding the facts together.

"But what exactly is worth killing for?" asked Jake.

"Apparently there is something that makes this a life-and-death issue." Tim was trying to figure out what that might be.

The door to the room adjacent to the control center opened and Alan walked in asking, "Now what's wrong?"

"There's an incredible mystery unfolding in our national politics, that's all," Jake asserted with a sarcastic tone of voice.

"And there's a lot more to it than you realize," said Tim, thinking now was the time to tell them what he had learned from Abraham Jahir. "There was a psychoanalyst at the meeting in Arizona. He was one of us who survived in the underground shelter. Man, did he lay an earful on me! It all smells of conspiracy. I just have to piece this together."

"What is his name?" Lyndsey asked him to repeat it.

"Abraham Jahir," Tim responded.

"Is he not a famous psychoanalyst?" Lyndsey asked, recalling that she had cited some of his writings in her doctoral dissertation. She saw Tim nod in the affirmative. "His name was mentioned in the report earlier. I'm familiar with several of his writings. Why was he in Arizona with you?" she asked.

"Apparently Jim Wallace wanted him to inform us about the zombies. Well…he insists that these zombies are an elaborate hoax," Tim began, "and I think I believe him. He said that Jim had an important piece of evidence for us, but we shall never know what it was. I'm trying to fit all of this together."

"That's a strange thing to say about these zombies. They are certainly real enough!" Zack wasn't able to reconcile the idea that the zombies were a hoax with the experience he and the others had at Jake's house.

"Here's something else that bothers me:" Tim was shaking his head. "Do you know that some people can't even see the zombies?"

"Really?" Jake asked with surprise. "How do you know that?"

"There was a Chinese national, a diplomat from Hong Kong, who was with us in Arizona. Unfortunately, he did not survive the attack. He was in the SUV with Representative Bartok and others on their way to the meeting. Well, they were stuck in traffic in Phoenix when zombies surrounded their vehicle. To make a long story short, this Chinese national never saw any zombies while the rest of them were freaking out. He needed a long explanation from all of us just to gain our trust."

"Oh, shit!" exclaimed Zack.

"Yes," continued Tim, "and he was not the only one who could not see the zombies. Dale George, a representative from the state of Ohio also killed in the bombing, relayed a long story about a zombie attack at his own house. He told his story with tears in his eyes. His father was with him during the attack but saw no zombies. His dad thought he and his wife were crazy, firing a weapon at nothing."

"How can that be?" asked Lyndsey.

"I learned much more from Abraham Jahir," Tim continued. "He works for the Haifa Software Corporation in Israel. He and two other scientists have created software that can make robots have feelings."

"What?" Zack, Jake, and Lyndsey all cried out simultaneously with disbelief.

"That's right," Tim repeated. "Ain't that just so cool?" he

said with disgust. "Robots that have emotions!"

"What is the value of that?" asked Jake quite seriously, expecting a rational response.

"Great fucking question!" Tim exclaimed, wondering himself what the value might be. Then he continued, "At any rate, the software was apparently stolen from the Haifa Software Corporation. Where it is Jahir does not know, but he and others are in the process of searching for it. Jahir believes they have a device that will guide them to the source of any signal it broadcasts."

"So, they can find the software?" Lyndsey queried.

"In theory at least," Tim continued. "But Jahir is in a quandary. After learning about these zombies, he wonders whether he and his colleagues should disclose the theft to the proper authorities. But he also made it quite clear that they would rather not announce the discovery under these circumstances."

"Well, who stole it?" Zack asked.

"That isn't clear to me," Tim said. "Jahir and his cohorts had thought they were the only ones knowledgeable about the software, but apparently someone else must know…unless one of *them* is involved."

"Software that makes robots have *feelings*? Holy shit!" Alan cried. He suddenly recalled what he had found in the fatty nodule plucked from little Michael's butt. "Did you guys tell Tim about the chips?"

Jake said, "Ahhh, that's right! Alan found two microscopic silicon chips in the mass that was removed from your son."

"What?" Tim was irate. He immediately wondered if they were related to this software. Suddenly, the function of this software was starting to make sickening sense to him. He felt as if he lived in the worst of Orwellian worlds. He looked at Alan. "You don't think that someone can send feelings to these chips?"

Alan was reasoning along the same lines. "Is someone trying to scare us?" he asked of anyone who had an answer.

Lyndsey was beginning to catch on, too. "Do you mean…" she began with her head turned sideways and her chin out. She was squinting forcefully with disbelief. "…that someone has programmed us to see zombies and feel fear?" She was first to express out loud what the group had collectively deduced. She stammered but went on, "You mean that zombies are a product of software and silicon chips, Tim?"

"I dunno. It's really hard for me to remember having seen them myself on the streets of Oakland after what Jahir has told me," Tim replied with an air of disbelief.

"We can explain the zombies, how?" Jake asked with doubt as he pointed to his head. "I have a scar on my forehead that says they were really there."

"But", added Zack, "they did disappear."

"You mean that they aren't there at all?" Jake tried to work out an understanding.

Alan's thoughts moved him to a different question: "How did the chips get into little Michael?"

They all looked at each other. "It had to have happened at the hospital," concluded Tim.

"A vaccine!" Lyndsey asserted with wonder and disbelief. "He had to have vaccines to leave the hospital."

"What purpose would it serve to implant silicon chips in a newborn? He wouldn't be able to see zombies! That doesn't make sense," Jake added.

"That's obviously true," Lyndsey thought out loud. "But was it to serve the same purpose years down the road as he grows older?"

"Sure sounds like a bold, long-term plan, if you're right!" Tim said.

"Why would anyone want us to perceive zombies that aren't really there…for generations into the future? What would be the point?" Zack wondered out loud.

Tim could not fathom an answer to this question. He conceived the problem from a different perspective. "What if someone could make us feel whatever they want us to feel?" he asked with a shiver that chilled him to the bone. From within this chilling shiver the voice of paranoia spoke to him, arousing his defenses. First, he wondered whether someone was trying to steal his privacy. But then he thought about Clare and Michael. Someone was trying to steal his entire family's privacy! Tim could feel an increasing determination empowering him to solve this mystery.

"One problem at a time!" Alan demanded. "How did these chips get into us, assuming they are in fact in us?"

"It had to be the mandatory Ebola vaccine!" Tim insisted with an eerie feeling. "Everybody had to have it as of last week. Michael couldn't leave the hospital without it."

"That makes sense. Zombies started attacking about a month or so ago," added Zack. Then he found need to joke, given the despair he was feeling. "The vaccine was administered for no cost; we should have suspected something sinister!"

"Oh, my word! What should we do about this?" Lyndsey sought a plan for action.

"Won't others also find out?" asked Jake.

"We just happen to know about the software," Tim mused out loud. "This could eventually be found out, especially if Jahir alerts the authorities. What about the chips...has no one else found them?"

Jake got up and went to his liquor cabinet. He wanted a drink to calm his nerves. Then he glanced out the window. "Shit!" he exclaimed. "Zombies coming this way. God damn it!" he griped and went straight toward the weapons case.

"Wait!" standing at the window, Tim could see three zombies traipsing through the field more than a hundred feet from the house. "No weapons!" demanded Tim. Listen to me! Keep calm. I'll go down and get the women and children, *calmly*. Don't let on that anything is wrong. You got that?" He asked Jake with hands on his shoulders. "Okay?" he looked toward the others with an air of determination. They nodded in agreement. "I'll get the others and tell them we are gonna discuss a trip to the zoo. Get ready to share some *good* feelings with the children."

Tim ran down the steps to the basement. He asked Greta and the kids to come upstairs. "Rinna, Jeffrey, Phillip, come on now! We have to talk about a trip we are gonna make. Come on, hurry up!" Tim tried to rush the children without alarming them. He said, "You can go back to the bicycles in a few minutes." Then he asked them to follow him as he went to get Clare and Michael. Clare had just changed Michael's diaper. "Honey...come on upstairs. We have a surprise we wanna discuss."

"Right now?" she queried.

"Yes, and we sort of need to hurry, babe. Lyndsey has to leave for work soon," he added, picking up Michael from the bed and turning to go upstairs.

"Alright," she agreed and went toward the stairs following Tim closely. Greta and the children were right behind them.

While Tim had been gathering the women and children, Zack, Alan, and Lyndsey paraded past the window to get a glimpse of the zombies that Jake and Tim had seen. "I see three of them," Alan said, making room for Zack and Lyndsey.

"Yeah, I see 'em," added Zack. But when Lyndsey got to the window she had to ask where they were. "You don't see 'em? Right over there," Zack pointed to the field to the left of their shed. "They are coming right this way. Don't you see 'em?"

"No, I don't see anyone," Lyndsey exclaimed. "Oh, my word, I don't see them." For only a moment she couldn't understand why, when everyone else had seen them. It was enough to help her feign being shocked. Perhaps at some later time she would have to make a confession. If what she was thinking was true, then neither she nor Rinna would be able to perceive the zombies.

"Lyn, what do you mean you can't...." Jake was interrupted by Tim.

"Are you'n's ready? Here we come," Tim wanted to alert the gang upstairs so they wouldn't give him away. Now the entire crew was in the attic.

Jake didn't want the children playing with the control devices for his monitors, so he suggested that they go into the attic bedroom and play with the video console in there. Greta followed them. Looking back toward the adults in the control center, she asked, "Where are we going?"

"We wanna plan a trip to the zoo." Jake declared, trying to play the game through toward some discussion point.

Tim glanced at the adults to verify that they were not showing any signs of fear. He winked at Alan and Zack, who appeared a bit apprehensive. Lyndsey had a confused expression, but only momentarily. "Okay," said Tim, gesturing toward Clare to sit in the chair next to the attic bedroom. "Here you go," he said handing Michael to her. He looked over toward Rinna and the boys, and said, "Do you children know how important you are to us?" He paced pensively, lifted his head, then he said proudly, "We have little Michael now, but all of you are our future. Our whole purpose is to raise you so that you learn what is most important in life. We wanna teach you to do your best to make life good. Good health, happiness, and good friends are the most important things in life. Right?"

Tim was just passing the time, trying to create positive feelings for all of them to share. He remembered how Abraham Jahir emphasized that feelings of fear and aggression create the problems with zombies. According to him, these were not merely the feelings *produced* by the perception of the zombies, but they were the very emotions needed to *conduct the collective perception*, creating a shared experience of a zombie attack. Now was the perfect time to test Jahir's claim that the attitude of fear and domination needed to be replaced with an attitude of respect and cooperation.

Then Rinna interrupted his thoughts. "Yeah," she said, "so you are gonna make us happy and take us to the zoo! When are we going?" she asked with playful exuberance.

Then Jeffrey spoke up and asked, "Can we go today?"

"Yeah, can we?" begged Philip, bouncing up and down on his toes.

"Lyndsey has to go to work, so she can't go today," Jake replied, temporarily dampening their enthusiasm. "But perhaps we can all go tomorrow." Jake was prepared to change any plans that he and Lyndsey might have had to spend time with the children. For the time being, he was happy to play along with whatever it was that Tim was trying to do.

"Maybe we can go tomorrow," replied Tim, "but *all* of us have to be able to go. Is there anyone here who cannot go tomorrow?"

Alan spoke first. "Greta and I can go tomorrow."

Then Karen asked, "Zack, we could go, couldn't we?"

"Sure!" said Zack, "I think it would be a lot of fun!"

"Lyn, would you like to go with all of us to the zoo tomorrow?" Tim asked her, knowing that she would agree.

"Sure, I would!" Lyndsey replied jubilantly, as if she were as excited as the children.

"What about you, Aunt Clare?" asked Rinna, "Do you and Michael wanna go?"

"Oh, yes we do, Rinna. Thank you for asking," Clare replied as if she knew exactly what to say in support of her husband.

"Well, then," Tim began, "I believe that everyone here has agreed that tomorrow we shall go to the zoo. Is that right?"

All the adults looked around and nodded toward each other indiscriminately. Meanwhile, Alan and Jake had already sensed that there was no imminent attack coming from the zombies. Tim also wondered to himself, "*Surely, if we were going to have trouble we would have by now.*" He walked cautiously toward the window, not wanting the children to realize that he intended to get a view outside. "Well, then," he turned back toward the children, "what must we do to be prepared to go to the zoo tomorrow?" Tim wanted to keep everyone thinking together to make a plan for the next day.

Rinna was hovering over Michael, who was still in the arms of his mother. She was first to speak again. "We have to get the diaper bag ready for Michael, and make sure he has milk to drink because he can't eat what we eat."

Lyndsey walked over toward Rinna and put her arm around her. "You are gonna be a great mommy when you grow up, sweetheart!" She hugged Rinna tightly and kissed her on the cheek. Then the boys clamored for some affection from their parents. Both Karen and Zack obliged, lavishing Jeffrey and Phillip with hugs and playful smiles. All of them shared the feeling of love that is a genuine source of unity among families and friends. Tim saw this as an opportunity to look out the east window where the zombies had been seen earlier. There was none there. He picked up a controller in case the children were watching him, then moved toward the west window in the attic bedroom, passing the families as they showed their affections for one another. He peered through the window, surveying the surrounding area. Nothing.

"Okay, boys and girls! I believe we are going to the zoo tomorrow. If no one has any objections, then we can go back to what we were doing," Tim said, as if to adjourn the meeting.

"Yay!" the children cried in unison and ran down the steps.

"Hey, wait for me!" yelled Greta, trying to keep up with them.

"Can we go back downstairs and ride the bikes?" Jeffrey asked from the bottom of the steps.

"Greta, will you go with them?" asked Jake.

"Sure," she agreed as she tried to keep up with them.

"I'll head down there, too," Karen suggested as she descended the stairs.

"Honey," Clare called to Tim, "I'm gonna close the door and feed Michael."

"Alright," he said, happy to have some semi-private time with Jake, Lyndsey, and Zack. He went over and kissed her, then followed her into the attic bedroom. He looked out the window there. All was clear. "I'm going out to talk with Jake, babe," he said with a smile. She returned the smile as he walked out the door and closed it gently.

Jake was already searching out the east window. Zack had gone to the corner of the room and picked up his drone with camera attached. "I'm gonna send this out to sweep the area, alright?"

"Good," said Lyndsey, "I'll be leaving shortly."

Zack opened the window. There was a level ledge just outside the window, balanced upon the downward pitch of the roof. He placed the drone on the ledge, then sent it skyward. As it propelled to scan the area around the house and neighboring properties, Zack picked up his phone and connected it with the camera on the drone. It was a hot, clear day, and there was nothing to interfere with the view of the landscape that it provided. Zack could see that Jake's neighbor, Paul Branch, was outside riding his lawn tractor, but no zombies could be seen anywhere in the vicinity. "Your neighbor is mowing his grass, but I do not believe that he is a zombie today," Zack joked, referring to that frightful night when his wife, Karen, thought for sure that one of the zombies attacking at the downstairs bedroom was Paul Branch. "Otherwise, I see no monstrous threats."

"I think Jahir has given us valuable advice," Tim deduced. "Whenever you see zombies, you must not be alarmed. He said to avoid the feelings of fear and aggression as much as possible and adopt an attitude of respect and cooperation. Jahir said the worst thing to do is live in a 'heroic attitude' and allow the aggression to arise in you with an intention to destroy the zombies. Aggression is essential to the attitude of domination. This is what gives life to the zombies. In its absence, they cannot bother us. Our external senses have been tricked, sending our private, internal sense on a flight to fear!"

Zack was still puzzled. He mumbled to himself, trying to sort out the facts. "What is real now? In order to wipe out the zombies, we have to avoid the heroic attitude? And this is consistent with the attitude of domination…and *that* is the enemy?"

Lyndsey was close enough to hear him. "I believe that is his thesis," she added, sitting forward. "Jahir has contributed many insights to the world of psychoanalysis, but this is a more recent one."

Tim responded, "It would have to be if it has been developed to eliminate the zombies. But our new party is warring against the attitude of domination. It is not our goal to be 'masters and possessors of nature'.[4] We must not forget that *we* are under *its* power! Native Americans had a healthier relationship with nature. It was alive with their ancestors.[5] It was to be cherished and respected. Today, Americans have denied their earthly heritage with the same ignorance and deception that they reject the real self. The Cartesian ideal is a grand deception. No doubt it has brought us to this age of great technological discovery. Unfortunately, it has also taught us to exploit the natural world, especially each other, to the point that some of our most vital resources have grown scarce, and we can no longer unite in spirit to solve life-threatening problems. The attitude of domination is out of control in our society. We must usher in a new age. Somehow, we have to make a virtue of the necessary; cooperate with each other, while preserving nature and helping it to flourish. We seek a totally different way of life than one ruled by the attitude of domination."

"So, it would seem," Lyndsey thought out loud, "that our battle against the zombies correlates with the new party's aims. Right?"

"Yes, it seems a bit ironic," Tim replied. "In both cases we are up against what Jahir calls the heroic attitude. The latter is an aggressive orientation to the world in the mode of domination. It requires various types of force to sustain it. It is a habit wherein people have developed a taste for winning competitions of all sorts – even those of their own fantasy – pitting themselves against other people of their own imagining. Hence, it is marked by self-deceptions, built upon comparisons of oneself with both others and the natural world as a whole."

Then Lyndsey replied, "We have been talking about empathy, and how self-comparison is presupposed in it. Empathy is a spontaneous and natural element of conscious life. This self-comparison is definitely taken for granted, but it is always present at those times when one is sharing someone else's feelings. However, the heroic attitude is marked by a different kind of comparison wherein one aims to *differentiate* oneself from others."

"That's right!" Tim responded. "Many people develop the habit of imagining their own superiority over others. This habit is essential to the heroic attitude. It is learned in societies whose citizens are trained to imagine other societies as weak in comparison to one's own. It is an attitude which might begin with the thought, 'Our nation is better'. But this quickly transforms into 'I am better than you', or 'I can do this better than you', and then, ultimately, 'My car is better than your car.' It is a slippery slope."

Lyndsey then added, "This heroic attitude is an aggressive form of self-deception. An imagined 'ideal self' is believed to have powers over and beyond others. Others are weak, relative to oneself. I would argue that this is a negative reaction to an experience of sympathy, which becomes an act of pity."

"Pity?" asked Jake. "Isn't that the same thing as sympathy?"

"It is not. I mean it as something different."[6] Lyndsey explained, "Pity is compounded upon sympathetic experience. It adds something to it. Sympathy spontaneously and naturally attunes my internal sense to share in the suffering of someone else. It reminds one of one's own weakness as one perceives the weakness of the other. But the act of pity adds another component. Pity includes some form of expression wherein one confirms for himself/herself '*it is the other who suffers, and* not *myself*'. It is a denial of one's own weakness which compounds sympathetic experience. In an act of pity, self-comparison *differentiates* the other from the self. The act of pity expresses superiority. It might say, 'I feel sorry for *you*'. Therefore, an act of pity is a form of self-deception, resembling an 'attack' on the other. It's as though one pities the other because that other has reminded one of one's own weakness, and this has created resentment which must be avenged."

"Nietzsche certainly suggests that pity is vindictive."[6] Tim said, nodding. He was the one who interested Lyndsey in Nietzsche.

"Basically, this act of pity is twofold," said Lyndsey. "It originates with sympathy to share the other's suffering. But it also includes a repressive function. It denies the real self and casts it out from conscious awareness, positively identifying the other as the one who suffers."

"How, then, is pity a part of the heroic attitude?" Jake asked.

"It is intrinsic to it." she responded. "Start with sympathy. One must admit that a sympathetic transfer of feelings carries the essential possibility of itself being deceptive, insofar as there is a lack of correlation between the feelings one has and the other's feelings. But pity is something else. It involves a *deliberate* self-deception over and above the basic flaws intrinsic to human sympathy. Subsequently, the heroic attitude compounds even more aggressive deceptions on top of pity. Consider this: The zombies motivate one to imagine that the ideal self wins all sorts of battles and competitions. In the heroic attitude, one compares oneself to someone else…or others in general…and imagines oneself, or some group including oneself, as better than the other or others. Generally speaking, pity is a combination of sympathy and self-denial. Furthermore, the elaborate construction of an ideal self as heroic and superior is not natural but learned. In the heroic attitude, others determine how one is to feel and think and act."

"Jahir claims that the heroic attitude is a response to fear," Tim added.

"Yes," said Lyndsey, "there is at least one other psychoanalyst who defends that position. But he claims that the fear of death is natural, and the heroic attitude is a natural response to the fear.[7] Anyone who claims this is also likely to emphasize that sibling rivalry is a *natural* form of competition. But I am not completely convinced that sibling rivalry is not learned from parents and society. It is quite difficult to distinguish the extent to which our competitive spirit might be natural from what is learned. I do not know Jahir's position, but I do not believe the heroic attitude *develops* naturally. Rather, it appears to be something learned from others. I would insist that our primordial repression of anxiety and helplessness is a private experience of every human born of woman. It is certainly natural and universal among the species. However, fear of death arises from social experience. It is learned. Arguably, those of us who have grown up as Americans have been trained in a way that this primordial anxiety is transformed into fear of death. This is the foundation for conscience and guilt in our society as we know it. The heroic attitude is the grease that lubes the contemporary capitalistic machine."

"It sounds as if you are implying that the heroic attitude is a massive program of self-deception encouraged by our society." Jake concluded.

"I am, absolutely!" said Lyndsey, "And it works because of primordial guilt.[8] Arguably, everyone experiences a *natural* guilt. It results from an awareness of one's own deceptive intentions to avoid conscious acceptance of one's own vulnerability. The entire scheme of conscience in society is founded upon this denial of the real self. Secretly, one knows that one is a weak animal, but we prefer to be infallible. So, we create an ideal self on the stilts of our own deceptions to avoid the quagmire below. Religion is but one tool that lends its support in one's personal creation of the ideal self. Society shows us many tools that we can use to nourish the ideal self in a community built upon the heroic attitude."

"How could we ever overcome this attitude and embark

upon a different path for humans in a new age?" asked Zack.

"That's the trillion-dollar question!" Jake was wanting to ease away from the psychoanalytic details.

"We have to change our collective attitude toward life. It is the policy of respect and cooperation that we must establish as a healthy approach to natural life," Tim began. "We have always been taught that the public good must be preferred over anyone's private good. But this is questionable as an absolute principle. One problem is that "health" cannot be properly fitted in this scheme of thought. A healthy public first requires healthy individuals – body and spirit. A healthy society can be nothing more than the collective health of its citizens. The heroic attitude is not conducive to the health of individuals. Its utility is to support and preserve our public *entities*."

"Many of our public institutions are exploiting our private lives!" Tim insisted. "The information age has yet to be oriented toward public health. Rather, it has gradually transformed our private lives into a public entity. I have a virtual duplicate who is my personal double!"

"We are losing our own selves, our own health and wellbeing!" Lyndsey exclaimed.

"But can we reclaim these things?" asked Jake.

"Good question! One might have to accept one's real self. But awareness of one's own weakness causes anxiety, and that is undesirable. The best outcome is for one to face the anxiety and overcome primordial guilt," Lyndsey claimed boldly.

"What would that look like? Or feel like?" Jake wasn't sure what Lyndsey was suggesting. At times he felt as if he were unable to follow her thinking, and it bothered him.

"We would be seeking the source of a special unity, a self-identity." Lyndsey could always sense when she was taxing Jake's patience with the details of her psychoanalytic theories, so she knew either to speak in simple terms or move on to something else. On the other hand, Tim was very much into the philosophical end of the discussion. She knew he would ask questions if he did not follow her reasoning. However, she was entering the grey area of her theories, and she had work to do to clarify her own understanding. Nevertheless, she had some ideas what such a situation might look like. "It would be marked by a noteworthy lack of self-deception.[9] If we could collectively accept our true identity, and we could tolerate our anxiety, we might ultimately dispense with the fear of death. I cannot accept the psychoanalytic position that fear of death cannot be unrepressed."[10]

Lyndsey had barely finished speaking when Tim's phone rang. He got up and went down the stairs to answer it in privacy.

"Well, I have to head downtown to the institute," Lyndsey said, noticing the time. "I have a session with a new client this afternoon. Zack, I need a favor."

"Sure thing, Lyndsey. What is it?" he asked, not recalling any such request from her in the past.

"I want you to make sure that Tim's car is parked in the garage after I leave. We don't want anyone snooping around here looking for him, if you know what I mean." Lyndsey was thinking that if there was an investigation into a conspiracy, then someone might come to their house in search of Tim. She did not want any such visitors.

Suddenly, Tim ran up the steps and threw open the door to the attic. "Lyn, are you driving into town?" he asked with urgency.

"Yes, I am about to leave shortly."

"Can you drop me at the Hillman Library?" he requested.

"Okay, but we'd better get going now, so that I'm not late

for my appointment," she cautioned, rising to make the preparations quickly. "Leave your car keys right here," she pointed to the table in the attic.

"Okay, but one more thing…" Tim interjected, "I need those silicon chips."

"They are in a vial in the medicine cabinet in the hall bathroom, downstairs," Alan said proudly. "I made sure to keep them both."

"Great! I'll take 'em!" Tim said, exuding confidence. He went in to tell Clare what was happening. She had dozed off with Michael in her arms. He wasn't sure what to say to her because he realized that, given the events of recent days, there seemed to be a surprise around every corner.

Chapter 13

Tim's Search for Understanding

"There she is!" Tim alerted Lyndsey with a tap on the shoulder, and a finger pointing in front of her face, to the left of her view through the windshield.

"Okay, don't get too excited, Tim," Lyndsey cautioned, "I dunno where I should go to get you there."

"I can get out here, Lyn." Tim was close enough to maneuver his way on foot through the swelling crowd. There were thousands of people participating in a protest on the streets of Oakland. It was larger than he had ever seen before, but it seemed to be peaceful. A lot of people were carrying signs, and some were chanting.

He could see past the Cathedral of Learning and Forbes Avenue. The entire parking area in front of Hillman Library was wall to wall people. No cars were likely to be parked in the lot today. Tim could not even see the whole group of protestors from his vantage point. They had flooded across the street at the back of the lot. The Carnegie Museum was completely surrounded, as if there was something there that everyone had gathered to see. There were still more people streaming back toward Phipps Conservatory, even onto the hill behind

Carnegie Mellon University. Within Tim's immediate perspective, he could see that protestors lined Forbes Avenue, from the businesses across from the library to as far as he could see toward CMU. The crowd was packed tightly on the street in front of Stephen Foster Memorial, and all the way toward Tim's current location near the Cathedral of Learning. People were lined up along the sidewalk on Fifth Avenue toward Heinz Memorial Chapel on the corner.

When Lyndsey had first noticed the crowd, she was in the leftmost lane of Fifth Avenue, where she was likely to get bogged down. She would have to drive around the crowd to travel just a couple of blocks to the parking garage at the institute.

Tim could barely see Kayla Bruster at the corner near Hillman Library, across Forbes Avenue. But he saw the dress with the luminescent yellow trim that she had told him she would be wearing. "I guess I'll talk to you later, Sis," he said.

"How will you get home?" Lyndsey thought she had better find out if she was supposed meet him later.

"I don't know. Can I text you?" he asked.

"Alright, but I expect to be working into the evening." Lyndsey guessed about her own schedule to see what Tim's plans were. Tim noticed that the crowd had begun spilling onto Fifth Avenue in front of the Cathedral of Learning.

"You'd better go while you still have a path to the right," Tim said as he got out of the SUV, shut the door, and ran around the front toward the sidewalk where the crowd had suddenly expanded. He blew her a kiss and smiled as she moved into the right lane to make a turn and go on to work.

The crowd was vibrant, and people were close together. It seemed to Tim, though, that it was orderly and respectable, so far. He noticed that some signs opposed specific companies, and many signs demanded respect for our natural environment.

Others demanded stronger restrictions on the production of greenhouse gases. One group he passed had outlined a detailed plan for recycling waste, salvaging every piece, whether it was plastics, metals, ink, batteries, or whatever. These people were collectively picking every piece of foreign matter out from the natural environment, as if to separate each in kind. "*It is pretty clear,*" thought Tim, "*why mandating recycling, and creating the corresponding organizations to accomplish the task, is so slow to happen. It is essentially opposed to the frivolous and wasteful consumer habits of our society. We produce mountains of garbage, pile it up and cover it with dirt, or drop it into the not so vast oceans. An infrastructure focused upon recycling is simply deemed to be too costly. A 'restructuring of the typical' would require unusual and undesirable changes to our everyday lives. Not only is there no profit to be reaped from these endeavors but, in fact, they have to be funded by some charitable person or group, if they are to be funded at all.*"

Tim was on the lookout for any signs referring to the International Alliance. He had seen none, as yet, but had once again located Kayla Bruster. She seemed to view him coming in a momentary eye contact, but then she turned, and walked from the corner of Hillman Library where she had been standing, back toward the entrance to the library. The crowd was densely packed there. She had only taken a few steps when Tim couldn't see her anymore.

"*What the fuck?*" Tim objected in private. Then he thought that she might want him to meet her in the library. So, he just kept walking in the direction he had been going, watching for her out the corner of his eye from behind his sunglasses, which everyone needed on this particular day. Then he saw her again, along the wall by the downhill ramp to the entry doors. She took something from her pocket. "*What is she looking at...?*" he queried, "*Oh, it's her phone, you ass,*" he thought to himself, as if to jog himself awake. "*Maybe I should call her?*" he wondered. Before he could answer his own question, she made his phone ring.

"Hi there!" she said gleefully as soon as he answered.

"Hey!" he said casually.

"Wait where you are," she said with a muddled voice that was hard to understand. "Everything is out!" she added, hoping Tim did not interrupt. She continued quickly so as not to give him that chance. "You are a hot property!" This statement was crystal clear. "You have questions to answer," she added. "Don't come any closer to the library. Stay on Forbes. Wait…" Then, back to the muffled voice, "Call ya back." Click.

"*Oh, shit!*" Tim exclaimed to himself, making sure he didn't actually say it. He could see her step away from the wall, move toward the parking lot, then penetrate the depths of the crowd and disappear.

He walked toward Primanti Brothers on Forbes Avenue quite slowly, subconsciously enjoying a whiff of the aromas. Along the way he had been avenging himself with the thought, "*So…someone has contrived a conspiracy against our coalition. Do they intend to prevent us from forming a new party on the basis of a global alliance? Why? Because we defend the tenets of the International Alliance? What is wrong with that? We are creating a party that represents a growing number of American people who think that we must reprioritize our lives and recreate our infrastructure. There has been no crime committed. On the other hand,*" he thought, "*with the evidence we have, the Coalition could demonstrate that someone has created the zombie conspiracy against the American people. But who? And what kind of crime is this? Sending zombies from software through chips implanted in our bodies… This is a crime against humanity! It is the piracy of our privacy!*"

Then his phone rang again. "Hey, what's up?" Tim answered casually.

"A lot!" she exclaimed as she worked her way through the crowd.

"I have a textbook for you," Tim said. He didn't know exactly what he should say in order to make her aware of the evidence he had. He had planned to give her the silicon chips.

"Okay," Kayla replied. "Over by the stairs leading up to the back of the museum. Go there now!" Click.

Tim looked in that direction, but he could not see the stairs through all the people. He began to maneuver through the crowd in the parking area toward the steps at the rear of the museum. He removed his jacket, flung it over his shoulder, and carefully turned and twisted through the crowd, trying not to make contact with others where possible.

The vial with the silicon chips was in his side pocket. He had hoped to give it to Kayla Bruster as soon as possible to have her initiate an investigation. He also wanted to give her the names of Abraham Jahir and the Haifa Software Corporation and tell her about the software. But he did not want to share any information by electronic means, if possible. He believed there was no privacy using any electronic means of communication. So, he wanted to meet personally with Kayla Bruster to show her the evidence that he believed might incriminate the Eternity Corporation, since they had manufactured all the new Ebola vaccines.

He knew that the facility where these chips were being infused into the vaccines had to be found, thinking that if someone could test the shipments in search of silicon chips in the vaccine, then proof of a conspiracy should be found. The company had made substantial profits selling the first vaccine, not only throughout Europe and Asia, but also in the United States. However, no other countries had interest in the second, more effective vaccine that was distributed and administered in the United States. None of the foreign countries which had used the first vaccine had experienced any return of the virus. But, in the U.S., a handful of hospitals had seen new cases, and these were found not long after the first vaccine had been deemed a success. Apparently, there was some rogue cell that could infect the next generation born from the carrier. That was when the Eternity Corporation had vowed to create a new and perfected vaccine that would no longer allow any of the Ebola cells to survive as dormant.

Suddenly, Tim heard a chant, "Join the Alliance!" At first, he froze and avoided glancing in that direction. Then, he needed to turn sideways to pass several people carrying signs saying, "Save our Farmland". Tim nodded in their direction, and muttered, *"Damn right!"* under his breath. That gave him the opportunity to look forward through his dark glasses as he produced a smile for the protestors. He saw more than a dozen signs with the letters IAPN in the hands of the people chanting. He wanted to meet them to talk and chant with them, but he would have to do that another time.

"There she is!" he silently exclaimed to himself. She was on the third step leading up to the rear entrance of the museum. She must have been looking over the top of the crowd just long enough for Tim to see her. That made him want to feel more comfortable, but he didn't. He was only about a hundred feet away from her. Then she stepped down to the sidewalk, turned away like she didn't even see him, and started walking briskly toward Phipps Conservatory. He picked up his own pace to keep close. The crowd gradually thinned on the other side of the bridge near the Conservatory, so he could keep her head in view. The bridge itself was covered with chanting protestors, but the sidewalk was passible.

"Holy shit, not again! Where the fuck do I have to go?" he wondered as he followed her. She walked with a purpose, head down, hips swinging in a slight rocking motion. For a moment, Tim had a good view of her, because the crowd had thinned on the walkway approaching Phipps Conservatory.

"Where the hell is she going?" he said under his breath. He was perplexed as he pretended to be interested in the sign on the sidewalk in front of the Conservatory. Then, she crossed the street right in front of a moving car and ran uphill into the open field behind Carnegie Mellon University.

Tim stopped at the sign advertising the upcoming programs at the Conservatory. He tried not to stare at her. *"I feel like a spy in my hometown!"* He pivoted and glanced around at the crowd. It was primarily pedestrians, but there were a few parked vehicles, and a few more attempting to maneuver away from the bridge, which they certainly could not cross. It was an end point for all vehicles to turn around and go back the way from which they had come. Out the corner of his eye, he saw Kayla Bruster gazing over the crowd from the hillside. She tilted her head back, taking a drink of water from a bottle she produced from the book bag hanging from her left shoulder. Tim turned and walked toward the door of the Conservatory, pretended to glance inside, then turned back to take the walkway toward the street. He was surprised to finally see Representative Bruster coming toward him.

"Hi," she smiled as she spoke to Tim. Kayla Bruster was 45 years old. She was thin, but very athletic, as Tim was finding out just trying to keep up with her. She reached toward him with both hands, greeted him, and then turned and walked briskly toward the bridge behind the museum. Tim followed as she turned to cross the street, toward Carnegie Mellon University. As Tim caught up with her, she slowed her walk and said, "The FBI is on campus. They are looking for *you*! You could be detained."

"I have a vial to give you with two silicon chips that were surgically removed from my baby."

"Okay," she said, delaying for time to think through her plans. As Tim reached into his pocket for the vial, she added, "Keep it for now."

Tim left the vial in his pocket. Then he decided to drop a name. "If you contact Abraham Jahir, he can tell you about a newly developed software that must be related to these chips. I think that they have been injected into people with the Ebola vaccine." But then his confusion surfaced in convoluted reasoning. "That is what has created the zombies to make the populace so fearful."

"What? A little slower please!" she needed to hear that once more just to understand all that was packed into Tim's claims.

"Abraham Jahir," he said again, "from the Haifa Software Corporation in Tel Aviv. They can make robots have feelings. Their software transmits a signal to these microscopic circuit boards. I believe these chips are implanted into everyone who has had the second Ebola vaccine."

Kayla was nonplussed. She hesitated before speaking. "I know that name…Jahir…but he is accused of leaving the country to avoid further questioning." Then she stopped, gazed in the opposite direction, and wondered if it was wise to go any closer to CMU. She knew not to walk back toward Hillman Library. She was protecting Tim from being detained, but neither did she want to be seen with him. In fact, there was a man who had entered the library earlier whom she did not want to see either of them. That was why she walked toward the Conservatory.

"Can you go to the Eternity Corporation production facility?" She totally blew Tim away with this question.

"What?" his eyes shifted upward, then he moved them from side to side upon hearing the request. "Where?" he added in the next breath.

"Just outside Columbia, South Carolina," she said. "That is where the vaccine is produced. Then it is shipped to various warehouses to stock the pharmacies. We have to examine the supplies at these warehouses and various pharmacies."

"I can't do that!" Tim gasped, insisting it was beyond the realm of his possibilities.

"You don't have to do *that*. I need you to transport the new President of the IAPN there. Give him that vial you have…he will know what to do with it. Take my SUV." She handed him a key fob. "Scan the fob with your phone to find the car; it is not too far away. Travel on I-79 South to the first rest area in West Virginia. Stop there. You will see a man with a cigar, wearing a South Carolina Stingray hat. He'll let you know the plan."

"What? *Now*? Get your car?" Tim stammered, surprised by the abrupt request. He wasn't sure what he was getting into, but he was already in this predicament over his head. He felt obligated, even as he wondered what he would say to Clare.

"The name of this man is Jakob Fuerst. He is here to gather the evidence we need. We need your help, Tim." Then, she paused before she offered a secret to seal the deal. "Jake told me you would do it."

"Jake?" Tim wasn't certain what to make of her allusion to Jake.

"Jake told me that you had found the chips in your baby, and that Abraham Jahir was with you at the cabin." She really piled on the persuasive effort because she had no time to assist with proving a conspiracy. She would be too busy advising the first-ever candidate of "The People's Party". She didn't want to have to explain to Tim that Senator Anne Feinman from the state of Minnesota had originally listed her party as independent but was about to announce that she was a candidate who represented the new party. Moreover, they had already adopted the platform and selected the name "The People's Party". It had become necessary to launch the party immediately based on the platform as developed to this point.

"I'm taking your car to pick up whom?" Tim didn't remember the name. He was overpowered by a chilling feeling flowing from his legs up toward his head. It came from the belief that he was involved in some kind of espionage.

"Jakob Fuerst." She spelled it for him with an umlaut. "He will have…."

Tim interrupted her, "Yes, yes…a cigar and a Stingray

hat."

"Go toward Forbes Avenue, around the front of the museum. The SUV is in a parking garage between Forbes and Fifth. Drive safely. Good luck!" she wished Tim as she turned and picked up her pace to cross the bridge.

"*Well...*" he thought to himself as he watched her hips swing until they were lost in the crowd along the bridge, "*I gotta go around the Carnegie Museum.*" He connected his cellphone with the key fob. A map showed on his phone's screen, guiding him to the SUV. It would be a little more than five blocks if he went around the museum.

Once again, his phone rang. It was Kayla Bruster. "Hey," he said.

"Don't come this way across the bridge. Find a path through Carnegie Mellon University. Act like a college guy! The FBI is at the museum. I'd get going!" She didn't mince words. The man she was looking for from the hillside across from the Conservatory had been found. He was an FBI agent who knew Kayla Bruster well. Every move she made served to avoid being seen by him. When she saw him climbing the rear stairwell toward Carnegie Museum, she quickly maneuvered into the crowd.

Tim picked up his pace and trotted up a gradual hill past the dorms at the CMU campus. Then he cut between two buildings on the campus and slowed his pace as he found his way toward the main entrance of the university. He could see on the map that the parking garage was not too far away. The shadows grew longer as evening was passing. Tim ran past the traffic across Forbes Avenue in front of the university. He knew he was about to make a road trip that would change his life…and perhaps all of America.

Chapter 14

Seeking Material Evidence

Tim had begun to feel safe once again behind the wheel of Kayla Bruster's Marauder. He took the time to calm himself and decide what he needed to do. He decided to leave Oakland by means of Bigelow Boulevard. From there he made his way through the evening traffic around the Hill and through the Strip District. Traffic was not particularly heavy. He sought the quickest and easiest route across the Fort Pitt Bridge and through the tunnel.

On the other side of the tunnel, he found himself in the fading light of day. He thought about calling Clare…knew he had to call her soon. *"What am I doing?"* he chastised himself. He had just returned to his family life after the crisis in Arizona but had barely spent a day with his wife and son before leaving them again. He tried to envision what to say to her, but he couldn't find an acceptable reason to offer. He simply felt obligated to continue the work of the Alliance. Consequently, he fumbled to find the words to comfort his wife.

Clare sounded heartbroken to think that Tim would travel so far away and not take his family. It made him sick to his stomach as he tried to explain that it was quite unexpected. He couldn't help but feel guilty for having left without notice. It was so hard for him to continue the conversation with Clare that he told her he would have to call her back once he settled into the drive. Then, he called Lyndsey. She always seemed to calm his anxiety when he needed it. He recalled how his Mom and Dad had suffered with the Ebola virus, and Lyndsey had been their best friend. She helped to calm him once again, and he even asked for her help settling Clare. But nothing seemed to prevent that sick feeling from recurring off and on for a couple of hours, until he met with the man who was so important to Kayla Bruster.

When he had first picked up Jakob Fuerst in West Virginia, the man had noticed Tim's stressful condition. He urged him to stop at McDonald's to eat and get a milkshake. Tim was feeling miserable as he pulled into the lot of the fast-food chain. Fuerst told him to drink a lot of water and get plenty of food and drinks for them both. He gave Tim his payment chip, saying that he would wait in the Marauder. Tim guzzled two large cups of water while he waited for his order. That alone went a long way toward settling his stomach. He also bought several burgers and fish sandwiches for the ride. Tim was thankful, realizing this new acquaintance of his had sensed that he had made himself sick by not eating or drinking when he was so stressed.

Jakob Fuerst was a man of sixty-eight years. He had a medium frame, about 5'10" and 165 pounds. His blondish-grey hair curled out from under his cap on the sides and in the back. He was clean shaven and handled himself with an air of dignity and confidence. His gait reminded Tim somewhat of his own father and he took comfort from the relative similarity. Realizing that Fuerst had sensed his difficulty, he felt as if this man was really concerned for his wellbeing.

Finally, after each of the men had quickly disposed of a fish sandwich, Tim's passenger asked, "Can I open another one for you?"

"Yes, please," Tim said as he guzzled some more water.

"You'll be stopping again a few miles down the road to piss out all that water," Fuerst quipped and laughed, looking over at Tim. Tim laughed and thanked him for his concern. Then the man further endeared himself to Tim. "I am from Dusseldorf," he began. "I was a colleague and close friend of the late Jan Greisfeld." Somehow Tim was pleased to hear that. His spirit began to rise as a result of momentarily feeling reconnected to the world with a purpose. But that good feeling was abruptly lost in his recollection of what must have happened to Jan Greisfeld. The last time Tim had seen him through the floating dust and debris of the cabin, he couldn't pick himself up to get on the shoulder of LeShaun Brinson to escape through the back door of the conference room. The rat-a-tat-tat of the AK-47 that Tim had heard as he was going into the underground tunnel might have been what sealed his fate. Just hearing his name relit Tim's passion for the Alliance and what it symbolized. He thought of a flame that had flickered out being rekindled. Then, Fuerst continued, "I have been in contact with Abraham Jahir and Amir Awad. They are trying to locate the source of the signal that activates the zombies."

Tim was pleased to hear this. "Have they made any progress?" he asked after swallowing a mouthful of fish sandwich.

"We shall have to find out when we meet Amir Awad," replied Fuerst. "Right now, we are going to a hotel near Orangeburg, South Carolina. I have my radar zeroed-in on the location. There we shall meet three people, one of whom has worked for the Eternity Corporation. She is a chemist and lab technician. One is a private investigator...used to be FBI...but you need not worry about him. He wants to get a closer look at these vaccines. The other works at a warehouse where the boxes of individual vaccines go before being shipped out to the pharmacies. He drives pickers and forklifts, and other machines, but he has samples from recent incoming shipments. What do you have for me?"

"The vial with the silicon chips?" Tim asked without hesitation.

"Two of them were removed from your baby?" Fuerst asked with disbelief.

"That's right."

"I believe one belonged to your wife;" Fuerst guessed, adding, "she probably got the vaccine during the time that she was pregnant."

Tim had a feeling of having been violated. That alone made him want to expose the conspiracy. But who was the source of this calamity? Fuerst did not seem to know, but he did seem certain that they would soon be rid of the zombies. Tim wondered cluelessly about this for a long while during the drive. A lot of time passed in silence, and the hours went quickly as the SUV hugged the contour of the road, up and down the mountains. At one point, Tim thought out loud: "These are *real* mountains, quite unlike the rolling hills covered with saguaro cactuses of South Mountain in Arizona." He realized this as he found the need to accelerate more than usual to climb the Appalachians. "I could have *run* over the top of South Mountain in less than an hour!" He laughed at the comparison.

Fuerst had only smiled in response to Tim's comment. He was silent for at least ten more minutes, until he broke the monotony of the drive for Tim. He had been quite busy using his phone, until out of nowhere he said, "You might like to know that The People's Party has its first official candidate for the office of President of the United States."

"Wow! Already? I thought that the party would not be involved in this election?" Tim asked, surprised about the late entrance into the race. "Who is it?"

"Senator Anne Feinman from Minnesota. She has already seen your writings in support of the party platform. Actually, she thought you might like to be her Vice-President," Fuerst said quite nonchalantly.

"Yeah..." Tim responded with sarcasm, until a glance from Fuerst indicated that he was dead serious. "Are you shitting me?" Tim was flabbergasted by the thought. "I haven't a vice-presidential bone in my body!"

"Well, Mr. Austin, you would be a noble correspondent for the Alliance," Fuerst offered no persuasive effort. His tone was matter of fact. "I'm sure there is someone else Feinman can choose...that is, unless you change your mind."

"You can be sure I shall not be changing my mind!" Tim wanted to be quite clear, so he started over. "I want to live a private life. I'm a simple man who wants to raise his children to celebrate the simple realities of life. It's just that I want my children to begin with important things like health and friendship. I want them to enjoy nature, you know, and to live a full life with self-knowledge." Tim was about to merge onto I-26 toward Charleston. He was finally finished traveling on I-77.

"It's a few more miles to the hotel just outside of Orangeburg," Jakob reminded him.

"What are the plans for meeting with the people you mentioned?" Tim wanted a reminder while he tried to figure what exactly his role was to be. It was too late to decide that he didn't want to be involved. He just wanted to determine whether he would be getting into more trouble. It was hard enough to believe that he was being sought by the FBI in Pittsburgh. He was beginning to get anxious again, until he realized that Kayla Bruster and Fuerst must already have a plan for action. It was easy for him to convince himself that he was merely part of a master plan. Consequently, he was thinking he might have to do just whatever was asked of him...other than run for Vice-President.

"They're going to meet us and compare ideas, you might say," Fuerst said with a smile.

"Will we get a chance to sleep a bit?" Tim was exhausted.

He wanted to rest after this stressful drive of nearly eight hours.

"If you hurry to get there and lie down," Fuerst laughed with a little sarcasm of his own. Then he changed his tone. "I'm getting warnings about a weather report. There is a hurricane several hundred miles across the Atlantic that is moving very quickly. It is traveling at 30 mph…" he paused in surprise, "Can that be right? Anyway, it seems to be making a beeline toward the Carolinas." Fuerst was not a meteorologist, but he was certain that was terribly fast, relatively speaking. "I'll keep an eye on it."

Finally, he pointed to a passing sign. "The next exit is our destination." Tim was relieved to hear that; it was after 3:00 am. He was thinking that he would love to shower and rest for a while.

"Our friends should be awaiting us at the hotel," Fuerst replied as if he wanted to prevent Tim from resting. "Right here."

Tim made the right turn and Fuerst directed him to park next to what appeared to be an ambulance. Tim wasn't bothered that he had parked at the far end of the lot, some distance from the office. He wanted to walk and loosen up.

"Gotta get out, stretch my legs." Tim stepped out and clasped his hands high above his head, then he bent backwards and forwards trying to loosen his spine. "A lotta stress comes from bad posture!" He slammed the door of the Marauder.

Fuerst hopped out of the passenger side, looked over at Tim and shifted his eyes to the back of the ambulance. Then, he walked over and opened the back door, gesturing to Tim to get in. Tim hesitated a moment in surprise, then resigned himself to a further delay in getting some rest. Tim climbed in first and a man dressed as a medic came around to the back of the van to shut the door behind Fuerst. There were two empty seats waiting for them. The inside of the van looked like a miniature laboratory with electronic scopes and video screens. There were two other seats; one had a woman strapped in it, and the other a large man who was built like a wrestler. The van started moving and the woman said, "Hello, I am Natalie Vincent. I would like to have the vial you brought." She gestured toward Tim.

Fuerst pulled the vial from his shirt pocket and handed it to the chemist. Tim watched the woman carefully, searching for clues about what was happening in front of him. Then, he spied a face peering through the window toward the lab from the back seat of the cab. It was a penetrating gaze from a man with a serious expression on his face. "Must be the cop Fuerst mentioned," thought Tim.

Natalie Vincent gestured toward the man in the other seat. He produced a box of vials that were about two sizes larger than the vial Tim had. They contained individual doses of the second Ebola vaccine; the one that was touted as being 100% effective. He had brought them from the warehouse near Charlotte. The chemist had already placed the specimen from the vial given to her by Fuerst into one of the scopes and turned on the video. Tim could see two circuit boards, amplified for visual detail. She emptied a vial from the other man onto a different scope and turned on the video screen adjacent to the first one. Only one circuit board in the vaccine. Ms. Vincent further amplified the scope. All three chips were the same. Each had a symbol which identified the semiconductor producer who had made them. Tim thought that the symbol seemed vaguely familiar, but he couldn't quite place it. The chemist reached out for another vial from the large man who sat beside her. Then she exchanged it with the one that she had just scoped and adjusted the intensification. It had one circuit board that looked just like each of the two from Michael. She compared it to a picture of the one she had just removed from the scope. All four of the chips appeared to be the same. She repeated this process, removing individual vials of vaccine from various boxes brought by the warehouse worker. Every vial contained one circuit board in the vaccine. They were all the same type of chip.

Natalie looked over at Jakob Fuerst, then Tim, and said, "One of these was injected into your wife, I believe. Did she have this vaccine while she was with child?"

"I think so." Tim said dully, his fatigue from the drive was increasing rapidly. He was befuddled over the circumstances surrounding the need for poor Michael to have surgery to remove silicon chips from his backside.

"That is probably why two were found in your son," Ms. Vincent deduced. "Each of the new vaccines that I have scoped contain only one, and they are all the same kind of chip."

The forensic van went back to the hotel parking lot; the man in the cab had apparently received the signal he had sought. When the van came to a stop, the driver opened the back door to the parking area. Fuerst got up and gestured for Tim to follow. They got back into their SUV and Tim drove it closer to the front desk as the ambulance left the property. "Alright, Tim," said Fuerst, "we shall check in so that we can rest a while."

"I need to talk to my wife!" Tim was wanting a little private time.

"Yes, you can rest and talk to your wife. Wait here. I'll check in." Jakob walked into the lobby, wondering whether their plans would be complicated by this approaching hurricane. The season for hurricanes in the Atlantic Ocean had only just begun, so this one was early. Even though it was still far out into the ocean, it was traveling very quickly, and it was quite large. While hurricanes had become more frequent along the east coast over the past few years, it seemed that every year at least one hurricane would cause record amounts of damage to properties along the path of its destruction. Fuerst was hoping that this was not one of them.

When he returned, Fuerst had more news from the sources that were feeding him information over his phone. "The general location of the electronic source transmitting to these chips has been found. We shall be searching for it tomorrow." Then he added, "The chips removed from your son have been taken to another location to try and receive the satellite communication. They will be placed into robots with sensitive capability. If they are activated by the specific transmitter identified, then it will enable the robot to express specific feelings – we expect fear and aggression – and then we shall have completely traced the circuit which makes the zombies."

"But we still don't know who is doing this!" Tim exclaimed, so as to elicit a response from Jakob Fuerst.

"But we are well on the trail," Fuerst replied again in that calm, matter-of-fact tone, which made Tim feel as if he needed to be more objective and less emotional. "Amir Awad is coming to Charleston tomorrow. We are going to help him find the source."

Tim expected that he would continue as the designated driver, but he needed some rest before he could get behind the wheel again. Fuerst opened the door to the hotel room and he and Tim entered. It was a large room with two king size beds. Tim threw his jacket onto the floor next to the first bed on the way in, then went straight to the toilet to empty his bladder. The force of the stream sent water splashing all around the commode. When he got back to the bed, he took a deep breath, kicked off his shoes, and laid down. He couldn't count to ten before he had sunk into the semi-conscious state that was rest.

Chapter 15

The Matter for Creating Zombies

Tim was waiting impatiently for Fuerst to return with the engineer who was a good friend of Abraham Jahir. He had parked the SUV along the curb at the very end of the building where the new arrivals would deplane, then walk out to curbside and seek their transportation away from the airport. It was already hot and steamy at ten minutes before noon in Charleston.

The humidity was so oppressive that, just getting out of the vehicle to stretch his legs and take a short walk about the area, Tim had worked up a sweat. He had lost sight of Fuerst shortly after he left the Marauder and had not seen him since. He wondered if Fuerst had the necessary credentials to enter the building and get through the rigorous airport security system. Tim was quite certain that he, himself, would be detained if he had attempted to pass through security to enter the building – especially if the FBI was seeking him nationwide. In fact, as he stretched his legs, he was careful to stay far enough away from the exit doors to avoid any exposure to electronic identification sensors.

Although it had only been fifteen minutes since Fuerst had left the SUV, Tim was tired of waiting. He thought about calling Clare, but the timing did not feel right. Then, he could see Fuerst and another man walking briskly toward the car. He also noticed that everyone at the passenger pick-up area had begun to move with greater haste, so he opened both passenger doors and the cargo door on the SUV and prepared to leave quickly, as he became concerned that there might be good reason to do so. Fuerst was carrying one large bag, and the man with him had two others. Without a word they loaded the bags and got in.

Jakob was the first to speak, addressing Tim. "This is Amir Awad. He is a close friend and colleague of Abraham Jahir at the Haifa Software Corporation." Then he gestured toward Tim, and said, "This is Tim Austin. He is our American correspondent. Unfortunately, closer acquaintance will have to wait. We have to move quickly."

Tim started the SUV and drove away from the curb. "What has made everyone move so hurriedly all of a sudden?" he asked Fuerst.

"It seems that this hurricane means business! Winds have been measured at 180 mph. It is spinning tightly and continues to move directly toward the coast at a whopping speed of 30mph. It could be here much sooner than we wish. We must go inland quickly!" For the first time, Jakob Fuerst had shown an urgency in his speech and actions.

"What is our plan?" asked Tim. While he waited at the traffic light, he took a closer look at Fuerst in the passenger seat beside him, to see whether he appeared worried, but he did not.

"The Governor has declared an emergency. All lanes of I-26 are now going west," Fuerst replied.

Traffic was somewhat slow exiting the airport. Tim was watching for signs to get onto I-26. When he glanced into the rearview mirror, he noticed that Awad was removing items from one of the bags he had brought. Although his view was restricted, it looked as if he was assembling electronic equipment on the seat beside him. Fuerst was examining the traffic situation from his laptop.

"I am going to get onto the main highway, right?" Tim wanted to be sure.

"Yes," Fuerst replied, "but, be sure to remain in the westbound lanes for the time being. We shall need to exit the highway at some point, and that might not be possible from the eastbound lanes. Awad will be searching for the signal. It cannot be too far away."

Awad was working as quickly as he could to assemble the tracking device that he had created to locate his own software. Awad affectionately referred to his software as SAI, an acronym for Sensitive Artificial Intelligence. When he had first assembled the tracker back home in Tel Aviv, it had indicated that the signal from SAI had been broadcast from an area on the east coast of the United States. When he attempted to locate the signal more precisely, he was directed toward the city of Columbia, South Carolina. So, he gathered everything he needed to find the precise location, and a few more items he would need once he found it, then made his way to Charleston. He was not entirely sure that this tracking device would work well enough to find the exact location. But it was the best he could produce in haste.

It had been more than five years since the accidental discovery that had ushered in a new age of electronic communications. Certain rare earth materials, when fused together with the heat of lasers and integrated into the circuit of a silicon chip, were capable of receiving electronic signals in a way that made the broadcast of television via satellite look like a dinosaur from the Mesozoic Era. The need for giant antennas to receive the signal and transmit it to separate satellite dishes had been completely sidestepped with this invention. And this signal did not travel through the usual radio waves, but by means of a newly created...or rather, discovered...current. This unique current interacted differently with physical things.

There was still a lot to be learned about it, but research was slow. However, the most remarkable distinction about this current was that it did not communicate merely sound and video to the new circuits. It opened a communication channel capable of carrying odors, tastes, and tactile sensations!

The foundation for the new technology had been harbored in secrecy at the university where it had been created. Those who had invented it were not willing to share what they had found with anyone. They preferred to conduct extensive testing and make an evaluation of its potential applications. Instead of publicizing the discovery, work had continued with the aim of constructing a complete system that would send a signal to a direct broadcast satellite, which in turn would ultimately open a channel within the unique current to a multiplicity of microscopic antennas designed to receive it. After some discussion, it was agreed that the first component of the system, which had to be designed and built, was a communications satellite with a unique and incredibly powerful transponder. It had taken nearly four years to complete that project, but when it was ready for launch there was no hesitation by government officials to attach it to a rocket and send it into the earth's orbit. As far as they knew, it was a new generation of communications satellite, albeit with a unique transponder.

While the satellite was being constructed, a number of scientists worked to develop and assemble sending units and other devices needed to complete the system for broadcasting a signal. To satisfy their curiosity, they were told that they were constructing a new generation of communications satellite. But they were not privy to the function of the new chips, and these were what distinguished the entire system. The genius behind the design of the new circuit was Salaam Vendali. He knew well how he manipulated the materials that produced the microscopic antenna, but he had no intention of sharing his knowledge with the other researchers. Instead, he baited their curiosity, confident that his secret was safe.

Whenever Salaam Vendali was not at the university, he

could be found at the Haifa Software Corporation in Tel Aviv. He had been working there for years with Amir Awad to create software for artificial intelligence when they had a major breakthrough. Awad and Vendali had witnessed an extraordinary change in their experimental robot when they were trying to find a way to make it respond to situations of danger. One day, when they were testing their software, Vendali had clumsily fallen against his table, knocked a glass beaker to the floor and fallen upon it, lacerating his hand and buttocks. He cried out in pain. To their astonishment, it seemed as if the robot had "sensed" Vendali's pain. They were astounded as they witnessed its speech. Its expression was flushed with emotion when it asked, "Are you alright, Sal?" It approached him, reaching out with its robotic arms to help him up. Both men were in awe; it was the very first time that a robot had ever expressed feelings.

Awad continued working on the software, trying to make the robot express other feelings, but his success was limited. Different feelings were displayed at times, but haphazardly, and out of context. That was when he sought the help of Abraham Jahir. Jahir had become a friend to Awad by means of a professional relationship that had endured for more than ten years. Jahir was Awad's therapist. Over a period of several years, he had helped Awad overcome personal problems dating back to his childhood. As a result, Awad had learned to treat him like the father he never had. When Awad had asked Jahir to come to Haifa Software Corporation to help him correlate his software with human feelings, Jahir was both intrigued and honored to be considered for the task. Haifa Software had been seeking a corporate psychologist and, when Awad had introduced Jahir, he was hired immediately. Jahir found this work to be more enriching than his private practice, and he was inspired by the challenge to help Awad and Vendali accomplish their aim for the software.

While Awad and Jahir worked to create feelings for robots that were appropriately correlated with those of their human owners, Vendali was seeking a producer for the new chip, since he was fully satisfied that his sensibility circuit had been successfully integrated into the circuit with the microscopic antenna. He had been working with a company in Silicon Valley, called Alt-X, to have his new circuit mass-produced.

It was by a stroke of luck that he had learned about this company. He had met an attractive American woman at the university who claimed to have a friend whose parents owned and operated a semi-conductor company in California. Her name was Kayla Bruster. Vendali frequently went out of his way to befriend her, and to try and persuade her of the value of these chips in the world of communications. After an entire semester having conversations with Vendali, she promised to try and pull some strings to help him finance the production of the chips. When she had finally told him that engineers from this company wanted to meet with him, Vendali could not believe his ears. He traveled to California with detailed plans for the circuit he had designed. Once he had arrived there, he was pleased to find them eager to produce the chip. He didn't know how she had managed to do it, or where the money had come from, but the preparations were underway to build the equipment needed for mass production of the circuit.

Finally, Awad had completed the assembly of his tracking device in the rear of the Marauder. "Alright. Yes," he said. "I'm getting a signal several miles from here in the direction that we are currently traveling."

"Then we should stay on this highway?" asked Fuerst.

"I believe so. I shall tell you as we get closer," he said.

Tim kept driving. His stomach was getting that nauseous feeling once again. He thought about Clare and Michael, and he yearned to be with them. He also felt apprehensive from not knowing when and how they might avoid the hurricane. "It'll all work out," he kept thinking to himself.

Chapter 16

Lyndsey's Search for Understanding

Lyndsey finally found a few moments to relax alone. She decided to try and open Tim's laptop. She slouched into the chair in the den and opened it from the very place where it was designed to rest. She had not planned to make a trip to her childhood home the previous evening. In fact, she had been concerned over not having heard from her brother after dropping him off at the University of Pittsburgh campus. But, as she was preparing to leave the office, she finally received a call from Tim. He told her that he needed her to get his laptop from its hidden location at home because it contained all the work he had done in correlation with the International Alliance. He said that it should also have a recently delivered letter explaining how to prevent the zombies from further disrupting their lives. Tim had insisted that she get it as soon as possible. He effectively made her feel that she had better act quickly, because he had become concerned that it could fall into the wrong hands. If the FBI were to access the data within his laptop, it would incriminate not only him, but also Abraham Jahir, among others. So, Lyndsey had gone directly from the institute to secure it.

Retrieving the laptop was an adventure for her. When she arrived at the neighborhood of her youth, she encountered a ruckus at a house on the end of the road, three blocks from her destination. It was directly in front of her to the right. Her immediate perception motivated a flashback to Jake's house during their clamor with zombies. Her flashback helped to inform her about what she was seeing...or not seeing...now. This experience was even stranger to her than the previous one.

She saw two people aiming their handguns, and another swinging a scythe. At first, she thought that one man with a gun was aiming at the man wielding the scythe, but then she realized that was not actually the case. *"These houses are too close together for this,"* she muttered aloud. She didn't bother stopping at the stop sign while she could still pass this calamity before it could affect her. But this was not the only strange behavior she would encounter. At the next block, she approached five people walking on the road heading in the direction whence she had just come, armed with all sorts of weapons. They were local homeowners, defending their neighborhood. She raised the window on the Marauder and slowed to a coast, so as to pose no danger to the gang. Then, she saw four more people twenty-five feet or so to her right circled around the side entrance to a house. One fired a pistol into the ground by the door, and that made her jump. Another man thrust a long spear into the ground behind the shooter. Lyndsey felt like she was in a war zone. *"I feel so alienated,"* she quivered, *"It looks like a charade."*

She arrived at her parent's house, now the home of Tim and Clare and Michael, with no further problems. Just for a moment, she was afraid to get out of the car. The armed people living in a world of zombies were only a few blocks behind her. But she took the key to the back door in hand, jumped out of the SUV, and quietly but swiftly hopped up the steps and ran around the side of the house to the back door. She was quite familiar with this door. She knew the key functioned smoothly and she could get right in, shut it, and run up to the back bedroom. She retrieved the laptop from its location inside the closet wall. Wasting no time, she was back out the door in less than two minutes. More shots were fired down the block where the charade was being played out, so she quickly hopped in the

SUV and had it moving almost immediately.

Suddenly, several police cars were racing straight toward her SUV as she was traveling away from the victims of the zombies. It made her feel like she was in the way, so Lyndsey moved over behind a parked car. Two mini-SUVs zipped past her. A large police van was traveling in her direction, so she sat still. As it slowly passed her, she momentarily imagined that she might be arrested for having Tim's laptop. Finally, the van eased away from her and she was able to escape the neighborhood onto a winding, hilly road that would deliver her to the main route home.

As she entered the password, Tim's laptop opened to reveal the documents enclosed. But her thoughts drifted to reflect upon a conflict that she needed to resolve. *"Jake wants to know why I can't see zombies. I'll just tell him the truth: we got the first vaccine before we had learned that Mom and Dad were sick with the Ebola virus. The doctors assured us that we were protected, though it was probably too late for our parents. Neither Tim, nor Rinna or I got the disease from Mom and Dad, so we didn't need another shot! While Tim had decided that getting the new vaccine would be harmless, I was not willing, so neither Rinna nor I have gotten it."* But Lyndsey knew that Jake would wonder how she could get away with that. Her virtual file would not identify her as having the new vaccine. If that were the case, then she could never enter any government or hospital building, or her own office, for that matter. She did not want to tell him how she had managed to evade that obstacle.

Then, her attention shifted back to an appreciation of her dead parents. *"Mom and Dad were so proud of their children...majors in Philosophy and Psychology were certainly appropriate for us. It was the best way to learn about life, and the 'nature' of the world we live in. Dad said we would be good guides for the human spirit. His warning was also good advice; he had said that too many people were specializing in STEM, and that a rounded education is not possible without extensive studies in the liberal arts. He always insisted that a one-sided emphasis on STEM would contribute to the demise of our country."*

"*What is this?*" A document suddenly appeared entitled, "Response to the Heroic Attitude". It aroused her interest, so she sat up in the chair. Just then, Jake came down the stairs, stealing her attention, to alert her about the potential danger to her brother.

"I don't suppose you were listening to any news reports on that thing?" he asked gesturing toward the laptop.

"No, what's up?" Lyndsey asked.

"There is a gigantic hurricane making a beeline straight toward South Carolina. I hope Tim, and whomever he's with, are smart enough to get the hell out of its way!"

"I'm sure they will have some place to hunker down," Lyndsey said with confidence.

"I'm not so sure, Lyn!" Jake exuded caution in his tone of voice. "Hurricane Alfonso is not the average hurricane! This is one of the 'ultra-canes'. Looks like one of the biggest ever, and it is moving at an unheard-of rate of speed. It'll start to affect Charleston sometime this evening."

"Just don't say anything to Clare." Lyndsey warned with a whisper. She and Michael were sleeping, and she could find no good reason to alarm her before it becomes absolutely necessary. The women had cancelled the trip to the zoo when the other families decided to return home. Only Phillip and Jeffrey were disappointed. Rinna was satisfied to be with Michael.

Jake smiled lopsidedly and nodded. He knew the routine. There was a lot he would not tell Clare. Jake even had some things he would not tell Lyndsey.

Jake Altmeyer was seven years older than Lyndsey. He had

known her years earlier, but they lost touch during her parents' illness. Jake had been dating Kayla Bruster before he had met Lyndsey. He knew Kayla from high school in Western Pennsylvania, but they had never associated with each other until about seven years ago, when he met her at a social event. After that, Jake would go out with her on occasion. Once she had returned from her studies overseas, they had become more intimate, and spent some time together. After a couple years of dating Kayla, Jake got to know Tim at the university in Pittsburgh and became acquainted with his sister. He found Lyndsey attractive, and he felt something special about the way that she cared for people, especially her daughter. And he loved spending time with Rinna, who was barely four years old. She was so happy when Jake would read books to her. It made him wonder how the father of this little girl could have left her.

But there was a great fear of the Ebola virus. Lyndsey's parents had the virus. She cared for them during their illness, even as she had begun work at the State Psychiatric Institute. She raised Rinna, practically by herself. Tim had provided some help for Lyndsey after moving back home to be with his ailing parents. While Lyndsey's parents had the virus, Rinna's father had the fear of it. He could not accept that Lyndsey wanted to help her parents, so he completely avoided the Austin home. At that point, Lyndsey had decided that she wanted nothing more to do with Rinna's father. He wasn't exactly begging for them to come back anyway. Instead, he offered her a lump sum of money to be spared of any future responsibility for the little girl.

Besides Rinna's father, Jake Altmeyer also had the fear of Ebola. It had prevented him from getting to know Lyndsey and Rinna. He, too, had stayed away from the Austin house for quite a while. It was not until after the Austins died, when Tim, Clare, Lyndsey and Rinna were all living together, that Jake had offered Lyndsey to come and live with him in a country setting outside of the city. Jake had inherited his property from his parents. They had practically given it to him once they had decided to live out their senior years in the Western desert. After all, they had accumulated substantial wealth. His father had founded a thriving technology business in Silicon Valley, so he and his wife had the means to own property anywhere they wanted.

When he first got the house, Jake wanted a live-in companion. Unbeknownst to Lyndsey, he had invited Kayla Bruster to live with him at his house. But she was independent, and while she would stay for a while, she would also disappear for long periods of time. That didn't fit Jake's style. He wanted a companion on a daily basis. He knew that Kayla Bruster was a busy woman with an agenda, and he never made any effort to change her. She always wanted to be in control, and she had specific ideas about her own future.

Jake knew that he was attracted to Lyndsey Austin, but he did not have the courage to ask her for a date. He was also concerned that Rinna might not remember him after so long. It was not until Tim told him that Lyndsey would go out with him that Jake had become confident enough to ask her. Once he had spent some time with Lyndsey and Rinna, he decided to forego further relations with Kayla Bruster. Instead, he made his top priority to help Lyndsey raise Rinna. The little girl was so happy when he would come to get her at the daycare. He would take her for dinner and ice cream, and to play in the park, whenever Lyndsey had to be at the institute. This made Lyndsey extremely happy. Her little girl finally had a loving father figure. She was so pleased with Jake's treatment of Rinna that she accepted his invitation to live with him. And, after nearly two years of cohabitation, Rinna was showing a much greater self-confidence due to the relationship he had developed with her.

Lyndsey tried to focus once again on Tim's laptop. She had closed it when Jake interrupted, and that had closed the document. As soon as the laptop rebooted, it blinked with a message. It was a direct link opened to contact Abraham Jahir. "*Oh dear!*" she exclaimed under her breath. She looked more closely at the link. It was recently opened. "*Jahir wants Tim to call him,*" she thought. Realizing she had inadvertently contacted this renowned psychoanalyst, she took the computer into the basement and connected to the link again. She felt a bit naughty doing so. "Hello," she said, wanting simply to disclose the facts, "I am Lyndsey Austin, Tim's sister. I have contacted you through his laptop. He is…"

She was interrupted by a response on the other end. "Lyndsey? Lyndsey Austin?" was all she heard.

"That's right. I have Tim's laptop. I have contacted you by accident. I'm so sorry."

"No, no, that is good! Thank you very much! I am Abraham Jahir. Tim has told me about your studies in psychoanalysis."

"Yes, I am familiar with some of your writings," she was proud to say.

"Lyndsey, I am currently traveling with the man who saved us at the cabin. With the help of my Native-American friend, I found a quiet place on the Pima Indian Reservation, until he indicated that he would have to seek new employment, given the fire at the cabin. Then I asked him to take me eastward and he agreed. He has the transportation, and I have some money, and we both have a love for nature. It has been exciting to share the beauty of the American landscape with a man who feels and breathes the nature of your western lands. Unfortunately, these reports that I am wanted for questioning have made me feel like a fugitive from the law. I was recognized at a restaurant in Missouri. We have been on the road since then, and we need a place to rest."

"Where are you currently?" she asked.

"We are on I-70 heading east toward Indianapolis."

"Well," Lyndsey began, "the best I can do is to offer you respite at our humble abode. But you will be driving a while before you get here. I'll give you the address."

"Is it in Pittsburgh?" Jahir remembered that Tim spoke

affectionately about the city.

"It's a few miles to the north of the city." Then, she told him the address.

"Have you heard from Tim?" he asked her.

"No, and I'm worried," she replied.

"It will be necessary for them to find safety from the hurricane as first priority. I shall be in contact with him soon. One more thing," requested Jahir. "Have you read the article that you opened?"

"What?" Lyndsey didn't know how to respond to this question.

"I opened my phone line through the article I sent for Tim. That is how you contacted me." He wondered if he had sensed apprehension on the other end, but then he decided it might be his own, so he added, "Please read it if time permits. Thank you for the invitation to your home. I shall contact you when we are near. Good-bye now."

"Yes, good-bye now," Lyndsey repeated.

Chapter 17

Seeking the Source of the Zombies

"Do we still have enough time to escape to the west? This traffic is not moving too quickly!" Tim was reminding Amir Awad and Jakob Fuerst of their dwindling prospects for outrunning the hurricane. They expected that the eye of Hurricane Alfonso would hit the east coast after 7pm, but damaging winds and torrential downpours would be arriving in advance of that. While they all believed that they were far enough inland to avoid ocean flooding, this hurricane was extremely dangerous, and it was moving directly toward Charleston. It was already past 3pm and Tim was only fifty or sixty miles inland, near Orangeburg. This would certainly not be out of harm's way if the hurricane made landfall at Charleston. If the current course and wind speeds were correct, then he would need to travel several miles further inland to avoid the devastating effects of the winds and rain.

Awad thought that he had found the signal transmitted from his software. He had guided Tim into the docking area of a shipping company, but Awad's equipment must have been malfunctioning, or perhaps the signal was being scrambled. "I had been getting a strong signal right in this area, but now it has faded," lamented Awad.

"Well, what do we do?" asked Fuerst. He still had that matter-of-fact attitude about things. Tim, quite frankly, was wishing Fuerst would show the same urgency he had expressed when they were leaving the airport.

"Drive around the area while I attempt to relocate the signal," Awad requested. He was in the rearmost row of seats in the Marauder. His radar and detection equipment were set up around him. But the signal was no longer detected. Tim drove toward the front of the building. It was a small shipping company called Top Transports. It had a handful of trucks in the front. "I think we have the wrong place," said Awad. "I'm getting a signal that is some distance from here."

"Are you sure?" Fuerst asked. "We are cutting things close. I see that in the eye of the hurricane the winds are 180 mph! It is traveling in our general direction."

At that moment, looking outside the SUV, the winds were deceptively calm. "I think I was getting a phantom signal," insisted Awad. "I believe that I was intentionally misled. I am not surprised by that. However, if that was a phantom, then the signal I am receiving now must be sent directly from the software. It is about twenty miles from here to the west northwest. We shall have to go that direction to find it."

"Would that be wise?" Tim wondered. "Are you confident we can get far enough away from the hurricane in time?"

"How long would it take to get there?" asked Awad, glancing toward Fuerst.

"It's in the right direction – that is, away from the coast," Fuerst acknowledged.

"Should we get back onto I-26 toward Columbia?" asked Tim.

"I'm not sure," Fuerst wondered himself. He had been attending to the map on his phone. On I-26 they would have to stay in the westbound lanes and hope that they could exit without traveling all the way to Columbia. But some exits were not open. He sought an alternative. Eventually he guided Tim along local roads, through residential areas dotted with small businesses. The land had begun to rise ever so slightly as they had exited the low country. The area was full of pine trees and oaks that thinned out only where development had removed them. By the time they had found the signal, it was almost 4:00 pm.

"Wait, please!" Awad urged.

"Wait? Just stop, and pull over?" Tim asked.

"Yes. We are very close. Please, stop somewhere! My radar is fluctuating with motion." Awad spoke confidently. Tim stopped on the street alongside a gas and charge station. No one was around, and the station was empty.

"Can you clarify the source, please? We are short on time. Perhaps we should drive north or south. If we were to travel as far inland as possible to the west, even into the mountains, I'm not sure that we would escape the wrath of Alfonso." Fuerst was trying to determine the best direction to travel to avoid the worst of the hurricane.

Awad lifted a wire toward the skylight in the roof of the Marauder. "It is several hundred feet on the other side of this charging station."

"I just have to find a way there, right?" asked Tim.

"You are fine, son," Jakob Fuerst replied assuredly. He realized that he might have to help Tim manage his stress. "Continue the way we are headed. Make a right shortly ahead."

"Yes, we have to circle back now," said Awad.

"I'm on it," Fuerst said. "Right again," he instructed Tim. After the right turn, he found himself facing a triad of possible options. On their left was a road traveling through what looked like a nursery of tall pine trees grown closely together. It was difficult to see through these pines. They obscured the view of a large building behind them. The middle road was the main road. It would continue around the sharp bend in front of him to wherever. On the right was a gravel road leading to some residences.

Suddenly Tim's phone rang. It was Clare. He hesitated to answer.

"Shouldn't you answer that?" Fuerst looked at Tim.

"It's my wife," Tim responded. The phone continued to ring.

"Answer it, son," Fuerst insisted. Tim obliged him at the same time Awad attained a clear indication where the signal was coming from.

"Through the pine trees on the left!" demanded Awad just after Tim had pressed the button to receive Clare's call. Awad's command was the first thing she heard.

"Tim? What…?" She wasn't really sure what she heard.

"I'm here babe! Good to hear your voice!" he said in earnest. "Should I drive between the trees?" Tim asked Awad.

"What?" Clare asked.

"Babe, I am driving, and I'm not sure where I am. Someone else is giving me directions. I'd better pay attention here. We have to escape this hurricane. I love you, Clare, but I'll have to call back later."

"I love you, Tim!" she cried. "Can't wait till you get home! Bye." The line went dead. But once again, just hearing Clare's voice stirred his passionate desire to be with her and Michael. He promised himself that he was going to spend some quality time with them both as soon as possible.

"I'm sorry, son." Fuerst sensed Tim's disappointment over not being able to converse with his wife. But he was quickly interrupted by Awad.

"The signal is definitely being transmitted from somewhere on the other side of these pines," Awad asserted with complete confidence.

Tim wound his way along the road between the pines. For the first time, he had begun to notice that the breeze moving the trees had gotten stronger. His concern about the coming hurricane made the motion of the pines appear more pronounced than it really was.

At the end of the road was a parking area. It was at the back of a very large building; an old-style, indoor-outdoor mall surrounded by a substantial parking lot. The entire complex, and the road between the pines that led to it, was on a slight uphill grade. As Tim turned toward the right side of the building, he noticed three SUVs parked at the bottom on the opposite side. The hill crested at the front of the building, and gradually declined as one exited the mall in the front. This mall was elevated just enough to provide a scenic view of the valley to its north. One could see for some distance into the valley, where there was a residential community filled with homes interspersed with a few businesses. Tim and Jakob Fuerst could see some people hastily covering the windows of their homes with plywood and shutters. Others had already made such preparations, and some homes were without any alteration.

"Well, what are we gonna do here?" Tim's concern was shared by Jakob Fuerst.

"It is 4:30 now." Jakob was calculating the odds for their escape. The eye of the hurricane is expected to make landfall around 8:00 pm. We could be experiencing increasing winds, upwards of 100 mph, before that. The winds are 180 mph at the eye. Where it goes once it hits land is not certain. It is traveling at 30 mph, so it may well move straight towards us."

"We have to get the hell out of here!" Tim insisted. "We have less than three hours to run from it!"

"Unless we could shelter somewhere nearby," Awad suggested as he hopped out of the Marauder. "Please allow me a few minutes to look around." He was sizing up the giant building whence the signal had originated. It appeared to be three full stories high, at least in the rear. The front of the structure was partially underground. Signs identifying each individual business were located along the outside, but it seemed everything was closed. There were two open corridors running crisscross through the center of the lower level of the building. Entrances to these corridors were centrally located on all four sides of the square building.

Awad walked around the side they had just passed in the SUV, then entered the corridor on the south side of the mall. He walked at a fast pace, looking from side to side to get a quick view of the inside. He could see that there was a roof over the entire second level. Offices and businesses were wall to wall on both the first and second floors. Stairwells to the second level could be found along each side of the corridors. Much to his surprise, he saw people inside two of the businesses. He didn't focus on that because he was more interested in finding an entrance to the third level. But the third floor was not obviously accessible from inside the corridors. Awad suspected that the third floor was where he would find the equipment sending the signal.

He continued walking through the corridor from the back of the building toward the front. At the front he had to climb six steps to exit the north end of the corridor to the parking area. Awad calculated that the ground at the front of the building was about six feet higher than the rear. He knew that was important, but he was still focused on how to get to the third floor. He saw Tim and Fuerst waiting in the Marauder, so he picked up his pace once again, walking away from them, and around the far side of the building.

On that side, he spied an outdoor metal stairwell, complete with handrails, going up the rear of the building. On the second story it came to a level platform, splitting the stairwell into separate flights. One end of the platform led to a door on the second story, and the second flight went to a door on the third floor before it turned and went up a few more steps to the roof. Awad was sure that he would find the transmitter and other equipment up there, so he turned and trotted back toward the Marauder.

"What do we have?" asked Fuerst as soon as Awad had climbed back into the SUV.

"Let me check something," Awad replied, picking up his laptop while making adjustments on some other device that looked like a graphic equalizer to Tim.

"Is there a safe place to hunker down in there?" Tim asked, growing more concerned by the minute.

"I am quite certain that my software is somewhere in this building. The signal is strong and consistent. There must be a sending unit near the roof of the building. I did not go up there, but I found a stairwell to the roof." Awad waited for a response from Fuerst.

"Is there any place that we can find safety in this building to wait for the hurricane to pass?" Fuerst asked Awad.

"I think so. We shall have to look more closely along this northern end of the corridor. The lower level of the building is concrete construction. It is partially underground in this corner," Awad pointed directly in front of the men. "It would likely provide safety, but I did not find a specific location that would protect us." Awad shrugged his shoulders. Then he remembered, "There are some people inside a couple of the businesses on the lower level. Perhaps, they could help us to find safety…that is, if they know about a safe location?" Awad was grasping for hope because he wanted to find a way to the third floor of the building. He was hot on Vendali's trail for the first time since the man had betrayed his partners. Awad expected that he might have to kill him personally. But, just as important to him, he hoped for the opportunity to pirate the system that Vendali was using to transmit the counterproductive signals which had produced the zombies throughout America. He knew that he could use the very same equipment to send his own signals. The chips were already in place, and he and Jahir had been working to make specific adjustments to the software. If he could not appropriate the system for his own use, then he would have to permanently disable it.

"It is almost 5:00 pm; we'd better make a decision immediately!" insisted Tim. He was watching the sky darken and the pines to his left bend and sway more and more as the minutes passed.

"Drive to the rear of the building, and we shall see what those people are doing here," Awad suggested.

"Yes," said Fuerst, "I believe our best option is to seek protection at the lowest level of this building." Tim didn't waste any time. He maneuvered the Marauder to park at the end of the corridor at the rear of the building.

"I need to get my equipment," Awad insisted.

"Can't you wait until we find a place to hunker down?" Tim was getting impatient with Awad. As he opened the door to the Marauder, a gust of wind yanked it from his hand and blew it wide open. It hit its limit and bounced back toward Tim, who pulled his hand away just in time to avoid injury. "Shit!" he cursed.

"I have to take at least one bag now!" Awad reached behind him and pulled out the smallest of the bags he had brought. "Okay, let's go," he said. Rain began pelting the ground just as they closed the doors to the Marauder. Each man turned simultaneously to make a dash through the wind and rain into the corridor.

When they got into the giant hallway, they had escaped the rain and the worst of the wind. They were in a corridor about forty feet wide. There were a few metal chairs several feet into the corridor, arranged for seating around large planters at its center. At the other end of this corridor, several hundred feet due north, was the six-foot stairwell going out to the parking area at that end. The wind flow was slightly cut off in the north-south direction due to the stairwell. But when they arrived at the middle where the perpendicular corridors intersected, the wind was whipping at speeds higher than the gusts in the valley to the north. The eye of the hurricane was supposed to be a couple hours away, but the winds were already getting strong.

"Right over here!" Awad pointed toward a doorway beyond the midpoint where the light was on. There were two men about to cover the large glass doors with pre-cut sheets of plywood.

Tim ran to the door and yelled, "Are you staying to ride out the storm? We need shelter." Tim had barely finished when one of the men inside yelled back at him as he shook his head from side to side.

"No. Leaving as soon as we put up these boards." The man backed away from the door and helped his cohort lift the plywood into place.

"Let's go!" Jakob yelled to Tim as he waved at the men.

"Go where?" Tim was looking around at the building, as was Jakob.

"There were more people in this other store," Awad exclaimed as he proceeded northward through the corridor. Light was protruding from holes in the plywood covers over the glass windows of an electronics store. Tim ran over with Awad to peer inside. Peering through holes in the plywood, Tim thought he could see people moving things, but they quickly escaped his view.

"This way!" Jakob was yelling with his hands cupped around his mouth from the northernmost end of the corridor. Tim had barely heard him over the howling wind and pounding rain that echoed throughout. He was motioning for his companions to follow him. Tim and Awad glanced at each other then ran toward him. As they approached, Fuerst turned toward one of the stairwells to the second level.

"We should not go upstairs!" Awad insisted, waving his arms in the air. But Fuerst ignored Awad who was still fifty feet away from him. Tim had approached Fuerst, also reticent to go upstairs. What was not apparent to Tim or Awad was that there was a restroom several feet behind the stairwell on the lower level. "Let's see if we can shelter in this men's room." Fuerst gestured in the general direction. Tim followed him around the stairwell. By that time Awad had caught up to them.

As the three of them walked into the men's bathroom, it was apparent that it was almost entirely underground at the northeast corner of the mall. Tim noticed that two small vents opened to the outside near the top of the east wall. His attention was drawn there because the strongest gusts whistled through the vents. The outer walls appeared to be strong enough to withstand violent winds. They were concrete block covered with plaster. Also, the interior surrounding walls were concrete construction all the way around to the metal entry door.

"This place will have to do." Jakob Fuerst suggested.

"I have to get my equipment from the SUV!" Awad informed them. Quickly the three men ran back toward the SUV. The wind continued gusting incrementally higher. It forced huge drops of rain directly into their faces as they opened the doors of the Marauder and jumped inside.

Once they had sat down, Fuerst advised, "We should drive the SUV into the corridor. It will fit easily through one aisle." Tim didn't waste any time. He started the Marauder. As he turned the wipers on full blast, he watched the long needles from the pine trees get pushed to the bottom and sides of the windshield. Then he sped along the rear of the mall, passing the corridor in which he intended to park the SUV. He shifted into reverse and backed the Marauder all the way to the crossing corridor. There was room to spare on either side as he passed the decorative planters.

"Go a little farther, past the intersection a short distance," said Fuerst. "I believe we should park close to this intersection. We would have three possible ways to exit." Tim nodded, believing that to be a good idea. He backed away from the intersecting corridor, easing the Marauder out of the crosswinds that clashed at the center of the building.

"I'll climb out your side," Tim said as he parked with the driver's side right up against the wall at Jarvis' Office Supplies.

Fuerst and Awad flung open the passenger side doors.

"Help me bring my equipment," yelled Awad. As the men dragged the bags out of the SUV, it was shaken by a violent gust of wind, and a loud crack echoed in the hallway. A branch from a large oak tree had snapped and fallen onto the parking lot not far from where they had been just a few minutes earlier.

"Let's go!" Tim exclaimed.

As they approached the door to the men's bathroom, Awad drew close to Fuerst. "I might walk up those stairs to find access to the roof," he yelled, as if he were oblivious to the severity of the wind.

"You can't go up there!" Fuerst insisted. "It is time to take shelter, right now!" Awad frowned and nodded, and the three of them entered the shelter.

"We should be safe in here," Tim thought out loud.

"I like that it is mostly underground and protected at the corner of this building," replied Fuerst, "and that we can hear each other speak."

"Does that door lock? We need to anchor it somehow." Tim went over to the door. The wind was whistling a frightful tune through the vents above his head, and the door was moving ajar, then shut, in repetition. At times, it sounded like someone was pounding the wall outside of the vents. Among the whistling and the pounding, Tim envisioned ghouls playing a wicked march to enliven evil spirits. He blinked hard as if to erase that image from his mind, and pushed the bathroom door closed against the wind, then turned the latch, locking it shut. An immediate result was a more restricted air flow through the vents, and the pounding was dulled. The temperature in the room was relatively cool. A constant drip of rainwater had begun to fall from each vent.

Awad carefully placed his bags along one wall and sat down beside them. "Maybe we can get some rest," he said.

"How the hell can we rest here?" Tim doubted the possibility. But the more he thought about it, he decided that might be the best way to spend this time of waiting. He listened to the wind as it whistled through the vents and watched a trickle of water run down the wall, forming a small puddle that flowed into the floor drain. Then he and Fuerst sat down aside Awad and leaned against the wall near the sinks. Not one of the three men had any expectation that this hurricane was going to allow them to rest.

Chapter 18

The Unconquerable Forces of Nature

Lyndsey was restless and stressed. She was alarmed by the simultaneous occurrence of so many natural disasters across the globe. She felt as if the entire earth were under siege. The evening news reports had disturbed her deeply. The international and national events created a background for her perception of what was happening in Western Pennsylvania.

Along with the usual reports of drought and fires in Australia, and the rising water in Venice, Italy, a number of oil fields in Saudi Arabia had flooded. But the events in the U.S. were much more threatening. A series of powerful earthquakes had been felt up and down the west coast. The amount of structural damage throughout California, and north through Oregon and Washington into Canada was staggering. No death toll was available, but many people were missing and feared to be injured or killed. Those near the affected areas were in recovery mode and struggling to help each other. The damage was estimated to be in the trillions of dollars. The earthquakes had initiated a gigantic tidal wave that was racing toward the Japanese islands, where people had been warned to flee the coast. The earthquakes were probably related to recent volcanic action at Mount Saint Helen's. A lava flow had begun days earlier with only a minor eruption. It had been spewing smoke and ash, but now a larger flow of molten earth was reshaping the landscape surrounding the volcano.

The east coast was dealing with its own problems, and these were of primary concern of Lyndsey. She had been unable to contact Tim since he asked her to get his laptop. The hurricane had brutalized South Carolina, where flooding up to ten feet deep extended several miles inland from the force of ocean water. Thousands of people were believed to be drowned or washed away. The tops of buildings could be seen by helicopter from above the flood waters near Charleston. The ocean shoreline had moved significantly westward, at least for the time being. The eye of the hurricane had carved out a path thirty miles wide with winds well over 100 mph, until it met a powerful line of severe thunderstorms coming from the west. The line of severe thunderstorms had spawned dozens of tornados as it moved eastward. But Alfonso, having weakened somewhat after moving inland, was heading directly toward it. These were two unusually potent storms that collided head on. The affects from their collision were incalculable and unpredictable for the national weather experts.

Lyndsey was currently sheltering from tornados at home with Rinna, Jake, Clare, and Michael. They were all in the basement for maximum protection. The experts had scrambled to alert the public about the powerful weather events, the likes of which had never before been witnessed. The warning for the greater Pittsburgh vicinity had come from the local weather service, but not until 9:00 pm. They said to expect tornados in the area for the next few hours, and perhaps also straight-line winds up to 100 mph.

Radar had disclosed that when the line of severe thunderstorms had met with Hurricane Alfonso at the mountain range in the Western Carolinas, the hurricane exploded outward in every direction. Alfonso was moving so fast that it never made a turn. It hit the eastbound storm at the mountains like water slamming against a brick wall. The force of the winds ricocheted upon the collision and scattered, cutting paths mostly northward and southward along the mountain range, with some turning back toward the east coast. What worried Lyndsey was that the dangerous tornados and straight-line winds were traveling so fast that they would be arriving in Western Pennsylvania before midnight, limiting the amount of time that people would have to prepare.

Jake had been working hard, knowing that a line of severe thunderstorms was coming. He had been rushing to install storm windows throughout the house. While he had originally intended to install this protection when he replaced the broken windows, he had procrastinated, and left the work undone. This coming storm had forced him to install them quickly. He also had to dismantle his entire computer system in his control center to put it in a safer place. He did that first.

He had a most unwelcome surprise while he was installing the storm windows. It turned out to be an adventure that would test his virtue. The glass panes were easily manageable when the winds would cooperate. Early in the day there had been only a gentle breeze, but the winds had begun to pick up by evening.

Jake was trying to finish quickly. However, as he reached for the second pane to cover the window in the back bedroom, he saw three zombies heading right his way. They were about 150 feet into the field toward the home of Paul Branch. "Shit!" He cursed, disgusted. His immediate thought was to go for a weapon. Then he stopped and glanced back in the direction of the field. The zombies were slogging straight toward him at a slow pace. He thought for sure they were looking right at him, moaning as a response to having seen him. His stomach turned sick. "I have to protect myself!" he thought aloud. He watched them dragging ever closer, but slowly.

Then he stood up straight and turned directly toward the zombies. He wondered, *"How did Tim do that?"* They were still a hundred feet away, but appeared as real as ever to Jake, even as he told himself, *"These fuckers aren't real!"* His fear was building, and he was facing a desire to flee. Eighty feet away and closing. Seventy. Jake forced a swallow and decided he would run into the house. But, before he could move a muscle to execute that decision, the zombies had miraculously disappeared. He moved his eyes from side to side in their sockets, facing in the general direction of where they had been. Nothing seemed to be out of the ordinary. The zombies were gone. He felt a sense of relief, and pride, believing that he was able to overcome an illusion of zombies with his own will. However, he was deluding himself, for, at the very moment that the zombies had disappeared, the system sending the signal to satellite had been destroyed by Hurricane Alfonso.

After the zombies had disappeared, Jake moved quickly to pick up his tools and put them away. Still, he kept a wary eye on the area around him. By the time he had returned to the house, the wind was beginning to circle and gust, and rain began pelting against the storm windows. *"I don't even have to clean 'em off!"* he quipped to himself as he ran inside to lock in the storm windows and nail the barricade boards back onto the window frame. He rationalized that he might still need the barricade to block out blowing debris from the storm…not so much for zombies.

When he had finished, darkness had arrived with the storm and he adjourned to relax in the basement. He thought it best that he got some rest before Jahir and Redfeather arrived. Two more people would be staying at his house, but he didn't mind. There was plenty of room, since Alan and Zack, their wives, Philip, and Jeffrey, had all gone home. Alan and Zack felt much more confident about staying at their own homes, believing that the zombies were only a strange sort of hoax.

"We are going to have to stay down here until these storms pass," Lyndsey told Jake and Clare. "If we need to stay here all night, we have food and drinks. We also have enough relaxing furniture for each one of us to recline."

"When is your company getting here?" Clare asked Lyndsey.

"He is close now." Lyndsey was speaking of John Redfeather, the driver of the Chevy truck that was bringing Abraham Jahir. "But their timing is scaring me." The wind was whipping, and there was a torrential downpour at the moment. The rain had been sporadic until now. Lyndsey walked over to the vents in the glass block windows, shutting them tightly. The rain was pounding hard against the vents, and water was seeping through, making narrow streams down the wall.

She went back to the recliner she had been lounging on and opened Tim's laptop to the article by Jahir that had initially connected her with him. She requested a response.

Jahir answered, "Yes, Lyndsey Austin?"

"Where are you?" she asked. Then lightening lit the sky and thunder reverberated through the ground beneath the basement floor. "Oh, dear!" she exclaimed.

"Hello?" Jahir could hear nothing.

"Are you okay?" Lyndsey wasn't sure what had been struck by the lightening, but it was something nearby.

"We are stopped on the road we were traveling. We can't see. But I'm sure we are very close to your driveway."

"Drive all the way to the garage, and park anywhere. Come in through the man door on the right side of the garage," Lyndsey instructed Jahir. "It is not locked. Someone will guide you into the house."

"Once we can see again. Hopefully, that will be soon. Goodbye now."

"Goodbye," said Lyndsey, hoping they would arrive soon. But she felt her expectations for the future slipping into the unknown as her stomach lifted up toward her lungs. "*These storms are real,*" she thought, while unable to forget the rest of the events that were reshaping the national landscape. "*We can *be sure of these!"*

Chapter 19

The Zombies Unmasked

A delightfully bright ray of sunlight was piercing through the gloom and doom. Morning had begun to penetrate the holes in the wall, which had been dispensing water the night before. At the time of the heaviest rains, the water was pouring in through each of the vents at a rate comparable to an open water faucet. What made it worse, the drain in the floor was inadequate for taking the water as quickly as it entered. Once they noticed that the drain was not functioning, Awad quickly picked up his bags from under the sinks and placed them on top. The others followed with their bags. The water had gotten to be a couple inches deep before it started flowing under the thin gap beneath the door. Tim waded through it and pried off the perforated drain cover with a piece of metal from the privacy door that had been in front of one of the toilet stalls. Then a whirlpool began that would eventually take all the water from the bathroom.

It had been a challenge for them to stay dry, but at least the men had been safe inside of the bathroom. It was impossible to relax during the storm until the wee hours of the morning when the winds had abated to tolerable gusts. The floor was wet, and they had only one roll of hand towels that was dry, but they were safe.

Unfortunately, they couldn't lie down, and even if it were possible to lie on the floor, none of them could have slept. The winds made a constant pounding sound against the vents in the wall, until it sounded like something had broken inside and the pounding had stopped. Then there was the most horrifying noise that echoed for too long. It sounded like a rocket blasting off above their heads. Each of the three men had to cover his ears and eyes as he huddled within his own private toilet stall on top of a commode. The concrete dividers between the commodes created a sense of safety. However, each stall had a metal door which shook constantly even after being latched.

The door on the end stall was directly in the line of the winds gusting through the vents. It had been torn from its hinges and bounced around the room before coming to rest. Tim took it across the room and wedged it underneath the entry door. Still, it continuously tapped up and down on one end. Crashing sounds with braking glass could be heard throughout the evening, along with snapping trees, until the point that the "rocket" had begun its take-off.

All these stress-inducing noises continued until after midnight, when the winds abated to a stiff breeze with strong gusts. The men were physically safe from the worst of the rain and the wind. However, the endless pressure from the wind, along with the water blowing throughout the bathroom, left each of the men wet and shaking, at least on the inside. Finally, they were prepared to leave their safe shelter to discover the extent of the destruction.

"It is after 6 am," Jakob Fuerst forced the air from his lungs to speak. He felt relief from the absence of noise, and the lack of water blowing through the vents. Each of the men was prepared to move on. The sunlight coming through the hole where one of the vents had been was beckoning them to go outside, and the wind was gradually fading back to a mild breeze. A calm, sunny day had arrived to displace the dark threats of the past night.

"I'll be glad to see more of the sun!" declared Tim,

standing with the other two men in the center of the bathroom.

"We can take a walk outside without the bags first. Someone can stay here at least for a moment, while one of us looks around." Jakob Fuerst wanted to go outside, so he opened the door. Tim followed, and the two of them ventured into an unknown world. They were expecting to encounter obstacle after obstacle outside of the bathroom. There was sunlight streaming through two more empty vent holes on the wall outside of the bathroom. A pool of water on the floor outside the door began to flow into the bathroom as soon as the door was opened.

The stairwell had become a barrier against which a mass of unrelated junk was piled. There was part of a wall, a thicket of pine brush, various display tables, a heap of electronics junk, specialty plumbing supplies, and ravaged portions of once stunning wedding dresses scattered about the wreckage. The garbage was stacked at least ten feet high in the corridor all around the staircase. Tim climbed up the side of the stairwell to peer over the top of the heap. Once he could see into the corridor, he realized that the entire roof was gone from both the north end where he stood, and the south end where they had entered. If there had been a third floor, it was no longer. Broken glass was spread throughout the debris, creating a hazard for climbing. He could also see down the corridor. Unfortunately, part of the upper walkway was missing, so it was not possible to avoid climbing over the heaps by walking along the second level. It appeared that they must do some heaving, lifting, and climbing, just to get near the SUV…assuming it was still where he had parked it.

"What's it look like?" asked Fuerst.

"There is debris all the way to the stairwell that exits to the parking lot," Tim began, searching for a way out the front of the mall. "The other side of the corridor is clear," he said as he noticed that the stores were now open to the outside on the second level, allowing the light of day to penetrate. Anywhere that there had been windows, there were no more. The hurricane had blown its way straight through everything except for the concrete walls making up the outer frames of the four, square sections of the mall. The winds had piled a giant heap in the northeast corner just in front of him. As he looked from the second level down toward the Marauder, he could see another heap of debris where they had parked, particularly where the corridors intersected.

"Looks like the SUV is covered. We'll have to climb over this very carefully," Tim judged.

"I'll get Awad and our bags," suggested Fuerst.

Tim led the way over the pile of debris that now abutted the stairwell, stacked up to the second level of businesses. He found the safest route through the pines, the merchandise from the stores, and the glass, then took the bags so the other men could follow his path. Once they had arrived on the other side, each of them paused a moment to examine the stairwell leading out to the front parking area. It had been packed full of debris so tightly that there was no view of the lot. It would be impossible to exit that way.

Each of the four, square structures separated by the two long corridors had been gutted. It appeared that the wind had blown from the west, clearing out the stores and leaving piles of debris only where the concrete walls remained. Most of the second floor, and the entire third floor, were gone. The sunlight was streaming in laser-like beams through the corridor as it danced and reflected from the twisted metal and shattered glass.

The men crossed over to the other side of the corridor and made their way in the general direction of the Marauder. From where they stood, they could see that the vehicle was underneath a variety of debris similar to what they had just climbed through. As concerned as they were for the condition of their transportation, each of the men took every step with caution, surveying his surroundings with care, and awe. There was nothing moving, other than a few pieces of metal framing, and the remains of dresses waving in the morning breeze.

When they approached the SUV from the opposite side of the corridor, it was not visible. Worse yet, the perpendicular corridor had some gigantic pine trees wedged into the opening at its eastern end. Caught in these trees were all sorts of office furniture, electronics, sections of walls, and various pieces of an above ground swimming pool. Back toward the SUV, which had been parked only a few feet from the center of the structure, there were several more branches that were much smaller. However, it appeared a large section of a roof had blown, or fallen, onto the SUV. As they approached their ride, each man dropped the bag that he was carrying in one general area.

"Where do we start?" asked Awad as he moved his head this way and that, trying to get a glimpse of some part of the Marauder. It was difficult to see anything with the sun just above the horizon, beaming directly into his face as he tried to peer through the brush and other debris.

"We have to find the SUV," Tim said, imitating Fuerst's calm and matter of fact style. To his right, if they could uncover the Marauder, the corridor was open to the west, except for a smattering of glass that they would have to drive over to freedom. "Here's the path we need to keep clear," Tim pointed toward the heap in front of the van, then tracked his route through the corridor with his finger. "What we move away goes there or there," he pointed behind the van and to the other side of the planter.

"Let's get started!" Fuerst bent over and grabbed a couple of branches that he could easily drag across the corridor.

"Look at this!" exclaimed Awad as he reached for something to remove from the pile of junk. He was tugging at a tangled mass of electronic equipment.

"This is the sort of device that would be transmitting a signal from our software." Awad replied with confidence.

"Remember, there was an electronics store, over there?" Tim reminded Awad that they had peered inside through holes in the plywood barricades. Awad looked in the direction Tim pointed. The store was now gutted and open to the outside. Almost everything that was inside had been blown away by the hurricane. Some of the equipment could be seen scattered or piled in various corners of the remaining shell of the building.

Tim and Fuerst were combining their strength to try and drag the trunk of a pine tree away from their transportation. It was more than six feet long and almost two feet thick. "How the hell did this get here?" Tim asked Fuerst, not expecting an answer. All three men heaved with their collective strength to move the tree trunk. They hadn't yet moved it far enough to clear a path for the Marauder when they had found a lifeless body behind the tree trunk, twisted and crushed against the front bumper of the Marauder.

"Vendali!" Awad expressed shock as he closely studied the face of the limp and contorted body. When they had pulled the pine tree away, the corpse had fallen from the top of the bumper. The face was still recognizable, but the head was turned around facing upward while the remainder of his body laid on its front side. One arm was twisted grotesquely aside him. His chest was crushed, but there was not a lot of blood, as though the storm had washed it away.

"You *know* this guy?" Tim asked.

"Yes," replied Awad regrettably, thinking he would never wish this kind of death on anyone, despite the fact he had been prepared to kill Vendali himself.

"This is Salaam Vendali? Is that right?" Fuerst asked with disbelief as he turned to get a better look at the body. Awad nodded as he rested on one knee beside his lifeless comrade. Fuerst knew that Salaam Vendali had partnered with Abraham Jahir and Amir Awad in the production of the software capable of creating feelings for artificial intelligence. He also knew that Vendali was the mastermind behind the invention of the silicon chips, while Awad had written the algorithms for the software.

Fuerst had initially learned what he knew about the new circuits from Jan Greisfeld several years prior. The two men were good friends, and he was aware of Greisfeld's rendezvous with Kayla Bruster at the university. Fuerst had not realized the intimacy of their relationship, until Greisfeld had openly informed him about their tryst and its value for the future of the IAPN. On the one hand, Fuerst was surprised that a man who was some twenty years her senior had aroused her sexual interest. But, on the other hand, he knew that Greisfeld, a teacher of Political Science at the university, was suave and debonair. Greisfeld had acquired a devoted friend who had dedicated herself to the recently founded International Alliance.

Once she had learned that he was a leading proponent for the German branch of the Alliance, Kayla had become willing to do anything in her powers to advance its cause. She remained a close correspondent with Greisfeld. After she had informed him about the discoveries that Vendali had bragged about, and that he was seeking to have his chips mass produced, Greisfeld jumped at the opportunity to gather his resources in support of the project. Confiding in Fuerst, Greisfeld sought more information about the people with whom he was conspiring, and it was Jakob Fuerst who was dispatched to secretly gather as much information as he could about Kayla Bruster, Salaam Vendali, and Amir Awad. It was his investigation of Kayla Bruster that had eventually led him to Jake Altmeyer and his parents' company, Alt-X.

Staring reflectively at the body of Vendali, Awad was deep in thought about the history of their relationship. He relived the time when they had first seen the emotional response of the robot. He recalled that he and Vendali had taken a vow of secrecy, which was later shared by Abraham Jahir once he had begun to contribute to the development of SAI. They had decided not to publicize the invention. Instead, they had agreed to perfect the software and prepare it for broad application. They had also decided that any future application of the software required a unanimous agreement among the three. But, Salaam Vendali had no intention of keeping the oath. Ultimately, he pilfered an incipient version of the software for himself and abandoned the other two men, despite the fact he was not able to further develop the software on his own.

Awad was remembering how Vendali seemed to have gone mad after their first success at producing feelings in the robot. He had begun to express delusions about using the software to rule the world. With the help of Jahir, Awad had become more aware of Vendali's passion for power and realized that he could no longer be trusted. When Fuerst had met Awad in Tel Aviv, he intimated that Vendali was already talking to others, and had made arrangements to have the chip mass produced. So, Awad had fully expected his treachery.

Under the guidance of Fuerst and Greisfeld, Awad and Jahir conspired to bait Vendali, so that they might collectively implement their own plan to achieve the goals of the IAPN. If anything were to go wrong, and the grand scheme was exposed, then Vendali would take the fall.

Fuerst had already learned that Kayla Bruster was quite an ambitious woman, and he had shared this fact with Awad and Jahir. To set the plan into motion, Fuerst sought Kayla Bruster in Philadelphia during a convention for political candidates in 2035. When he found her, he identified himself as a close friend of Jan Greisfeld. Then, he offered her the unique golden chain that Greisfeld had always worn around his neck, even when he would shower and when they were making love. She identified the chain immediately because she had often fondled it while they were in bed. She demanded further proof of Fuerst's sincerity, and he was well prepared to provide it. When he began to speak of the silicon chips, she no longer had any doubts as to his authenticity. She even confirmed for Fuerst that more than a half a billion of them had already been produced, and they were ready for shipment.

At the same time, the CDC had announced that the new Ebola vaccine was nearly ready for production at the Eternity

Corporation. When Kayla told Fuerst that she had a close friend who was a chemist and lab technician at that corporation, then he realized that everything seemed to be falling into place to extend the power of the IAPN over a nation that was unwilling to cooperate with the Alliance. He garnered Kayla's cooperation and made sure that the chips would get to where they needed to be, then returned home to implement the plan with his cohorts.

When the timing was optimal, Jahir and Awad joked about a mad scheme for the use of their discovery in the presence of Vendali, attempting to motivate his treachery. Awad had asked Jahir what might happen if the chips were placed in the new Ebola vaccine, which had been deemed mandatory for every American citizen. He dropped the name of Kayla Bruster, saying that she was an ambitious politician who had friends at the biotech company that was producing the vaccine. Jahir responded with a deep laugh, and Awad followed, as if it were merely a joke. But this was precisely the sort of purpose that Vendali had in mind for their discovery. It was only a few days later when Vendali had disappeared to America to determine the possibility for such an endeavor.

The ploy seemed to have worked like a charm. Natalie Vincent had received the chips and identified a stage in the production of the vaccine wherein one chip could be infused into each vial. That work had already begun. Kayla Bruster assured Vendali that every American would receive a vaccine containing the advanced chip he had created, making him believe that *his plan* was being implemented.

However, the scheme did not work to perfection. Initially, the group had intended that their signal would be sent from Jake Altmeyer's control center. But Vendali had put his own plans into motion and set up his own system to transmit a signal. He had broken contact with Kayla Bruster, and the group had no clue concerning his whereabouts. About the time that the production of the vaccine was underway, Greisfeld had dispatched his own people to find Vendali, but they were unsuccessful. In fact, Vendali had expected that he would be sought. He assumed that Kayla Bruster, or Amir Awad, would be tracking him. He began scheming as to how he might be rid of them.

In the meantime, he had been spying upon the operations at the Eternity Corporation in South Carolina, hoping to acquire evidence that the chips were being infused into the vaccine as promised. But he had difficulty finding that proof. He desperately needed a place to stay in the nearby area, so he took a job with a family who had an electronics business not too far from the Eternity Corporation. He couldn't have hoped for better; they had a room he could rent above the store that was not only affordable, but it was on the third floor of an outdoor mall, directly above the business where he had gained employment. He decided that he would set up equipment to transmit a signal from the software in his own room, where he had access to the roof.

After the vaccine was distributed, and American people had begun to receive it *en masse*, Vendali had tried to broadcast a signal from the software. He had hoped that he could render the American people subservient to his own demands by increasing the intensity of the signal. But he was unable to fulfill his delusions. After trying for several days to detect changes in the population, he thought that he had failed to transmit a signal. He had begun to consider returning to Israel, until he learned of the zombies. He knew that his transmission of the signal had to be producing the zombies, and he was giddy with the power he controlled to inspire fear and wreak havoc. He was preparing to seek an accomplice to help him increase his powers over the people when this disaster had blindsided him.

Now Vendali was dead. Hurricane Alfonso had stopped him and the signal. The zombies were also gone.

"Help me place the body inside the planter," Awad requested of either man.

Tim offered to help. The planter was practically emptied of all dirt, not to mention all flowers, which were nowhere to be seen. Tim and Awad placed the body of Vendali into the planter, then Tim went back to work with Fuerst to remove more of the debris from around the SUV. Awad took a long look at Vendali before he went over to help the other men.

"I'm sorry," said Fuerst. "Your partner deserves better."

Awad laughed gently. "He could never be patient enough to follow a stable plan. There was little he could do with the software." Awad gestured with his arms stretched, palms upward.

"He obviously sent the zombies!" Tim asserted confidently.

Awad shook his head and pretended to laugh. "Do you think he created the zombies, young man?" Awad asked, with a tone that made Tim feel belittled.

"Well didn't he?" Tim was genuinely confused. He looked toward Fuerst for guidance, but Jakob stared down to the ground at his feet.

"He knows..." Awad hesitated and reformulated his statement. "He knew nothing about the software!" Awad offered no additional information about the chip, even as he thought to himself about Vendali's expertise in designing it. He could see that Tim did not know about the grand scheme.

The three men walked over to the planter wall and either leaned against or sat on it. Tim opened a bag with sandwiches, but then his gaze settled on the body and he changed his mind. He offered the bag to the other men, who shook their heads. Fuerst said, "I couldn't right now." Tim took a bottle of water from the bag and turned toward Awad. "So...who created the zombies?" He asked the question with urgency.

"I can tell you what I believe they must be," replied Awad. He was trying to figure out how to explain the source of the zombies to Tim. He decided to speak openly about the signal that Vendali transmitted. "The software that Vendali had was only developed to the point of "neutral attunement". We had not programmed any specific feelings, except experimentally in our lab. With the help of Doctor Jahir, I had established a neutral setting for the software to correlate with the *nature* of human empathy. The production of specific feelings would require writing additional algorithms."

"I'm so glad I asked," Tim quipped as he failed to make sense of what Awad had just told him.

Awad smiled and continued, "No specific feelings have been transmitted. In the current state of the software's development, it could only reflect an existential reality among those who receive the signal."

"Are you sure about that?" Tim objected to the explanation. "No one perceives the zombies without the signal, right?"

"That's right," Awad confirmed. "Zombies were produced when the signal from the software was transmitted to the chips. However, the zombies are some crude representation of a spiritual reality in the lives of the American people. I believe they represent some kind of alienation. I would say that the American people are not only alienated from society, but also from nature and from themselves.[1]

"What do you mean?" Tim objected to Awad's characterization of Americans.

"No vaccines from this lot have left this country, and it would seem that all persons who have been vaccinated were, in theory at least, able to sense the zombies. The feelings that were produced were those that *belong collectively to the American people*. They are those feelings that are most widely distributed throughout the population. Neither fear of death, nor a feeling of superiority, was transmitted electronically to the chips, nor were the zombies. This collective orientation of the population was electronically interconnected by means of the broadcast, and the shared signal must have transformed the spiritual reality into a sensible reality – the zombies. Not to worry, though. It is possible that we can neutralize these dominant feelings in the process of recalibrating the software."

"That sounds fuckin' crazy!" Tim retorted.

"Maybe so, but the predominant feelings of Americans can be readjusted. Jahir knows how to correlate changes to the software in relation to human empathy." That was all that Awad would tell Tim at this time. But he decided to add, "We shall get rid of those zombies! Instead, the American people will perceive a beautiful and welcoming nature, enticing them to respect each other." Awad laughed.

"Sounds like utopia," Fuerst thought out loud.

Awad went over to the body of Vendali and checked each of his pockets carefully. He had his passport and a wad of American money in his shirt pocket. He was carrying thirty-five one-hundred-dollar bills. In another pocket he had a miniature notepad. Awad found locations in his own pockets for these things without an ounce of guilt or bad faith. Only after he had checked every pocket, and carefully tucked away each piece of evidence that had belonged to the man whom he had once respected, did he carefully place Vendali in the best possible position to make him appear to be resting.

Meanwhile, Tim and Fuerst had made progress at uncovering the Marauder, except for the large piece of roof hanging over the top of it. Tim was pleased that he had parked it so close to the building. Not only was it partially protected against the corner of the building, but there was less area to clear around it to make room for Tim to drive it through the corridor and outside.

The windshield, and all the glass on the passenger side of the SUV, was shattered, but that was only a small problem. "Let's put these bags inside," Tim said after opening both passenger side doors.

"Not yet. How will we get the roof off the top?" Fuerst

asked hoping to prevent any sort of accident. The three men stepped back and tried to survey the situation. Tim stood on the wall of the planter that held the body of Salaam Vendali. The roof extended well beyond the top of the Marauder onto the second level of the mall. It appeared that it might be well supported by the second floor, so that Tim might be able to drive out from under it. The problem was that it was hanging three or four feet over this side of the SUV.

"I got it. Let's get some wood pieces and use them for props along this side to push the roof up as much as possible on this end." Tim went looking for 2x4s or pine branches or display tables – anything he could find to try and support the roof. He was content after placing three props toward the back of the SUV. He had two remaining. "I'm gonna get in and try to drive this outta here." Tim said as he tried to gauge how much weight was still on the top of the vehicle. "If the engine starts, shut the door and use those two pieces to prop up this side as high as you can." He pressed the starter, but the security alarm sounded. He had to change the start mode to an emergency setting that would activate the fingerprint reading device in the steering wheel. Once it recognized his prints by comparison to its most recent user, the Marauder started. Tim pointed toward the pine branches. The two men struggled but managed to raise the edge of the roof only about two inches or so away from the passenger side of the SUV. However, part of the roof still weighed upon the vehicle, and none of them were certain that it was not stuck underneath.

"Get our stuff out of the way…and yourselves." Tim put the SUV in drive and removed his foot from the brake, but no movement. He pressed the accelerator modestly, but still no motion until he gunned it briefly. The most irritating screeching sound followed what sounded like a blast, and the vehicle lurched forward a few feet until Tim released the accelerator. He could see in the rearview mirror that the back door had been caught on the roof. The glass shattered as the top of the door bent away from the roof of the Marauder. Unfortunately, all the props had fallen, and the roof was still draped over the rearmost portion of the vehicle. Jakob and

Amir had to reset the supports for another try to escape from under the roof.

Finally, the Marauder was released from the clutches of the debris. It was broken and dented but seemed that it could still go down the road. The three men loaded the bags and climbed in, then they set out to establish direction through the aftermath of Hurricane Alfonso.

Part III : Therapy

Chapter 20

Tim's Vision of Social Unity

Once they had devised a way to clear the worst of the glass from the aisle that would be their road to freedom, Tim coasted the battered SUV outside to find a radically changed landscape. He stopped upon exiting the corridor. The pine forest to the west and south had been reduced to a few groups of trunks, strewn with the remains of what had been people's comforts, their shelter, the accommodations within, their different modes of transportation, and more. Ironically, the parking area was relatively clear of debris, except along the remaining walls of the mall.

Tim drove up the hill toward the front exit. Bright sunlight illuminated the absolute devastation. The housing community that was so neatly built into the valley floor was demolished and scattered everywhere. There was no visible structure in the valley that was still intact. Heaps of broken building materials, furnishings and automobiles were stacked all along the crest of the hill. But, similar to the place that had saved their lives, some of the concrete buildings still had part of their ground level. The three men were speechless as they gaped at the vast destruction. No one was seen moving anywhere in the immediate area.

"This is a nightmare!" Fuerst couldn't manage to expel enough air from his lungs to speak it audibly. "We survived this destruction?" He tried to breathe before he said that.

"Everything is blown away!" Tim said with amazement. Awad was in the back, already inspecting his electronic gadgets. But he, too, stopped and gazed all around with a sick kind of awe. There was no conversation among the men for several minutes, only an occasional gasp and sigh.

"I see no one!" Awad quietly broke the silence. He imagined momentarily that everyone had been killed. The scene in front of them certainly motivated fantasy in more ways than one. But this reality could not be imagined away. Mother Nature was conducting her business with much more violence than she was accustomed to exhibiting, and these disruptions were more widespread and frequent. Was it a sign to awaken delusional humankind to the *real* powers of domination? None of the three men in the Marauder was able to deceive himself about his relation to this powerful force.

Tim was searching for a way around the worst of the debris. He could see a path through the landscaping on the right that was close to the road. The hurricane did not leave a clear pathway along any visible roadways. Debris was scattered indiscriminately in heaps. Some of the piles were in long lines stretching for miles. It almost looked as if they had been arranged by a bulldozer. The rules of the road had no limits beyond the obstacles of wreckage. Tim would have to negotiate his own terms with whatever he encountered. Travel was quite slow, sometimes requiring Tim to reverse course and seek a different pathway.

They had just travelled through a residential area that was absolutely devastated. Tim was able to find paths around the remains of the homes that once stood there. He was entering a business district that was on the edge of what had been a thriving town. They were only a few miles from where they had found protection against the hurricane, but he noticed that the damage was not quite as bad here. Some roofs were still intact, and the roads were more passible.

Then, around the next bend, was the very type of scene that the men had hoped to avoid. It was a large two-story building that had been a hospital. There were three ambulances on the scene, doors open, with victims inside. People were scrambling around the ambulances, and over toward the building. The men could hear the voices of medics and victims yelling things that they could not make out. It was apparent to Fuerst and Tim that victims were being dragged out from one side of the building. Half of the roof had blown off the hospital, but the other part of it had collapsed, causing part of the second floor beneath it to fall onto the first. Some people at the collapsed end of the building had to be rescued. Much of the work at rescue and recovery had been finished as the three men arrived.

"Let's go!" Tim said as he parked the SUV. Fuerst nodded and was quick to get out to help. Awad made his way a bit more slowly. He had put his equipment back into the bags after having inspected each piece carefully. There were injured people lying and sitting outside of the building in the landscaped areas close to the ambulances. Along the front of the building were several bodies of people who had not survived. Three men and three women medics were tending to a number of injured, while also trying to rescue survivors. Two of the women were scrambling to provide aid not only to those in the ambulances, but also to the injured lying in the grass. As Tim approached the building, a man and a woman exited through an open doorway, carrying another man who was bleeding from his chest. "What can we do?" he asked of them.

"Go inside. Please! You will see two men who need your help," one medic yelled toward Tim and Fuerst. Now, Awad was running to catch up. He followed them inside, where they could see dust hovering in the late-morning rays of sunlight. A path was cleared through the lobby toward the other side of the building where the second floor had collapsed. That was where the other medics could be found digging into the wreckage, guided by a voice that could be faintly heard. There were two other men working as quickly as possible in unison with the medics. Each one helped in whatever way possible. Tim, Fuerst, and Awad each assessed the work that was needed, and began to assist. In a few moments, the medic who had spoken to them outside had returned with his partner.

"There is one more person in this room. We have gotten fifteen out; five did not make it. There is one more woman buried inside. We can hear her voice. Pile this shit over here." He pointed and went back to digging through the rubble which had been the building structure.

Tim could hear someone crying for help under the rubble. Two medics were pulling away the wreckage, but with more and more care as they were getting closer to the person behind the voice. Tim felt the intensity and emotion in the effort of the man who had given him instructions. He could sense the pain of this man's struggle. And, no less, he felt the suffering of the victims of the collapse. Every one of these people was sharing the same pain. Suddenly, he flashed back to a feeling that he had in the bombed-out cabin as he helped Jean Bartok to safety with John Redfeather. A sickening feeling of dèjá vu slowly evaporated, but he continued to reflect as if in a dazed state. *"The internal senses of individuals are attuned alike in catastrophic situations."* He thought to himself. *"Each person is anxious over the crisis at hand, but also immediately concerned for the health and wellbeing of the other victims."*

Then he had an insight that was illustrated by this life and death situation. *"This happens in the absence of sympathetic experience!"* he insisted to himself. *"It is not necessary in the collective experience of crisis."* Tim was awed by his recognition that in catastrophes there is an existential identity of feeling among victims that constitutes a transcendental unity. *"What does this say about human sympathy?"* he wondered. *"And what about our genuine concerns for public health? We seem to care most about health when we are in crisis, yet outside of the sphere of human sympathy. Do our most noble concerns arise from some alternative to sympathy? Or its total absence?"* His reflection was interrupted by the cries of a woman whose legs had become visible from underneath the rubble. The corrective brace on her right leg had kept it straight and relatively unharmed, but her left leg was broken, twisted, and bloody.

"Alright, you guys, carefully lift these things off. Don't put any weight on this!" That same medic pointed to the remains of a wall which was still covering the backside of the woman. "Let me get a good look at her before she gets moved." Everyone worked to expose the entirety of this woman from beneath part of a laboratory wall. The medic was first to place his own head where he could see the face of the sobbing woman. Her tears were mixed with blood and dust. One of the other medics came with a stretcher. The area immediately surrounding the woman was then cleared of debris so the others could maneuver the stretcher underneath her as carefully as possible. Their work was precise and undertaken with great care.

Suddenly, Tim was alarmed by the noise of a helicopter approaching overhead. "Go outside and wait for the medics in the chopper." The man who seemed to be leading the group gestured toward Tim, Fuerst and Awad, among others. "Help them, please." he added.

Tim went outside into the hot, humid air, still in a fog of bewilderment. He sat down on the curb away from the ambulances and the injured, while the chopper was landing. He put his head in his hands and his thoughts flashed to a memory of something that Victor Frankl had said about victims of the holocaust[1] – a horror of human design. Those who had witnessed the atrocities at concentration camps had no fear of death, nor could they feel pity. Tim wondered if something similar happens when catastrophic natural events occur.

However, "man-made" and "natural" faded into each other. He buried his face between his knees, tried to keep focus on his insight, and gently wept. *"Each individual's anxiety over his/her own weakness, experienced simultaneously among victims within the same crisis, creates a transcendental unity among them. It is a spiritual identity of men and women wherein all comparative differences between them are absent from conscious awareness. The common deceptions are lost because no one can conceal the immediate crisis. There is no need for sympathy, because there is no need to transfer the miserable feelings; everyone already has them. It might be natural to cast out the real self, but it cannot be ignored in the midst of a catastrophe. Is this what Lyn is referring to when she says, 'One has to accept the real self'?"* Tim wondered to himself. *"Is that what happens in catastrophes?"*

Chapter 21

A Healthy Perspective on Nature

Redfeather and Jahir had arrived just as stronger, swirling winds had begun to rotate through the neighborhood. Jake had removed his vehicle from the garage in preparation for their arrival, so that Readfeather's truck could be hidden inside next to Tim's car. The two men were welcomed into the safety of Jake's basement, and they were pleased to sit back in a recliner with a cold beer and a shot of whiskey. There were a variety of foods and drinks, arranged in a cool location in the rear corner of the basement next to a small refrigerator. In short order, each man had fixed himself a plate to go with his beverage, then returned to his recliner.

The flowing tension within the violent atmosphere was the only thing that conflicted with good social relations that lasted into the early morning hours. Intense storms slammed the area, one after the other, beginning before midnight and continuing their assault well past that hour. Powerful, gusting winds launched smatterings of rain mixed with a variety of other debris, all of which was pelting against the glass block windows for three full hours. The most frightening event came with banging and crashing noises upstairs that no one had ventured to investigate.

Everyone tried to stay calm by discussing their hopes for a new and healthier relationship to the natural world. But, given the existing environment, it was not too difficult to understand how to cooperate with Mother Nature. She had forced them to shelter in safety. The type of respect she demanded also acquired a vital significance. Once the storms had subsided, and they had grown too tired to speak, each had gone to visit the world of sleep. The entire group lingered in that peaceful place as time passed toward the noon hour.

Three had been dreaming about American Indians – specifically, how they might have lived on the pristine land centuries earlier. The final thoughts they had entertained in the wee hours of the morning, once Clare and Jake and Michael and Rinna were asleep, moved them to envision an idyllic world, which they visited for much too short a time. It was Redfeather and Jahir who had been talking about the American Indians and their vital orientation to nature. This subject arose from a natural order of events. All three of them had been motivated to focus on something other than their own apprehension, caused by the violent pounding against their protective shelter. Each one had tried to seek his/her own harmony in a new context amidst the anxieties.

The late-night conversation began before the constant pressures assaulting the glass block windows had first begun to subside. With a gentle smile on his face, John Redfeather facetiously suggested "Mother Nature is upset with us."

"We should learn a lesson from this man!" Jahir said to Lyndsey, nodding and glancing over toward Redfeather. "He has been well schooled by his ancestors about the value of the land. We have had interesting discussions about different territories of the West and mid-West, including national parks. I owe him greatly for having been my tour guide, a spiritual guide, and a safe driver." Jahir spoke with one hand over his chest and the other raised out toward Redfeather. Then he said, "I am particularly interested in this man you call Chief Seattle."

"He was a truly holy man. He wanted to preserve the way of life that is healthy and natural," Redfeather replied.

"Chief Seattle was a great leader, whom the settlers from the European world had to reckon with in order to survive in the west." That was how Jahir had understood Redfeather's account of the wise chief. "Tell them how his people interpreted their surrounding environment; how they envisioned their world of life."

Redfeather obliged, showing great pride in his response. "One should be attuned to nature with the same respect one would show for one's closest relatives. In truth, all people, and all of nature, are intimately related. The memories and heritage of a people is materialized in the land that they inhabited, where they farmed, hunted, and played. Chief Seattle warned the aggressive pioneers about the dangers of losing touch with nature and our ancestral heritage. Those men who wanted to buy the land of his people were not attuned to the environment. They were not interested in protecting and caring for the land. They were not nourished or raised in the Western frontier. The history of the land had been unknown to them."[1]

"Do you think we could return to an orientation toward nature that belonged to an indigenous people centuries ago?" Lyndsey felt the need to play the devil's advocate.

"We must redefine our relation to nature with a new attunement." Redfeather used a term that he had learned from Jahir. "We must follow the lead of Chief Seattle and teach every worldly inhabitant to love the land as one's own ancestral heritage."

"People have no respect for each other, let alone the rest of the natural world," insisted Lyndsey with a cynical feeling that made her uncomfortable.

"It is a different time, no doubt," lamented Redfeather, "but our lack of respect for each other is just another instance of our lack of respect for nature. We *belong to* nature.[2] That was

Chief Seattle's primary message. The new migrants believed they could *own* nature. They had a backwards view of their environment; they were not products of the local nature, but they thought themselves to be its possessors. The Great Chief considered them to be ignorant fools."

As the early morning hours had dragged them into sleep, the last things they expressed in speech were creative metaphors that painted a mental picture of the American Indians' vision of a nascent environment. It was an animistic dream world.[3] The spirits of their ancestors inhabited natural entities and forces. It was a world full of flourishing life.

But now they were awakening to the strange world of contemporary realities. Jake had arisen first. He proceeded to go upstairs to size up the damage from the freak storm. His hope was that he would encounter a minimum of obstacles to reconstruct his control center in the attic. He was wise to dismantle the components and put them in a safe place in case the attic could not withstand the force of the storms. In fact, he felt lucky that he still had an attic. One end of it was drenched from the rain that travelled along with the winds. The southmost facing window had blown in and shattered. It was reduced to dangerously sharp splinters that Jake had to pick up piece by piece as he started the long task of cleaning up the mess.

Back in the basement, Jahir had awakened to the pleasant indication that Awad, Fuerst and Tim were alive and well, but trying to navigate through a landscape of destruction. They would find a way to Pittsburgh, Awad assured him. To Jahir's surprise, this message ended with a short statement: "Vendali is dead." He had not given a thought to Vendali since leaving Arizona. While sitting in the underground vault of the cabin, he even wondered whether the fire-bombing and mass shooting had been Vendali's work. At the time he'd mused, "*it would be in keeping with his character to try and silence anyone who might try to stop him. But he could not have orchestrated that attack, could he?*" Then Jahir briefly thought of Jan Greisfeld and other victims at the cabin, knowing that Vendali had joined them in silence. For a moment, he wondered if Awad had killed him.

The news about Vendali had also moved him to recall how Jan Greisfeld's death had caused a significant change in their plans. Jakob Fuerst had wanted to remain behind the scenes, but the murder of his colleague had forced him to assume the position of President of the IAPN. However, that would not change the fact that Fuerst was the man in charge of coercing the most powerful countries of the world to join the Alliance. He had coordinated groups to work toward that end in two other countries where the people had been trained with an attitude of domination: China and Russia. But his first priority was to guarantee that the work in the U.S. was on course. There were bigger impediments to overcome to coerce the Chinese and the Russians to join the world in an attitude of respect and cooperation.

"I have good news for you," Jahir said to Lyndsey as he saw her eyes open, and her head turn in his direction. "Your brother is fine. He is on his way here now."

"Oh, that's great!" Lyndsey rubbed her eyes, then sat forward, emptying the remains from her water bottle into her dry mouth.

Clare sat forward with a grand smile, though her eyes were not opening easily. Michael had begun to wiggle on her chest, and this had brought her back to the conscious world just in time to hear the good news. She reached for her tear duct with her left index finger. "You hear that?" she gently tapped Michael's nose, then kissed it. "Daddy is coming home! Hooray!" She was pleased that Michael had allowed her to rest for so long. He, too, had slept for several hours straight through for the very first time. His long sleep had likely been induced by two hours of restlessness and unease during the noisy storms.

Before any of them could leave their makeshift beds, Jake had returned to the basement to give everyone the lowdown on the current state of his house. "The south wall of the attic is soaked. One of the windows blew out. Water ran into the walls down to the first floor, right in the middle of the house." Jake was shaking his head as he reported this damage.

"What about the control center?" Lyndsey asked.

"I disassembled it yesterday and put it in the master closet, covered with tarps. We were fairly lucky. Some water came in the roof, and we have some damage, but the equipment is dry," Jake reported this with a nod and pursing of his lips to indicate his satisfaction with the condition of his electronics. "I have a lot of work to do while it is daylight."

"How can I help, young man?" Jahir slowly stood up. He expressed his intention to do whatever was necessary so that they could get Jake's attic back to normal. The condition of the control center was as important to Jahir as it was to Jake. Building the hardware system was typically the work of Vendali and Awad back at the lab in Israel. However, Jake would prove to be an adequate replacement for Vendali. Taking care of the hardware would be his valuable contribution to their endeavor. This was his house, and his sophisticated home electronics already contained the most basic components needed to broadcast the signal. Jahir would rely on his expertise until Awad could arrive and complete the system.

"I'll let you know as I need the help," Jake replied. "First, I have to check the roof. I have to prevent any more leaks and dry the attic." Then, he turned to Lyndsey. "Lyn, can you make sure we have candles and flashlights for the entire house, in case we are still without electricity when darkness comes."

"Sure thing!" Lyndsey walked over and hugged him gently and kissed him on the cheek. He returned the affection modestly. "Is our upstairs livable?" She was tired of the dark basement.

"Yeah," Jake responded with ambivalence, "but it is wet along the wall at the base of the stairs to the control center."

Lyndsey went up to survey the damage. As she did, the others followed to the main floor, except for John Redfeather. He continued to rest a couple hours longer than the others. The trip from the Pima Indian Reservation had been a long one for him. It was quite pleasant in the beginning, while he was reminiscing about places where he had not been in fifty years. But Redfeather was 70 years old, despite the fact he appeared to be much younger. The long excursion had overwhelmed him. After all, he had driven all the way to Pittsburgh from Missouri, eleven-and-a-half-hours, only stopping so that he and Jahir might relieve their bladders, and grab drinks and snacks. Furthermore, his experience at the restaurant with Jahir, when he was recognized, was one of the first times he had ever felt that his own freedom was in jeopardy, as though he had done something wrong.

Lyndsey had found that the back bedroom on the first floor had also gotten wet. Something had happened to the window on the other side of the barricade. At least the boards had prevented most of the water from penetrating through the pane that had pulled away from its frame. She went out to get a better look, and to her surprise Jake had followed behind her.

"I can fix that easily," said Jake, realizing that he had not properly secured the pane into the window frame. He was looking around, trying to understand how the glass had not shattered. While Jake went through the necessary routine to reattach the bedroom window, his concern had returned to the roof. That was where he needed to make a closer inspection. He was getting help from Lyndsey, and Jahir who was working to clean and dry the upstairs. Jahir had also made a temporary cover out of cardboard for the open hole where the attic window had been. Once the roof and broken window were repaired as well as possible, and the drying process for the attic had begun, Jake turned his attention to the reassembly of his computer system.

But other technical work had to be done before they could broadcast a signal from a modified version of the software. Jahir needed to specify the psychological parameters that would guide Awad's re-attunement of the software. Ultimately, the aim was to transmit an attitude of respect and cooperation. Jahir was astounded by the results of Vendali's broadcast. Vendali did not know how to develop software. He could not use it to produce specific feelings in the population. He had only the original software, which had been fixed at a neutral setting. But somehow, his broadcast of that neutral setting had produced the zombies.

The neutral setting was specifically intended to produce no feelings whatsoever; it was simply *the ground* for further development of the software throughout the entire spectrum of human feelings. Jahir had determined this neutral setting for robotic sensitivity in direct correlation with the *nature of human empathy*. He would have to define creative movements of empathy that motivate specific feelings, and these movements would have to be translated into algorithms by Awad to produce those feelings in the targeted population.

However, SAI was not designed to produce feelings *in people*. It had been developed to enhance artificial intelligence. Nevertheless, Jahir had begun to conceive the changes that Awad would have to make to eliminate the zombies. As he engaged in this reflection, he wondered whether he might be going mad, as Vendali had, as he realized that the grand scheme to save mankind from self-destruction appeared to be within the realm of real possibility.

Chapter 22

Removing the Flagrant Deceptions

Lyndsey had finished preparations for the coming darkness without electricity when unexpectedly, but to the pleasure of all, the service had returned. Her community was reaping the benefits of having gradually converted all overhead electrical lines to underground. This was one of the rare occasions they had lost power since that change was completed. She left the bedroom where Clare and Michael were staying and walked into the den. Jahir had retired to the living room with his laptop. She saw him there and went to join him.

Jahir had been puzzling over this unexpected utilization of their invention. When he had initially begun his work with Awad and Vendali, Jahir had felt certain that the production of feelings in robots required that the neutral setting of the software should correlate with human empathy. He believed this was necessary for feelings to be shared comparably between humans and artificial intelligence. But now he wondered whether this decision had resulted in a compounding of deceptions and errors for the target population. Specifically, he was thinking about the potential for deception that accrues from the self-comparison essential to empathy. He wondered whether this had prevented a genuine, neutral setting for the software.

Jahir began to think aloud. "The extent to which empathy is ineffective for a transfer of feelings lies in its inability to result in a perfect sharing of feeling. The source of all deception and error might begin here. The shared feeling is not identical to the original. If this were a problem, how would I work around it to accurately identify the neutral setting for the software? Do we need an entirely different basis for neutrality?" He finally decided that these were questions that Awad would have to help him to answer.

Jahir opened his laptop to his writings on the heroic attitude. He knew that, to eliminate the zombies, they would have to neutralize the dominant feelings essential to this attitude. He would have to deconstruct society's shared internal sense, as if it were an onion with rotten outer layers but a good core.

"Hello, Doctor Jahir!" Lyndsey smiled with her usual charm.

"Ah! Hello, young lady," he responded. Redfeather entered and sat down quietly nearby, a bottle of water in his hand.

Lyndsey was concerned for the comfort of her guests as she looked around at the state of the house. She tried to ignore the fact that sunlight was barely able to penetrate the barricades covering the windows, and an unpleasant odor had begun to emit from the damp wall in the hallway. She turned her thoughts elsewhere. "There is still more of what we had last evening for food. We also have packaged meals that can be quickly heated. Please, help yourself to the kitchen, pantry and basement." She thought that no one should go hungry. "Do not expect me to get dinner. Even Rinna gets her own." Lyndsey chuckled, thinking about her daughter with pride.

"I have been eating ever since I awakened. I had some of the fruit with bran crackers. Please accept my sincere gratitude for your hospitality." Redfeather said with a bow toward Lyndsey.

"You are quite welcome. Continue to help yourself. Now that the power is back on, I have to put what was on ice downstairs into the fridge...but not until the fridge is good and cold." Lyndsey was reminding herself, not asking for help, but both men offered to help. That made her want to change the subject. Jahir could see that.

"Well, Lyndsey," he began to ask, "did you read the article attached to my contact line?"

"I did! I was fascinated, wondering how the zombies could be eliminated if the heroic attitude could be neutralized. But" Lyndsey continued, "I'm not sure I followed your thoughts on attunement."

"Well, I am talking about the software in that case. I believe that is not your expertise. You can follow the psychology, I'm sure?" Jahir asked. Just then Redfeather stood up and excused himself to see whether Jake needed any help upstairs. Lyndsey and Jahir acknowledged his decision and continued their conversation.

"Yes, I understood the psychology behind the heroic attitude, but the idea of attunement is perplexing. In addition, the idea of a neutral setting confused me," Lyndsey stated, not entirely certain that she understood what Jahir was trying to adjust.

"I am working with software which, I believed, was calibrated to a neutral setting and precisely correlated with human empathy. However, transmission of this signal to the target population produced the zombies, along with the fear of death and aggression." Jahir replied.

"I think I understand that. But I am confused by your plans to change those sentiments in people. How could you accomplish that?" Lyndsey asked.

"Yes...this is not yet clear to me, but I believe we can modify the existing software, and correspondingly change the dominant attitude among the population."

"What? I honestly can't believe that!" Lyndsey looked at him with amazement. "That's why you were distinguishing different levels of self-deception? Can fear of death and aggression simply be modified out of existence along with self-deception?" Lyndsey spontaneously made a short, breathless chortle.

"You could say that." Jahir began. "The phenomenal existence of the zombies seems to suggest that the neutral setting of our software does not correlate with a neutral orientation *in the American people*. In order to approach the latter, we would have to 'dial-back' through the centuries of training that has evolved into what exists currently. The artistic re-creation of human feelings via empathy is Western man's most significant legacy to himself. It is epitomized in the heroic attitude. The software indicates that this is the fundamental attitude of American society. This self-deceptive orientation to the surrounding world has to be stripped away layer by layer from common experience to make the adjustment."

"You aim to remove the aggressive self-deception intrinsic to the heroic attitude?" Lyndsey was trying to recall the specific deceptions.

"The tendency to envision others as weaker in comparison to oneself is a mental habit which founds a conscious orientation to the world that creates the zombies. One deceives oneself by imagining an ideal self, superior to others, and conceals the reality." Jahir reminded her.

"Yes, I recall. The ideal self is imagined to have special powers that define its superiority." Lyndsey spelled out what she thought he might say.

"The ideal self is epitomized within the heroic attitude. But I do believe that it is founded upon the act of pity, which is itself a compound of human sympathy."

"Yes, I recall that the act of pity has a very special significance for you," she said, hoping to hear an explanation of the claim that she recalled quite well.

"To eliminate the zombies, we have to go back through each of the levels of self-deception that make up the ideal self, until we arrive at the seed where a fear of death attains its root in the spirit of the American people." Jahir had mentioned the very concept she wanted to learn more about. "I believe that this fear is constituted within the act of pity. In pity one *decides* that the other is the one who suffers. Fear of death manifests within this intentional comportment to others. The self-comparison in pity is *not* purely *sympathetic*. If it were, then some specific feeling would have been sought for the sharing.

"Pity changes the fundamental sympathetic comparison," Jahir continued. "In this act of pity, a *difference* of feeling is constituted *in contrast to* the typical *identity* of feeling sought by means of basic sympathy. Empathy, in general, ideally aims for an identity of feeling. The comparison in sympathy occurs naturally. However, the comparison in pity appears to have a different origin. Therefore, I believe that I must neutralize this comparative *distinction* that conditions an act of pity. This is how we shall make an end to the heroic attitude."

Jahir's expression briefly softened to one of a man envisioning his ideal world, before firming with determination to make that vision a reality. "Imagine, if public expressions of such comparisons were forbidden! Use of this comparison by politicians is especially reprehensible, and most unproductive. It is, therefore, our intention to coerce our population into the desensitization of pity."

Lyndsey was trying to connect the ideas. "If we abort the side of self-comparison that differentiates self and other that is essential to an act of pity, then what remains of sympathy?"

"What remains is the basic self-comparison that strives ideally toward an *identity of feeling*. This is fundamental to empathy, no?" asked Jahir. *He* thought it was. That is why he had determined this to be the point of the neutral setting for the software, as if it were a *natural* zero setting. But he was no longer certain that this was the correct way to calibrate the neutral setting. Nevertheless, this would have to be his starting point for attuning the American population.

"So, if you could neutralize pity, you would still preserve sympathy but remove fear of death?" Lyndsey wanted to demonstrate that she was now able to follow what Jahir meant by attuning the American population. "Yes, and that would change the entire population's social orientation," replied Jahir, as though there could be no doubt.

"Is your goal what some psychoanalysts have referred to as 'fear of death unrepressed'?" asked Lyndsey. "Has this not been rejected as practically impossible?"[1]

"There are a few interesting opponents to that position from the 20th Century.[2] But, yes, fear of death unrepressed is critically portrayed as a utopian dream. No professional would reasonably claim that such a thing is possible. Anyone who does would be treated with contempt, and not taken seriously. But…times do change, no?" Jahir looked at her and smiled.

"And we would change drastically, would we not? Would everyone not be lost and confused, and feel that we have been thrown into a foreign society, if we were to have a sudden change of our predominating orientation to the world?" Lyndsey wondered how this new people would survive within the existing society. "How will that affect our social institutions? Will our society be able to change on-the-fly to match our new orientation to the world?"

"Unfortunately, it will be necessary to some extent. We have scholars addressing these issues, including your brother, Tim. Things will be quite different when the attitude of respect becomes predominant. The survival of traditional American capitalism and its institutions will depend upon its capacity to thrive on the grounds of the new conscience. Guilt will remain a formidable force for self-guidance. However, laws and moral principles will be ultimately founded upon respect and cooperation."

"We shall have to make significant changes!" Lyndsey smiled, until a lump formed in her throat, forcing her to swallow.

"Respect is goodwill toward other people and nature. It includes the wish, and the endeavor, for the flourishing of natural life. In that sense, the attitude of respect and cooperation fosters good health in general. Public health will be the primary aim of our institutions. The collective health of its citizens is itself incalculably profitable for any nation," Jahir claimed.

"If this is the guiding aim for reconstructing conscience, then what kinds of things will produce guilt?" Lyndsey asked.

"Overcoming the self-comparison peculiar to pity is paramount. It is the focal point for a new and different training, and a reconfiguring of conscience. We must unlearn, then forbid, the *spontaneous and habitual* use of self-comparison to express personal superiority. We must learn to be aware of this tendency to the point that we overcome the spontaneity, and subject it to scrutiny. We shall learn anew how to display our self-esteem. Expressions of *self-comparisons of distinction* in public will no longer be acceptable!"

Lyndsey had to hold her breath momentarily to prevent herself from bursting into laughter. "That will put a crimp on the practices of democrats and republicans! The usual Congressional speech will become taboo!"

"Yes," Jahir smiled. "To their demise, cooperation is bound to result. Conscience is to be reconfigured on this principle. And punishment has to be calculated and promulgated against these bastard comparisons. Perhaps the guilty should be placed into a *hall of distinction*, by himself/herself, exalted for all the public to see? We want the people in our society to feel shame for any self-proclaimed distinction. It is fine to be different, and excellent in one's own right, but self-*expression* of one's own excellence, or another's inferiority, should not be tolerated. People must learn to be satisfied with their own accomplishments in humility and abstain from making public comparisons to others."

"Well..." Lyndsey was feeling quite cynical now, "that would probably require a whole new religion to unite all people."

"That is correct, Lyndsey," Jahir began. "We have theologians working on one world religion. I am not an authority on this topic. However, I have been told about a Mother God, and a personal animism. There are also taboos I have heard. For example, there is no grim reaper. Mother Nature has her violent tendencies, but she does not seek our death. Rather, she has given us life, nourishment, and shelter, to have a place with her. The opting for a Mother God epitomizes the rejection of the traditional dominant, masculine divinity. Moreover, the new religion will be more attuned to the natural experience of the human being. There is no omnipotence or omniscience predicated of the Mother God. She is alive, embodied, and makes our home."

"An honest and realistic agreement about our place in the universe might just bring us together," Lyndsey deduced.

"As a family, we must begin a practice of seeking self-knowledge," continued Jahir. "Our new training will require a cultivation of privacy, a form of transcendental self-discovery. We must help our children to accomplish a self-awareness based upon truth, but also with respect for the mysteries of conscious life. Specifically, each individual must attune one's unique and personal self to its natural environment with respect. This is absolutely essential to creating public health."

Lyndsey was confused because she was trying to envision daily life in this new world. "How will everyone work together? Or will life be spent more in reflection and play among one's loved ones?"[3]

"That is a very good question. I do not have a complete answer," Jahir had to honestly admit that he had not worked out all of the solutions. "Certainly, we must begin with special care for our children and our elderly as we do the work that we must. Family care must be integrated with healthcare and the workplace. This is the most important social problem to work out. With the rise of artificial intelligence, and the more prominent use of robots for all sorts of jobs, it is not entirely clear how we shall be spending our time, but we must be oriented toward a wider sense of family and devoted to public health and the flourishing of nature."

"And that is the aim of our laws, and our new constitution?" asked Lyndsey.

Jahir was trying to comprehend the changes this would require for legal institutions in the new American society. He was no lawyer, but he had always appreciated some of the processes of the American legal system. However, the laws themselves would acquire a new foundation that would ultimately create conflicts with the old constitution. "There are scholars working on this too. We could speak of changes in particular laws. For example, making respect for others a legal and moral necessity will forbid the *exploitation* of weakness and ignorance for profit."

Jahir had hardly finished saying this when Lyndsey laughed out loud. "Advertisers will have a major challenge in our new society! The production of ads has become an art of manipulating feelings. Perhaps we should adopt strict guidelines for the presentation of a product that is for sale. Only facts are relevant. We must return to what is most important in an ad."

"Yes, you are quite correct," said Jahir. "Information about the product must be clear and accurate, and persuasive efforts minimal and overt."

"It seems only fair that no one's weakness should be manipulated for profit. This is consistent with the fact that the sick and the elderly must be respected in our society," Lyndsey deduced. "Neither can there be any minorities created by prejudice in language or deeds. On principle, everyone is equal in deserving basic respect."

"We must acquire new insights into how one makes recompense for the strength and good health that one enjoys, and the care one receives and provides unto death. At no time can anyone become prey for vultures who produce their lifelines." Jahir spoke as if there could be no doubt about such a principle. "The values of products and public entities are subordinate to the health of the people they serve. It seems that the ultimate calculation and distribution of profits in our society – particularly in the world of medicine – ought to be determined over a lifetime, and not by point of contact purchases."

"What about our ultimate weakness?" Lyndsey asked. "It is your aim to remove the repressed fear of death from our American society. That is, you intend to forbid the mental activity which produces it? That definitely suggests that something must be wrong with the way Americans are oriented toward death. Therefore, we shall have to ask what understanding and 'feel' for death is appropriate."

"This is a most important question!" Jahir stated emphatically. "A collective, repressed fear of death can be no more. We must take care to represent death for what it is, especially in speech. Furthermore, our expectations about death in life need to be suitably managed. Might we doubt whether it is *absolutely necessary* that one must die?"

"Well…we have to be realistic. But just because everyone who has lived in the past has eventually died, there is no *absolute* necessity that all of us alive today will die."

"That is true…*logically,* that is. It might provide a ground for *mystery*, no matter how remote the possibility, to say that death is not absolutely necessary."

"No one can know the future!" Lyndsey insisted.

"Death is most strange as an event in life. It happens only once, to mark the end of an organic life. No one can build personal experience about it. Yes, yes, we have personal experiences with the death of others, and this goes a long way toward forming our attitude toward death, but there is no personal experience of death *per se*. What do I honestly know about death, in terms of it being my own? We must be open to speaking frankly about this as a society and answer this question with honesty."

"There are definitely assumptions in our society about death! Religion claims to have the answers," Lyndsey exclaimed with authority. "We make every effort to prevent ourselves from openly dealing with death. It is not something that people speak about at length, even with family members. We have all sorts of rituals to wash our hands of close encounters with the reality. Our use of euphemisms disguises the facts with gentle, heavenly language. We need to take care with language to accurately represent death without the euphemisms. Basically, death is just another threat to our frail nature. If we could accept it as such, with just a moderate amount of concern and anxiety over it, would that mark a new starting point?" she ended with a question.

"There is much work to be done to build a healthy and realistic expectation about death," Jahir insisted, shaking his head.

Then Jake came bouncing down the stairs into the living room, Redfeather quietly following behind him. "We almost have my control center set up." That was welcome news to Lyndsey *and* Jahir.

Rinna and Clare approached them, Clare carrying Michael. The whole crew was present and accounted for in the living room, amidst the barricaded windows, all lights lit as darkness was soon to make its return outside. They all glanced around at each other for a moment without saying anything.

Suddenly, a knock at the door was "felt" like an explosion by the adults inside. Apprehension flowed through the group as if it were transmitted from Awad's software. Lyndsey immediately hushed Rinna and motioned for Clare to go downstairs. Both Redfeather and Jahir had arisen in silence with the rap at the door. Neither of them needed any guidance to follow Clare and Michael. They adjourned in an orderly fashion, hastily, down the stairs as a group.

Jake unlatched the locks and opened the door. On the other side was a vaguely familiar face. He was donning a badge that identified him as a member of the FBI.

"How do you do, sir?" the man replied. "My name is Salvatore Conte. As you can see, I am with the FBI." He looked past Jake to see Lyndsey standing behind Rinna, peering toward the door, her hands on Rinna's shoulders. "I am looking for Timothy Austin."

"He isn't here," said Jake.

"Do you know where he is?" the man continued.

"I do not." Jake was curt.

The man was quick to continue. "The reason I came here is because I believe this is the address of his sister, Lyndsey Austin."

"That's right," responded Lyndsey immediately. "But I have not heard from him since the attempt on his life in Arizona."

"Then you are aware of his associations?" the man asked.

"I am aware of everything that I have seen on news reports, and read online," Lyndsey intended to severely restrict any further questions. Jake walked outside, hoping that Conte would follow.

"It looks like you have all your windows barricaded?" Salvatore Conte said with an inflection that indicated a question.

"Yes, well, between zombies and storms we have been attacked from several directions." Jake replied.

"Have you been attacked by zombies?" Conte asked.

"We have actually suffered an attack." Jake added, "Zombies had broken my windows, so I made the barricades."

The man sensed that Jake's impatience was increasing, so he decided to leave. "Those wood planks probably saved you some trouble from that storm, too," he said as he spied numerous branches of various sizes strewn about the entire neighborhood.

"They didn't hurt." Jake was done talking now.

"Look, we only wish to question Mister Austin. If you speak with him, please tell him to contact us," the man added, handing a card to Jake. "I thank you for your cooperation."

As Jake received the card from the hand of Salvatore Conte, he remembered where he had seen him before. He and Kayla Bruster had met him once at a restaurant in the city. He recalled that Kayla seemed to have been a friend of this man. Since Conte had seen her with Jake in the past, he probably remembered Jake to have been acquainted with her. He watched as Conte turned around in his driveway, cautiously avoiding one large branch on the left side. Then he cruised slowly down the road. Jake watched as he drove away, then turned to go inside. *"It really is a small world,"* he thought to himself.

Chapter 23

The Search for New Leadership

The tires were rapidly approaching the pavement of the landing strip at the airport in Butler, Pennsylvania. It had been a rough ride in the small plane which Kayla had bought soon after she had acquired her license. Flying along the mountains, a dizzying turbulence literally and figuratively shook them to the bone. She could hardly assure the men that there was no immediate danger. But now she was glad to be landing. She thought about getting something to eat at her first opportunity, and her taste buds were watering with the thought. The plane bounced slightly upon contact with the runway, then she slowed it considerably, made a U-turn, and taxied past a couple of hangars toward an area where it could be parked for the short term.

Tim couldn't have been more pleased when Fuerst told him that Kayla was flying her private airplane to Rock Hill, South Carolina, to pick them up. It was the nearest airport to Columbia that was functioning. But, getting that far was a miserable adventure for the three men. Tim had not begun driving until nearly noon, after they had freed the Marauder from the debris that had hidden it from open view. Driving, and riding in, the Marauder was most unpleasant. The only windows remaining were on the driver's side; the rest were broken. Early in their journey they had to stop near a marsh, littered with the mangled wood frame of someone's roof, to tie the back door shut. Luckily, there was a long run of cable wrapped around a pole along the side of the road. Tim used it to bind the door shut from the inside so they could continue down the road without having to hear a constant banging.

It was hot, with scorching sunlight, and the air was strangely volatile. At times it felt as a clear, sunny day normally feels, except that on this summer day it was nearly 100 degrees already. A wave of sticky, smelly air passed through, and it was unbearable. With it, the humidity increased rapidly. It lasted for over an hour. There was no way to escape the sweltering sauna.

The men had begun their long journey from a small town outside of Columbia. They hadn't travelled far before encountering the hospital, where they had helped the medics load injured victims onto helicopters. When they had resumed travel they were soaked, mostly with their own sweat, and filthy. Once Tim had maneuvered the SUV around the many obstacles that slowed his progress, and travelled northward a few miles, there were less obstructions on the roads. But that didn't make the trip any more pleasant...especially in the absence of a windshield.

As soon as he had begun to encounter other vehicles on the roads, Tim had become genuinely afraid that he would get pulled over by the police. He had already warned Fuerst that he could be detained for any reason if his virtual file had been marked for apprehension. As this possibility sent him a chill, he wondered how and when he might have to take himself to the authorities and answer whatever questions they might have. "*Nah.*" He thought otherwise, without reservation.

Tim believed that he was due for a break from the gods – a little good luck. He had encountered one catastrophe after another, and it was beginning to weigh upon him. He wanted to be with Clare and Michael, and although he was feeling closer to them for the first time in a long time, they were nonetheless outside the realm of his immediate perception. However, his anticipation was strong enough to create a virtual reality.

Kayla parked the airplane near the building where a small crew was prepared to aid her and her passengers as they exited the plane. They were also prepared for refueling. Fuerst was the first to exit. When he stepped onto the tarmac, his legs wobbled, and he was lucky that a member of the crew had already been reaching for his arm as though the stumble was expected. Fuerst was thankful, then collected himself to slowly walk toward the building. Awad hopped off, carrying his bags with no difficulty. Then, Tim exited, and Kayla followed.

The late evening air in Butler was warm and muggy, but it was not as hot as the air had been in South Carolina. The men were all wanting to get washed and change into fresh clothes. On the way to the building, they were talking about allowing a cool flow of water to run over their heads. This was a small first step for them toward feeling refreshed. Inside the building was a dining area with a variety of conveniences, one of which was a dispenser complete with an assortment of meals. Kayla guided herself to the meal dispenser as the men excused themselves to an elaborate facility where they could wash and change clothes, if he had any to change into. Only Awad was thus prepared. He had clean, white t-shirts wrapped around his electronic equipment in the bags. However, there were also two clean shirts in Kayla's airplane, one each for Tim and Fuerst.

As Tim had come back from the facility, he approached Kayla Bruster. "You must have nerves of steel!" Tim said to her, raising his brow. "That was a most unpleasant flight!" He added with his eyes still wide open.

"I'm sorry," Kayla Bruster began, "but the turbulence was worse than usual tonight. I have encountered worse over those very same mountains, believe it or not."

"I would not want to feel that again. I've had a rough week. I want to go home and just lie around with my wife and son," Tim sounded delirious, almost to the point of whining. He knew he was within twenty miles of being able to fulfill that desire.

"I don't blame you," Kayla began, "and you are almost there now." She smiled warmly toward him.

"No one told me that The People's Party was going to have a candidate in this year's election!" Tim was looking for an explanation. He continued. "And was Fuerst serious in suggesting that I could be Vice-President?"

Kayla put the last bite of her meal into her mouth as if to prevent herself from responding. Then, she reached for the napkin on her lap, daintily wiped her mouth, folded it in half, and placed it on her empty plate. After she swallowed, she took a gulp of water from a bottle, cleared her throat, then clenched her hands on her lap.

"Sometimes the plans announce themselves as an opportunity arises, Tim," she used his name to try and achieve a more personal connection to him. "Perhaps you would reconsider?" she asked, not expecting him to change his mind.

"I want a private life. I could never be an elected official. I just want a simple family life…at least to the extent that it is still possible for me." Tim was wondering what exactly a normal life might feel like.

"Well, that is our loss. You are quite the type of man we need." Then she paused. "We have another problem now," Kayla stated with absence of emotion. At that moment Awad and Fuerst came around the corner toward their table. She waited for them to settle themselves before sharing the news. They placed their belongings beneath the table where Tim and Kayla were sitting and indicated that they were going directly to the meal dispenser. Tim and she sat quietly sipping at their bottled waters while they awaited their return. Once they had settled and begun to eat, Kayla stated, "Unfortunately, Anne Feinman has had a stroke."

Fuerst's head lifted, his attention shifting away from his plate. "I'm sorry," he began, "is she alright?" He had recently received a message that she had fallen ill.

"She has some paralysis." Kayla stated. "She has withdrawn her name from the ticket. We have to choose a new candidate," she relented. Just as she finished, Lyndsey Austin came walking into the cafeteria from outside. Tim's face lit up with joy. He got up and ran to meet her halfway with a hug.

"Hey, Sis!" was the only thing he said to her.

"I came to take you home to your family," Lyndsey said, brushing the hair away from his eyes.

"That's what I wanna hear!" Tim said jubilantly. They walked back to the table.

Lyndsey introduced herself. All present smiled and nodded.

Fuerst spoke first. "It is a pleasure to meet the sister of this man. He has made a valuable contribution to our cause. We had offered more, but Tim is happy to be the philosopher behind the scenes, if you will." He said that with a gentle smile, and a glance away from Lyndsey toward Tim. Lyndsey wasn't sure what more had been offered and she didn't ask. She was certain that Tim would tell her if he so wished.

"His family misses him very much," Lyndsey said, knowing her brother well. Then, she looked over toward Awad. "You must be Amir Awad," she said. "I know someone who is going to be really happy to see you." Lyndsey knew that Jahir was somewhat confused over how to proceed with the project, and that he expected Awad to save the day.

"Yes, ma'am," Awad stated with a wide smile, after swallowing a drink of water. He rose to clasp her hand in greeting. "And I shall be glad to see him!"

That left only Kayla and Lyndsey to acknowledge each

other. "Hello, Lyndsey," Kayla said, reaching out with her hand, "I'm Kayla Bruster."

"Yes, hello, Ms. Bruster," Lyndsey responded by gripping her hand gently, and slightly nodding. She knew Kayla Bruster to be a Senator from Pennsylvania. She also knew that she had been romantically involved with Jake, but Lyndsey had no jealousy or animosity toward her. After all, that had been before she had become intimate with Jake. Neither had Kayla harbored any ill feelings against Lyndsey. That made it possible for a friendship between them.

"I'm so appreciative that you could come. I hate to eat and run, but Jakob and I have another appointment tomorrow morning, and it would be nice to relax in my own bed for a couple hours before that. But you know…" Kayla acted as though she was being facetious, but it was typical for her to burn both ends of the candle. Then she seemed to fade into a daze of preoccupation for a moment. She was searching her mind to find a way to speak with Lyndsey in a more private setting. "Tell me, Lyndsey…" she fumbled for words, but couldn't allow the opportunity to pass. "I would rather not contact Tim directly. Is it possible that I might contact you if I need to give him a message of any sort?"

"Yes, I can carry a tune," she responded quickly. Seeing Kayla's phone on her hip Lyndsey offered to transfer her contact information to it. Kayla obliged by removing her phone from its carrier and touching it with Lyndsey's phone.

"There we go!" she said with a smile. At that point, each member of the party was ready to move in his/her own direction. Awad had the most baggage. Tim helped to move things more quickly by grabbing one of the bags filled with electronic components.

"You are all welcome to our humble abode at any time. We have ample space, and we would love to have you." Lyndsey said, speaking to Fuerst and Kayla Bruster. Kayla took that to heart. She didn't care how uncomfortable it might be, both her and Lyndsey in the same house with Jake. Kayla was not interested in him anyway.

Fuerst responded with a thank you, then deferred to Kayla Bruster.

"Thank you so much. I might surprise you sooner than you think." Kayla had good reason to return to Jake's house. She anticipated that she might need another strong spirit to help with her future endeavors. Jake had already been a valuable asset for the cause of the IAPN, and he wasn't even fully aware of the extent of his contribution. The semiconductor company his father founded in Silicon Valley had supplied the silicon chips, which had made possible the broadcast of a signal to the American population. Kayla had also convinced Jake to set up his own sophisticated computer system. He was happy to oblige. She had expected that one day it would prove to be instrumental for transmitting a signal. *"Yes, Jake has certainly contributed to the cause,"* she thought. *"But I might also need Lyndsey's strengths to support the party."*

Chapter 24

Founding a New Coercion

As soon as Lyndsey, Tim and Awad arrived at the house, Tim had excused himself for the night. It was after midnight, and he was looking forward to seeing his wife and son. He intended to shower, then retire to a comfortable bed.

He opened the door to the downstairs back bedroom and there was Clare, sitting up on the bed, her back against two pillows and donning a sexy negligee that provided little cover for her gorgeous torso. She had time to preen herself because Michael had gone to sleep on the bed beside her. Her long, flowing hair was neatly brushed and wrapped to one side, laying against her chest. Her nails were painted with the pink color that Tim liked. When Tim had entered, and first saw her lying there in the dim light, he felt a resurgence of his virility. It arrived along with a flash of who he had been prior to the past couple of weeks, and it reminded him of normalcy.

The two embraced briefly but passionately, until Tim excused himself to wash away everything which had a connection to the past few days. When he was finished, they had an exciting sexual encounter that eliminated all their collective stress, allowing them to rest peacefully. Tim passed out on the bed, snuggled up against Clare. The only time he moved all night was when Michael fussed and wanted nourishment. But then, he closed his eyes and went back to sleep, realizing that he felt satisfied for the first time in a long time.

Lyndsey, too, was tired upon her arrival at the house, but she had to make her rounds. She noticed right away that the barricades had been removed from the windows. It made her recall that the zombies were no more, despite the fact they never did exist in *her* perceptual surroundings. The thoughts guiding her current movements, though, were born from her concern for Rinna. Lyndsey gently pushed open the door to the small bedroom on the second floor. She could hear that Rinna was still breathing through congestion. Before she had gone to the airport, she had given her not only an oral medication, but she had also applied a topical salve on her chest and back with the hope of opening the airways of her bronchial tubes.

Once she was satisfied that Rinna would be alright for the night, she attended to Awad. He had gone to the basement with Jahir and Redfeather, but Lyndsey first took him to see the hall bathroom on the main floor. It was then she had noticed that some of the sheetrock in the hallway had been cut out and removed from the wall. It smelled musty, so she made a note to herself to light some candles to help cover the odor.

"I'm sorry for the condition of our house," Lyndsey said to Awad as they walked together toward the bathroom. "We were battered by storms, and they caused some damage."

"Please," he responded, "I am most thankful for these accommodations. One learns to appreciate the comforts he is afforded."

She had mentioned to him that they had only one private bedroom to offer, and no one to this point had used it. She showed the room to Awad, so he would know about it. Then she added, "You can sleep here, or downstairs if you wish, or there is a sofa in the living room. But, if you are like the other two guys, they prefer the basement. It has plenty of comfortable furniture, and an entertainment center, should you be so interested," Lyndsey expected Awad would follow the lead of the other two men. She left them to themselves and retired to the bedroom where Jake was already sleeping soundly.

Sure enough, Awad had decided to retire downstairs. Redfeather was asleep in his chosen recliner, but Jahir was fighting the urge to sleep so that he might speak with Awad. They had much to discuss, but Awad was quite tired and, after he had showered, he relaxed into a recliner with a bottle of water and a shot of whiskey. He spoke with Jahir for only a short time until his eyelids became heavy. Jahir saw that and allowed him to drift off to sleep.

The dawn came early the following morning. It was already hot and humid outside, and the air conditioner had been running full force most of the night to keep a comfortable temperature in the house. It was never quite as cool upstairs, so Jake had installed a portable unit into a window in the attic for his control center. It, too, had been running all night, so once he had arrived in the attic upon awakening, it was as cool as the rest of the house.

Jake had awakened at the crack of dawn. He was preparing to integrate new equipment as a functional part of his control center. Shortly after Jake had gone up to the attic, Awad had joined him with Jahir and Redfeather. Awad brought the bags that contained the electronic equipment he had been hauling around ever since he had left Tel Aviv. Surprisingly, nothing had been damaged. He unpacked and separated the components in front of Jake's control center and began to identify each piece, and its purpose. He distinguished those components needed for creating the software from the ones needed to transmit the new signal. Then, he and Jake went to work with the assembly.

"I shall first set up what I need to make the necessary adjustments to the software. Then we can integrate the sending unit, etc." Awad was mumbling, not so much to Jake, or anyone else, as to himself.

"What did you say?" asked Jake.

"Oh...nothing. I'm sorry," he said, "just talking to myself." Awad smiled contentedly.

Jahir had prepared for this moment to explain to Awad what he believed had to be done to transmit feelings of respect and cooperation. He had been fixated on the problems at hand ever since his arrival at Jake's house. He began by addressing Awad, "We must neutralize all feelings of superiority. These contain the deceptions which preclude the American people from establishing a healthy relationship to nature, and each other. These feelings, and their corresponding deceptions, must be forbidden. In this way, we shall deconstruct the heroic attitude, which is, essentially, the attitude of domination."

Awad laughed quietly under his breath, then responded, "In the grand scheme of things there are no heroes, only a plurality of contributors to a collective endeavor. Most people have a selfish purview that blinds them to the big picture. It is existentially relative that some people believe certain contributions are better, and more important. The mistake is to relate a specific creation with an individual, as if one person could be responsible for any invention. Many persons make significant contributions in the development of every creation."

Jahir didn't care to philosophize. He wanted to get right to the task at hand. "In order to eliminate the zombies," he said, "you must ultimately neutralize the 'comparison of distinction', which finds its source in feelings of pity."

"Yes, I understand. I must forbid feelings of pity." Awad did not exactly understand *why*, he only needed to determine *how*.

"That is absolutely necessary," responded Jahir. "Within the act of pity is a repressed fear of death. That must be neutralized."

"Is that so? I may have to take your word on that," Awad quipped, smiling.

Jahir placated him with an explanation. "Pity is a feeling wherein one elevates oneself as superior to those who suffer. That is why you must disallow it."

"Alright," interrupted Awad, "I must negate the feeling of pity." He was focused upon how to write an algorithm to prevent it.

"Pity is only one possible response to an experience of sympathy. It is marked by a rejection of one's own weakness *in the presence of another who suffers*. This is precisely the comparison of distinction which lies at the basis of the heroic attitude," Jahir said with total confidence.

Just then, Lyndsey came into the room. "Good morning, gentlemen. Please, don't let me interrupt you," she said noticing that they had stopped what they were doing to acknowledge her presence.

"Good morning." said Jahir. "No bother. We are discussing the tuning of the software."

"He is dictating instructions. I am trying to interpret them into software language." Awad explained.

"Yes," Jahir continued, "Perhaps you will have to write several algorithms, progressing one step at a time. Perhaps first, you can neutralize the feelings of aggression and superiority essential to the heroic attitude?"

"Yes, that might be my initial endeavor," Awad said pensively.

"That will eliminate the illusion of empowerment, and the aggressive deceptions essential to it," added Jahir.

"Allow me to take one step at a time, please." Awad smiled

gently as he glanced at his friend.

Jahir rose to leave so Awad could do his work. Before he left, he emphasized once more, "You must ultimately neutralize the 'comparison of distinction' that is born in the act of pity. This is the seed of the attitude of domination." He wanted this to be quite clear to Awad, as he believed that this was *the* necessary change to bring the feelings of respect and cooperation into prominence. Jahir could not fully fathom the work that Awad would have to do. All he understood was that it would be comparable to recalibrating the neutral setting which made it possible to develop the entire gamut of human feelings in future endeavors. In Jahir's mind, Awad had to prevent the possibility of the heroic attitude and pity in order to neutralize the dominant feelings of the American population. If they were to succeed, Jahir believed the end-result should be a predominant attitude of respect and cooperation.

Jahir nodded toward Lyndsey. They got up to leave the room. "I'll leave you and Jake to work together on this," he said. Lyndsey followed Jahir down the stairs and into the living room. They saw Redfeather working in the hallway downstairs. Lyndsey watched as he picked up the tools from the floor where the walls had been opened for drying.

"What are you going to do now?" Lyndsey asked Redfeather. He had already announced to Jake that he intended to take care of the soaked interior walls. He would make sure that no mold could grow inside of them.

"A man has to earn his keep. I have a cool, dry place to shelter, and plenty of food and drink," Redfeather said with a smile and a slight bow to show his appreciation. "I have experience with this sort of damage," he continued, pointing toward the damp wall. "You have to remove the sheet rock where the water has gotten inside to prevent mold. I hate to tell you, but I shall also have to open the ceiling in the basement beneath this wall."

"Oh, dear," Lyndsey exclaimed.

"If you do not, you will all get sick here," Redfeather warned. "Trust me. You can make repairs later, after it is completely dry." He adjourned to the basement with the tools to continue his work.

Lyndsey looked over toward Jahir. He was smiling, then shook his head gently. "Let him do the work. He wants to make a contribution of his own in a way that he is able," said Jahir. "The rest of us have other work to do."

Lyndsey was thinking about the plan to recalibrate the software that Jahir had been discussing. "Do you think that by removing the deceptions common to the heroic attitude that we could create a healthier society?" Lyndsey asked.

"I do strongly believe that!" Jahir exclaimed. "We have to try and return to our natural starting point…you know, before the collective orientation to the world had been misguided."

"So, what will the American people perceive and feel, if they are no longer duped by the feelings motivated by the zombies?" Lyndsey wasn't entirely certain that this was the question she wanted to ask, but she tried to figure it out along the way.

"If we could remove the essential deceptions peculiar to the ideal self, then individuals might be able to discover their true identity, and live and feel a natural unity with others," Jahir stated.

"I wonder?" Lyndsey expressed doubt.

"You do not think it possible?" he asked.

"I have doubts," Lyndsey said. This was something she had thought about herself. "I would say that self-rejection at birth is universal to all born of woman. I think that *this* is the starting point for the imaginative construction of an ideal self. A receptacle for the ideal self opens up with birth trauma. Within it is created, in great detail, over time, the ideal self, which is born and nourished with self-deception. Self-deception is the prescription that helps to keep away the anxiety that arises from looking squarely at the real self with full awareness. I find it hard to imagine that self-deception could be eliminated by preventing acts of pity."

Jahir was deeply moved by Lyndsey's account of the human situation. He believed that she might have deeper insights at her young age than he had as a man some thirty years her elder. It made him think that Jakob Fuerst would appreciate this woman's intelligence. Fuerst had to leave for China, because the opportunity had arisen to make inroads there to coerce the Chinese people to adopt an attitude of respect and cooperation. He was not comfortable leaving for Beijing until he was certain that an adequate location had been found where Awad and Jahir could transmit the coercion[1] for a new conscience to the American people.

However, Fuerst also needed to find suitable leadership for the new America. Jahir would inform him that this woman had what was necessary for the task. The new leaders of the United States would have to rebuild the infrastructure of American institutions. All changes would begin with a new means of coercion: a new conscience. The new conscience had already been worked out in some detail. That had been top priority for Jahir since it would be architectonic for reforming American institutions. He could see that Lyndsey had the wherewithal for carrying out this task.

"I hope that I did not offend you, Abraham," Lyndsey reached toward him with one hand.

"Excuse me, Lyndsey." Jahir admitted, "I was preoccupied. I heard you, and you are correct. Our self-deception is a direct result of our primordial repression." He then changed the subject without further examining the point she had made. "I suppose that every society takes advantage of each individual's self-denial. In your country, as in others, you are promised protection from alien powers. Society aims to help you to overcome your weakness in many ways that encourage the deceptions that create the ideal self."

"I can see that." Lyndsey agreed. "Our capitalistic society trains us to construct a common version of the ideal self in direct relation to the illusion of possession. Since each must make his/her contribution to society, one works to acquire wealth, and this is the primary means for the acquisition of power. We use our possessions to dominate and control. This is what brings happiness and satisfaction to the ideal self, thereby confirming the value of things, and capital. A vicious circle is formed."

"I agree with you, Lyndsey." Jahir was wondering about her interests for her career. "This society has evolved to the point that it is governed by the wealthy and powerful. The habits motivated by this society fuel competition, and promote the aggressive acquisition of things that empower, until intolerable disparities among the population arise and build to a crescendo, and there is some sort of revolution. Your country could be in danger of this now."

"Do you believe there will be some kind of revolution?" Lyndsey asked with genuine concern.

Jahir continued. "It does not have to happen at all. But it is close, because Americans increasingly demonstrate a lack of respect for each other and nature, as they collectively engage in the pursuit of wealth and possessions."

"I understand why you would want to change the dominant attitude of our society," Lyndsey admitted.

"Yes," said Jahir, "but we must have leaders to reform its institutions. It is inevitable that we experience conflicts that we shall have to resolve. Our scholars do not have all the foresight that we would like to have. The institutions of the future will have to result from creative inspiration over time as our fundamental changes are promulgated."

"Obviously, we shall have to begin with *basic* changes."

She searched her mind for an example. "We agree that religion is supportive of contemporary society. Christianity provides groundwork for building the ideal self to correlate with American capitalism. It coordinates the mythical roots for contemporary conscience, particularly in its teachings about death and male dominance, with political ideals. But in truth, the real self is lost in Christianity, along with one's living relationship to nature. Ultimately, the nature of conscious life is obscured. Christians also conceal their true identity, trading it for a collection of pleasant illusions."

"A new religion will be founded upon respect for natural life and oriented to the health of human beings in the natural world, and the indefinite expanse of the universe." concluded Jahir. "Religion must be the gateway to holistic health, not a gateway to heaven."

"That certainly is a noble plan," said Lyndsey. "Contemporary capitalism is blind to the health of individuals. Instead, the struggle for power and wealth creates the drive to exploit individuals for personal profit.

"Agreed," responded Jahir. "Public health has to account for every citizen. We cannot create minorities via prejudice, or outcast the sick and infirm. Nor can we forget how nature contributes to public health. It nourishes and protects us. Furthermore, we cannot be concerned only with the health of the body. The mental health of the citizens must also be protected, particularly against lies and deception, and ruthless manipulation."

"Huh!" Lyndsey forced a half-baked laugh. "How would we prevent that?"

"It seems that we might have to place specific restrictions upon speech and the use of images in advertising. But more important, a program of self-knowledge; self-reflection must be instituted to help individuals find their own private uniqueness," said Jahir. "Our families must create a specific agenda for daily reflection upon our nature as conscious beings living in an indefinite universe. This is an important first step in the production of mental health that our educational institutions must support."

"We must also do more to support the liberal arts, granting time and valuable resources to build an appreciation for the *context* of our inventions," Lyndsey emphasized. "The arts must be respected equally in correlation with the technical sciences that make our gadgets."

"Ah, you are prepared with an appropriate curriculum," Jahir said with a smile.

"We must also learn how our sports fit into the academic institution." Lyndsey added, "Perhaps they do not belong together? We need a makeover. There would have to be strict rules to teach how to show respect in competition, that's for sure. Furthermore, sports like American football, which tend to ruin the health of its participants, need to be purged. Perhaps it should be disassociated with schools, particularly universities, and instead have corporate sponsors thoroughly support the team and its athletes."

"All must be re-prioritized for the sake of our new everyday attitude, and the conscience to support it. Top priority is to be respect for nature, and cooperation to preserve it." Jahir had worked back to the beginning of their reflection.

Chapter 25

Leaders with Compassion and Insight

Kayla was feeling an alienated sense of déjà vu as she approached the door of Jake's house. She had not been there for nearly two years, and this time the circumstances were different. This visit was not an escape from her fast-paced life to a relaxing and romantic respite. This time, she faced a challenge to persuade a woman who was every bit her equal in intelligence to unite with her and run in an election that would mark a new beginning for the American people.

After Anne Feinman's stroke, Jakob Fuerst had surprised her with the request that she run as the first ever presidential candidate for The People's Party. The proposal had left her breathless and unable to respond for several minutes, during which time Fuerst, too, had sat quietly, awaiting her answer. When she had finally expressed her concerns with the endeavor, Fuerst recognized that she could be easily persuaded. He told her that he fully expected her to win the election, assuming that Jahir and Awad were to succeed at changing the dominating attitude of the American public. He added that her role would be vitally important. She would be responsible for guiding the reformation of American institutions, in accordance with the new conscience. Finally, she insisted that she would rather delay her decision until they could be certain that the software would perform as expected. Fuerst was not a forceful man, and he did not believe that it was necessary to make any further effort to persuade her. So, he asked her to consider it seriously, and not to linger at length without an answer. To gently urge her forward, he suggested that she consider a running mate…assuming she was willing.

So, here she was, besieged with memories that had reminded her whence she came. They were dashed once again as she recalled Fuerst had told her the day before that Awad had completed the alterations to the software, and they were ready to broadcast the new signal. It was imminent, if not already transmitting. He had also assured her that Jahir had been discussing issues with Lyndsey that were critical to the establishment of the new vision for the United States of America as an elite member of the IAPN. Jahir was so impressed with her that he told Fuerst that if Kayla Bruster had not already been so well known in the American political arena, then he would suggest that Lyndsey Austin would be their best option as a presidential candidate.

It was a hot and humid day, and the sky was threatening to burst with rain. A gentle breeze was transforming into more forceful gusts as the last morning hours faded on this summer day in late June. A couple of loose hairs were dancing around Kayla's forehead, having escaped from the bun heaped high above the top of her head. She moved them away from her eyes as she reached for the doorbell. To her surprise, Lyndsey opened the door before she had touched it.

"Well, hello, Senator Bruster," she replied energetically. "Welcome!" She reached with her right hand to help her into the house. "I didn't expect you to visit us so soon." Lyndsey said, despite the fact, deep inside, she had anticipated a visit from her.

"Hello, Ms. Austin," Kayla responded, reaching for her hand to enter. Thank you so much for your warm welcome." Rinna came running out to the living room to see who had come to their house. "Hello, young lady!" Kayla said to her, crouching to Rinna's level. "You are so beautiful."

"This is my daughter, Rinna." Lyndsey introduced her. "And this is our state Senator, Kayla Bruster."

"It is a pleasure to meet you!" Kayla said, making a fuss over her.

"Nice to meet you, too, ma'am," Rinna had been well taught to demonstrate respect for her elders. She politely excused herself to return to her game room.

Then Abraham Jahir entered the room. "Greetings, Senator Bruster," he said, as if he were in a more formal setting. He had expected her arrival at some point. Fuerst had warned him of her intent. "I am Abraham Jahir." He introduced himself.

"It is a pleasure to meet you, sir." She responded by extending her hand.

Once Tim had heard the introductions in the living room, he decided that it was safe for him, Clare, and Michael to venture back upstairs. He had made a dash to the basement with his family when he had seen the SUV enter the driveway.

"I believe you know this guy," Lyndsey said pointing toward Tim. "This is his wife Clare, and his son Michael."

"Hello, Tim," she said, turning to acknowledge Clare, and get a close look at little Michael. "You have such a beautiful family!"

"There are two more of us here," said Lyndsey. "I believe you know my friend Jake Altmeyer, and Amir Awad. They are upstairs, searching for evidence of the changes in the attitude of the American people."

Kayla was mildly surprised that Lyndsey had intimated that she knew Jake, but that evoked no emotional response in her.

"Oh…I see," she began, "so they have begun the transmission? Is it a success?"

It was then that Tim excused himself and Clare. He wanted it to be clear to everyone that he would rather know little or nothing about the project they were working on. Tim thought it was insane, and he was estranged by what he had learned regarding their intent. All he cared about was staying with his family. It was bad enough that he felt as if he could not return to his own home for fear of being detained by the authorities. However, he had been assured that things would change for him once the new signal was broadcast.

"They are trying to determine that. It might take a couple of days before we know for sure," Jahir responded.

Lyndsey excused herself to the kitchen briefly, leaving Jahir with Kayla Bruster. After several minutes she had returned with a pot of coffee, a bottle of brandy, some creamers, and a large pastry that she had cut into several smaller pieces. She placed them on the table in the center of the living room. "Please, help yourselves," she said.

Kayla looked around the house, noticing the damage to walls and woodwork since she had last been there. "How will they know if the transmission is a success?" she asked.

Lyndsey sat in the chair directly across from Kayla Bruster and stuffed some pastry into her mouth. She had nothing to say in response to this question.

Jahir responded. "We have only recently begun to broadcast the signal. We are watching for signs. It seems that there are no zombies. Hopefully, that problem has been nullified. May I ask, Ms. Bruster, have you received the vaccine?"

"Yes, I have," Kayla responded. "There was no way for me to avoid it. My career would have ended without it."

"Do you feel any differently over the past day or so?" Jahir asked her. Both he and Awad had already been questioning Tim and Jake about their feelings.

"Now that you mention it, I have not had the energy that I typically have, but otherwise, I think not," she replied.

"Please let us know if you notice any significant changes," requested Jahir. "Have you perceived anything unusual?"

"You mean like zombies?" Kayla asked.

"Well, no...I'm sure the zombies will not return. Their absence has been widely proclaimed nationally for nearly two weeks," Jahir responded, sensing that she had experienced nothing out of the ordinary to report. "We shall have to continue watching, I guess."

"What are you expecting?" she wondered.

"We are not completely sure. However, the fear of death and excessive aggression must certainly be absent. Furthermore, there should be no expressions of pity. There should be a complete absence of self-comparisons that promote one's own superiority over others." Jahir answered with the obvious changes that would correlate with the inner sense that Awad had attempted to neutralize in his rewriting of the software.

"If I understand Doctor Jahir correctly," Lyndsey began, "there should be a dominating attitude of respect and cooperation. We can look at public behavior to gather evidence or do as Jake and watch the national reports for clues. So far nothing is apparent."

Kayla laughed, and made her own suggestion. "Perhaps we should be watching the behaviors in Congress, and other political officials. Are politicians still making the usual attacks against the opposing party?"

After the three enjoyed a good laugh together, Jahir replied, "That is a very good suggestion." He excused himself and ran upstairs to tell Jake and Awad to seek any broadcast that showed Congress at work.

Kayla was searching for the words to ask Lyndsey to be her running mate. She couldn't find them yet. Instead, she decided to talk about a recent endeavor of hers. She had been spending a lot of time at the nursing home where her father was living his final days. "I have managed to avoid political contacts in the past two days," she said in a low voice.

"Oh?" Lyndsey wasn't sure what to say or think.

"Yes," she began, "my father has kidney disease. It will take his life soon, according to the physicians."

"I'm sorry to hear that," responded Lyndsey.

"He had been receiving dialysis for years, but now his health is failing. After all, he is seventy-five years old."

"It is not easy to watch your parents die," Lyndsey lamented. "Both of our parents died three years ago from the Ebola virus. I managed to care for them at home until the end."

"I wonder whether that is a privilege or a curse?" Kayla looked at her with her head tilted to the side.

"They were more comfortable to be at home with their children," Lyndsey replied. "It broke my heart, but I was proud to care for my parents. Timmy helped. It was obvious that they had accepted their fate. A change had come over them that one rarely sees in daily life."

"In what sense, Lyndsey?" Kayla used her name to establish a more personal connection with her.

"They just seemed to see the world with eyes wide open," said Lyndsey, shaking her head slowly back and forth. "It was as if they could see everything as it really is. They had no intentions to deceive themselves about anything…or anyone else for that matter. It made me think that the sick and the elderly have accepted the real self and face their weakness as fate."

"Yes," said Kayla, "it's very sad. My father speaks to me through the tube into his lungs with a gentle, and reassuring voice. He already shows signs of peace with himself."

"That's what I'm referring to," Lyndsey replied, noticing that Kayla was suffering the same pain that she had suffered.

"I can understand that your parents felt more at ease to die at home with you and Tim at their side," Kayla emphasized. "Nursing homes are so sad and impersonal." Lyndsey could see a tear stream from her left eye. "It is as though the sick and dying have become a pain in the ass, requiring services that they do not merit," she added, showing a touch of anger. Then she reached for some pastry. "In nursing homes, it doesn't matter who you are or what you had done in your younger days. Sometimes compassion is far from the minds of insensitive wage-earning caretakers."

Lyndsey could see that Kayla was not comfortable with the nursing home's treatment of her father. "It is sad and impersonal. No one can be paid to feel genuine sympathy for the sick and dying." Lyndsey was recalling her experiences at a nursing home outside of the city. "After one's health deteriorates, he or she becomes unable to serve oneself, and one's time on earth grows short, it is as though one had already become a non-human entity. However, I have witnessed some of the most compassionate behavior in nursing homes from the patients themselves."

"How is that?" Kayla wondered.

"I have seen many elderly people provide an inspirational example. The ones who have accepted their fate seem to clearly realize that health is what is most important in life, and they strive not only to use what remains of their own health, but even struggle to help others preserve what remains of theirs." Lyndsey was looking directly at Kayla as she said this. Kayla wiped a tear from her face and took another piece of the pastry.

Beginning to feel a strange bond with Kayla Bruster, Lyndsey decided to explain the psychoanalytic import of what she had just said. "Acceptance of the real self is accomplished by only a precious few people in everyday life. It is most common among the sick and the elderly. Such acceptance calms the inner turmoil, insofar as it includes a resolution of primordial guilt."

"I'm not sure I follow," Kayla replied with a sincere interest.

"Primordial guilt is something that every human has to deal with," Lyndsey began her explanation. "It is accompanied by shame over being a weak and helpless organism. The guilt is compounded by self-deception. It is painful at first to accept that one has deceived oneself for so long about the fact, especially when the fact can no longer be ignored. For the aged, deception is no longer needed; I suppose that it is ineffective. The truth can no longer be concealed from conscious awareness. Sickness and old age motivate a realistic orientation toward natural life."

Kayla was feeling genuinely enriched by the insights that Lyndsey had expressed. "Isn't it a shame that we cannot accept the truth until it is too late?"

"Yes, it is,' Lyndsey agreed. "But that could certainly be changed."

"What do you mean? By the software?" Kayla asked.

Lyndsey laughed, gently shaking her head. "Perhaps that *is* our only hope. However, I am more optimistic. I believe that we could employ a new and rigorous training, even if only to guide people in the right direction. If everyone became more tolerant of the *real nature* of life, then we might also overcome a lot of the tensions among us. I believe that we could establish a new institution of self-reflection to help people learn this."

"I'm very impressed with your knowledge," Kayla said sincerely. "I do appreciate the education." Suddenly, Kayla recognized what Jahir must have seen to recommend Lyndsey as her running mate. She was now ready to ask the big question.

Before she could, Lyndsey continued. "Actually, it is the same as accepting one's own birth, and the fact that one is a solitary organism."

"Yes…each of us is, in some sense, alone in the world." Kayla was sidetracked by her interest in Lyndsey's psychological insights.

"No one can go back to mother's womb to become part of her as one biological organism." Lyndsey explained. "Some psychoanalysts believe that everything we create is designed to simulate the protection of the womb.[1] I wonder whether we are somehow misguided into thinking that we can artistically recreate the womb? It certainly isn't necessary. Can we not see that we are in the womb of nature?"

"Well…" said Kayla, "your question is unusual."

"It is as if our internal sense got confused in our youth," Lyndsey insisted. "We could become more like the elderly earlier in life, if we could practice accepting the real self from a very young age. Everyone could be united transcendentally in a different empathetic comportment toward the world. This comportment would extend to nature, and not merely to cultural productions. It is the sort of self-knowledge that is necessary for mental health."

"Lyndsey, you are truly insightful," Kayla replied. Then she made her pitch. "We need your help to provide for the future of the American people. Perhaps you are aware that I am to be the candidate for President of the United States, representing The People's Party. You have been highly recommended to me, and I now see why. Please, be my running mate."

Lyndsey was speechless, but not so much surprised. Tim had told her that he was not willing to run as Vice-President on the new party ticket. He simply wanted to be a family man and use his philosophical expertise to serve the public. Lyndsey had felt that something like this might be in the works ever since the night at the Butler Airport. In recent days, Jahir had made it even more obvious in his conversations with her. She had wisely anticipated this. Over the past days, she had spent a lot of time with Rinna, trying to learn how she might react if her Mommy were to be in such a situation. She was not surprised as she realized that Rinna was mature well beyond her age. And she was satisfied that the girl could adjust to a new life with her Mommy.

"I am most honored!" Lyndsey replied. "However, my first priority in life goes to my daughter, Rinna. I could not accept your invitation without certainty that she will have the best in education and childcare in my absence.

Kayla was overjoyed. She felt a sense of unity with Lyndsey already, and she promised that Rinna would be provided the best of everything. As they were discussing the details, and what would follow as their immediate agenda, Jahir came back into the room. He could sense an air of unity among two proud women.

"Please, forgive Jake and Amir for not joining us. They are on the trail in search of the precise effects of the new signal," Jahir told them.

"We have a party ticket!" Kayla exclaimed. The three of them stood and hugged each other. "If you will forgive me, I must go now. I have important business that must be completed today. Please, keep me informed about the progress with the software," she said, looking directly at Jahir. Then she turned back toward Lyndsey. "Gather your necessities for a trip with Rinna to Philadelphia; I have a place for both of you. I greatly look forward to our new relationship!" She hugged Lyndsey once again, then walked toward the door. Lyndsey followed. "Keep in close contact," Kayla requested. Then she ran out the door into the tumult of swirling winds, accompanied by a few large drops of rain.

Chapter 26

Respect: Society Without the Attitude of Domination

Jake felt lost without Lyndsey. She had only been gone for one whole day and part of another, but it already seemed like an eternity to him. Jahir had tried to placate him, reminding him that he could travel with her if he should desire to do so. But this only made him feel guilty for not wanting to leave his own home for a life on the road.

To avoid feeling sorry for himself, he jokingly told Jahir and Awad that he had lost Lyndsey to another woman. Her leaving reminded him of the circumstances under which Kayla Bruster had told him that she could never be anchored to any one place, or man, for that matter. His feelings were similar now as they had been at that time. The great irony of this situation was that Lyndsey had left him to be with Kayla!

When he told Lyndsey that he would rather not accompany her right away, she had assured him that she would return, but that did not fill the emptiness in his spirit. The absence of Rinna enlarged that void.

And there was more. His control center was in constant use by Awad, who was working to transmit a signal that was supposed to coerce the American people to respect and cooperate with each other to preserve the natural world in the interest of public health. Awad had promised him that as soon as he could properly attune the software, his work would be mostly complete, and the broadcast of the signal would not tie up the majority of his system's functionality. But Awad remained at work at Jake's control center, even after the broadcast had begun.

On this day, Jake called upon his friend Zack LeVeille. Although he was somewhat disappointed when Zack told him that Jeffrey's little league team was playing in the regional finals and they were on their way to the game, Jake accepted his offer to attend the game with him and Karen. He thought it would be a pleasant diversion to spend time with his best friend, whom he had not seen for a while. They decided to make a day of it and attend both games, which would determine who would play on July 4th for the championship.

Before he had left his home, Awad and Jahir had made Jake commit to keep his senses heightened in search for effects of the signal being broadcast. Despite the fact he had limited clues regarding what he might be looking for, Jake agreed.

As they sat in the bleachers, Zack was telling Jake how much different the general atmosphere was on this day as compared to the playoff game that he had attended some three weeks earlier. It was obvious to him that people were not nearly as apprehensive over the possibility of encountering zombies. None had been seen anywhere in America for more than two weeks, and the consensus was that they had been only a temporary plague that would not return. But Zack had expressed concern that people might become complacent, and then have to face a horrific surprise when the zombies did return. He paid specific attention to Sylvia Lombardi, whose husband coached the team, because she looked like a totally different person.

"You see that woman there?" Zack asked Jake with a slight gesture toward someone sitting two rows in from of them.

"Yeah?" responded Jake, turning his attention away from the game toward Zack.

"She killed zombies. Her son was bitten, I think. She was frantic and paranoid as hell, sitting here in the bleachers three weeks ago, telling her story to anyone who would listen." Zack remained silent for a moment. Then he continued. "Look at her now. She shows no fear at all for zombies today. You should have seen her that day!"

"She got over it, I suppose," Jake concluded with a shrug.

"Maybe. But I can't imagine how she might have overcome the depth of fear she had expressed at that time," Zack said. "Let's see. Sylvia Lombardi," Zack called to her.

She turned slowly, gently smiled, and said, "Hello, Zack. Hi, Karen."

"Are we gonna win this game?" Zack asked her.

"Oh…we'll see," she said with a smile. "The kids have had so much fun this week preparing for the game. It's a beautiful day, not too hot. I am enjoying this," she ended, turning herself back toward the action on the field. Before Zack could say anything, she clapped and yelled, "Get a hit, Dennis."

"She's a *totally* different person, Jake; nothing like I remember," he said shaking his head from side to side. Karen vouched for what her husband had said by nodding.

On the first pitch there was a loud "*ping*" from the barrel of the metal bat making direct contact with the baseball. Dennis dropped the bat and watched the ball soar into the sunlight as he slowly ambled toward first base. He would not have to run hard on this occasion. Wally and Bridgett Mason were clapping and cheering for their son as he rounded the bases, having hit a long home run. His teammates greeted him with multiple encouragements as he returned to the dugout.

"What a slam!" exclaimed James Lombardi. "I haven't seen one hit that far in quite a while," he added, reaching toward Dennis' hand to shake it.

"Well keep watching me, coach," Dennis said with a smile and calm assurance. "Maybe I'll hit one even further next time," he added with confidence.

Everyone in the bleachers got a good chuckle from what Dennis had said. Wally Mason turned to the parents of his son's teammates and proudly said, "That's my boy!" One of the fathers reached over to Wally's head, knocked off his cap, and proceeded to mess up his hair with one hand. Wally laughed, and dodged him sideways, then picked up his cap, laughing. Everyone went back to watching the game.

Zack nudged Jake in the ribs with his elbow. "See that?" he asked Jake. What stood out to Zack was that Dennis' attitude toward the other boys had changed. As had his father's. They had demonstrated no aggression or animosity toward their peers, but only a playful teasing of them. The Dennis that Zack had known built and preserved his own self-esteem at the expense of others. Today, it seemed that the boy's competitive spirit had all but disappeared. He was more congenial than ever before. Zack lowered his voice to a whisper. "That kid is always aggressive and belligerent. I thought that nobody liked him, but his teammates rallied around him like a friend." Zack didn't understand the change.

"Really?" asked Jake, in awe. He began to realize that perhaps *this* was a sign that Awad's software was having an influence on society.

"Yeah! In fact, it seems that someone must have told the kids to behave themselves." Zack continued. "I've seen no excessive celebrations. These kids used to imitate professional ballplayers and celebrate their accomplishments with antics that some people considered disrespectful. Oddly, that is missing today."

All Jake could say in response was, "Huh?" He thought that the electronic signal might be working precisely as Awad had planned. He reflected upon what he had seen, and Zack's insight. Then he asked himself whether he, himself, was feeling different than usual. Suddenly, he blurted out, "I think it is the absence of the zombies!"

"What?" asked Zack.

"I believe the zombies had brought out the worst in us," Jake responded.

"That's for sure!" Zack emphatically agreed.

"Perhaps things will be different now," Jake insisted, knowing that he could not tell Zack what he knew, but yearning to assure his best friend that the zombies would not return. Then, Jake became much more sensitive, and attuned to his surroundings. He seemed to think that people were subdued, and expressing a limited ambition, and he certainly felt that way himself. It was as if the desire to excel above others had been weakened considerably, although it had not been eliminated. After the game had ended, and the players engaged in the congratulatory handshakes, Jake made a mental note that the children had displayed no aggressive or disrespectful behavior throughout the game, or after, despite the fact some of them did express minor antagonisms, albeit in a playful manner.

It was then that almost everyone present was overcome by the sudden appearance of numerous children all about them, playing joyfully with each other.[1] The children ranged between the ages of five and ten for the most part. Some were on the field with the players who were preparing to depart to the ice cream stand, others were around the bleachers, and some were in the parking area and about the woods. Children could be heard yelling, "Ha, ha, you can't catch me," among other things. Some were vying for possession of the various items with which they were playing, but not to the point of fighting among themselves. The parents in the stands, including Zack and Karen, witnessed this playfulness, marked by a gentle sibling rivalry.

But something else had changed with the presence of the children. The surrounding environment was inexplicably altered. It *looked* decidedly different than it had a moment before the children had appeared. There was a beautiful array of colorful flowers lining the edge of the woods, with a sweet fragrance hovering about the air. One could taste the sweetness, and the air felt as if it were enlivened by the sun as it gently caressed one's skin. There was the most pleasant feeling – a sort of "high" – that one had been reborn into a pristine and idyllic natural environment. What was most unusual was that nature seemed to be animated. The motions of the trees in the soft breeze, and the flowing of the stream on the edge of the woods, made sounds that resembled the voices of loved ones, enticing everyone to frolic and play. No one could fathom what was happening. Everyone was caught in a general feeling of "playfulness", as if their orientation to the world had been reduced to that of a child.

"Holy cow!" exclaimed Jake as he basked in the feelings of the moment.

"Is this really happening?" Zack asked, squinting his eyes, and pinching his arm to signify disbelief.

Not just the children, but also each of the parents in the bleachers had felt as if he/she had been transported back in time to an age when responsibility was something new and intriguing. But, before anyone could lose himself or herself in this new and welcoming environment, it disappeared, leaving only the strangest feeling of love and friendship, and the innocence of a child. Jake had become overjoyed. He almost exposed the project by telling Zack what he believed to be happening, but he managed to bite his tongue.

"This feels like utopia, doesn't it?" Jake asked Zack with an excitement he had rarely felt in his adult life.

"It has certainly left me feeling a mischievous sort of pleasure," Zack replied as the remaining parents rose from the bleachers to join the kids and imbibe in ice cream treats. As they all gathered for that purpose, there was a joyful innocence shared among them.

At the same time Jake was eating ice cream, many miles away Kayla Bruster was in Washington D.C. attending a special meeting of the congressional committee formed to discuss how to divide the costs associated with the new health care system. Some creative conclusions were necessary soon, so that payments for medical services would continue to flow, albeit according to a new set of guidelines. The most important characteristic of this health plan was that there was no longer any kind of payment to be made by the patient. There would be no more surprise bills that victimized someone who needed care and medications, driving him/her into unforeseen debt.

Kayla had expected this to be quite a contentious debate that was not likely to accomplish much. Someone was going to have to sacrifice something, and that meant the likelihood of a lot of name calling and character bashing. She expected that, in the end, the lobbyists would continue with their usual bribery of politicians, and this would be the deciding factor determining whom would bear the brunt of the costs.

In an ideal world, the costs would be distributed as evenly as possible throughout the entire system. They would be split among insurance companies, drug-makers, pharmacies, doctors, nurses, makers of the surgical robots, and more, not excluding the taxes paid by the American people.

As the debate progressed, it had become glaringly obvious to her that the usual guilt-slinging between democrats and republicans had been severely dampened. There was certainly opposition, but much to her surprise, the aggressive attacks on the opposing party had been reduced to disagreements in the most objective fashion ever witnessed by her. Rational argument had acquired greater import and replaced the infantile *ad hominem* attacks. She had begun to believe that Awad and

Jahir had succeeded with their endeavor to attune the software. It did, in fact, seem to her that respect and cooperation were dominating the meeting, despite the fact individuals were still being criticized at times, when only the argument should have been the target of refutation.

But something else was amiss. Creative inspiration seemed to be lacking in the debate. New ideas were extant, as if there were insufficient concern for and orientation toward public health within the very committee chosen for their expertise in health care and their collective determination to hammer out new approaches to cost sharing. Kayla sensed a general lack of dedication, and the absence of any urgency to finalize a plan.

She made notes to herself, identifying the most obvious changes in the congressional proceedings, and would be sure to inform Jahir as he had asked of her. But all in all, she had felt a substantial improvement that had, for the first time, motivated her to actually enjoy a process which had always been disgustingly tedious with endless backbiting and was, ultimately, doomed to failure.

Chapter 27

Crisis in Paradise: The Problem with Self-Comparison

Awad had just shut down the signal and disconnected the sending unit from Jake's control center. He was feeling dejected, but not defeated. The initial feedback he had gotten certainly felt promising. The adjustments that he had made to SAI appeared to have elevated the feelings of respect and cooperation as the guiding orientation of the American people. Kayla Bruster's report on the proceedings at the congressional meeting was exactly what he wanted to hear. He seemed not only to have eliminated the zombies, but also the aggressive self-deception peculiar to the attitude of superiority.

While minor antagonisms still prevailed, the violent deceptions and emotions that had fueled animosity and divisiveness were nowhere to be found. This was a welcome improvement, which moved Awad to believe that he may have provided a new beginning for the social fabric of American capitalism. Hatred, killing, profound jealousy and the like, were absent in the daily behavior of the people during the time in which the signal had been broadcast. The result was that the most violent emotions, which had divided the nation, appeared to have regressed back to a state of mere natural capacities lacking development.

There was also the report from Jake and what he experienced with his friend Zack. He had told Awad that the interactions of the kids on the baseball diamond, and the relations among the parents, had improved noticeably. Jake had specified that the typical celebratory behavior displayed after successful hits was missing. When he heard this, Awad sought his own confirmation in a competitive context by watching a Major League Baseball game. While he had limited knowledge of the sport, he could nonetheless look for the antagonistic behavior that marked an expression of competitive superiority. He saw none of that. In fact, the game that he watched, while it was exciting for the home team to come from behind in the ninth inning, revealed that the players seemed to show respect for each other.

Awad was particularly moved by the perceptions of children playing together within a beautiful and animated nature that had been seen by numerous people. When both he and Jahir had heard reports of the same experiences among people throughout American society, Jahir was reminded of the teachings of Chief Seattle, which he had learned about from John Redfeather. For that moment, he thought that they had transported the American people to an earlier period in history when the natural world was able to motivate a profound awe and respect. The two men had been so pleased with this outcome that they had drank a toast with the bourbon from Jake's alcohol closet. At first, they both believed they had eliminated the aggressive deception which dwelt in the spirit of 21st Century American capitalism. Jahir was so excited that he had contacted Lyndsey to brag about their success.

Unfortunately, there was one unacceptable consequence that would send Awad and Jahir back to the drawing board. Several reports on the national news had indicated a serious setback. It was specifically related to the recent catastrophes on the west coast. The effects of SAI upon people who survived these catastrophes clearly showed that Awad had failed to complete the project as Jahir had directed. In fact, the two men had become so dejected that they wondered if it would be possible to achieve their goal.

The problem was that the survivors of the earthquakes, and its severe after-affects, were not responding to help those in need. It was as if no one cared, or the healthy survivors seemed not to understand the gravity of the situation. Most people avoided getting involved in rescue and recovery efforts. It was as if they knew not what to do, or they were so fearful that they had decided to flee for their own safety. The failure of Awad's efforts was epitomized in the many expressions of *pity* which had become the dominant response of survivors toward those who were suffering. On the one hand, it was obvious that SAI had reduced the level of aggression and ruthless self-promotion back to a level associated with innocent and playful children. But, on the other hand, *that* appeared to be the reason why people had failed to respond as responsible adults to alleviate the suffering of their fellow man. Distraught, Awad sought an explanation from Jahir.

"These people are behaving as if they lack all life-experience and have not yet matured sufficiently to accept the facts. They behaved as children who flee and absolutely repress the anxiety." Jahir shook his head, continuing to analyze the problem in the search for a solution.

"Well, my friend," Awad started, "what do you prescribe now?"

"Let us carefully review the situation," Jahir said, feeling as if he were repeating himself.

"I mean..." Awad stammered slightly, "we do have a very limited success."

"It is not enough," Jahir lamented. "These surviving victims prefer to save themselves it seems. They are obviously sympathetic, but the numerous expressions of pity indubitably indicate the failure of our project."

"That is apparent," Awad said, as if Jahir had simply stated the obvious.

"Let's see…" he continued, reflecting to himself. "We observe childlike behavior instead of responsible action. Most children are without recourse to do otherwise in times of crisis, so they simply flee from their anxiety. For that reason, their sympathetic feeling was followed with pity."

"Yes," insisted Awad, "and we remain at square one."

"That is true. Obviously, a repressed fear of death also remains, lurking beneath the surface in the American people, and so the foundation for conscience, as it had been, still reigns. Self-deception continues, despite the fact it is not so aggressive as before." Jahir was collecting the facts.

"I do not understand how we could have a partial success that looks so promising, yet fails so miserably in a most supremely important context?" Awad questioned.

"We seem to have compounded misbehavior in crisis." Jahir evaluated this problem. "We have made it difficult to tolerate the stress of catastrophic events. There are reports of emotional breakdowns, an increase in alcohol consumption, and bizarre sexual relations, to release the stress being felt. These indicate that the anxiety motivated by the catastrophe is intolerable."

"What is worse is that these behaviors have already started to bring about bad feelings between people, increasing antagonism." Awad began to think out loud. "I thought that I had eliminated the possibility of feeling pity. But obviously it still exists. Therefore, the seed for aggressive self-deception is alive and well in the American spirit."

"Perhaps I was wrong." Jahir had personal difficulty admitting that possibility. "It could be that a repressed fear of death *is* a fixture of human nature." It was painful for him to even suggest this. He experienced and demonstrated frustration and confusion over his uncertainty, forcefully rubbing his forehead with the palm of his hand.

"That would also doom the political project to restructure American institutions," Awad added. "Alterations to existing institutions would prove insufficient to prevent the attitude of superiority from returning over time."

"I shall not give up!" Jahir expressed his determination, standing to pace around the attic as he thought. "Obviously, the 'comparison of distinction' still exists, despite your effort to eliminate pity from the spectrum of possible feelings. I am certain that this sort of self-comparison is the bogie that haunts the American people. We *must* find a way to neutralize it."

"Yes, but how must I proceed?" Awad asked.

"Let me think," Jahir responded out loud, rehashing the psychological facts for his partner to hear. "The primordial repression of the trauma of birth marks the original rejection of the real self. This is the infant's repression of the anxiety that arises in its earliest human experience of utter helplessness. Okay," he continued, "the experience of sympathy marks the return of the real self to conscious awareness through the medium of the other who is perceived to be suffering. Certainly, the child, not to mention most adults, responds to the sympathetic experience by forcing the repression anew. This is what we call pity. It necessarily evokes the self-comparison of distinction, which is the source of self-deception and the seed of the heroic attitude."

There was a long silence as Jahir paced all around the attic. Awad had opened the files of the software. He was staring at it, wondering what changes he might have to make to complete the project. Suddenly, Jahir's face lit up with an "Aha!" moment.

"I know that I have made a mistake somewhere. Perhaps I have found the source!" he said with hope. "Perhaps I have identified the wrong source of deception, whether self-deception or otherwise. It is obvious that the comparison of distinction is the basis for the aggressive self-deception peculiar to the attitude of superiority."

"Yes," said Awad not really giving his full attention yet. "You have already said that."

"But" insisted Jahir, "all deception is related directly to our original self-rejection. Is it because the real self becomes 'not me' at birth that the transfer of feeling in sympathy is inadequate? Perhaps full awareness of the other's suffering is somehow prevented due to this original self-denial."

"Okay, what does that entail?" asked Awad.

"Don't you see?" Jahir was pleased with his insight. "It could be due to our self-rejection that there can be no *identity* of feeling transferred in *any* form of empathy. To the extent that the real self is "not me", but other, a complete transfer of feeling is also rejected. In sympathy some part of suffering must belong exclusively to others, and not myself. Hence, self-denial prevents the perfect sharing of feelings. Ultimately, deception begins within the natural experience of empathy, and thus, too, in sympathy. Therefore, the ground of deception lies within our natural tendency to empathize for the sake of sharing the feelings of others."

"How does this truth, if it is so, determine the work that I must do to adjust the software?" Awad's concern was obviously with the writing of algorithms.

"Let me think." Jahir furrowed his brow and continued pacing with his hands clasped behind his back. "I'm not sure," he admitted pensively.

Then footsteps were heard coming up the stairs toward the door. It opened, and Jake came in with Tim. Jake glanced at his control center, then toward Awad and Jahir. Not only did he notice that his computer system was idle, but he could sense that the two men were in deep thought.

"Gentlemen," replied Jahir with a faint smile.

"You've shut down the signal," replied Jake without even a

hello.

"Yes, we have problems," answered Jahir, while Awad worked with the problem of rewriting the software.

"Really?" he asked. "It seemed to me that the boys and girls on the field were competing respectfully. Isn't that what you wanted?"

"Please," said Awad, with a slight wave of his hand, "it was not enough." He looked back toward the algorithms he had written, subtly indicating that he did not wish to discuss it further.

Jake grabbed a controller and turned on the video screen at the upper left corner of one wall. He saw images of damage to buildings caused by the earthquake in California, so he turned up the volume. The report went on to say that the scope of destruction was massive, and thousands of people on the west coast were missing and unaccounted for. All four of the men listened intently, gaping in disbelief at the extent of the disaster. They were silent, until the end of the report when it was said that the hopes for rescue were diminishing, and it remained only to recover the bodies of the deceased.

Jahir put his head down, gently shaking it. "There is the reason for our failure."

"What?" asked Tim and Jake simultaneously. Jake lowered the volume.

"You saw children playing, did you not?" asked Jahir.

"Yes," responded Jake, "it felt like some kind of utopian world."

"Well, it certainly is not," replied Jahir, briskly sweeping away Jake's recollection of the good feelings he had at the kids' ballgame. "The response in crisis is absolutely inadequate. It is what you would expect of children, not responsible adults. We have made a critical error that we must correct, otherwise, our endeavor is doomed to failure."

"I don't understand," replied Jake with disappointment.

"People are fleeing the danger, instead of helping their fellow man," Jahir emphasized, raising his voice while looking directly into Jake's eyes.

"Well," Tim began, "that certainly doesn't match what I have experienced in times of crisis."

"What are you saying, young man?" Jahir asked, knowing that Tim not only helped him to escape the attack on the cabin with his life, but he also survived the destruction of Hurricane Alfonso – all within the same week.

"These disasters represent crisis on a large scale. I mean…" Tim hesitated for a moment, "catastrophe is a crisis for many people at once in the face of the same life-threatening event. By my experience, and what I had witnessed in other reports of such occurrences, all survivors are with and for each other. No one is simply 'for-oneself'. Neither is there is any petty opposition dividing people. There is no antagonism. This is overcome when everyone suffers the same crisis at the same time."

"That is very insightful," answered Jahir. "It is for this reason we know that what has happened out west is an abomination created by SAI. Something we have done has altered the typical human response in these situations. And this outcome is absolutely unacceptable." His voice trailed off at the end.

"I see," Tim responded, then a silence followed before he continued. "Surely you remember what happened to us on South Mountain. After the bombing, those of us who were able went to the aid of the injured. It seems to me that whenever a catastrophe of that sort happens, *each survivor cooperates and coordinates in the search for victims.*" He gestured toward

Awad. "We witnessed the same thing at the collapsed hospital building in South Carolina. Everyone was concerned for the *individual health* of every other potential survivor. It appears to me that whether the common crisis is a hurricane, bombing, earthquake, or whatever, the health and wellbeing of everyone involved is sought as top priority from within some sort of catastrophic attitude. This is demonstrated time and again. No?"

"You are so right, Tim," Jahir said with pride. "We all had the same feeling of urgency to help each other. Yes…you have something there, young man. It does appear that this experience of catastrophe brings one nearest the absolute ideal of human sympathy to share an identical feeling of suffering." Jahir wondered whether he might be onto something that would help Awad to correct their error.

"Sympathy?" Tim retorted. "I would question whether, in fact, sympathy is even experienced in these disastrous events. Multiple people experience the same crisis – this manifests a catastrophic attitude, which creates a transcendental unity of feeling in crisis, shared by each victim. Who needs *sympathy* to share the suffering?"

Jahir looked at Tim with the promise of a future. Awad had also sensed that Jahir had gained an important insight from his philosophical friend. He sat forward to pay closer attention to their conversation.

"Yes…perhaps… Yes! Yes!" Jahir was suddenly flushed with excitement. "You are absolutely right. No one involved in the catastrophe must make a self-comparison to others to share the suffering of fellow victims. The internal senses of the victims are attuned alike in the catastrophic attitude, *despite the absence of human sympathy*. While there is not a sympathetic transfer of feeling, there is nevertheless a transcendental identity of feeling. Everyone is united by an anxiety over his/her human frailty in response to the immediate threat. This attunes and connects everyone involved with their environment in crisis. *It is an existential unity of the most natural kind.*"

Jake also sensed something like euphoria building in Jahir. "What have you just learned?" he asked.

"It was there all the time!" Jahir exclaimed. "The real unity of the species is manifest in this catastrophic attitude. This is true because *the necessity of crisis in conscious life is universal.* With that in mind, I may have a solution to our problem!" Jahir was overjoyed.

"Well, what is it, man?" Awad begged.

Jahir walked over to Tim, clasped his head in his hands, and kissed both of his cheeks.

A mischievous grin surfaced upon Jake's face. He gestured toward Awad to follow him. "If you two want us to leave, we can, boys," he quipped. All of them roared with laughter. Jahir's laughter was fraught with relief. Awad had never seen his friend so animated.

Then Jahir said, "What is unique about catastrophic situations is that the deceptions inherent to human sympathy are absent because *there is no self-comparison. All* deceptions about life are abandoned in this attitude."

"What must I do?" Awad asked, ready to start rewriting the software again.

"Just a minute," Jahir requested, "let me think." He began pacing back and forth in front of the window. Jake and Tim sat quietly watching him.

After about ten minutes, he spoke. "We were trying to neutralize the comparison of distinction essential to pity. That was the wrong approach. *We must neutralize all self-comparisons.* The comparison of oneself to others is the source of all self-deception! But how do we neutralize this? How can we use SAI to program Americans to live within the catastrophic attitude?" It was beyond his ability to solve the problem with the software.

Then Awad said, "I believe we can still use SAI to accomplish the original goal. I shall remove the previous changes and begin with the package that Vendali had used to transmit the zombies. Subsequently, I need only to make one alteration. The transcendental identity of feeling essential to the catastrophic attitude should be the zero setting. That should achieve our purpose.

"Please, again?" responded Jahir.

Awad complied with an explanation. "The final tuning of the software will require that I neutralize the *self-comparison* that you had believed to be natural within human empathy. This is the comparison which moves us empathetically to feel like the other feels. *It* must be neutralized as *the* condition for the possibility of the transcendental unity of the human spirit."

"Yes, yes!" interrupted Jahir with encouragement for him to begin right away.

Awad continued. "Every conscious orientation to the world is a modification of the catastrophic attitude. Everyone will endeavor to live with anxiety, facing the realities of life without self-deception."

"This is perfect!" raved Jahir. "That would mean that our original unity with each other, and all of nature, is directly related to anxiety over personal weakness without self-deception!"[1]

"That would be how we elevate respect and cooperation as the dominant orientation to the natural world?" Tim was asking. "It makes sense that anxiety over one's own vulnerability is the motivating factor in the goal of *public health*. It moves each person to seek not only one's own health, but also the well-being of everyone else."

"The unity shared by all within the catastrophic attitude would seem to be the nearest natural equivalent of returning to the womb," Jahir said with a smile, looking at each of the other men.

"How is that?" asked Tim.

"It has always been the desire of mankind to return to the womb. All that we create is made to simulate the protective environment of the womb,"[2] said Jahir.

"Really?" asked Jake.

Jahir was pleased to offer an explanation. "Many psychoanalysts agree on this point. Some believe that the womb is the lost source of our protection that we try to recreate with every cultural product. I would emphasize that mother and fetus share their feelings as the biorhythms of one *natural*, biological entity. The same feeling flows through mother and fetus as if through an electrical current. This is the ideal aim of empathy that our nature cannot achieve in reality."

"I don't understand all this talk about returning to the womb," said Tim. "Does it have some greater significance?"

"Yes. We should use this symbolism to reinterpret our relationship to nature. It is an error to believe that humans are born with a fear of nature, as though she were a sort of grim reaper, seeking our misery and death. This foolish belief moves us to interpret our cultural creations as the means for our protection. We must revisit that assumption. We might attain valuable insight by using an analogy of proper proportionality: mother is related to her fetus in the same way that Mother Nature is related to humanity. Mother suffers a violent birth to deliver her newborn, just as Mother Nature suffers a violent birth in delivering humanity into the world. But this is necessary and good, because, without it, human life does not exist. It is discomforting at first, but one must learn to understand and accept the reality of birth and love it for what it is, because it is the condition for the possibility of our humanity." Jahir finished, his voice flushed with excitement, "The effort to re-create our original life source is an expression of our self-deception, and the augmentation of our suffering."

As their discussion continued, Awad had already begun to make the proposed changes to SAI. He couldn't help but notice on the margin of his consciousness that Jahir seemed to be criticizing the very project in which he was engaged.

Chapter 28

Crisis, Catastrophe, and Our Unity with Nature

As dawn arrived on the morning of the July 4th holiday, and Americans across the nation had prepared to celebrate the anniversary of the birth of their nation with cookouts and fireworks, no one could anticipate the profound changes that had begun to materialize. An entirely new nation was to be born, reducing the old one to nothingness.

Awad had finished adjusting the neutral setting of the most divine of all cultural creations so that it would be founded upon the catastrophic attitude. It was set to transmit one and the same orientation toward the natural world to each and every American who had received the second Ebola vaccine. All the electronic hardware was in place and additional precautions had been taken, ultimately with the intention to make the broadcast permanent.

Awad and Jahir had made these preparations in defense, considering that Mother Nature had become increasingly volatile and unstable. On this particular day, storms were in the area and lightning bolts flashed about the sky, electrifying the atmosphere. The natural environment was threatening to wreak havoc upon the weak and feeble animals that relied so heavily on it for their nourishment and preservation.

The alteration of the software was easily achieved by Awad, and the signal had been transmitted for nearly twenty-four hours. It was to be expected that the changes in attitude programmed into the software would need some time to thoroughly engage and activate the chips collectively, and thus echo the predominating attitude of Americans. But, certainly, the signs would show soon. All the men were searching in every possible direction for any indications of the new reality. Kayla Bruster and Lyndsey had also been alerted to watch for changes and asked to report back to Awad. Even Alan Gustavsson and his wife, Greta, had been invited to Jake's house to share what they all expected to be a utopian world, even better than the one witnessed personally by Jake and Zack at the children's regional finals.

But children playing delightfully and innocently in a pristine and idyllic natural world were not to be transmitted as a reflection of a new spiritual reality of the American people. That was not what anyone would perceive. This time, pity would be nowhere to be found. Neither would empathy function to transfer feelings among the people. Self-comparison would be permanently eradicated from all memories of conscious life as the plague creating all enmity.

Awad's re-attunement of SAI had at least one unexpected consequence: The primordial repression of birth trauma had also been eliminated, i.e., *repressed self-rejection* had been banished from conscious life, by programming Americans to live in the catastrophic attitude.

The anxiety over helplessness, endured by everyone born of woman, was kept from the time of birth. Newborns would squirm and scream and not rest comfortably, even after exhaustion had overcome them. How this would affect their development was yet to be seen. However, adults would accept and embrace anxiety as an essential and valuable part of conscious life that motivated them to seek public health. Every member of the population who was oriented within the catastrophic attitude would simultaneously accept the real self into conscious awareness. This seemed to be the only way to unite a diverse people in a common orientation to the natural world for the good of the species. SAI was certainly not able to help one return to the womb. However, a biorhythmic unity of mother and fetus had been established among all people by means of an electronic representation of the transcendental unity of the species.

American conscience had been collectively united into one, electronically programmed to be identical for every individual on the grounds of respect and cooperation. Fear of death had been unrepressed, and thereby rendered a non-factor in conscious life. There was something markedly fulfilling within conscious experience in the catastrophic attitude, abstracted from the crisis. It was only in this attitude that each human being could *find himself/herself* as *one, completely united with others in community spirit*. The bonds of unity among the people had become stronger than one might have imagined to be possible. This was so because in the catastrophic attitude there exists not only a conscious identity of each human with every other member of the species, *but also a self-identity* insofar as everyone accepts his/her real self. This would be SAI's gift to humanity.

When Kayla Bruster arrived at Jake's house with Lyndsey, many of those who had contributed to the creation of the broadcast signal were present amidst the electronic equipment that was assembled to give birth to the new nation of Americans. Besides Kayla and Lyndsey, there was Jake, Amir Awad, Abraham Jahir, Tim and Clare, Alan and Greta, and last but certainly not least, Rinna and baby Michael. They gathered in the control center around the powerful new invention they had brought to life.

Lyndsey had been thinking a lot about the project that Jahir, Awad, and the others, had undertaken. It was she who had clearly expressed what seemed to be the ultimate truth underlying the endeavor. "We are conducting a grand experiment with the American people. But what we are trying to do reveals a profound truth about the species as a whole. If humans are programmed to *feel* as they would in catastrophe, then and only then would there be a transcendental unity of the species oriented toward cooperation and mutual respect for all nature, such that our main concern becomes the health of all people."

Tim interrupted her, "That's true, but I think that perhaps we are missing the big picture. Was it not your original intent to overcome the attitude of superiority which makes it impossible to cooperate and respect each other, and nature as a whole? This project was initiated so that everyone would work together to protect and preserve the nature that nourishes us. Is it not a supreme contradiction that, in the aim to overcome the domination of nature, we must utilize an artificial power to *change* our nature? Is it not ironic that *human nature* must be changed to achieve this goal? We had to prevent by electronic means the possibility for all comparisons of the self to other people so that we could unite the people with and for one another in the absence of self-deception. It certainly seems to me that your technology has given birth to a new human nature."

Jahir came to the defense of his project. "It seems that human nature had to be changed because empathy is insufficient to unite us as a species. I believe that humans subconsciously know this. Unfortunately, empathy is the means that our nature provides to unite our collective will for the good. Ironically, this defect in our nature blinds us, and prevents us from realizing that *Mother Nature is the womb of our creation*. She gives birth to us, but we alienate and exploit her to create an *artificial* womb. In the end we create our own divine realm, rejecting the only divinity which has given birth to the species. It is our only choice to use creative techniques and technology to change ourselves into the ideal we prefer."

There was a long silence, as no one voiced a response to his assertion.

Chapter 29

The Ruling Power

The evening air at The Point was stifling with humidity, but the crowd didn't seem to care. Everyone had their mist spray, and other cooling devices, as they waited where the three rivers met for the fireworks on the July 4th holiday. The festivities were intended to celebrate the 260th anniversary of the founding of the United States of America.

There was a strong scent of cannabis in the air, and the smoke was held close to the ground by the heavy atmosphere. It wafted about the people. Thankfully, the rivers were fairly well behaved. Water lapped against the retaining walls that traversed the banks of the rivers throughout the city. It rose to two feet from the top of the wall at its peak. But, given the recent storms and the unstable atmosphere, the rising levels of the Ohio, Allegheny, and Monongahela Rivers appeared as though they could be a threat to the dry ground in the not-too-distant future.

The whole gang had crammed into the Marauder, and Jake drove it to a parking garage near The Point. Kayla, Lyndsey, Rinna, Tim, Clare, Michael, Alan, and Greta had all decided to join the crowd for the festivities. Amir Awad and Abraham Jahir preferred to remain at Jake's house, rather than carouse within the bustling crowd. It was Lyndsey and Jake who had suggested the excursion into the city. Awad and Jahir had encouraged them to go, so that they might witness firsthand any changes that had been affected by the new signal being broadcast. Awad had insisted that the changes should soon be recognizable. The group had cast their blankets upon the earth and sat down with snacks and beverages.

Rinna was bubbling with excitement. She caused Lyndsey and Jake to pay particular attention to her as she wanted to run among the festive and happy crowd. There was no apparent reason for them to be concerned for her safety because everyone Rinna approached had warmly welcomed her presence. It was as if the marijuana smoke had distributed a "high" among the people, all of whom were friendly and pleasant with excited anticipation.

Tim and Clare leaned against each other, holding the tiny bundle of joy who was their future. Somehow little Michael was sleeping between them as they nestled their heads together to kiss and cuddle. Clare had prepared Michael for the noise by inserting plugs into his tiny ears.

Alan and Greta were sitting on their own blanket with their arms wrapped around each other romantically as they dreamed of their hopeful future as parents.

Kayla behaved as her usual self; she was utterly independent. She walked about The Point, looking at the people in the crowd with a smile, displaying the pleasant demeanor that had endeared her to practically everyone she had met.

Abruptly, the festivities that everyone had gathered to see began with a bang and a whistle, then multiple explosions resulted in the colorful lights dancing across the sky. The crowd was in awe, everyone simultaneously gaping at the sky, sharing the pleasures of their perception.

This continued for more than an hour, until the rapid fire of explosives which indicated the grand finale. However, after the final explosion of lights had occurred, no one wanted to leave. People continued to mill about, enjoying the good feelings, obviously unwilling to let go of them and depart.

It moved Lyndsey and Jake to discuss the apparent unity of the people as though it were the influence of SAI upon the crowd. Kayla, too, had returned to the group, also having sensed a different sort of unity among the people present at The Point.

Suddenly, the fireworks continued. But this time they were not an artistic production. Mother Nature had begun to fire lightning bolts across the sky, one after the other. These were quite a bit more spectacular than the ones that had been launched from the barge just off the shore of the Ohio River.

Lightning continued to fire across the sky, creating a brilliant spectacle that was looked upon by the crowd with an awe far surpassing their experience of the fireworks. It was easy to imagine a collection of divinities in the heavens waging war with arrows of light.

But the collective feeling of the crowd had changed. Along with the awe, there was an apprehension flowing among the individuals, which had not been present during the artificial light show. People had begun to gather their belongings and retreat to search for a protective area to shelter. However, there was little recourse to any such protection, at least in the immediate vicinity, other than a narrow tunnel beneath a bridge which supported the highway leading to the Fort Pitt Tunnel.

While there was certainly anxiety building among the crowd as a result of the electrical storm, there was no panic among them. Everyone was quickly, but carefully, maneuvering to escape toward the downtown area where there was adequate shelter for all. Much to the disbelief of Lyndsey and the rest of the group who had picked up their blankets, diaper bags, and backpacks, the people were leaving The Point in an unusually orderly fashion, making sure each person could escape safely through the ubiquitous tunnel under the highway back toward the city buildings.

Strangely, there was no rain falling, but the astounding firing of lightning bolts continued for several minutes as the crowd collectively exited The Point.

Finally, Mother Nature's light show ended just as abruptly as it had begun. The milling crowd stopped all at once to gaze toward the sky with anxious anticipation. The lightning bolts had ceased, but there was a strange humming sound. It sounded like a giant transformer echoing all about the atmosphere. Everyone looked about in confusion, searching for its origin, but the source was not to be found in the immediate vicinity.

Along with the humming sound, all the people thought that they smelled something like an electrical fire. Nevertheless, the orderly endeavor to seek the protection of shelter continued. But the humming and the odor permeated the city, until another light show began that was entirely distinct from the earlier firing of lightning bolts across the sky. This time the sky was lit brightly, as if it were daylight at 11pm.

The entire spectrum of colors displayed in rapid succession. First yellow, then green, and blue and red, until every color known to man had adorned the heavens in a rolling cycle that kept repeating itself. This continued for several minutes, during which time people had dropped their belongings, and grabbed their loved ones with inseparable clutches.

Everyone could feel their hair standing away from their skin, and the surrounding environment seemed to be full of electrical current. But every person, including Jake's gang, had stopped in their tracks, rendered immobile by the most profound feeling of *awe* ever shared so widely among mankind.

It was then that the earth had begun to rumble, until everyone expected to see a train streaking down railroad tracks toward them. But no trains were to be found.

Once again, the sky lit with the revolving colors of the spectrum, making night into day. The smell of electrical current was so strong that people were licking their lips, trying to remove the taste of it from their mouths.

The anxiety could be cut with a knife, but no one was afraid. Everyone simply held each other tightly with awe as their senses were bombarded.

The humming and the vibrations of the earth beneath their feet was increasing, and the people came ever closer to each other in physical space without even having tried to move themselves. As everyone had crammed close together with anxious anticipation, all the perceptual events that had converged to produce the anxiety, the awe, and the physical proximity, had ceased. The senses of everyone, both external and internal were put to rest, but only momentarily, as the signal from SAI finished synchronizing all of the chips to produce one common, sensible experience.

Before they had loosened their grips on each other, everyone had begun to feel something like a vacuum pulling at them. It came with a deafening echo of voices that sounded like innumerable people singing loudly in a chorus.

The sky once again began to lighten. It got brighter and brighter. The voices got louder and louder, but the singing had stopped. Now, the voices appeared to be yelling a warning, but no one could make out the words. The light kept getting brighter, even to the point of creating blindness. The warning echoing from the depths of the universe had deadened everyone's ability to hear.

Heat was increasing beyond the human capacity for tolerance. The odor and taste of an electrical fire moved from one's lips and nostrils to his/her stomach.

Then the rumbling became a violent shaking, until every entity upon the earth had begun to bounce upon its surface. Every human sensation had become unendurably intense.

At that moment, *conscious life on earth had been absolutely united as one internal sense*, and the entire planet had been launched across the universe into another solar system where conscious life would establish a new beginning.

Endnotes

Part I, Chapter 1

1. Chapter 1 is a dramatization of the initial crisis in a human life, from the perspectives of both the newborn and the mother. It is based on ideas discussed by Otto Rank in *The Trauma of Birth,* and also Sigmund Freud in *The Problem of Anxiety*. In particular, Rank refers to the newborn's experience of birth trauma as a "primal repression" on page 8 of *The Trauma of Birth*. Also, Sigmund Freud refers to the anxiety of the newborn as an "expression of helplessness" on page 76 of *The Problem of Anxiety*. I have borrowed the concepts of "primal repression" (from Rank) and "primal anxiety" (from Freud), referring to them in this novel as "primordial repression" and "primordial anxiety," respectfully. I have specifically characterized the newborn's denial of its original human experience as a rejection of its "real self". What is rejected is the anxiety that is directly correlated to the immediate threat of helplessness and vulnerability at birth.

Birth trauma is the starting point for the phenomenological and psychoanalytical interpretations developed in this novel. I am thus deeply indebted to the psychoanalytic expertise of Otto Rank and Sigmund Freud, among others. My own interpretations of "repression" and "unconscious" are somewhat liberal and might be inconsistent with contemporary psychoanalytic theory.

Chapter 6

1. Freud, Sigmund. *The Problem of Anxiety;* translated by Henry Alden Bunker, M. D. New York: W. W. Norton & Company, Inc., 1936, p. 76. Freud refers to the separation from the mother as the source of "primal anxiety." I have used the term "primordial anxiety" to refer to the anxiety experienced by the newborn in the trauma of birth.

Otto Rank in *The Trauma of Birth,* page 5, suggests that the client during therapy is reliving birth trauma.

2. Ernest Becker, *The Denial of Death.* New York: The Free Press, 1973, p. 15. The thesis underlying this novel is strongly opposed to Becker's view of human nature. See also note #7 in Chapter 12.

3. In *The Problem of Anxiety*, Freud indicates that "nothing similar to death has ever been experienced..." (p. 66.)

4. See Ernest Becker, *The Denial of Death,* p. 103. Becker provides an account of Freud's proclivity to imagine his own death in terms of what his mother, father, and friends might have thought or felt about it.

5. Refer to note #1 in Chapter 1.

6. Martin Heidegger, *Being and Time*, translated by John Macquarrie & Edward Robinson. New York: Harper and Row Publishers, Inc., 1962, page 332. What I have called "primordial guilt" is derived from Heidegger's account of a "primordial Being-guilty which belongs to *Dasein...*" However, my interpretation of it in this novel is my own and does not necessarily follow Heidegger's reasoning.

Chapter 9

1. See note #1, Chapter 1.

Part II, Chapter 11

1. This paragraph is a representation of a typical (Husserlian) phenomenological reflection that focuses upon the Cartesian *ego cogito*. See Edmund Husserl, *The Cartesian Meditations: An Introduction to Phenomenology,* pages 18-19. I have chosen to represent transcendental consciousness as the privacy of one's internal sense.

Chapter 12

1. In this novel, I have developed my own idea of empathy, both its definition and a theory of its origin. These ideas are born from a combination of phenomenology and psychoanalysis. The idea that "empathy presupposes a self-comparison" is based on the phenomenology of Edmund Husserl. See, e.g., Edmund Husserl, *Cartesian Meditations*, pages 90-92. Husserl accounts for our experience of others *as conscious beings*. One recognizes the other as conscious (like oneself) by means of an association of one's own self as animated with the other who is perceived. See also page 94 which reads, "The other is...an analogue of my own self and yet again not an analogue in the usual sense." The theory of empathy that I have developed in this chapter assumes this self-comparison as a spontaneous and essential aspect of *empathy*. I speak of this self-comparison as a *comparison of identity*, i.e., insofar as empathy is a spontaneous and natural attempt on the part of conscious life to share the other's feeling as genuinely as possible. This comparison is not to be confused with the *comparison of distinction* that I shall speak of later.

I have emphasized that this self-comparison is not always deliberate. Rather, it is originally spontaneous, and *a natural form of association* that is not part of one's immediate awareness. Therefore, I am not claiming that one necessarily *infers* the feelings of others by means of it. The other's feelings *can be inferred intentionally* by comparison, but they are not necessarily. A scholarly, phenomenological account of different views on empathy can be found in *The Collected Works of Edith Stein,* Volume III, *On the Problem of Empathy*, Third Revised Edition, translated by Waltraut Stein, Ph.D. Washington, D.C.: ICS Publications, 1989.

Throughout this novel I have referred to empathy in relation to sympathy. Sympathy is a special type of empathy. Empathy is a sharing of feelings in general. But I am primarily interested in *sympathy* as the *sharing of pain and suffering*. My goal is to connect the phenomenological fact of self-comparison with one's own experience of weakness and vulnerability in the experience of sympathy. I am suggesting that in the experience of sympathy one spontaneously associates one's own weakness and helplessness that had been originally repressed with the trauma of birth. A major theme of this novel concerns the human experience of crisis, and my aim is to represent this by suggesting that the primordial repression resulting from birth trauma is part of a spontaneous and natural self-comparison that is essential in every act of sympathy. Therefore, my thesis on sympathy is conceived by means of a combination of Husserl's transcendental phenomenology, and Otto Rank's suggestion that the trauma of birth is echoed in every human crisis.

See also note #6 in this chapter. Friedrich Nietzsche provides an account of "pity" (quoted below) that correlates well with the phenomenon as I have described it. However, I have spoken of "pity" in this novel as something essentially different from sympathy. I have noted this distinction with specific reference to Nietzsche.

2. Whenever I use the term "coercion" I mean it in a specific context. See Sigmund Freud, *The Future of an Illusion*, translated by W. D. Robson-Scott, edited by James Strachey, (New York: Anchor Books), 1961: "It is in keeping with the course of human development that external coercion gradually becomes internalized..." (p.13). The formation of conscience is the goal of this external coercion.

3. It is my intention to develop a possible theory of the origin of a "repressed fear of death". My thesis is that over the course of our training in society, the primordial repression of one's anxiety over helplessness is transformed into a repressed fear of death. That thesis is developed in this chapter, and again later.

4. See Rene Descartes, *Discourse on Method* and *Meditations on First Philosophy*, p. 33. The endeavor to control nature is referred to as "the Cartesian ideal" later in this paragraph.

Also, what I have called "the attitude of domination" is discussed in detail by Herbert Marcuse, *Eros and Civilization: A Philosophical Inquiry into Freud*. See, e.g., pages 113 and forward.

5. See Chief Seattle, Susan Jeffers, *Brother Eagle, Sister Sky: A Message from Chief Seattle*. The words of Chief Seattle symbolize all of nature as alive with the spirit of our ancestors. Susan Jeffers depicts this truth in her beautiful paintings.

6. I have derived my idea of pity as something different from sympathy based upon Friedrich Nietzsche's discussions of "pity" in *Daybreak: Thoughts on the Prejudices of Morality*, pages 83-94. Nietzsche seems to distinguish two decisive moments to "pity," especially in section #133, pp. 83-85. He cites different examples that call for pity, then he says, "Or an accident and suffering incurred by another constitutes a signpost to some danger to us; and it can have a painful effect upon us simply as a token of human vulnerability and fragility in general." This is an essential element of the phenomenon of sympathy as I have described it, involving a spontaneous self-comparison, which is likely a natural occurrence. However, in the very next sentence, Nietzsche adds something that I am referring to as "pity" in this novel. "We repel this kind of pain and offence and requite it through an act of pity; it may contain a subtle self-defense or even a piece of revenge." This "self-defense" that he refers to is likely to be *the denial* of one's own weakness (which is absent in the basic experience of sympathy). This is why I have distinguished an act of pity from the phenomenon of sympathy. Nietzsche also says that "there is something elevating and productive of superiority in pitying…" on page 88. I have borrowed this idea from him and marked *pity as an expression of the fear of death* in what follows. Ultimately, I have distinguished "sympathy" from "pity" on the grounds of Nietzsche's discussion, but I do not want to suggest that this is necessarily what Nietzsche had intended.

7. Ernest Becker, *The Denial of Death*, page 15. Becker insists that the fear of death is natural. On page 11 he says that

"heroism is first and foremost a reflex of the terror of death." He had already (on page 4) claimed that the "urge to heroism is natural." The latter is impossible to refute absolutely. However, I have made the effort to emphasize that the "the heroic attitude" is learned and strengthened as one grows in American society. Becker's guiding thesis in his book is that we naturally endeavor in life to be heroic in response to our natural fear of death. This novel was motivated as a response against this claim.

8. Refer to note #6 in Chapter 6.

9. Martin Heidegger, *Being and Time*, p. 358. Heidegger's notion of an authentic *Dasein* is characterized by an "anticipatory resoluteness" insofar as *Dasein* faces *Dasein's* own mortality "without Illusions" and with a "sober anxiety". Contrast this with Becker's idea that human character is built upon a collection of illusions that conceal from us our natural fear of death. Arguably, these are two diametrically opposed orientations toward life.

10. This position that a repressed fear of death is both natural and necessary is defended by Ernest Becker, *Denial of Death*, pages 260-268. Becker lays out his arguments against both Norman O. Brown, *Life Against Death: The Psychoanalytic Meaning of History*, Second Edition, and also Herbert Marcuse, *Eros and Civilization: A Philosophical Inquiry into Freud*. Brown and Marcuse defend the possibility of an unrepressed fear of death.

Chapter 19

1. This statement resembles a Marxian thesis developed in his early writing, "Alienated Labor". See *Karl Marx Early Writings*, translated and edited by T. B. Bottomore. New York: McGraw-Hill), 1964.

Part III, Chapter 20

1. Viktor E. Frankl, *Man's Search for Meaning*. Part One, translated by Ilse Lasch, (Boston: Beacon Press), 1959, p.18: "The prisoner of Auschwitz, in the first phase of shock did not fear death." And, on pages 21-22: In the "second stage", "...Disgust, horror and pity are emotions that our spectator could not really feel any more."

Chapter 21

1. Chief Seattle, Jeffers, S. *Brother Eagle, Sister Sky: A Message from Chief Seattle*. Redfeather's entire discourse about Chief Seattle is a summary that includes some paraphrasing of this book.

2. ibid. This is almost an exact quote from the page that reads, "The earth does not belong to us. We belong to the earth."

3. ibid. The beautifully detailed artwork of Susan Jeffers in this book has helped to inspire the idea that nature for the Suquamish Indians, and perhaps also other native Americans, is animated with spirits.

Chapter 22

1. See Chapter 12 note #10. I have Ernest Becker in mind.

2. Again, see Chapter 12, note #10. The reference is to Norman O. Brown and Herbert Marcuse. However, I would also include Martin Heidegger as having conceived his authentic *Dasein* in the absence of a repressed fear of death.

3. Norman O. Brown, *Life Against Death*, pages 32-33. Brown refers to the child's life of play as a sort of utopian world that adults might wish to revisit.

Chapter 24

1. See note #2, Chapter 12.

Chapter 25

1. This is a fundamental thesis of Otto Rank. See, e.g., *The Trauma of Birth*, page 97.

Chapter 26

1. This idea is derived from the utopian world discussed by Norman O. Brown. See note #3 in Chapter 22.

Chapter 27

1. See note #9 in Chapter 12. The reference here is to Martin Heidegger's view on authentic *Dasein*.

2. Refer to the note in Chapter 25.

This novel is a dramatic representation of an unpublished manuscript I have written, entitled, *Not Fear of Death: Reconfiguring Conscience for a New Age*. Many of the following sources were documented in the writing of it. Additional references have been included for the writing of this novel.

Bibliography

Becker, Ernest. *Escape from Evil*. New York: The Free Press, 1975.

Becker, Ernest. *The Birth and Death of Meaning*, Second Edition. New York: The Free Press, 1971.

Becker, Ernest. *The Denial of Death*. New York: The Free Press, 1973.

Chief Seattle, Jeffers, S. *Brother Eagle, Sister Sky: A Message from Chief Seattle*; Paintings by Susan Jeffers. New York: Dial Books, 1991.

Brown, Norman O. *Life Against Death: The Psychoanalytic Meaning of History*, Second Edition. Hanover, NH: Wesleyan University Press, 1959.

Choron, Jacques. *Modern Man and Mortality*. New York: The Macmillan Company, 1964.

Clavell, James. *Shogun: The Epic Novel of Japan*. New York: Random House, 1975.

Descartes, Rene. *Discourse on Method* and *Meditations on First Philosophy*; translated by Donald A. Cress. Indianapolis: Hackett Publishing Company, Inc., 1980.

Frankl, Viktor E. *Man's Search for Meaning*; Part One translated by Ilse Lasch. Boston: Beacon Press, 1959.

Freud, Sigmund. *Civilization and Its Discontents*; translated by

James Strachey. New York: W. W. Norton & Company, Inc., 1961.

Freud, Sigmund. *The Ego and the Id;* translated by Joan Riviere. Edited by James Strachey. New York: W. W. Norton & Company, Inc., 1960.

Freud, Sigmund. *The Freud Reader*; edited by Peter Gay. New York: W. W. Norton & Company, Inc., 1989.

Freud, Sigmund. *The Future of an Illusion*; translated by W. D. Robson-Scott; Edited by James Strachey. New York: Anchor Books, 1961.

Freud, Sigmund. *The Problem of Anxiety;* translated by Henry Alden Bunker, M. D. New York: W. W. Norton & Company, Inc., 1936.

Freud, Sigmund. *Reflections on War and Death*, Chapter II, *Our Attitude towards Death;* translated by A.A. Brill and Alfred B. Kuttner. New York: Moffat, Yard & Co., 1918*;* Bartleby.com, 2010. www.bartleby.com/282/. [October 2017]

Freud, Sigmund. *The Interpretation of Dreams*; translated, 1955, and edited by James Strachey. New York: Basic Books, 2010.

Gawande, Atul. *Being Mortal: Medicine and What Matters in the End*. New York: Metropolitan Books, 2014.

Hanh, Thich Nhat. *No Death, No Fear: Comforting Wisdom for Life*. New York: Riverhead Books, 2002.

Hegel, G. W. F. *Reason in History: A General Introduction to the Philosophy of History*; translated by Robert S. Hartman. New York: Macmillan Publishing Company, 1953.

Heidegger, Martin. *Being and Time*; translated by John Macquarrie & Edward Robinson. New York: Harper & Row Publishers, Inc., 1962.

Husserl, Edmund. *Cartesian Meditations: An Introduction to Phenomenology*; translated by Dorion Cairns. The Hague: Martinus Nijhoff Publishers, 1960.

Husserl, Edmund. *Zur Phänomenologie der Intersubjektivat*, Dritter Teil: 1929-1935. Herausgegeben von Iso Kern. Den Haag, Netherlands: Martinus Nijhoff, 1973.

Kierkegaard, Soren. *The Sickness Unto Death: A Christian Psychological Exposition for Upbuilding and Awakening*; edited and translated by Howard V. Hong and Edna H. Hong. Princeton: Princeton University Press, 1980.

Lacan, Jacques. *The Seminar of Jacques Lacan, Book XI, The Four Fundamental Concepts of Psychoanalysis*; edited by Jacques-Alain Miller, translated by Alan Sheridan, 1977. New York: W. W. Norton & Company, Inc., 1981.

Marcuse, Herbert. *Eros and Civilization: A Philosophical Inquiry into Freud*. Boston: Beacon Press, 1955.

Marx, Karl. *Karl Marx: Early Writings;* translated and edited by T. B. Bottomore. New York: McGraw-Hill, 1964.

Merleau-Ponty, Maurice. *The Primacy of Perception and Other Essays on Phenomenological Psychology, the Philosophy of Art, History and Politics;* edited by James M. Edie. Evanston: Northwestern University Press, 1964.

Nietzsche, Friedrich. *Daybreak: Thoughts on the Prejudices of Morality*; translated by R. J. Hollingdale. New York: Cambridge University Press, 1982.

Nietzsche, Friedrich. *On the Genealogy of Morals* and *Ecce Homo*; translated by Walter Kaufmann and R. J. Hollingdale, (*Ecco Homo* is translated by Walter Kaufmann); edited by Walter Kaufmann. New York: Random House, Inc., 1967.

Nietzsche, Friedrich. *The Birth of a Tragedy* and *The Genealogy of Morals*; translated by Francis Golffing. New

York: Doubleday Anchor Books, 1956.

Rank, Otto. *Art and Artist: Creative Urge and Personality Development*; translated by Charles Francis Atkinson. New York: W. W. Norton & Company, Inc., 1932.

Rank, Otto. *Beyond Psychology*. New York: Dover Publications, Inc., 1941.

Rank, Otto. *Psychology and the Soul: A Study of the Origin, Conceptual Evolution, and Nature of the Soul;* translated by Gregory C. Richter and E. James Lieberman. Baltimore: Johns Hopkins University Press, 1998.

Rank, Otto. *The Trauma of Birth*. Mansfield Centre, CT: Martino Publishing, 2010.

Rank, Otto. *Truth and Reality*; translated by Jessie Taft. New York: W. W. Norton & Company, Inc., 1978.

Rank, Otto. *Will Therapy;* translated by Jessie Taft. New York: W. W. Norton & Company, Inc., 1978.

Refabert, Philippe. *From Freud to Kafka: The Paradoxical Foundation of the Life-and-Death Instinct*; translated by Agnes Jacob. London: Karnac Books Ltd., 2001.

Solomon, Sheldon, Jeff Greenberg and Tom Pyszczynski. *The Worm at the Core: On the Role of Death in Life.* UK: Penguin Books, 2016.

Stein, Edith. *The Collected Works of Edith Stein*, Volume Three, *On the Problem of Empathy*, Third Revised Edition; translated by Waltraut Stein, Ph.D. Washington, D.C.: ICS Publications, 1989.

Made in the USA
Middletown, DE
26 February 2021

34427604R00192